Consequences

by
Laine Highsmith

authorHOUSE™

1663 LIBERTY DRIVE, SUITE 200
BLOOMINGTON, INDIANA 47403
(800) 839-8640
WWW.AUTHORHOUSE.COM

First published by AuthorHouse 11/28/05

ISBN: 1-4259-0061-5 (sc)

Library of Congress Control Number: 2005909756

Printed in the United States of America
Bloomington, Indiana

This book is printed on acid-free paper.

Acknowledgements:

Writing the acknowledgements is probably the hardest part of this process. So here goes... First and foremost, I give all the Glory, all the Honor and all the Praise to my Heavenly Father. You are my source, my provider, my healer, my friend, my confidant, my everything. I love you Lord and thank you for loving me.

Next, I want to thank my family. You all mean the world to me and although we don't see each other as often as we used to and we don't spend as much time together as we used to, nothing has changed when it comes to my love for you.

Next, I want to thank all of you that have in someway touched my life. Relationships are the cornerstone of this journey we call life. With some relationships, you meet people that you never imagined you would ever have anything in common with and they become lifelong friends. Some relationships take you to places; you never thought you'd go and you learn something valuable and rewarding in your travels. Some relationships may cause you pain, but when all is said and done, you find that it was an experience you had to go through in order to grow. Some relationships bring you love, a love like you never thought you'd ever have because you thought it only existed in your dreams, or in the movies you watch, or in the songs you listen to or in the books you read.

I want to be careful not to forget anyone; so to prevent that I won't mention any names. Let me let you all know that I love you all (my family, my friends, my acquaintances, my email buddies, my new readers, the book clubs, my co-workers, prayer partners, my encouragers) and I thank you all for your love, support, and encouragement. My words could never adequately express what you all mean to me.

And last but not least, to my special gift from God. I don't know what I did to deserve such a blessing. I can finally say that I found that love that I see in the movies I watch. I found that love that I hear in the songs that I listen to and I found that love that I read about in all of the books that I read or try to write. I found that love in you. Thank you.

Consequences

The Choices you make sometimes lead you to a place where you will have to make some hard Decisions, but be careful because you will ultimately have to deal with the Consequences that follow.

Chapter One: Derrick

It was after eight when we landed, Matthew was waiting with the car so we could immediately go over to Selina's to pick up Lily. Raven seemed overly anxious; I had hoped that the eight-hour flight from Hawaii would have calmed her down. Having made love for most of the flight, I thought that she would have relaxed some; instead she remained fretful. I called my voicemail to check messages while Raven called her sister. My attention was directed to my wife's phone call when I heard her tone of voice change.

"What's the matter with her?" Raven shouted into the phone. I ended my phone call and turned all of my attention to her.

"No Wesley, don't take your time. I would like to pick up my daughter so my husband and I can get back to our honeymoon." She said placing her hand into mine; within a few moments she hung up the phone and I waited for an explanation.

"I messed up again." She said.

"Come here." I leaned over and she laid her head on my shoulder. The car stopped just outside of Selina's mailbox.

"Take a deep breath, calm down and think good thoughts." I offered trying to calm her.

"It's not working." She whined.

"Close your eyes."

"Derrick, I don't feel like…"

"Raven, listen to me; you cannot control this situation. From the looks of it Wesley is not here yet, so you are just going to have to wait. Why do you want to stress yourself and everyone else out? Calm down. We are not in a hurry. We will go inside and we will wait." I spoke in a calm tone to camouflage my true feelings. It is getting harder and harder to deal with Raven and her need to keep Wesley lingering between us.

"Hello Selina." I spoke when my new sister-in-law opened the door.

"Hi." She stepped back inside and opened her arms for a hug.

"Get in here so I can kick your butt." Selina said to her sister from our embrace as Raven walked in and closed the door.

"Hello you two; I didn't think you would be back so soon." Winston said coming down the stairs.

"The spoiled brat had to come home early because Wesley took Lily to South Carolina." Selina interjected.

"Selina, we've had a long flight. Can I bother you for something to drink please?" I asked hoping to ease the tension building in the room.

"Sure Derrick." She led me into the kitchen.

"We both know Raven is overreacting about Wesley taking Lily to South Carolina. A lot has transpired in the last few days; help me defuse this volatile situation; please?" I asked softly.

"I'll try, but Derrick she has to realize that Wesley is entitled to take his daughter to his home whether it's here or in South Carolina whenever he wants to. She can't control where that man wants to spend time with his child."

"I agree and I will talk with her when we get home. Just help me get through this and..." The beeping of the security alarm interrupted me. When Selina and I returned to the living room; Wesley was handing Lily over to Winston before walking out the front door again. Winston in turn gave Lily to Raven.

"Hi beautiful one." Raven spoke softly as a new aura came over her when Lily was placed in her arms.

"Excuse me." Wesley said trying to get back inside the door. Raven stepped aside and I asked Wesley if he needed any help.

"No thanks. I got it." Wesley placed the diaper bag and Lily's overnight bag on the floor and then a third bag he must have bought for her. I walked over to see Lily.

"How's daddy's girl?" I asked and Raven handed Lily over to me. I looked into the beautiful eyes of this innocent child who in turn blessed me with a smile. Even though we were still in the room, it seemed like we had been distanced from all of the drama. I heard words being exchanged and when I heard my wife's voice raise another octave I knew it was time for me to step in.

"Raven sweetheart, can I see you in the kitchen for a moment please?"

"Not now Derrick. I think we need to end this stupidity right now. Wesley, I am sick and tired of going through this with you. I've tried being a friend to you. You couldn't handle it. I've tried to be civil, now all of a sudden you can't handle that either. What do you suggest Wesley? You want to hurt me Wesley. Fine, take your best shot. I bet it won't hurt any more than the last time. You do remember that, don't you? You were the cause of us not working out. You. Face it." Wesley started to say something but Raven raised her hand to stop him.

"If you had been man enough to tell me the truth about Samantha, then we probably wouldn't be here having this simple ass conversation. You made a choice. You made the decision. Now you have to live with the consequences. I am tired of you and your threats. I am tired of you trying to get back at me. You want a fight? Fine, then take me to court; I'll meet you there. But you can bet your simple ass that you won't get anywhere near my daughter again unless a court orders it."

"Raven, that's enough." Selina shouted and Lily started to cry. I took her out of the room to calm the both of us. When I returned to the living room and found my wife crumpled to the floor that was the last straw.

"Princess, it is time to go." I said as I handed Lily over to Selina so I could help my wife up to her feet. Raven didn't put up any argument, which was probably best under the circumstances. After saying goodnight, I walked my wife and baby out to the car. Matthew went inside to get Lily's bags while Raven fastened Lily into the car seat.

"I'm sorry." She said softly.

"What are you apologizing for? The way you behaved or how you feel? You will have to tell me because I don't want to be accused of assuming the wrong thing." I knew after saying those words that I should have waited until I calmed down but it had to be said. Raven is my wife now and she is going to have to get past Wesley if she expects our marriage to last. My cellular phone rang before Raven could respond.

"Derrick Kincaide." I answered just as Matthew pulled onto the highway. Bob was a welcomed diversion and I purposefully stayed on the phone to avoid what was going to be an ugly conversation. All of the diplomacy I have developed in my lifetime was not going to pull me through this situation. Bob caught my attention when he mentioned Shayla's name.

"I'm sorry Bob, what did you just say?"

"Shayla's benefit is in a few weeks. I was planning on coming in early with Vonda. Are you free on that Saturday, maybe we can get a few rounds in before the benefit?"

"I'll have to get back to you on that."

"Are you all right?"

"Yes. I'm just tired it's been a long day and a long flight."

"I understand, please give that beautiful wife of yours my love and I'll talk to you later."

"Will do; good night." I looked over to see that Lily had fallen asleep; Raven seemed lost in thought elsewhere. I closed the cover on my phone and Raven turned to look at me but she didn't say anything. Matthew parked the car and came around to open the door. After helping Raven get out, I handed the car seat over to her.

"Hello, I wasn't expecting you until tomorrow." Mrs. Hill dressed in her robe greeted me at the door.

"We had a change in plans. How are you?" I asked before placing a kiss on her cheek.

"I'm fine. Can I get you anything?" She asked.

"No thank you. It's late; I think we are all going to call it a night. I'll see you in the morning. Good night."

"Good night." She smiled and walked back towards her room. I turned to hold the door as Matthew placed the last of the luggage inside. I said good night to him before setting the alarm and then looked up the stairs towards our bedroom wondering if I should give Raven some more time before we were faced with this discussion. Opting to keep the peace, I walked into my office and powered on the computer.

Barbara had faxed over the agenda for the board meeting, I walked over to the fax machine to glance over it. She had made all of the revisions I wanted and now I was sure that everything was covered so that Raven's appointment could be voted on and approved immediately. Victor and I agreed to nominate Geoff Grainger from Advertation for the Vice President of Business Continuity. All of the executive staff of Advertation was invited to the meeting and we were planning to make the announcement of the acquisition as well as unveil the new organizational chart.

"New mail has arrived." The computer announced and I walked over to my desk. The first thing I saw was that there were seven new messages from Regina and I sighed at the thought of having to deal with this again. There are not many times in my life when I knew before I did something that it was a mistake and did it anyway, this is the one time I wished I had heeded my own warning. I deleted the messages and closed my eyes while I waited for the inbox to return.

The next message was from Shayla and I read it aloud in my best imitation of her voice.

"Derrick, I have informed the committee that you will be presenting the annual check for the foundation. They needed to know the contribution amount so they could complete the check copy for the photos; I thought $250,000 would be a nice round figure for this year. I will pick up the check at the board meeting."

I had to laugh since I should have known that she would pull something like this especially after the way she performed at the wedding. Heaven only knows what else her little mind has in store for me. I deleted the message, answered a few emails and was about to power off the computer when another message from Regina came in. My watch showed that it was after midnight. What could she possibly want at this hour? Once again I ignored that feeling of don't do it and clicked to open the email.

"Are you coming to bed?" Raven's voice startled me because I hadn't; noticed that she had come into my office. She motioned for me to get up.

"It's been a long day and we have a lot to talk about in the morning. I know that I behaved badly tonight and I owe you an apology. Please don't think that I am not respecting you or your feelings." She spoke softly.

"You're right it's been a long day, let's talk about this tomorrow." I said powering off the computer and taking my wife by the hand to follow her to bed.

***

Lily's soft gurgles over the monitor woke the both of us.

"I'll go. I need some time alone with my little lady anyway." I said sliding out of bed.

"Okay." Raven responded but I was sure she was talking in her sleep. After grabbing my robe, I walked into the bathroom to wash my face and brush my teeth. My reflection revealed that I was badly in need of a shave. Raven liked the look of the beard coming in but when I looked in the mirror at the gray hairs, it only reminded me of the difference in our ages. I ran my hands across the beard that was sure to come off today and then went in to spend some quality time with my little darling.

"Good morning Princess." Lily smiled and kicked out in anticipation of me picking her up. I decided to change her diaper first figuring that when we sat down for her feeding it would not be interrupted. I placed the bottle in the warmer while I changed her and within a few minutes we were in a synchronized rhythm of my rocking and her sucking on the bottle.

***

My mind darted back and forth between what was going on at the office, the board meeting and how I was going to handle Regina. The day we met at Carlson and Co., I had already been told of her antics. Against my better judgment I tried to give Regina the benefit of the doubt and that was a definite mistake. She proved to be all that I had been warned of and then some. It is really a shame because she is a smart girl; she just doesn't have any confidence in her intelligence. I closed my eyes rocking Lily back to sleep and that day came back to me like a dream.

"So let's put on a new face." Regina delivered her closing statement with a bright smile.

"Are there any questions?" She looked around the room and our eyes met. The President of Vera asked a few minor questions that she answered with ease.

"Anyone else?"

"Yes, if I may. I was wondering who primarily is the target audience you have in mind here. Right now Vera has a great market share in the 18-25 demographic, but we need to hit the other areas. What about this campaign will draw the others in?" I asked and watched as Regina lost the cool composure she'd displayed throughout the presentation. Her eyes darted back and forth between Victor and Raven.

"Raven, perhaps you could help us out with this question." Victor said to Raven who was not pleased at all that he asked for her help.

"Sure." Raven said before she stood and took center stage at the head of the table. She was so poised and confident in her answer to my question. At that point it became clear that this was Raven's concept and Regina had for some strange reason taken over the presentation. It couldn't have been that Raven was not able to speak in front of a crowd her presentation skills were excellent.

"Yes I like that and it makes a lot of sense. Good Job. Miss..." I smiled.

"It's Raven... Raven McNeill." She returned my smile and I caught a glimpse of her deep dimples before she went back to her seat. Victor gave a closing statement and I was about to make a move over to Raven to acknowledge her excellent proposal but Regina reached out her hand to formally introduce herself.

"Mr. Kincaide, it is a pleasure to finally meet you. Mr. Truell has spoken so highly of you. I look forward to working with you."

"Thank you Regina."

"So I understand that you are in town for a few days while you are finalizing the acquisition. Perhaps we can get together for dinner one night, I would love to show you around the city as well as hear your vision for the company."

"I'll have to check my schedule." I looked around the room and saw that Raven had made a quiet escape.

"Mr. Truell, help me convince Mr. Kincaide to join me for dinner tonight." Victor smiled and obliged her. He told me that Regina would be the person he would recommend to bring me up to speed on all the accounts presently held by Carlson.

"Regina, I'll have my assistant Barbara give you a call to schedule something before I leave." I gave in mainly because after spotting the time on the clock above her head, I realized I was going to be late for my appointment with Larry.

"If you two will excuse me, I have to go now." I picked up my briefcase and headed down to the lobby where I caught sight of the celery green suit that Raven was wearing exiting to the parking garage.

After meeting with Larry in the restaurant at the hotel where I was staying I decided to go up to my room and call it an early night. I had scheduled the jet to leave at seven a.m. so I could make it back to Los Angeles in time for Rick's interview with the admissions group at Stanford. After answering a few email messages and returning several calls, I realized it was after eight p.m. and I hadn't eaten. Hating to eat alone, I decided to go against my better judgment and asked Barbara to forward me a number for Regina.

"Hello, this is Regina, I am sorry that I have missed your call. Please leave your name and number at the tone and I will return your call at my earliest convenience." Her machine answered and I debated on whether or not to leave a message. The beep came forcing my response.

"Regina, this is Derrick Kincaide. I was hoping I could take you up on that dinner invitation tonight before I leave in the morning. I'm sorry I missed you." I hung up the phone, grabbed the room service menu and called in my dinner order. Within a few minutes there was a knock at the door, I answered thinking it was room service.

"Hello. I got your message and came right over." Regina stood outside of my door in a dress that was barely there. The flesh toned colored dress hugged her body so tightly you had to look hard to see that she actually had clothes on. She smiled as she made her way past me and into the room.

"How did you?"

"Caller ID. I called the hotel and got your room number and came right over."

"Regina..."

"I'm hungry, what do you have a taste for?" She asked taking a seat on the sofa.

"Actually, I just ordered from room service. Um, I can cancel it if..."

"No, we can stay in. I don't mind."

"Take a look at the menu there and order something."

"Thanks. I'm a little parched, could I have something to drink?"

"What would you like?"

"A gin and tonic would be great." She said and I looked at my watch thinking it was getting late for a stiff drink. The last thing I needed was Regina getting intoxicated while in my room. Regina called down to room service to place her order as I poured her drink.

"Yes this is the Hamilton Suite and I'd like to add to the order that was placed earlier. Yes, I'd like an order of the oysters with a side of saffron rice and asparagus topped with hollandaise sauce. Also send up a small dish of Beluga Caviar. Thank you." She said as I sat the drink down on the table.

"They are going to bring both orders up together, I hope you don't mind."

"No, not at all." I took a seat in the chair next to the sofa she sat on.

"So, why don't you bring me up to speed on the accounts?" I said.

"Well, Jameson Foods is our largest client to date. They have the potential of growing to a twenty million dollar account provided that we can find a way around Gerber. We also have Klein Jewelers, Weaver Electronics and..." The knock on the door interrupted her spiel.

"Room Service." The young lady called out from the opposite side of the door. I walked over to open the door and let the young lady in. She wheeled the cart over to the sofa and Regina watched as she set the carafe of the Chardonnay

Regina ordered on the table. Regina poured the wine in the glasses as I gave the lady a tip and closed the door behind her.

"Here's to…" She handed me a wineglass.

"It's a little late for me…"

"Come now, you aren't going to let me drink alone are you? Just take a sip, one for the toast." She said with a smile.

"Very well. Here's to a successful, profitable business venture." I offered.

"And to things to come." She added and clanked her glass against mine. We ventured into eating our respective meals but Regina was insistent that I try a taste of her meal as well. I tried to get some other business related questions in but Regina kept changing the subject to personal matters.

"So I hear you are separated from Mrs. Kincaide."

"That's correct."

"That has to be hard on you. I mean a man like you with all that you do and accomplish daily; you need someone to comfort you at the end of a long day."

"Regina, it's getting late and…"

"And by now, you should welcome a pair of open arms."

"Regina…"

"Derrick…" She stood and her dress fell to her ankles, exposing her firm beautiful body covered by a flesh colored piece of lingerie. She walked over to where I was sitting and kneeled down in front of me.

"Let me show you how a man of your stature should be treated after a successful business meeting." Regina ran her hands up my thighs and cupped my growing erection in her hands.

"Just as I thought, this is exactly what you need." Regina unzipped my pants and took possession of my throbbing member.

"Regina, I don't think…" Before I could speak another word, she had covered me with her mouth. It had been such a long time since I had an intimate encounter, all rational thought left my mind and I sat back to enjoy whatever she had in store for me.

"Why don't we move into the bedroom where we will be more comfortable?" Regina said when she finally came up for air.

"Regina, this has gone much too far already."

"Derrick, don't you find me attractive?"

"Yes, but that's beside the point."

"I know what your head is saying, but your body is saying something entirely different. I think you enjoyed the appetizer, why not have a taste of the first course? Come." She stood up and extended her hand to me.

"No. Regina this really is not a good idea. This will compromise our working relationship at the office."

"The relationship I am concentrating on right now has nothing to do with the office."

"Regina, this has to stop."

"You don't really mean that." She grabbed me and stroked me again to the point of climax.

"Wouldn't you rather feel me around you instead of my hand?"

"Regina…" My words were cut off when I could no longer hold my release.

"See what I mean? Derrick we are two consenting adults. What goes on here tonight will stay strictly between the sheets and these walls." With a slight tug, she pulled and I followed like an animal on a leash. Regina's appetite was insatiable and I had to wonder how much of that was due to the oyster dinner she had or the Chardonnay. I was satisfied from head to toe as far as my body was concerned, but my mind had to wonder what this night of pleasure was going to cost me in the long run.

***

I was awakened from my trance when I heard Raven entering the nursery.

"I'm going to lay her back down and you come back to bed." Raven said after taking Lily from my arms to lay her down in her crib. Lily fretted a little and Raven rubbed her back until she went back to sleep. I got up and walked into our room, I was sitting on the side of the bed when Raven came in.

"How are you feeling this morning?" I asked as she crossed the room and took a seat at her dressing table.

"I'm good. What about you? Are you jetlagged?"

"Not really. I was actually speaking of your emotions; you put on quite a display last night."

"I apologized for that already." She said as if she was getting upset with the direction of the conversation.

"But you never said exactly what you were apologizing for. Was it your behavior or your feelings? You know we've been here before and I don't want to get the wrong idea."

"Derrick, where is this going?"

"Let me be direct. I didn't appreciate the display you put on last night. It was pretty evident that all of that emotion came more from your unresolved feelings for Wesley than from Lily's whereabouts. I thought your surprise wedding ended that chapter of your life. I guess the real surprise is that it didn't. How are we going to deal with this? I told you before; if you weren't sure about your feelings for me that you should not proceed with this marriage. You said you were sure. I guess your actions are speaking louder than your words."

"Derrick?"

"Please let me finish. I love you Raven. Nothing about my feelings for you has changed, not one inkling. But I deserve the same from you. I will not be a part of another loveless marriage. If this marriage was another one of your rash decisions, then I would rather end this now than to suffer the consequences later."

"Are you done?" She asked turning to face me.

"Yes."

"Then please let me say a few things. Derrick I love you and marrying you was not a mistake nor was it a rash decision. Yes, I behaved badly last night. These last few weeks have been nothing but a roller coaster ride of emotion. Yes, there have been times when I've acted without thinking. But it has never been my intention to hurt you. I recognized last night that I never once considered how you would feel after seeing all of that. It is true, I do still care for Wesley because he is after all is said and done the father of my child, but I love you. There is no question there. I love you. I am upset that Wesley wants to fight me for custody. I am afraid of the outcome of that mainly because I think deep down inside I knew that Wesley was Lily's father long before it was confirmed but I didn't want to hurt you." She walked over to where I sat and kneeled down before me.

"You had been so supportive of me during the time I was going through all of that and you were very vocal about your feelings. How could I look you in the eye and say that I care for you but I am pregnant by someone else whom at that time I still loved? Was that wrong? Probably but after you take that first step it's often hard to try and turn around and move in the opposite direction. But last night when I laid here replaying everything in my mind over and over again, I realized that if the situation were reversed, I would have bolted a long time ago. You haven't. I realize how much you have given up so we can be together and that means a lot to me." She took a deep breath.

"You're right actions do speak louder than words and your actions have been screaming at me telling me that I need to step up to the bar, and act like a woman who loves and appreciates the man that loves and protects her. Please forgive me. I promise that this is the last time Wesley is ever going to come between us." She looked like she was about to cry. I heard her words but I wasn't quite sure if I believed them. I pulled her up to her feet and then wrapped my arms around her and kissed her softly.

"We are going to have to take this one day at a time." She said softly.

"That's all we can do." I agreed with that sentiment and then proceeded to show her that I was willing to try. I removed the strap from her shoulder and placed a kiss on her collarbone.

Chapter Two: Wesley

I didn't sleep much; Naquia was on my mind. I tried to call her a few times and got the answering machine. She wouldn't return any of my pages so after sunrise, I drove non-stop to get home to try to reconcile with my wife. My mind replayed conversations and now I could see what she was saying about Raven. Other than me wanting to be an active part of Lily's life, I could see where maybe I wasn't being fair to Naquia and I knew if I wanted to save my marriage, then I needed to fix this.

***

I pulled into the empty driveway hoping to see her truck parked in the garage. It wasn't. I picked up the phone and called the hospital. The duty nurse said Naquia wasn't on call. I paged her and again she didn't return the call. I started to dial my mother-in-law Marjorie's number but decided to drive over there instead. I turned onto Marjorie's street and parked in front of her door. I looked at the front door wondering if my wife was in there and what she may have told her mother. Whatever it was I couldn't say anything because if I had listened to Denise I probably wouldn't be in this position now. I got out of the car and my mother-in-law met me before I could ring the bell.

"Oh hi. I thought you were Naquia."

"Sorry to disappoint you. I was hoping I'd find her here. I called the hospital and they said she wasn't on call."

"I haven't seen her in a couple of days. She said she was going with you to the city to take your daughter back."

"Oh." I was about to say something else that was cut off when Marjorie's phone rang; she asked me to come on in.

"Hello? Hey, Wesley and I were just talking about you. Yeah. Oh. Okay. You want to… Oh okay then. Bye."

"Naquia?" I asked.

15

"Yes. She said she needed to get away and that she will call you later. I knew she was taking your cousin's death kind of hard, but I didn't think it would affect her like this."

"Did she say where she is?"

"No. She just said to tell you that she will call you later."

"Okay."

"Wesley, I'm worried about her. She told me about the situation with you wanting to fight for custody of your daughter. I guess I'm to blame for her feeling the way she does because she's never had to fight for anyone's attention. She was always first in my life and now she doesn't understand that it's not always going to be about her."

"Marjorie, I don't think…"

"Listen to me. My daughter has always relied on her looks to get her what she's wanted and for most of her life it has. There were times when I've watched her manipulate people because they too were caught up in her looks as well. She didn't do that with you, and I hoped that things would be different when she met you. I'm afraid of what will happen to her if this marriage doesn't last. She's never gotten over her father leaving us, and now with the death of her patient. I just don't know." Marjorie was on the verge of tears. I opened my arms to her to comfort her.

"I'm not ready to give up on my marriage. I love your daughter and I am going to do right by her. Don't worry." After a hug and a kiss on her cheek, I said goodbye and went home to wait for my phone call.

***

It has been two days and Naquia hasn't come home or called. I called the hospital and found out that she was on duty. The nurse asked me if I wanted to have her paged, I decided against it and headed over to the hospital to see my wife. When I walked through emergency, I didn't see anyone I recognized so I walked back to the residents' quarters. I smiled and nodded at a few faces that looked familiar or seemed to recognize me. When I walked past the swinging doors, I felt my anger begin to rise because my wife was sleeping or trying to, on a cot. It made me mad to see her sleeping like this when she could be home and sleeping comfortably in our king sized bed, instead of being here balled up in a knot.

"Doc." I whispered hoping not to startle her.

"Hmm?" She responded but she was still very much asleep.

"Come. Let's go home and get you to bed."

"Wesley?" She stirred and opened her eyes.

"What are you doing here?" She asked in the middle of her yawn.

"We'll talk about that later. Come on let's go home." I reached out to pull her up to her feet.

***

"Are you feeling better?" I asked my wife who had just awakened from her more than five-hour nap.

"Much better." She said after a long stretch.

"You hungry? I have some stuff; I can make you a salad."

"Thanks, that sounds great. I'm gonna take a shower, I'll be right back." She said before leaving to go back upstairs. I walked into the bathroom to wash my hands. It was good to have her back, she sounded like my Naquia and not the woman I had been at odds with for these last few months. I had the football game on in the den and the Carolina Panthers was putting a hurting on the Colts. Keeping my eye on the game, I set a place for Naquia on the coffee table and brought in the salad dressing when she walked in wearing one of my jerseys. My eyes left the game and traveled up those long brown legs that I missed being wrapped around my waist.

"You like?" She smiled as she turned around to give me a complete view.

"Always have." I said walking up to her and taking her hand.

"Sit." I said and Naquia sat in front of the place setting. I went into the kitchen to add the warmed chicken to her salad.

"What do you want to drink?"

"Water's fine." She started to get up.

"Sit. I'll get it." I walked over to hand her the salad and then went back into the kitchen for a bottle of water.

"You're not eating?" She asked before taking a bite.

"Not hungry." I said taking the top off the bottle and pouring the water over the ice in her glass.

"That's too bad." When she leaned over, I caught a glimpse of her nakedness under the jersey.

"What do you mean by that?" I asked intrigued by what her answer could possibly be.

"I've missed you. I know we have a lot to talk about but it doesn't take away from the fact that I miss my husband and his touch. Wesley, I love you and I don't want to lose you."

"I've missed you too and you are right we have a lot to talk about, but…" She interrupted what I was about to say.

"I want to come home; I'm tired of being mad. I know I haven't been fair to you in all of this. Call me selfish, I just don't want to share you with anyone, especially not Raven. I just think we deserve the chance to be happy and live our life together without Raven and her child."

"Babe, I love you. There is no one other than you that I would rather be with. But Lily is my daughter and I love her too. I will not choose one of you over the other. I want the both of you in my life. Yes, I have to consider your feelings about your career and not wanting to be a mother figure to my daughter. I don't like it but I have to respect it. But I cannot live with you not wanting to be around when my daughter is here because you are thinking that I am making you second. There is no first or second, you are both important to me. I want us to work through this now while she is not old enough to sense the tension. I don't want there to be any tension, none. My lawyer has already advised me that trying to get custody of Lily is going to be difficult. I don't like it but I have to respect that too. So while I may have to give up that fight, I am not giving up on being a major part of my daughter's life. And I want my wife to get over whatever ill will she has regarding my baby because she doesn't like her mother. Lily has nothing to do with that." I looked at her to try and read her face for her reaction.

"In the meantime, I am going to try and sit down to talk with Raven and Derrick and work out some type of regular schedule where I can get her one-week out of the month. That will give you three out of four weeks alone with me, but that one week I need you to be here for me, with me and with Lily. Can you do that?"

"I'll try." She said softly.

"Then that's all I can ask. Thank you." I said and Naquia leaned over to kiss me. I could see that things were going to get back on track.

***

Naquia and I made love for a few hours before she had to go back to the hospital for her shift. When I stopped in front of the emergency room she said she would be home probably around noon.

"That's cool after my appointment with Ken, I'm going over to Father's, I told him I'd help him do some stuff to the house."

"Then I'll see you when you get home, I'd like to pick up where we left off."

"Not a problem; we can do that." I smiled before kissing her lips again.

"I love you."

"Love you too Doc." I leaned over to get one last kiss before getting out to open her door. After watching Naquia walk into the hospital, I drove over to the lawyer's office to keep my appointment. Mrs. Bellamy looked exactly like Flo from Alice this time when I walked into my lawyer's office. I had asked his advice about the custody situation. Basically, he said I really didn't have much of a leg to stand on when he petitioned the courts for the complaint I'd given to Raven at her wedding. He was hoping it would be enough to scare her into some type of compromise.

"Good morning Hun, go right in he's expecting ya." She smiled and went back to her phone call.

"Thanks." I knocked on the doorjamb before going in.

"Hey Wesley, come on in." Ken Lindsay stood to greet me.

"Good to see ya. How's it going?" He shook my hand.

"Not too good. I don't think our tactic worked." I said taking my seat across from him.

"The last time when I went to pick up my daughter, I walked into Raven's wedding. She was getting married that day which was why she was giving me a hassle about picking up Lily."

"So tell me, what happened?"

"Now after thinking about it, it probably wasn't the best time to spring the petition on her."

"You didn't."

"Yep, I did. I guess some of my hurt feelings resurfaced. I mean damn, I just found out that she withheld the fact that she was pregnant with my baby from me, then her former boss who is now her husband tells me that Lily is my daughter and then she lets me walk into her wedding like that. Damn, she could have just said something and then we could've made other arrangements." I felt myself getting angry again so I stopped talking.

"I know this is hard for you Wesley but you realize that she probably is just as angry with you. You did after all get married not too long after you two broke up. Women don't deal well with situations like that. Neither do they forget." Ken smiled as if he had first hand experience with what we were talking about.

"So go ahead what else happened?" He asked.

"We had words the other night; she came home early from her honeymoon because she found out that I brought Lily home here to South Carolina. Now she's threatening that the only way I'll see my baby is if it is court ordered. I ain't trying to hear that and we need to do something."

"I'm already ahead of you. Unfortunately as I told you before, legally there really isn't much that we can do. You are not going to like this but I am going to advise you to talk to her and you two work something out. If that doesn't work, then I will see if I can get a mediator to hear your case; a judge isn't going to come anywhere near this." He closed what must have been his notes on my case.

"Did you hear what I just said? She's pissed off; there ain't no talking to her when she's mad. Believe me, I've already been there."

"What about her husband?"

"What about him?"

"Talk to him."

"Man…"

"Wesley, when you are in a position like this, you have to use whatever angles there are to your advantage. I am sure that man wants to make sure he has his wife's full attention instead of having her every thought of you and how to hurt you. That is all that any of this is about, you two are trying to hurt one another." He got up and walked over to my side of his desk.

"Man, swallow down that hurt pride for a minute. Try to talk to her in front of her husband. If she doesn't budge, watch his reaction. I guarantee you; he will have something to say about this even if he doesn't say it to you." He patted my shoulder before walking back over to his side of the desk. A part of me knew he was right but I just don't like the idea of giving in to her. I have always been the one to try to make things right, she needs to realize her shit stinks just like the rest of us.

"Call her and tell her you realize that you handled this badly, and you want to work something out because in the long run all of this is going to hurt your daughter."

"I guess you have a point and my baby should not be the one to suffer because of our stupidity." I stood and shook his hand.

"Thanks Ken, I'll call you and let you know how your advice goes over."

"Just be cool and watch him. He'll get her to compromise." Ken smiled like he knew already that he was right. He walked me out to the car and told me it was all going to work out. I smiled and said goodbye. When I got in the car, my phone was ringing.

"Hello."

"Wesley, it's me." Vicky sounded scared and like she had been crying.

"Vicky, what's wrong?" I asked turning the volume down.

"I need to get out of here. Terrence has gotten worse; he won't listen to me or to the doctors. He told me to get out today and this time I'm going to take him up on his offer. Can you help me?"

"Are you sure Vicky, you know the last time…"

"Wesley, I'm sure."

"I'll make the arrangements. The ticket will be waiting for you at the ticket counter."

"Thank you."

"You're welcome."

"I'm getting out of here before he comes back."

"Call from the plane so I'll know what time to come get you."

"I will. Thanks again Wesley. Bye."

"Bye." I disconnected the call and the phone rang in my hand again.

"Hey doc." I peeped the caller ID before answering.

"Hi honey, listen I've got some bad news." Naquia was about to cancel.

"What? I'm not going to get my after dinner quickie."

"No silly. This is serious."

"What's up doc?"

"Mason is not doing good. He may not make it through the night."

"Really?"

"He's in the final stages, his condition has worsened and all we can do now is keep him comfortable."

"Damn. I'm sorry to hear that baby. This is the little boy right?"

"Yes." She said softly.

"You gonna be all right?" I asked.

"Yeah baby. I just don't want to leave him right now. You understand don't you?"

"Of course. Call me if you need anything. I love you." I heard Naquia's name being called in the background.

"Honey, I've got to go. I'll see you later okay?"

"Sure thing baby."

"Bye." She hung up and I sat there for a minute with the receiver in my hands thinking this AIDS thing ain't no joke. Naquia had told me about this little boy who must have been born with the virus. His mother had been on drugs and had been brought into the emergency room one night after almost overdosing. Naquia had struck up a friendship with the girl and promised to watch over the little boy while his mother was in recovery. Naquia had been spending a lot of time with the little boy just like she had been with Preston before he died.

Preston, Samantha and Terrence. Damn. That's when it hit me. No. Can't be. Preston has been sweet all his life; he wouldn't have gotten with Samantha. The question is did he get with Terrence. Oh shit. All of a sudden everything was falling into place. I made a U-turn and went to see Samantha. I needed some answers. I parked in the front of Mrs. Nelson's house and saw Samantha sitting outside on her grandmother's front porch. It was over ninety degrees outside, but she had an afghan draped across her lower body. Samantha had always been small, but now she looked like a skeleton with just skin covering her bones.

"Wesley?" Her voice was hoarse.

"Yeah. How are you feeling?" I asked surprised that my anger towards her had subsided enough for me to actually care about her well-being.

"As well as can be expected I guess." She responded before coughing. "What are you doing here?"

"I need to ask you something." I took a seat on the top step.

"What?"

"To your knowledge, were Preston and Terrence involved?" I watched Samantha's face give me the answer I didn't want.

"I think that's pretty obvious now. Look at us."

"Damn Samantha, when are you going to come clean with Vicky?"

"I've tried Wesley."

"Stop trying and do it. She's coming home later today. I know she's going to want to come by here. You have to tell her the truth. I mean all of it the whole truth. This shit is serious."

23

"Don't you think I know that?" She began to cry and with all that we'd been through, I was surprised that I still had compassion for her. I still felt like she couldn't be trusted but when I watched where this disease had taken her; I realized that this was worse than any type of punishment I could've ever even wished on her. We sat in silence until she spoke up.

"Wesley, I am sorry for all the pain and confusion I've caused. You do believe that don't you."

"I wish I could say that I do Samantha." I got up to leave.

"One day I hope you can forgive me." She said sadly.

"Yeah, me too." I took the last step down and got into my car.

***

Vicky came off the plane looking like a California girl; her hair was blowing in the breeze, her big dark shades and her designer luggage. She caught the eye of several men as she walked by. I wondered if she even realizes how beautiful she is; how she could find a good man who would love and respect her. Vicky found me in the crowd of people waiting to meet their loved ones. I waved to her and she walked right into my open arms.

"Hey you." I said hugging her tight and kissing her cheek. I grabbed her luggage and led the way to the car.

"How was the flight?" I asked as we waited for the shuttle.

"Long."

"Why? Did you get delayed?"

"No, it's just a long way back home." She said quietly. I could tell by her mood she was going through changes. I got her settled in the car and took her back to my house. This was the first time she'd been back to the house since Preston's funeral. She had gone back to California to collect her things and Terrence had obviously pulled a number on her to get her to stay. But it wasn't much longer before the news broke about Terrence contracting the virus.

Vicky was quiet the whole ride, I thought she might have been jetlagged in addition to whatever she was wrestling with internally. She didn't say anything when I didn't take the exit to Father's house; I thought she might've been sleeping.

"This is a lot of house for two people." Vicky shifted in her seat as we parked.

"It won't be for too much longer."

"What do you mean? Is your wife expecting?"

"No. Hopefully Lily will be here with us on a part-time basis."

"Who?"

"My daughter. Lily."

"Oh yeah, I forgot about her. How old is she now?"

"She just turned three months. Can you believe it?"

"Time waits for no one." She said solemnly. I got out to open her door but she didn't wait for me. She grabbed her bags from the backseat; I had to stop her.

"Hold up. You know you don't carry anything in my presence if my hands are free." I could tell she was no longer used to being treated like a lady. I handed her the keys.

"It's the silver one." I said getting the suitcase from the trunk. Vicky opened the door to the utility room and stepped inside. I sat the bags down and punched in the security code.

"Come on in." I picked up her bags again and walked through the den and down the hallway to the guestrooms.

"Which one?" I asked and Vicky pointed to the first door. I stood to the side so she could open the door. We walked in and I hit the switch to illuminate the room. Vicky looked all around at the modern furnishings Naquia used in decorating this room. I sat the luggage down in front of the closet and turned to take a good look at my baby sister. She reached up to remove her sunglasses just as I noticed her black eye. When our eyes met, she turned away in shame.

"Just tell me you're okay." I said quietly trying to hide my anger.

"I am now." She said and walked past me into the bathroom and closed the door. I went into the kitchen to pull together some dinner; it was almost nine so I went with something light. I pulled fresh vegetables from our garden out back. I made vinaigrette dressing and put it in the refrigerator to cool. Vicky never came back out so I called Father to let him know that Vicky was home and that we'd see him and Natalie tomorrow. I retired in the den to wait up for Naquia, when I woke up it was after 2am. I paged her and she called me right back.

"Why aren't you here with me and asleep?" I asked.

"Mason needs me. We've been playing memory games and he's winning all of them."

"That's good. Why isn't he asleep?"

"I don't know; he's probably afraid to close his eyes. I just want to be here with him so he won't be afraid. He hasn't let go of my hand since I've been here. I feel so bad. I wish there was something more that I could do."

"I'm sure he appreciates you just being there. You want me to come and keep you company? I can hold your other hand."

"No, but thanks. I know you aren't fond of hospitals. I'll be home as soon as I can."

"Call me if you change your mind. I love you Doc."

"You too. Good night." She disconnected the call and I headed upstairs to our room. I heard the television playing in Vicky's room when I walked by. I tapped lightly and when she didn't answer, I figured she was asleep so I stepped inside to turn off the TV. She looked like an angel, a battered angel. Her black eye also had a cut on the same cheek. It must have been hidden under her makeup. I closed the door and took the stairs up to my bedroom. The lights under the stairs lighted the loft leading to our bedroom. I set the timer to turn them off in an hour and to turn on the motion detector. Our bed seemed a whole lot emptier tonight.

***

"Good morning." I felt Naquia's lips brush my cheek. She stepped out of her pants and shoes and walked into our bathroom. She turned on the water and was about to step into her shower stall when I walked in.

"You okay Doc?" I asked as she closed the door.

"Yeah." She said quietly.

26

"You need some time alone?"

"Yeah, just a little."

"Okay. By the way babe, Vicky's here."

"She is?"

"Yeah. She said she needed to get away. I don't know if she is going to stay with us or go home to Father's. I just wanted to let you know."

"Is she all right?"

"Don't know. I'm gonna make you some breakfast now, we'll talk later." I washed my face, brushed my teeth and gargled. I left Naquia just as she was turning off the water. Knowing she's not a big breakfast eater, I made her a bowl of cereal with some fresh fruit and juice. The television was on again in Vicky's room when I walked past with Naquia's breakfast tray. Naquia was sitting on the edge of the bed when I returned to our room, looking down into her hands. She held onto a key.

"I remember just a few months ago, Pookie asked me to pack up his place and donate all of his things to a shelter. Now Mason, who should have been wondering which sport to play this year has fallen victim to this dreaded disease. He was just an innocent child; he didn't deserve this. I am so sick and tired of people doing things that other people have to suffer the consequences for." She looked at the tray.

"I'm not hungry."

"Then lie down and get some sleep." I sat the tray on the floor and pulled back the covers from her side of the bed. Naquia climbed into bed and I lay down beside her. I held her in my arms as she cried herself to sleep. After she'd drifted off, I carefully removed my body from her, picked up the tray and went back downstairs.

After taking everything back into the kitchen, I poured a glass of orange juice and knocked on Vicky's door.

"Come in." Vicky sat up in the bed, pulling the covers up to her chin.

"Mornin', how'd you sleep?" I asked handing her the juice and sitting down beside her.

"You have to ask? This bed is so comfortable." She sipped the juice and I noticed a bruise on her neck.

"Vicky, I don't want to start any arguments or anything."

"Then don't." Her tone changed.

"Are you okay? I mean I can see something has taken place, are you okay? Have you been checked out?"

"Wesley, we had a fight. It got physical, and it got out of hand. He is not himself right now, he's under a lot of pressure, and he's going through something so I have to be patient and understanding. I have to make sure he is okay and that he has his medication and is taking care of himself."

"What about you?" I asked.

"That's where I'm having problems. See right now I am feeling guilty about leaving Terrence alone. I'm feeling bad about getting mad and starting an unnecessary fight that caused him to hit me."

"Vicky..."

"No Wesley, you don't understand. I love Terrence. I really love that man, and a lot of our problems come from me being silly and insecure. I know none of you understand that. Terrence is the only man I have ever loved. I can't leave him right now when he needs me the most. I needed a break; I needed to get away for a minute. But instead out of my silliness, I flew cross-country because I was mad at something he said. Now I know what he means about me being immature. I know now why he doesn't want to get married."

"Sis, let me tell you something. Love doesn't hurt it's not painful. Even though some things are said and done that may hurt or are painful, they don't last; it doesn't linger on; it's temporary. I can see that you love Terrence, I don't understand it but I have to respect it. What you just said proves to me that you really love that man, but does Terrence love you? Do you think Terrence is sitting at home right now trying to figure out where you are? What you might be feeling or if you are okay? I will bet you he hasn't called Father to see if you are here or if he has seen or heard from you. I'm not trying to talk him down; I can't tell you what you should or shouldn't do. I just want you to really open your eyes to your situation. I want you to see your relationship for what it really is and not what you want it to one day be. You are a beautiful woman. You deserve to be treated like the precious, priceless treasure that you are. But until you recognize it for yourself, nobody else is going to see it." I caressed her cheek.

"If you want, we can call Natalie; maybe she knows some nurses in LA and we can make arrangements to get someone to go by and check on Terrence to ease your mind. In the meantime, I want you to take this time that you are here for you. I want you to hide out here, relax and get some rest for your mind and your body. You don't have to worry about going anywhere or doing anything. I will get you whatever you need. Can you do that for you and for me?"

"But..." She was about to find an excuse not to take me up on my offer.

"No. Take a few minutes, go take a long bubble bath and give what I just said some thought. I'll call someone to come here and give you a massage, come and do your hair and stuff and then you tell me if you don't agree with what I've just said."

"Okay." She said as if she was giving up on her end of a battle.

"Run your bath and I'll make a few calls." I kissed her cheek and left to go upstairs to get dressed.

Naquia was out of it; I closed the blinds to darken the room for her and switched on the ceiling fan to keep the room comfortable. I thought about what my lady must have been going through having lost two of her patients in a short period of time. It had to be one of the downsides to being a doctor. She had shared with me, how they try to teach them to detach themselves from the patient. She said that was the one course she was destined to fail.

"Umm..." She cleared her throat.

"What are you staring at?" Naquia rolled over to the center of the bed.

"My beautiful wife." I lay down beside her.

"Have I been asleep long?" She asked.

"No, it hasn't even been an hour. Go back to sleep."

"You want to put me to sleep?" She ran her hand across my chest.

"Nothing would give me more pleasure but you'd probably fall asleep on me midstream." I kissed her forehead.

"You're probably right, but tonight it's on. I picked up a little something for you. I can't wait to see your face." She smiled.

"Oh yeah? Then I've changed my mind."

"No, get out of here. Wake me around two please?"

"Sure baby." I kissed her nose and left her side to get into the shower.

***

"You know I could get lost in this place. You are going to have to give me the tour of your mansion again. It's a good thing my bathroom is in my bedroom or else I'd be lost and wandering out here trying to find my way. How many rooms in this place again?" Vicky was standing on the stairs like she didn't know whether to go up or down.

"It's four guestrooms with baths, the kitchen, dining room, living room, den, Lily's room and playroom, the gym, utility room and up here is our loft and bathroom. Other than the powder room that's pretty much it. Take your time and wander around. As long as you stay inside, you should be able to find your way back to your room."

"I told you, this is too much house for two people." She said taking my hand.

"Hungry? I can whip up some omelets or we can go out if you want?"

"Where's Naquia?"

"She's sleeping; she just got in a little while ago."

"I'll take one of your omelets now and maybe I can take you two out later for dinner."

"Sounds good but I'm not sure she's off. We can find out later." I led Vicky to the kitchen where I sat her down and pulled out all the fixings.

"I want to go and see Samantha. Could you take me over to her grandmother's house?"

"I told her yesterday that you were coming home. Take my car; I'll put the keys in it for you. So you can come and go as you please. I want you to feel at home here."

"You went to see her?"

"I had something I needed to ask her after Naquia and I talked yesterday."

"I'm glad to see that you are trying to…"

"Don't get it twisted. I'm not trying to do anything where Samantha is concerned. I think we'd better change the subject."

"Whatever you say." Vicky handed me the green peppers and onions she had chopped up and I poured them into the egg mixture. Our omelets were delicious and Vicky cleaned the kitchen before she left to go visiting.

"The keys are in the car with my phone in case you need it. I'll call you when Naquia gets up. Be careful with my baby." I said.

"You men and your cars. Bye." Vicky waved as she walked out to the garage.

***

I called everyone so they could come over to welcome Vicky home. We were all out back when Naquia woke up. I could tell that she had showered again because her hair was damp and I smelled the fruity smell of that stuff she kept in her shower.

"Hi everybody." Naquia embraced me from behind.

"I'm starving." She whispered in my ear and I pulled her around in front of me and sat her in the only vacant chair.

"I'll get you something." As I walked away I heard Naquia telling them about her patient passing away. I pulled together a salad and topped it with the remaining grilled chicken breast strips. I sat the plate on her lap and handed her a napkin.

"Thank you baby." She smiled before digging in. Natalie, Father and DJ brought out the homemade ice cream and we spent the afternoon laughing at old stories, sharing memories and making new ones. Everyone started leaving when the sun started going down. Vicky informed us that she had made arrangements to spend the night with Samantha. I started to say something but Naquia stopped me. So instead I gave her a spare key to the house and the security code to keep with the keys to my car. After walking everyone out to their cars, Naquia and I went inside to give each other something we have been promising one another for the last couple of days.

***

There were no words spoken except those sung from the stereo. The candles provided the only light we needed and our love gave our minds and bodies all the direction needed. We began with the sensual touching of one another's body, kissing, tasting, and touching everywhere. As the intensity grew, our passion took control; we were about to ride this wave all the way until Naquia stopped.

"Wesley, we need a condom."

"Huh?"

"A condom. Do you have one? Where's the box?"

"Naq…"

"Excuse me." She got up and went into the bathroom. I sat up in the bed and watched her. When she came out, she handed the box of condoms to me.

"What's up doc? What's this about? Mason? You know we've both been tested; we're fine. So what's up?"

"I'm ovulating."

"Yeah."

"Well I want some extra protection. I don't want to get pregnant. I'm on an antibiotic for my sinusitis and I don't trust my pills alone."

"We're back to you not wanting to get pregnant."

"Yes. I haven't changed my mind."

"Doc, I thought we had settled this. Especially considering how you took to Mason. You're almost finished with school; how much longer are we going to wait?"

"I don't know."

"What is it?"

"I don't have any reason other than I'm just not ready."

"But we've talked about this."

"Yeah I know and like I said, I've had a change of heart."

"A change of heart?"

"Yes, I don't want my child to have to compete for your attention or affection when your precious daughter is here. It wouldn't be fair."

"Naquia, I would never…"

"Wesley, my mind is made up."

"Now you're telling me we can't even talk about this. Where is all of this coming from? I thought we settled this."

"I don't know maybe Mason's death has caused all of this to resurface. When I think of what Pookie went through, how it must have felt to love someone who wouldn't even admit to him on his deathbed that he cared for him. That same someone he loved, lived and died for wouldn't even come forward to be there for him in his final hours. Pookie felt like he had wasted his life and his love for Terrence who claimed he loved him. All because Terrence was involved with your sister and didn't want his dirty little secret to come to light." She cleared the emotion that had crept in her throat.

"Pookie had to compete for his lover's attention, his time, and his love because Terrence wasn't man enough to admit that he loved Pookie. I know how that feels; I know we've made a lot of progress, and you love me, I can feel that. But I don't know what would happen if Raven were to come here one day saying she's single and available. I don't know in my heart that you wouldn't leave me. And with that uncertainty, I cannot bring a child into that confusion."

"So all of a sudden, I'm just like Terrence and I wouldn't acknowledge you and my love for you. Damn, how long have you been holding all of this inside?"

"Wesley…"

"No Naquia, listen. I don't know what else has to be said or done here. I love you and I can't keep defending myself for something I haven't done and have no intention of doing. I thought we were past all of this. Raven and I have

33

nothing between us but Lily. Other than Lily, we have nothing to talk about. Now if you're trying to talk about her sister. Cee and I are friends and that has nothing to do with Raven. Naquia, we can't keep doing this. I can't take this back and forth shit." I got up out of frustration stepped into a pair of sweats and went outside for some air. It seemed like now that she had me believing everything was cool, she turns around and sucker punches me. It was still early; we couldn't have been inside for more than an hour. I knew I had to get myself together; I would have to go back inside eventually. I felt Naquia as she closed her arms around my waist.

"I'm sorry." She said and kissed the back of my neck.

"I don't know where all of that came from. I'm scared. Wesley, I can control every other aspect of my life except you. I love you and I know how you felt when we first got married, but now with your reaction to Raven getting married, I'm not so sure. That day I knew that even though you said you loved me that you were still into her too. It hurt then and it still hurts now. I know you haven't given me one reason not to trust you, but when it comes to her, I don't trust you. I'm scared to death that if we were to have a baby, our baby wouldn't be good enough. You have your daughter perched up so high on that pedestal, where would our baby be?"

Chapter Three: Raven

I finished brushing my hair and then walked into my closet. Today was the day for the board meeting and I didn't want Shayla to have anything to use against me. I chose my new Dolce & Gabbana suit. I fell in love with the Camel color and when I saw that the inside was lined with a leopard print, I knew it was perfect. Even though it was wool; it didn't look like I was wearing it out of season. It's August now so the fitted button front jacket with the high collar and matching skirt with a back zip and slit was just what I needed on a day like today.

"Princess, I'll be in the office. We should get to the office early so we can get you prepared."

"Okay, I'll be right down." I sighed at the thought of facing Shayla and her cohorts. I'm sure she has found a way to get them all on her side. I would feel better if Derrick just chose someone else. He was totally against that idea; he was dealing with this like it was some type of mental chess match with her that he refused to lose. I zipped up the skirt, sprayed a little perfume, checked my makeup again and then headed into the nursery to kiss my baby goodbye.

"You look nice, is that new?" Mama asked.

"Yes, it was one of my wedding gifts." I reached into the crib to tickle my angel, she cooed and smiled at me.

"Bye lovely one, Mommy will see you later okay?" Lily kicked her feet and giggled.

"Wish me luck." I said to Mama as I reached over for a kiss.

"Luck is not needed when you've got God's favor. It's already done." She sounded just like Bishop Long.

"Thanks. See you two later." I closed the door to the nursery and headed downstairs. Derrick was on a call when I walked into his office.

"Let me make this clear for you. I don't need any test and this is the last time I will have this or any conversation with you about this. Do you understand me?" He sounded angry.

"Honey, I'll be in the car." I said while tapping lightly on the doorjamb. He nodded in response.

"Good morning Ma'am." Matthew saw me coming out and jumped out to open my door.

"Good morning Matthew." I slid into my seat and opened my briefcase to go over the fact statement Barbara had prepared for me. Derrick wanted to make sure I had all bases covered in the event someone wanted to come at me with some historical information about the company. It was amazing to see how Derrick had taken his initial advertising agency that was run by himself and two other people, to turn it into this $90 million dollar company. I watched as my handsome, successful husband opened the door and walked over to the car, dismissing Matthew when he got out to greet him. Opening the door, I slid over to let him in.

"Everything okay?" I asked.

"Yes." He nodded.

"Are you ready?" He asked.

"As ready as I'm going to be." I said.

"Well you look beautiful and that alone should get you half the votes." He leaned in and kissed my cheek.

"Thanks. I wish it were that easy."

"Princess, you have nothing to worry about. Shayla thinks she can manipulate this but I won't let that happen. We have too many things to do than to entertain another one of her machinations. Now let's go over some of these points."

***

By the time we pulled in front of the building, thanks to Derrick I was prepped and ready, I knew KCI inside and out, and for anyone who didn't know better, they would think I was one of the initial players. It didn't dawn on me until we walked into the lobby that this was the first time we were back in the office since the wedding. The congratulations banner in the lobby brought a smile to both our faces.

"Good morning Mr. and Mrs. Kincaide." George the security guard said with a smile.

"Good morning." We responded in unison. Derrick pressed the button on the elevator and I greeted a few more people who came in while we waited. I was pleasantly surprised by the reception we were receiving, I thought we would still be in the whispering and snide remarks stage. When the bell rang for my floor, Derrick said he'd see me at ten, which was good because I was worried he might want to put on a performance for the other riders in the elevator.

"Okay." I said and walked out to find another banner hanging outside my door. Valerie stood with a small gathering of people, I figured that George must have called upstairs to announce my arrival.

"Good morning Mrs. Kincaide." They all said sounding like a third grade class.

"Good morning." There was an awkward silence like I was supposed to say something else.

"What?" I asked curious to see what this was all about.

"Since we were not privy to your surprise wedding, we didn't have the chance to give you a proper shower, so..." Valerie pressed a button and the strip tease song came on and Brian from the mailroom popped out from around the corner and started dancing around like a maniac. Brian is a sweetheart but a sexy dancer he is not.

"Do ya'll want me to take it off?" He said over the music.

"No." Was the resounding response from all of the ladies gathered there outside my office. Brian faked a look of disappointment and continued this so-called dance until I begged Valerie to turn it off.

"Please stop him before he hurts himself." I said wiping tears of laughter from my eyes. The music stopped and then they presented me with a gift.

"Thank you." I sat down and opened the beautiful ivory colored wrapped box to uncover a Sterling Silver frame set.

"That's one for your hubby and one for the baby." Valerie announced.

"Thanks everyone, this is so beautiful and it really means a lot." I said fighting back emotion. I gave hugs to everyone I could get to before they all

37

started to leave. Monica picked up the wrapping paper and frames and took them into my office. Valerie and I joined her after I hugged the last person standing outside my door.

"I have a nine o'clock, so let's get to the juice first." Monica said as Valerie closed the door.

"There are no words to describe it." I said remembering the pact that Derrick and I had made on our honeymoon.

"Oh no sistah girl, you ain't getting off that easy. Tell me something good." Monica said shaking one of her manicured fingers at me.

"Where'd you go?" Valerie asked.

"We went to Hawaii after a brief layover in Beverly Hills."

"Ooh that sounds nice, tell us more." Valerie grinned after taking a seat.

"Derrick decided that he wanted to surprise me for the honeymoon since I had surprised him with the wedding. He got us a suite at The Regent Beverly Wilshire; you know the hotel from the movie Pretty Woman. Aside from the hooker thing, he treated me just like Julia Roberts." I said smiling at the recollection of what happened.

"No it's because of the hooker thing, he treated you like Julia Roberts." Monica slid in and we all had to laugh.

"After shopping like crazy, we left the next day to fly to our new house in Hawaii."

"What?" They both said sounding like a choir.

"He bought us a house over there so we wouldn't be disturbed while on the island. It was the most romantic time I've ever spent with anyone in my life. Everything was great until we got back here."

"What happened?" Valerie asked and then I remembered that they didn't know the truth about Wesley being Lily's father.

"Nothing worth repeating. So what's going on around here?" I asked hoping that we could change the subject. Monica and Valerie filled me in on the commotion after the wedding was announced in the paper. For the most part it was all good; it was funny when they told me that before the announcement in the paper, someone had actually started a pool on the date when we would get married and that Lynette Lemore was the person who won the pool which ended up being over $2500 dollars.

"Maybe I should ask for my cut." I joked.

"Well you're glowing and looking nice girlfriend; Julia must have spent a pretty penny on Rodeo Drive." Monica smiled.

"Thank you."

"Thank you? That's it? Valerie I don't know if I like the new Mrs. Kincaide. She keeps secrets." Valerie laughed with Monica.

"If you ladies will excuse me, Mrs. Kincaide has a meeting with the Board of Directors in about fifteen minutes."

"See? It's starting already. New suit, new attitude, meeting with the board." Monica teased.

"Get out of my office." I said as I picked up my portfolio and started towards the door.

"Call me when you're done, if you're not too busy maybe we can do lunch." She said before heading off to the stairs that led up to her office.

"Do you have everything you need?" Valerie asked.

"Think so. Wish me luck?" I said and then remembered what Mama had said earlier.

"What luck? You're the boss's wife, it's a done deal." She said as if that would really make a difference.

"I'll see you in a little while." I said as the elevator bell rang and the doors opened. The ride up to the executive suite seemed shorter than normal and before I could finish looking at myself in the mirrored walls, the doors were opening to the outer cove of Derrick's office. Barbara smiled when she saw me stepping off the elevator.

"Good morning Mrs. Kincaide or is it McNeill-Kincaide?" She asked.

"The answer to that question better be Kincaide or else you will have a bigger fight on your hands than this meeting." Derrick joined us and placed a kiss on my cheek.

"I guess that answers your question. How are you Barbara?" I asked as Derrick walked back into his office.

"I'm good. You look great and he looks happy. I would say all is right with the world. Coffee?"

"No thanks."

"Let's go get settled in the conference room." Derrick said putting his jacket and when he turned to face, he kissed me as I straightened his tie.

"Derrick you really are going to have to do something about this inappropriate behavior in the office. What if Gavin or another of the other board members were with me?" Shayla's annoying voice interrupted the moment.

"They would just see a happily married man being attended to by his beautiful wife." Derrick responded by kissing my lips again before taking me by the hand to walk off towards the conference room.

"*Ouch.*" Angel said and I had to agree.

"Before we get started do you have the check?" Shayla asked when she caught up with us.

"My accountant is delivering it today."

"That wasn't necessary, I could have delivered it." She said sounding like he had spoiled something. Gavin and few other board members were escorted in and Barbara directed them to the continental breakfast buffet. Derrick came over to whisper in my ear.

"Don't let her get to you. You are beautiful; you know this company inside out and that is all that matters. I love you."

"Thanks." I said noticing Mr. Truell walking in with several people I didn't recognize. The remaining board members all came in and within minutes Derrick was starting the meeting.

"Good morning everyone." Derrick said and smiled. He looked extremely handsome in his cinnamon brown colored suit. I wondered how many women thought that we had planned our attire for the day. Derrick asked everyone to look at the agenda for the meeting and he began with old business. When no one had anything to add to the reading of the minutes, we moved into new business. Derrick announced the completion of the Advertation acquisition.

He went around the table and introduced the unfamiliar faces that were members of the executive staff of Advertation. Derrick went over the new accounts that were coming aboard as a result of the acquisition and then gave an update on the company's standing and year to date net worth.

"I am assuming that there are no objections to anything I have just shared with you." Derrick said with a smile.

"Not yet." Shayla said and a light chuckle came from a few people.

"Then next on the agenda are the two open positions. I would like to appoint Raven to the position of Vice-President of Operations. You have all received her dossier of accomplishments for your review. There is one addition that should be communicated. She has accepted the role of Mrs. Derrick Kincaide since our last meeting." Derrick smiled and Shayla fumed under her poker face. A few people congratulated us and then Derrick went back to business.

"Before we put this to a vote, are there any questions?"

"First of all, let me congratulate you on your nuptials. I have read Ms. McNeill's long list of accomplishments but I still don't see anything that says she is the best possible candidate for this position." Joyce Mitchell spoke up and my heart sank down to my feet.

"In all honesty, I believe we should perhaps look outside the company for a viable candidate." She finished.

"Joyce what is it exactly that is making you so uncomfortable? Raven has all of the operations experience we would require of someone outside of the company for this position. She has a solid relationship with the clients as well as the staff here. She has the educational background in marketing and proven work experience in advertising. Enlighten me on what's missing." Derrick asked and most of the people turned to look at Joyce for her response.

"I don't disagree that Raven is a valuable asset to the company, but I am not convinced that she's seasoned enough for the role of Vice-President. We are as you have just announced a $120 million dollar company. We should not jeopardize any of that because you've taken a new bride." She said and I took a deep breath probably because I too questioned if I was ready for this responsibility.

"Joyce, you have been a member of my board now for what ten or eleven years. When you were appointed it was because of your work within the community and none of it had anything to do with the advertising world. You were chosen because of the skills, knowledge and abilities you possessed. You were successful in providing educational resources to the less fortunate and for your ability to make sure their needs were being met. We looked outside of your background or "seasoning" as you put it so eloquently. What is so different now?" Derrick's demeanor and his tone of voice commanded everyone's attention and agreement to his point of view. Joyce could not respond and Shayla seemed displeased. Gavin then took a shot.

"That all sounds good Derrick, but let's examine all that has transpired in the last year that could have negatively impacted our position in the arena. There have been rumors of scandalous affairs within this office involving you and women within your employ. Not to mention the unplanned pregnancy and all that transpired at that press conference. Now you have pulled off this secret marriage. Quite frankly, you are acting as if you have something to hide now and we never experienced any of that when you and Shayla were married."

"Gavin, I am surprised that you would choose this forum to voice your concerns regarding my personal life. Normally, I would not address something like this in a board meeting but since you've opened the door, let me walk in. First things first, to settle your mind and anyone else who may subscribe to the theory that all of a sudden I have lost all of my business sense; Raven's appointment is one that has been carefully considered by myself and other members of my executive staff here at KCI. We are in agreement that she has more than proven her worth here and that there is so much more that she can add heading up our Operations. Secondly, as you've stated those rumors could have had a negative impact but in fact they did not. Lastly, my personal relationship with Shayla in the past or Raven now has never impeded my judgment or ability to run this company. So neither my marriage nor the birth of my daughter has any bearing on KCI other than the fact that they have brought me great joy which in turn makes my coming to work here all the more gratifying. So if there are any other valid points of contention to discuss I am more than willing to entertain them, if not. I would like to put the appointment of Raven Kincaide to the position of Vice-President of Operations to a vote. All in favor please respond with aye." Seven of the ten members raised their hands with aye.

"Those opposed, please respond with nay." Derrick said and Gavin, Joyce and Shayla responded.

"Thank you. Please let the minutes show that Mrs. Raven Kincaide has been appointed the Vice-President of Operations for KCI effective immediately." Barbara scribbled her notes and Derrick proceeded.

"Next is the position of Vice-President of Business Continuity. Geoff Grainger is an internal candidate from Advertation. You were all forwarded his dossier as well. Are there any questions or comments regarding Mr. Grainger's appointment?" No one had anything to say, so it was put to a vote and passed as well.

"Is there any other new business?' Derrick asked. No one had anything so he adjourned the meeting and people started to leave.

"Mrs. Kincaide, it's a pleasure to meet you." The man who was just named Vice-President of Business Continuity extended his hand to me.

"Raven please. And it's nice to meet you as well." I said shaking his hand while eyeing an exchange between Derrick and Shayla in the corner.

"I'm really excited about this new opportunity with KCI. Mr. Kincaide is a mastermind and I have been following his career for years. I know there is so much I can learn from him." He said and I think he realized he didn't have my full attention.

"I'm sorry Mr. Grainger, would you please excuse me for a moment?" I said trying to get to my husband who looked like he was ready to grab Shayla.

"I didn't orchestrate anything; perhaps if you'd keep your zipper closed you wouldn't be faced with these accusations." Shayla increased the volume on her voice when she noticed me approaching.

"Derrick, sweetheart can I speak with you for a moment please?"

"I need a minute Princess." He said never turning his attention away from Shayla.

"Honey, it's important." I placed my hand on his arm and he turned to face me after delivering his last verbal blow to Shayla.

"I gave you twenty-five percent of my company to get you out of my life and pockets once and for all. Don't fool yourself into thinking you have some type of control or that you can actually maneuver anything around here. So I would advise you to let your friends Gavin and Joyce know that if they cannot remain objective they can and will be replaced. I don't think they are going to like you being in their pockets as well."

"Just remember my darling husband; everything done in the dark eventually comes to light. I'm going to make sure it's bright enough for everyone to see." Shayla smiled and walked away. Derrick was about to say something but took a deep breath instead.

"Yes Princess?"

"I thought things were getting heated so I figured I should come in and rescue you for once."

"I don't think I'm the one you would have been rescuing this time." We walked out of the conference room and into his office. Derrick closed the door and placed a kiss on me that said he needed much more.

"Wow." I said trying to catch my breath.

"Where did that come from?" I wiped some of my lipstick from his lips.

"From the depths of my heart; you don't know how much I need a woman like you in my life." I sensed that he was feeling something more than what this meeting and his words with Shayla had brought on. I hugged him tightly.

"Well you're kinda stuck with me now, at home and at work."

"And I wouldn't have it any other way. We have to get you and Valerie moved up here."

"Why? I can stay in my office."

"All of the executive staff is on this floor, why would you be any different?"

"Okay I won't fight you on this, after the battles I've witnessed today I'm sure I have no chance of winning."

"Good. What's on your calendar today?"

"We're trying to finish up the final details for the launch party. I've got a few client calls to make but other than that I'm open."

"Can we get out a little bit early today? I want to go home have a good meal and time with my ladies."

"Sounds good to me; call me when you're ready to leave."

"I will."

"I love you." I said before walking out.

"Thanks I needed to hear that right now." He smiled before picking up the telephone. I closed the door to his office.

"Barbara, keep an eye on him for me please, he's having a rough one."

"Sure thing Mrs. Kincaide."

"Stop that." I said while pushing the elevator button.

"Okay Raven." She smiled.

***

Mr. Truell was making introductions on my floor when I stepped off the elevator. I excused myself and walked into my office. I powered on my PC and checked my emails. After being out of the office for seven days I had accumulated a total of one hundred and seven new messages. Glancing through the names, I picked the ones that may have needed immediate attention and left the remainders to be opened at another time.

"May I come in?" Geoff Grainger stood just inside my door.

"Sure." I rose to greet him.

"I'm sorry about earlier." I said.

"No problem. This is a nice office you have here."

"Thank you. Have a seat." I said and sat back down.

"Thanks."

"So Mr. Grainger…"

"Geoff please."

"Okay Geoff, how long have you been with Advertation?"

"A little over five years." Geoff continued and shared with me all of his hopes, his dreams and his desires to conquer the advertising world. He shared how he did a term paper on Derrick and decided he was going to work closely with him some day. Now that dream was coming true. His soliloquy was interrupted by Monica's entrance.

"Knock knock, sorry to interrupt." She said with a smile. I watched as her sexy girl personality surfaced.

"Monica let me introduce you to Geoff Grainger. Geoff this is Monica Redding." I said.

"Nice to meet you." Geoff said and Monica smiled.

"Raven, I wanted to know if we were still on for lunch." Monica said sounding all professional.

"Sure. What time?"

"I'm free whenever you are. Call me when you're finished here."

"Actually Geoff if you don't have any plans why don't you join us, Monica is the Vice-President of Financial Affairs and I am sure you two will be working closely together very soon."

"Oh?" Monica asked turning to face Geoff.

"Yes, Geoff is the newly appointed VP of Business Continuity." I said watching my girlfriend at work.

"Congratulations and welcome aboard. Let me grab my purse and then we can go." Monica said before leaving.

"Monica, why don't you meet us in the lobby?"

"Okay." I noticed Geoff's eyes following her as she walked out of my office.

"Geoff, I'm going to call Derrick to see if he can join us." I said picking up the phone to call upstairs.

"Hi Barbara, is he available?"

"No he had to run out, is there a message?"

"I wanted to invite him to lunch. Is he at least in a better mood?"

"No."

"Okay. Would you give me a call when he returns please?"

"Sure thing." I hung up the phone and told Geoff I was ready. Then a brainstorm hit me.

"Uh hold on a minute." I said as he pushed the down button for the elevator. I walked over to Valerie's desk.

"What's wrong?" She asked.

"Call me on my cell in two minutes." I heard the bell on the elevator ring. "I'm coming Geoff."

"What?" Valerie asked looking totally bewildered.

"Just do it please." I said running to catch Geoff in the elevator.

"Sorry." I said to everyone waiting in the elevator. There was one stop before we reached the lobby and I was hoping we'd make it to the lobby before Valerie tried to call. Monica was standing at the guard's station when the elevator doors opened. She had touched up her makeup and I shared a knowing glance with her. As we were about to go my phone rang.

"Hello?"

"It's me crazy lady, why am I calling you?"

"Hey Valley, no I'm still in the lobby."

"Of course you are because you couldn't have possibly gotten any further in two minutes."

"What happened? No we need that resolved today. Eric will have a conniption fit if we don't...never mind, I'll be right there." I said closing the cover on my phone.

"I'm sorry guys; I'm going to have to ask for a rain check." I said looking to Monica hoping she would catch on.

"Is everything okay?" Geoff asked.

"I'm right in the middle of a big launch party for one of my clients and unfortunately we are having problems with the caterer. You two go ahead and have lunch without me and I'll catch up with you later."

"You want us to bring you something in?" Monica asked catching on to my scheme.

"No thanks, I'll get a salad or something from the cafeteria. Go. You two enjoy yourselves." I said turning to walk towards the elevators. Monica and Geoff left and I went back upstairs to my office.

***

"I need to see you in my office please." I said as I walked passed Valerie's desk.

"Yes Mrs. Kincaide." She said giggling.

"You want to tell me what all of that was about?" She asked as she closed the door to my office.

"I'm trying to hook Monica up."

"With Mr. Grainger?" She said putting a British accent on his last name.

"You are so silly. You know you are going to have to get serious if you want to continue to work for me."

"Continue to work for you? Monica was right you have changed."

"I have to, now that I am the new Vice-President of Operations, I cannot continue to play around. As a matter of fact, we need to get this office packed up for my move." I said in a serious tone not cracking a smile.

"I'll get right on it."

"And I need you to get me all the materials I will need to get my executive secretary up to speed on all of my accounts." I could tell that statement stunned her because she hesitated before she responded.

"And lastly, I need you to make up your mind if you'd like to continue to be an admin or if you'd like a promotion to be my executive secretary." I said with a smile.

"You know you make me sick right?"

"What?"

"You come in here playing games and everything; nobody knows when to take you seriously."

"Well?"

"Well what?"

48

"Okay so you want to stay here and be an admin, I understand."

"You'd better stop playing." Valerie smiled and hugged me.

"I have to talk to Derrick because I'm not sure when the office will be ready, but that will give us time to get organized at least."

"I guess I'm going to need a new wardrobe too. I have to start dressing like I've got a real job now. I peeped that new Dolce & Gabbana suit." She said tugging at my jacket.

"Okay, let's change the subject, where are we with the launch party?"

"Everything is done, unless you are about to add something new. Are you?"

"Calm down. If Eric is happy, then I'm happy." I said taking my seat.

"Have you decided what you're wearing?" She asked taking the seat opposite me.

"No, I asked Eric to design something for me but I haven't heard from him."

"Just have Rodeo Drive send you something to wear."

"I don't have it like that."

"I beg to differ, you are Mrs. Derrick Kincaide now and all you have to do is..." The ringing of my phone cut off Valerie's statement. We both reached to answer it.

"I've got it. Raven McNeill." I said automatically.

"You mean Kincaide don't you?" Cee said into the phone.

"Hey sister; what's up?"

"I hadn't heard from you so I thought I'd give you a call. You still mad?"

"No just busy. How are you and the rest of my family?"

"We're okay. I wanted to know if you had some free time today. Maybe we could go out for a couple of hours."

"Actually today wouldn't be a good day, can we make it tomorrow?"

"I don't know. I'll call you."

"Are you sure everything is okay?"

"Um hmm." She didn't sound very convincing.

"I'll call you later." She said softly.

"Okay. Bye." I hadn't heard my sister like this in quite sometime. Is it a full moon or what, first Derrick, now Cee? When I hung up the phone Valerie went through all of the preparations for the party. We had covered everything Eric had requested and then some.

"Girl you've been busy." I said jotting down the last of my notes.

"I guess I'm going to have to give you a raise with that new position."

"A big one." She laughed.

"Got you covered." I looked up and noticed Monica coming towards us. "Say thank you Raven." I said when she stepped into my office.

"Thank you Raven." Monica smiled and took a seat beside Valerie.

"How was lunch?" I asked.

"Delicious." She responded.

"Now we could take that in a number of ways." Valerie said.

"And all of them would be accurate."

"You didn't." I said.

"Come on now, I'm not Regina. He at least has to wait until the second date."

"Oh so this was the first?" I asked.

"No, the first will be dinner tonight." She said with a big grin.

"So I wasn't imagining things. I thought I saw something there."

"You did. Good looking out." She laughed. I hadn't seen this side of Monica in a long time. Not since she and Samuel parted ways. I knew losing her first love had taken a toll on her but losing him to someone she trusted, her white neighbor was more than either of us could stand. I wanted to pull off my earrings, rub myself down in some Vaseline and give her a good ass kicking myself. Samuel was such a coward he didn't have the decency to tell her that things were over between them, he actually continued a relationship with the both of them until Monica came home early from a business trip and walked into her house to find this tramp in her bathrobe, cooking breakfast in her kitchen for her husband.

"No problem." I smiled at my girlfriend and walked her back to her office to get more details. She promised me a phone call after her dinner full of details.

"Well Mrs. Kincaide, excuse me VPO."

"What?"

"Vice-President of Operations. Geoff told me you got appointed too this morning. Congratulations"

"Thanks."

"You know what this means right?"

"I'm lost. What does it mean?"

"Now you're gonna see how I earn that fat paycheck you keep talking about."

"Bye girl, have a good time tonight. Wait a minute; let me fix that. Behave yourself, keep your hands to yourself and all of your clothes on and fastened."

"What are you trying to say?"

"You know exactly what I am saying, not trying to say. Behave yourself."

"I will. Girl scouts honor." She held up three fingers.

"The closest you've ever come to a girl scout is buying some cookies." We both laughed. Monica's phone rang and I left to let her answer it since Travis was away from his desk.

Chapter Four: Derrick

The sight of another email from Regina took me back to that feeling of regret again. I reluctantly opened the email since I didn't get a chance to read the last one.

"Derrick you cannot continue to ignore me. I need to speak with you it is an urgent matter. Please call me and I will come to you." I pointed the mouse to the delete button and clicked. I picked up the phone and looked in my Rolodex for the number but Rick walked in before I found it.

"Dad, you have to talk to that woman. She's gone off the deep end again." Rick shouted as he entered.

"That woman? She was your mother last time I checked." I got up and walked over to the mini-bar.

"I knew she wouldn't be pleased but honestly, if she makes me change; I'll drop out." He said angrily.

"It won't come to that." I said handing him the soda and taking a seat in the chair facing my desk.

"Thanks." He said from his seat in my chair.

"Son, your mother just wants what she thinks is best for you. She thought you would automatically want to run the business."

"I don't want the headaches you have to deal with on a daily basis. I don't want people always coming after me for money. You never have time alone..." Rick stopped speaking when he noticed Regina standing in the door.

"I'm sorry Dad; I didn't know you still had meetings." Rick stood up to leave.

"No son. Regina, this is unexpected. Did we have an appointment?"

"I'm sorry to interrupt. I was in the building and wanted to know if we could speak for a moment."

"Right now is not a good time."

"Dad, we can finish this later. I'll go over to Dave's until I hear from you." He smiled at Regina and waved goodbye on his way out. When Rick left, I got up and walked over to take the seat behind my desk again.

"What is it Regina?"

"I've been trying to reach you for days now. You haven't responded to any of my messages."

"This is not a good time." I said noticing Barbara's return to her desk.

"Derrick we have to talk." Regina's voice began to rise.

"And we will later." I said before pressing the intercom for Barbara.

"Barbara, what's on my calendar after three?" I asked.

"You're free for the rest of the day." She replied.

"Good, I will have to run out for a few minutes then, so please don't schedule anything."

"Okay."

"Thank you." I released the button and looked over to Regina.

"I'll come by your office at three."

"Good. We'll talk then." She rose to her feet and I walked her to the door to keep up appearances for Barbara's sake.

"Thanks for coming by Regina, it was good seeing you again." I said when the elevator's bell rang. Barbara handed me a stack of scouting reports and asked if I wanted any lunch.

"Just something light, maybe a sandwich."

"Turkey on rye?"

"Sounds good. Thanks." I reached into my pocket and pulled out a twenty.

"Get yourself something as well."

"Thanks I will." Barbara got up after forwarding the phones. I walked back into my office and placed the reports on my desk. I walked over to the window to look out onto the city below. My mind went back to where all of this began almost a year ago.

***

"Thank you. I think you deserve a raise after that one." I smiled at my secretary who had once again rescued me from another unpleasant episode with Shayla. She has been my guardian angel for the last twenty years.

"So you keep telling me." Barbara headed towards her desk and closed the door behind her. I used the next few hours of solitude to finalize the acquisition and to plan the new organizational chart. Barbara asked if I wanted her to forward the calls to my voicemail since she was leaving for the day.

"No, but thank you again for taking such good care of me; I tell you if you weren't married, I'd divorce Shayla immediately and drag you to the altar."

"Promises. Promises. Good night." She smiled and placed the messages she'd taken on my desk.

"Good night." I thumbed through the messages and smiled at the one from Suzanna. The number she left told me she was still in England and any thoughts of seeing her tonight were quickly dismissed. I dialed the number on the message slip and smiled at the warm greeting I received on the other end.

"I was hoping when you called you'd be back in the states." I said.

"Sorry darling, it's been raining for two days so we are behind schedule."

"I got the tickets to that premiere you wanted to attend."

"You did. Why am I not surprised? You really are a man that gets what he wants."

"I want to make love to you tonight."

"Fuel up the jet and come over."

"Don't tempt me. I have the acquisition signing in the morning. When do you expect to be back?"

"Probably Friday, Sunday at the latest." Suzanna said and I heard her name being called in the background.

"Derrick, I'm sorry darling but I've got to go. Miss me?"

"More than I will ever admit."

"I'll see you soon. I promise I will make it worth your wait when I see you."

"I'm going to hold you to that. Have a great shoot. Goodbye." The click disconnecting our call ended my hopes of having a relaxing evening. I don't know why but instead of going back to work reviewing the files of other companies I wanted to scout for future acquisitions, I picked up the phone to call Regina.

"Derrick, how are you?"

"Fine thank you and you Regina?"

"I'm better now. I thought you were going to call me."

"I've been busy."

"Too busy to finish what we started?"

"Regina…"

"Derrick, meet me at Hamiltons at seven, I have the same suite."

"I don't think that's a good idea."

"That's not the head I want you to think with. I'll see you at seven." She hung up before I could respond. I hung up the receiver and finished what I was working on. When I got into my car, I toyed with the idea of fueling the jet and going to see Susanna but driving across town was easier.

"I was expecting you at seven; it's nine now and…" Regina spoke as she took my hand and ran it up her thigh and under her skirt to reveal that she wasn't wearing any panties.

"Regina…" Before I could finish she reached up and covered my mouth with hers. Her tongue surveyed the inner most parts of my mouth as she inched her body in between my legs. Her hands began to massage me and before I recognized what I was actually doing, I had Regina bent over a chair and I had entered her from behind. It was as if I was having an out of body experience because I knew better but I was doing it anyway. The more she moaned, the harder I pumped and within a few minutes I shot off what felt like a missile full of tension into her body. We both quivered and didn't speak or move. I stepped away from Regina zipped my pants and walked into the bathroom. Feeling disgusted with my animalistic behavior, I refused to look into the mirror. I washed my hands and headed back to face Regina.

"Regina, we have to talk." I said motioning for her to take a seat on the sofa.

"What has taken place between the two of us has been…"

"Derrick, we don't need to rehash all of this. Like I said before we are two consenting adults and I am sure you would agree that we should be able to handle ourselves with the proper decorum." She stood. Barbara coming into my office with my lunch was a welcomed interruption to my thoughts.

"Here you are." She placed the sandwich and a bag of chips on my desk next to the files.

"Thank you." I took a seat and opened the file.

***

"Derrick Kincaide for Regina Jameson." I said to the security guard seated at the desk. Carrying my briefcase as if we had a scheduled meeting was the only protection I had in the event I ran into anyone here. Regina dressed in a black suit that was tightly molded to her petite body walked out to meet me.

"Mr. Kincaide, nice to see you again." She extended her hand to solidify her act. I smiled and followed her into the elevator. Once behind closed doors, her demeanor changed.

"I didn't think you were coming." She said running her fingers through her hair.

"You don't expect me to believe that."

"Derrick, I don't understand why you…" She stopped speaking when the elevator stopped. She stepped off and I followed her to her office.

"Can I offer you anything to drink?"

"Regina, I just want to deal with this situation for the last time and cut off any further communication or interaction between us. So if you want to offer me anything, offer me the assurance that this is the end of this nonsense."

"Derrick, if this wasn't important, I wouldn't be bothering you. You do recognize that I did not create this situation alone. It takes two to tango and the two of us tangoed quite a bit. Now that you have become involved with Raven…"

"This has nothing to do with my wife. Is this another one of your competitive jealousies? I can tell you now, you won't win."

"Jealousy? Please there is nothing Raven has that I would ever be jealous of."

"And the point of all of this is what exactly? Regina you are a married woman and you knew I had no real interest in you. Whatever it was that we had was purely of a physical, sexual nature. At your prompting, if I recall correctly, you wanted to show me how a man like me should be treated. I did not deceive you; I did not mislead you. You were involved in a relationship and so was I."

"And if I recall correctly, you never once tried to stop it. There is no need to continue to rehash all of this; we see things very differently. You should know that someone else knows about us."

"There is no us and whatever anyone thinks they know is strictly speculation."

"Actually it's not, they saw us together." She said taking a seat behind her desk and pulling a large manila envelope from her desk.

"What is this?" I asked as she handed the envelope to me. I opened it and pulled out three large photographs, I just looked at the one of Regina and I in a compromising position.

"This arrived while you were on your honeymoon." She handed me a note that read, "I'm sure your husband would be interested to know whether or not he really is your son's father." I folded the note over and handed it with the photographs back to her.

"You don't have anything to say?" Regina asked obviously irritated by my silence.

"What would you like me to say?"

"You don't seem worried about this?"

"Should I be?"

"Derrick, what kind of question is that? I don't know about you but I don't want to lose my family."

"Then I would suggest that you stop playing these childish games and move on with your life. Are those pictures supposed to scare me? Regina, let's cut to the chase, what do you want from me?" Before she could answer there was a knock on the door and it opened immediately.

"Regina, I..." Mrs. Jameson stopped short when she saw I was in the room.

"Mr. Kincaide, I didn't realize you were here. Did we have a meeting?" She said coming in and closing the door behind her.

"Actually, Derrick stopped by to make us aware of some organizational changes over at KCI." Regina spoke up before I could respond.

"Oh. That wasn't necessary; you could have sent a memo. After all you are a busy man, not to mention a newlywed. Congratulations on your recent nuptials."

"Thank you. You are one of our biggest clients so I felt a personal visit was in order." Regina looked relieved that I didn't contradict her story.

"Yes, I'm sure you did. Regina, we are having dinner tonight at the club and I wanted to know if you all could join us."

"Sure, I'll let Richie know."

"Derrick, it's nice to see you and please give your beautiful bride my best." She extended her hand to me.

"I will." I said shaking her hand.

"Regina, I think we're done here." I got up to follow Mrs. Jameson out the door.

"I have a few more questions." She responded and I noticed that Mrs. Jameson had stopped at the elevator.

"I'll have Raven give you a call. She would probably be better suited to answer your account specific questions. Mrs. Jameson would you hold that elevator please?" I walked away and rode down to the lobby with Mrs. Jameson.

"You know I thought I saw something that night we all had dinner, I guess I was right." Mrs. Jameson said.

"Really?"

"Yes." She said with a smile.

"I guess we are all surprised, but it's a good one." I said just as the elevator door opened to the lobby, I turned to look at her.

"Yes, I'm sure it is. Take care Mr. Kincaide." She smiled before the doors closed and I walked out to the car.

Chapter Five: Raven

When I looked at my watch it was going on five and I still hadn't heard anything from Derrick. I powered off my computer and decided to wait for him in his office.

"I moved everything until tomorrow afternoon so we can meet with the decorators in the morning." Valerie said as she laid some mail on my desk.

"Okay."

"Are you all right?" She asked pulling her purse onto her shoulder.

"I'm fine." I said with a fake smile.

"Give that baby of yours a big kiss from me." I said picking up the mail.

"Ditto. Good night." She said.

"Night." I picked up the phone and dialed upstairs.

"Derrick Kincaide's office, Barbara speaking."

"Hi Barbara. Is he back yet?"

"No, but he called about thirty minutes ago and said he was en route."

"Good. I'm on my way up, are you on your way home?"

"Actually I was waiting for him; I've got some things to go over with him before I leave."

"Are they urgent?"

"Not really."

"Then it can wait until morning; go home."

"But..."

"Barbara."

"Yes Mrs. Kincaide." She said with a laugh.

"Have a good evening."

"Thank you. You too." I picked up my purse and briefcase and headed up to Derrick's office. Barbara got on the elevator I came up in and I went into Derrick's office. I sat on the sofa and waited but after fifteen minutes I started to get antsy so I picked up his phone and dialed his cellular.

"Derrick Kincaide." He answered.

"Hello Derrick Kincaide. How are you?"

"Fine thank you and you Mrs. Kincaide?"

"I've been better."

"What's wrong?"

"My husband is missing in action and I'm a little bit worried. The last time we spoke he mentioned something about going home early to spend some time with me, but that never came to be."

"I'm sorry Princess, but something came up that I needed to take care of right away."

"Are you finished?"

"Unfortunately no."

"Well honey, go ahead and handle everything, I can call a car and just meet you at home."

"I appreciate that, but I have handled enough KCI business for one day. It's time to handle something else now."

"Oh really, and what did you have in mind?"

"I was hoping I could leave all of that in your most capable hands and just enjoy whatever you can think of."

"I'll give that some thought on my way home."

"We will be in front of the building in about five minutes."

"I'm on my way down." I hung up the phone and just as he said, when I stepped off the elevator, the car was waiting. Derrick stepped outside to greet me.

"Hi honey." I gave him a kiss as he grabbed my briefcase.

"You call that a kiss." He said after he was in and the door was closed. He closed the partition and began to slowly seduce me. Derrick placed a kiss on my lips as his hands unbuttoned my jacket to reveal my camisole. His lips left mine and traveled down to the breast he exposed.

"Ahh..." I said hoping it came out as a whisper. Derrick sucked on that nipple as if he were a hungry nursing infant. I closed my eyes to enjoy the moment, and as the sucking intensified, he reached under my skirt. He stroked my soaking wet mound and then decided he wanted a change. Derrick pulled my panties and hose down in one swift move. He inserted his finger into me and my back instinctively arched. When Derrick's eyes met mine, I saw a flood of passion and emotion that was different than any other time.

"Derr..." I started to say something but it was swallowed back when he stroked me and a wave crested. I reached for his slacks and unzipped him and within seconds we had switched positions and I mounted him to give us both the fulfillment we craved.

"Mr. Kincaide." Matthew's voice came over the speaker and we both stopped like two teenagers who'd been caught in the act.

"Yes Matthew, what is it?"

"There appears to be a traffic jam on the highway, would you like me to find another route?"

"We're not in a hurry Matthew, whatever you choose is fine."

"Very well sir." Matthew switched off the speaker and turned up the music. We both laughed.

"We'd better call Mama and let her know we're gonna be late." I reached over to get my phone from my purse.

"Hold on a second." Derrick said as I removed myself from him and sat on the seat beside him. Derrick dialed a number on his phone.

"Hello. Do you have any plans this evening? Would you mind keeping an eye on your little sister for a couple of hours? Good. Call a car for Mrs. McNeill and we will see you in a little while. No go ahead. Okay son, thank you." Derrick ended his call.

"Rick's going to take Lily out on her first date. Call your mother and let her know a car is on the way to take her home." I did as I was told and Derrick got dressed again. Opening the partition, he instructed Matthew to find the nearest exit as I dialed home.

"Hi Mrs. Hill, how's everything?" I asked.

"Fine. Everything is fine."

"Good. Can I speak with my mother please?"

"Sure. Hold on please." After a few clicks Mama picked up the line.

"Hi baby."

"Hi Mama, listen we're stuck on the highway. There must be an accident or something. A car is on the way to take you home and Rick is going to watch Lily until we get there."

"Are you sure? I can stay; your father's dinner is already prepared."

"Thanks but I think Rick wants to take Lily out and show her off to his friends."

"All right then, I'll see you tomorrow. You two be careful out there."

"We will, see you tomorrow. Good night Mama and thanks."

"You're welcome baby." I ended the call and Derrick informed me that we were at least two miles away from the next exit and basically stuck.

"That's too bad." I said.

"What do you mean?"

"Well it was different when we were riding and Matthew had something else to concentrate on. I really don't think I want to give him a peep show here in the limo." Derrick laughed but I was serious.

"You're not trying to be coy with me now are you?"

"Call it what you like, but it ain't happening buddy."

"Have it your way." He said with another chuckle before dialing his phone. After checking his messages, he opened his briefcase and tried to act like he was concentrating on what he was reading. The soft jazz playing in the car was creating a romantic setting as the sun began to set. Matthew inched as much as he could but when he informed us that we were waiting on a MediVac to come to the scene of the accident which was about five miles away from us, we knew we were going to be there for a while.

"So what are you working on?" I asked.

"Reviewing some scouting reports."

"You're still looking to buy another company?"

"Maybe. Why? You don't think we should?"

"It's not that, it's just that when I joined Carlson and Co., it was a small company with a family feel. Our clients felt like they were important and that they would receive personal attention."

"You think we've lost that?"

"I don't know it just seems like the bigger we get… never mind."

"No Princess, tell me your concerns. There may be something that I haven't considered."

"I just think we stand to gain a lot with the little clients as well as the large ones. When I think about Jameson and how they have come up the ranks and now they are actually giving a big name like Gerber a run for the money. It just makes me feel good to know that I was part of that. When you are dealing with someone that already has an established name and their own recognition, it's like we are just pushing paper and shuffling money. Am I making any sense?" I asked hoping that Derrick wouldn't laugh himself silly. Derrick looked at me and closed the file he had on his lap. He moved in closer to me and placed a light kiss on my lips.

"What you said is just another reason why I love you and why you are the Vice-President of Operations. You don't know how happy this makes me. I am finally able to have an intelligent conversation about my business with a woman who understands. I never imagined I would find someone like you in my lifetime. You are intelligent…" He kissed my cheek.

"Caring and compassionate." Another kiss.

"And sexy as hell." This kiss was deeper and much more passionate.

"And smarter than that; I haven't changed my mind." I said catching on to his ploy.

"Too damned smart sometimes." Derrick retreated back to his side of the limo. Within a few minutes we were moving again and Matthew found an alternate route to get us home. I left Derrick in the limo on a call and walked into an empty house. Mrs. Hill left a note on the counter saying Rick had taken her and Lily out for a little while. Dinner was warming in the oven and smelled delicious. It then dawned on me that I hadn't eaten all day. I decided to go upstairs, shower and change into something more comfortable hoping Derrick would be in from the car by the time I got back downstairs. I stripped out of my suit and turned on the water in the shower. The steam quickly fogged the mirror and I stepped in closing the door behind me and took a seat on the bench in the shower. Just allowing the steam to open my pores and relax me.

"Mind if I join you?" I was startled by Derrick's voice since I had closed my eyes and focused on the music playing.

"Not at all." I watched as my 6'8 giant kneeled down to lay his head on my lap.

"Do you want to talk about it?"

"About what?"

"Whatever has you in this mood. Whatever caused you to disappear. Whatever you and Shayla were arguing about earlier."

"It's nothing new. Shayla is just being Shayla. I'm tired of people questioning me as if I have all of a sudden lost all of my business sense and..."

"What? Talk to me."

"And I love you and that settles it."

"All righty then. The man has spoken." I said with a soft chuckle. Derrick laughed as well.

"How do you feel about everything that transpired today?" He asked.

"It wasn't as bad for me as I thought it would be it was more like they were trying to discredit you. I really wish you didn't have to go through all of this."

"Princess, KCI is still my company and nothing is going to change that. Shayla can try and make ripples in the water if she likes, but it will be just that; ripples. She can't do anything or change anything; I've made sure of that. And that is enough talk about business, I'd much rather pick up where we left off in the limo." Derrick rose to his full height and pulled me into his arms, where our love dance began again.

Chapter Six: Wesley

Naquia had just pulled her third twelve-hour shift in the last five days. My baby was finishing the last of her classes for the semester, going through her internship rounds and then giving time at the AIDS hospice every other day. When I waited outside the resident's quarters to pick her up this morning, she looked like she was dead on her feet.

"Hi baby." I opened my arms to her and she walked right in. I picked her up and carried her to the car; she rested her head on my shoulder. I let her down so she could get in the car. Two seconds after starting the car, I could tell she had fallen asleep. When we pulled into the garage, I nudged my wife to get her to at least make it inside to the den and I'd take care of the rest. She curled up on the sofa and I pulled a throw blanket out of the linen closet and covered her. I turned off all the ringers on the phone and went outside to shoot some hoops.

The ball bounced off the rim and I ran to chase it down, when I reached the end of the fence a trance came over me. It was like déjà vu, my mind when back to the first time I saw Raven and Trey in the park. Trey was chasing his ball and Raven ran up behind him. She caught him and tickled him until he fell to the ground in a fit of laughter. I still find it hard to believe that it was almost a year ago when we were meeting and falling in love. Now we are at each other's throats as if we've been bitter enemies from the beginning. We have to come to an agreement about Lily, I don't care that we will never be together again, but I can't live without being a part of my beautiful daughter's life. My trance was broken when I heard a car horn in my driveway. Vicky got out and walked over to the court. She looked good, like she was finally getting herself back together. It didn't take much convincing for her to realize that she needed to stay away from Terrence. We convinced her to go and get tested after that mess with Terrence and Preston. Samantha must have used her illness and pulled on my sister's heartstrings. Even if I had been there to witness it in person, I still wouldn't believe that she wants to forgive Samantha.

"Let me take a shot." Vicky said as she walked up to me in her suit and high-heeled shoes. I bounced the ball to her.

"Don't break a nail." I said as she caught the ball and tried to setup for her shot. She threw up an air ball that I caught under the basket.

"Maybe it's the shoes." I said and laughed.

"Where's Naquia?"

"She's asleep; she just got off a little while ago."

"Oh."

"What's up?"

"She said she was going to help me pick up the stuff for Father's birthday dinner and then we were going over to the hospice."

"Well I can help you with the birthday stuff, but that's it."

"Wesley, you are going to have to face her sooner or later."

"Why would you think that?"

"Let's change the subject? So how are things with you and Naquia?"

"Everything's cool."

"That's good to hear."

"How are you? What's going on with you?"

"I'm still trying to keep a low profile. Being back here I feel like the town idiot. But it's getting easier. I actually have a date."

"A date? Who is he? You know he has to pass my inspection before there will be any dates going on."

"I'll be sure and tell him that tonight at dinner." Vicky laughed and it felt good to see her happy again. If she had only listened to us years ago maybe we could have spared her some of this pain. But as Mother always said experience is the best teacher. My mind drifted off to Mother and the talks we had before she died. I guess if I had listened to her, I would have been spared my pain.

"Did you hear me?" Vicky nudged me.

"No. What did you say?"

"Where did you go?"

"I was just thinking about Mother."

"Yeah, she's been on my mind a lot too probably because of Father's birthday. Do you think having this dinner is a good idea?"

"I think so; you know Mother always had a way of making our birthdays special. I'm sure she would've done something big if she were here."

"Yes and with a new grandbaby, she would have really gone all out. How is my little niece?"

"She's good. I am going to make a run up to see her this weekend. I am going to sit down and talk with Raven and Derrick to see if we can come to an agreement with the visitation and squash this whole court thing."

"I hope everything works out. Why don't you see if you can bring her back for Father's dinner, I am sure he would love that?"

"I think I will."

"Let me go, I've got some extra time to get dressed for my date. Tell Naquia to give me a call so we can reschedule."

"I will and you make sure you're home by ten."

"Ten?"

"And not a minute after young lady." I shook my finger at her and she waved me off before getting into her car.

***

"Hey." I woke up when I felt Naquia's lips brush against my cheek.

"I didn't mean to wake you." She spoke softly.

"Where are you going?"

"I just got paged; they need me back at the hospital."

"What time is it?"

"Almost seven."

"Doc, you haven't even had eight hours sleep. Damn, are they that busy?"

"Short staffed. I've got to go. I'll call you later." She kissed me again and headed out to the garage. I picked up the remote control and flipped channels for a while finally settling on a NBA classic game on ESPN. I noticed the blinking light on the caller id box and reached over to the phone to turn the ringer back on. When a long distance commercial came on, it reminded me to call Raven about getting Lily.

"Hello." Derrick answered.

"Derrick, it's Wesley. How are you?"

"I'm good Wesley and you?"

"Everything is good. I'm hoping to make a run up there this weekend to spend some time with my little girl. I want to talk to you and Raven, I'm hoping we can figure out a visitation schedule and squash this whole court thing."

"That sounds like a good idea. We'll see you this weekend then. I'll tell Raven when she gets in."

"Thanks. How's my Lily?"

"She's growing more and more everyday. They went over to Selina's."

"Oh, okay. I'll see you all on Saturday. Bye."

"Goodbye." Derrick said and disconnected the call. I dialed Cee's place.

"Hello?" Trey answered the call.

"Hey little man, it's Wesley. What's up?"

"Hi Westley. Are you coming to take me to Chuck E. Cheese?"

"Not today, but soon okay?"

"Okay."

"Can I speak to your mommy please?"

"Mommy, Westley is on the phone." Trey sounded as if he was screaming at the top of his lungs.

"Hey there stranger. Are you in the city?"

"No, I'm at home. I heard my little lady was over at your place."

"She is, as a matter of fact, I have her right here. Say hello."

I could hear my daughter breathing on the other end of the phone.

"Hi sweetheart." I began talking to her and telling her how much I loved her and missed her.

"Yeah, I miss you too. When are you coming this way again? You manage to come and see Lily, but what about me, I thought we were friends?" Cee said when she came back to the phone.

"I am coming this weekend and I will make your house my first stop."

"Liar. You know you ain't coming here first. But that's cool, pick up Lily and then you won't have to rush once you get here."

"Sounds like a plan. Can I speak to your sister for a minute please."

"Hold on." Raven must've been sitting right next to Cee because her voice came immediately on the phone.

"Hello Wesley. What can I do for you?" She sounded like she had an instant attitude but I had to remain calm.

"Hi Raven. How's my little lady?"

"She's fine."

"Good. Listen, I called because I wanted to talk to you and Derrick about this custody situation."

"As far as I'm concerned, there is nothing to talk about. Anything that needs to be said can wait for court."

"Raven..." I took a deep breath before continuing.

"We really don't have to go there."

"You took it there so it's a little late for that now isn't it."

"Raven, I don't want to fight with you."

"Then why did you call?"

"Because I thought two adults could come to a resolution about this. Maybe I would have been better off talking to Derrick." I took another deep breath to calm myself and I heard Cee saying something to Raven in the background.

"I just wanted to let you know that I'm coming up this weekend to see Lily."

"Okay."

"And I was hoping I could bring her here for a few days next week, we are having a birthday dinner for my father."

"Okay. Are you going to take her back when you leave this weekend?"

"Yeah if it's not a problem."

"No problem." She said sounding eerily calm. I haven't had a calm conversation with Raven in months and this was scaring me.

"All right, then I guess I'll see you Saturday."

71

"See you then. Bye."

"Bye." I said and she hung up the phone. I looked at the receiver before hanging it up, wondering if I had dreamt the whole thing.

***

Naquia was getting ready to spend the day with Vicky, picking up stuff for the birthday dinner and spending time with Samantha at the hospice. They are still trying to convince me to go and see Samantha because her health is steadily deteriorating. To get them off my back, I agreed to think about it. I'm thinking about it all right, I'm thinking it ain't happening.

"What time do you think you'll be home?" Naquia asked fastening the buttons on her shirt.

"I don't know, if it gets too late, I may stay in the city until morning." I looked to see if she had a problem with what I had just said that she wouldn't articulate to me.

"I was going to suggest that." She said with a smile. I walked over to her and placed my arms around her waist.

"Oh you were? No more jealousies or insecurities about Raven?"

"Nope. Not a one."

"Good." I placed a kiss on my wife that was interrupted by Vicky's voice from downstairs.

"Be careful. Call me when you get there and let me know what you've decided."

"I will. I love you."

"I love you too." Naquia blew me a kiss before leaving our bedroom.

***

When I took the exit to Raven's house, I called to let them know I was about ten minutes away. The housekeeper said she'd give them the message. The gate to their driveway was closed so I had to call again. This time Raven answered.

"We're out back, come in through the front door and then through the kitchen." She said. I heard Derrick saying something in the background and then the gate opened. I parked the car and followed Raven's instruction. I had prepared what I was going to say to her about Lily and the visitation. I practiced out loud so I could make sure it sounded right. The last thing I wanted was to cause another explosion. Things were finally peaceful and that was for the best. It still blows my mind to know they are living like this. When I walked through the French doors to go out to the backyard, I could see that some construction had been started since the last time I was here. Lily was in the middle of a blanket with Raven and Derrick on opposite sides of her.

"Hi." I spoke as I approached them.

"Hello Wesley. Good to see you." Derrick stood to greet me with a handshake. Raven smiled and picked up Lily.

"Look who's here to see you." She said standing and handing her over to me. Lily smiled at me.

"Hey baby. How's my little lady?" I kissed her cheek and she reached for my nose.

"I'll go get her bags." Derrick announced before leaving us alone.

"Would you like something cool to drink?" Raven asked.

"No thanks."

"How was your trip?"

"Cool, not much traffic."

"That's good. How is everyone?"

"Everybody's good."

"You said you're having a party for your father's birthday?"

"Not really a party, just a family dinner. Aunt Ruth and Mr. Henry are coming so I'm sure they are going to be excited to see my little lady."

"That's nice." She said in that calm voice again.

"Father's birthday isn't until Wednesday, so I was thinking I would just bring Lily back on Thursday."

"Oh, I packed enough so she could stay the entire week. But if you want to bring her back on Thursday, that's fine."

"No, I just thought…"

"Wesley, I owe you a big apology. I have been acting so stupidly these last few months. I have not been fair to you and I have no right acting like Lily is my child alone. I don't know it's just that I was all caught up in crazy mixed up emotions. I was mad at you and at me. I was being stubborn and bullheaded and ultimately I was only hurting myself in the process. So please accept my apology, I am sincerely sorry that I was acting like such a bit…"

"The name calling is not necessary, apology accepted."

"Thanks." She said as she watched Lily running her fingers over my lips. I kissed her fingers and she giggled. Raven just smiled.

"What?" I asked wondering what was going through her mind.

"She is just like her mother, mesmerized by that killer smile." She smiled and I was surprised that her statement didn't faze me. I guess I had finally reached that point where Raven no longer affected me. Derrick came back with Lily's bags and they walked us to the car. After Derrick placed Lily's bag in the trunk, I handed Lily over to him so he could say his goodbyes. Derrick wished us a safe trip and then left Raven, Lily and I alone again.

"Is everything all right?" I asked wondering if this was the reason behind her change in attitude.

"Yes, why do you ask?"

"Never mind. We'd better get going." I said opening the car door. Raven fastened Lily into her car seat and gave her a kiss.

"Be good for your Daddy. Mommy loves you." She kissed her again and then closed the door.

"I'll call you when we get in so you'll know we arrived safely."

"Okay. Be careful." She said before walking away towards her house. I watched for a moment still wondering if something was going on that I wasn't aware of. I started the engine and looked over at my gorgeous daughter, who yawned and let me know she would be asleep momentarily.

Cee was standing in the door waiting for us when we pulled into her driveway. It started storming when we got on the highway so I called when we got to her exit. She walked over to meet me with an umbrella to keep my sleeping beauty dry.

"Hey stranger." She gave me a kiss on the cheek while I unfastened the belt securing the car seat. I took the umbrella and she took Lily upstairs to lay her down. After placing the wet umbrella in the powder room's sink, I was tackled by Trey who looks like he's grown another five or six inches since the last time I saw him.

"Hey Westley."

"Hey little man. I guess I can't call you that anymore you are getting so tall. You are going to be just as tall as Shaq man. You gonna play for the Lakers?"

"No, the Knicks." He said with a smile. I gave him a high five and asked about Tyrese. No sooner than I spoke her name, Tyrese came barreling into the room in her walker going about ninety miles per hour.

"Slow down speedy, you drive just like your auntie." I stooped down to place a kiss on her cheek.

"I'm gonna tell her you said that." Cee said coming down the stairs with the monitor.

"I know you will." I said watching Tyrese go barreling off to the kitchen.

"So what's up? It's been so long since I've seen you." Cee took a seat in the recliner.

"Nothing, I'm just trying to be a good husband and keep the peace with your sister."

"Yeah that's enough to keep you away; are you two at least being civil?"

"Believe it or not she was cool. Kinda spooky though, you know how she is when she's quiet."

"I think she realizes she's been acting like an ass. Derrick has probably put her in check. I never thought I'd say this but he's been good for her. Maybe now she'll finally grow up."

"Maybe."

"I'm sorry that was insensitive of me. You know I wanted you two to…"

"Cee, it's cool. Whatever we had, we had. It's past tense. She's married and happy and so am I."

"Really?"

"I don't know about her, but I am. Naquia and I are cool, I'm doing the right thing and she's meeting me half way. That's all I can ask."

"If you say so."

"I say so. So what's up with you? How's Winston?"

"Let's change the subject." Cee's mood changed dramatically.

"Nope. You're always making me talk; now it's your turn."

"Winston has turned into a workaholic. We don't do anything; we don't go anywhere. I'm tired of sitting around here alone day in and day out."

"Have you told him that?"

"Has he heard me is the better question? You know I don't have a problem speaking my mind. He just ain't listening."

"You want me to talk to him."

"Oh hell no, you know that would hurt his manly pride to think that I said something to someone. He would rather have everybody thinking we're the Huxtables."

"Who?"

"You know from the Cosby show." I started to laugh but Cee didn't even crack a smile, which let me know that this was very serious to her.

"Okay. So what are you going to do about it?"

"I'm leaving him." She spoke in a serious tone and for a minute I believed her until I saw a smile creep up on her face.

"Gotcha." She said with a big grin.

"I knew you were lying."

"The only thing I'm lying about is leaving him."

Chapter Seven: Raven

I watched as Wesley pulled off with Lily and tried to hold back the tears. I wasn't sure why I was feeling so emotional today. Maybe it was time for my cycle again. When I walked into the house Derrick was in his office on the telephone. I took advantage of this moment of solitude and decided to go into the den and do something I haven't done in a very long-time, recreational reading. Lately, all I've had a chance to read are marketing reports, scouting reports, and budgets. I picked up this book I started a while ago called Choices. It was really good, but it hit a little too close to home so I had to put it down. I figured I would just start over and try to get back into it.

"What time do you want to leave tonight?" Derrick asked coming into the den.

"Where are we going?"

"Shayla's benefit; I have to make the presentation."

"Derrick, I really don't feel like…"

"Princess, I need my wife by my side tonight. I promise I'll make it up to you." Derrick placed a kiss on my forehead and extended his hand to help me up to my feet.

"This is going to cost you." I said with a smile.

"I think I can afford it."

"Don't be so sure." I pinched his behind as we walked towards the stairs. Derrick's cell phone rang when we reached the first landing.

"Derrick Kincaide." Derrick answered as we finished the last of the stairs.

"I'm sorry Bob, but something came up. No, we're getting dressed now, I'll see you there."

"Did you have a meeting or something that you forgot?" I asked walking into my closet.

"We were supposed to play golf today but I thought it would be better if I stayed here since Wesley was coming."

"What does Wesley coming have to do with anything?"

"I just thought it would be best if I were here."

"What are you trying not to say Derrick?" I pulled out one of the many things Derrick had picked up for me in Beverly Hills. This particular gown was an Iridescent Taffeta wrap top with collar, two-piece with self-tie sashes. I thought the coral would look good against what was left of my suntan. Derrick walked into the dressing room as I held the gown up in front of me in the mirror.

"That's a great choice."

"Thanks but you haven't answered my question."

"Wesley mentioned that he wanted to talk about the custody issue. I thought that talk would take place today. I wanted to be here for you in case things turned ugly."

"I told you that..." I felt my anger rising.

"Princess, please let's just get dressed and make this appearance."

"Derrick we have to talk about this. It's obvious that you don't believe me when I say I will handle this."

"All right, I won't say another word." He turned to walk into the bathroom. Derrick started his shower and I laid out all the essentials I needed to pull off this outfit. In about an hour we were walking down the stairs and heading out the door.

***

"Matthew, wait a minute." The car stopped and Derrick ran back into the house. I checked my makeup in the mirror and looked for anything that Shayla could use to pluck my nerves. Derrick was back within a few minutes and our journey began. The ride over to the Grand Ballroom was quiet; I figured Derrick thought I was angry with him. It's not so much that I'm angry; I'm just tired of dealing with all of this. I'm going to call Larry in the morning and ask him to draw up an agreement and I'll give it to Wesley when he brings Lily home next week. Derrick caught my attention when he tapped my thigh.

"Have I told you how beautiful you look tonight?"

"Not yet." I said with a smile.

"You are absolutely stunning but there is something missing."

"What?" I said pulling my compact out again.

"Calm down. I just want to add something to your ensemble." Derrick handed me a velvet jewelry box.

"Happy anniversary." He leaned over and placed a kiss on my cheek.

"Anniversary?"

"Yes, it's been a month since we exchanged our vows." He said with a smile.

"Honey, I'm sorry, I've been so busy with Eric's launch party and everything, I..."

"You don't have anything to apologize for. Open it." He sat back waiting for my reaction.

"Oh my go..." The necklace inside the box looked like the ones I've watched the stars wearing when they were being interviewed on the red carpet on their way into the Oscars.

"Breathe." He said reaching for the box.

"Derrick..."

"I love you and I want you to look and feel like the most beautiful woman in the room tonight."

"I don't know what to say."

"You don't have to say anything."

"Thank you honey; I love it and I love you." Derrick fastened the necklace around my neck and then kissed my neck. My hand reached up to touch the weave styled necklace that lay flat on my neck perfectly in the cut of my gown. With this necklace there was no way I would not feel like the most beautiful woman in that room tonight. The car stopped and Matthew came around to open the door. Derrick got out first and then extended his hand to me.

"Mr. Kincaide, do you think your wife will surpass the two million dollars she raised last year?" A reporter shouted before all the others fired off their questions. Derrick kept walking without answering any of them. We entered the foyer of the ballroom and saw that many of the attendees were socializing there. Derrick tried to make his way over to the registration table pulling me along like a toddler caught up in all the sights of the Christmas lights decorating a New York City street. I overheard a conversation where the ladies were praising Shayla for outdoing her last event.

"I heard she got Preston Bailey to do the ballroom. That's why we're waiting out here, so she can announce the opening of the room." A lady dressed in a shimmering gold lamiae gown that was probably at least one size too small stood in a line beside where Derrick was conversing with Gavin Harding from the Board.

"At twenty five hundred dollars a plate, I wouldn't expect anything less." This woman was dressed sophisticatedly in a silver sequined jacket with a pair of black Palazzo pants.

"Raven, it's nice to see you again." Gavin extended his hand to me and the ladies who were speaking all turned to look at me.

"Hello Gavin." I said and Derrick excused us before heading over to the registration table.

"Good evening, Mr. and Mrs. Derrick Kincaide." Derrick said to one of the ladies seated at the table.

"Good evening Mr. Kincaide." The woman looked down onto her roster and then looked up at Derrick.

"I'm sorry sir; there must be some kind of mistake. We only have a seating assignment for you sir, since your wife is chairing the event."

"My wife is standing here beside me. My ex-wife is chairing the event." Derrick seemed bothered by this obvious attempt by Shayla to embarrass me. The woman at the table showed her discomfort with the situation and excused herself for a moment. Another woman who knew Derrick came over to greet him.

"Derrick, good to see you again." She extended her hand.

"Melissa, there seems to be some type of misunderstanding with the seating arrangements tonight." Derrick spoke sternly while shaking her hand.

"Shayla gave me the names of the contributors who would be seated at the head table. The other seats were assigned as the plates were purchased. She didn't mention that you would be bringing anyone."

"Melissa, this is my wife Raven. I wish to be seated next to my wife at a table near the front of the room so that I can make the contribution to the foundation and make a quick exit. I have already written one check for a quarter of a million, you can either find me a table with two seats, or I can just buy a table. Either way, I wish to be seated immediately." It was apparent that Derrick was upset, but he didn't raise his voice or make a scene. Melissa smiled and excused herself. Within a few short moments, we were being escorted into the ballroom.

***

The doors opened to a room filled with tables elegantly decorated with flowers of all colors. Every other table had a tall tree like centerpiece, which carried your eyes up to the chandeliers. Everything sparkled and I had to give it to Shayla this was spectacular.

"Chanel, how are you sweetheart?" Derrick's voice brought me back to reality.

"I'm fine. What are you doing here?" She asked with ice in her voice.

"You know I always support your mother with this event."

"I wasn't talking about you." Chanel looked at me and rolled her eyes.

"Chanel, you are going to have to accept the fact that Raven is my wife and you will respect her as such."

"That will never happen." Chanel walked off. Derrick wanted to go after her but I stopped him.

"Not tonight. Let's just get through the evening and we'll deal with Chanel at another time. Okay?"

"Yes." He kissed my lips before Shayla's clearing her throat interrupted us.

"Can't you two control yourselves? Who let you in this early?" Shayla seemed irritated by our being there but I figured it was more by my presence than Derrick's.

"Good evening, nice to see you too Shayla." Derrick dignified her with a response as he walked around to embrace me from behind. The look on her face showed her disapproval.

"What is she...?" Shayla was interrupted when one of the attendants asked if it was okay to open the doors.

"Yes." Shayla said after composing herself.

"Derrick we are seated at the head table." She extended her arm to point in that direction.

"Actually, I just got a table for Raven and I over here." Derrick pointed to our table.

"You are going to throw off the balance of the room. What am I supposed to do about the photographs?"

"Find someone else for that seat." Derrick said taking me by the hand and walking away from Shayla.

"That was a little harsh." I said as he seated me.

"Nothing that wasn't warranted."

"Derrick, I need to speak with you." Shayla followed us because she obviously wasn't finished.

"What is it now?" He sat down beside me.

"This night is too important for me to have you pull a stunt like this."

"What is that old saying...turn about is fair play? Now you are getting a taste of your own medicine. Doesn't go down quite so easily now, does it?"

"You're going to pay for this." She scowled.

"I already have." Derrick kissed my hand and Shayla turned to walk away. People started to file into the room and began to take their seats at their assigned tables. After a few minutes the girl named Melissa asked everyone to be seated and she welcomed and thanked everyone for coming.

"Tonight we are going to be graced by the wonderful sounds of Cassandra Mills as our featured vocalist. There will be a scrumptious meal prepared by Chef Jacques Oliver who flew in especially at the request of Mrs. Kincaide. I know I am not alone when I say that I am excited to see if Mrs. Kincaide has surpassed her monumental achievement last year. Without further

ado, I introduce to some and present to others, the phenomenal Shayla Kincaide."
Melissa started the round of applause and Shayla made her way to the podium.

"Thank you everyone. Tonight is a night that I look forward to each
year. It is a night of glamour, of excitement and most of all a night of sharing and
giving. Tonight is the third year that I have chaired this event and believe it or
not I still feel like I can do more. Many faces that I see here tonight are familiar
and many are new. But bottom line, I see your hearts and I see the smiles on the
faces of all the family and friends of the people that we are helping by raising
these funds for a silent killer in our community. Tonight we are going to provide
the means for further research so doctors can one day stop this cell that seeks to
destroy our children and our future. Tonight we will come one step closer. So
relax, eat, drink, dance, and mingle. After dinner we will make the presentations
and calculate our final tabulation. I believe we will surpass last year's total by a
landslide. Again thank you all for coming and thank you most of all for giving."
There was a thunderous amount of applause and Chanel started a standing ovation
for her mother. I knew right then and there that Shayla could give any actress a
real run for their money if she decided to pursue an acting career. I was surprised
to see my husband joining everyone in the standing ovation after the exchange
that had just taken place between the two of them.

The wait staff began serving the dinner, which was decorated in such
a fashion that it looked too pretty to eat. But when you tasted it, any thought
that you may have had about spending too much money on this night quickly
disappeared. Champagne flowed freely throughout the room and Derrick
introduced me to many people who were new to me but a part of the circle that
he and Shayla once shared. I sensed something coming from most of the wives
that were introduced to me. Bob came over to greet us and I felt a little bit better
when he approached.

"Hi. How are you holding up?" He asked.

"Isn't it written all over my face?" I asked trying to plaster a fake smile
in case the one I thought I had on had disappeared.

"Yes it is. I could take all of your money tonight if we were playing
poker." He smiled and I laughed at his comment.

"Why don't we get out of here and go test your theory?" I whispered in his ear just as my eyes locked with his wife Vonda's. If looks could kill, I'd be dead on the spot.

"Bob, it's time for the presentations." She grabbed his arm and pulled him away. Bob mouthed the words I'm sorry as walked away. Shayla approached the podium and asked everyone to be seated.

"I know everyone enjoyed that scrumptious meal. Thank you Chef Jacques, you are truly a gift. Before we begin, I would like to thank everyone who helped me pull this affair together. Please give my staff a round of applause." She motioned for them all to stand and we all applauded them.

"Now let's begin the presentations. Our first presentation will be made by Little Miss Taylor Anderson." The audience applauded as a little girl dressed in a beautiful wine colored taffeta dress walked up to the microphone.

"Hello my name is Taylor Anderson and I am the Sickle Cell Anemia spokesperson for this year. When you look at me you probably can't tell that I carry the cell. Many of my friends and classmates don't even know that I suffer from this illness because they have never seen me when my condition flares up. I am here tonight for two reasons. The first is to thank you all for caring enough to share and the second reason is to present Mrs. Kincaide with this bouquet of roses and a check for two thousand dollars. Since the benefit last year, we have held penny rallies at the end of every month at my school and this is total amount we've collected." Taylor handed the flowers and a check to Shayla who hugged her and placed a kiss on her cheek. Taylor received a standing ovation from everyone in the room.

"Thank you Taylor." Shayla handed the roses over to someone seated near her and then asked the corporate sponsors to report in alphabetical order.

"Princess, would you please do me a favor?" Derrick whispered into my ear.

"Sure honey, what is it?"

"I would like you to make the contribution for KCI." Derrick said and pushed the envelope over to me.

"Derrick, I don't think that is a good idea." I whispered.

"I'll be right by your side."

"No, you will not use me as a pawn in this silly little game you are playing with your ex-wife."

"Princess, I want to put Shayla in her place once and for all. This will put an end to her shenanigans."

"Or add fuel to the fire." I pushed the envelope back across the table to him.

"And now KCI." Shayla said and started the applause. The spotlight came over to our table. Derrick stood and extended his hand to me. Not wanting to bring further attention to myself, I placed my hand in his and together we walked up to the podium. Suddenly I felt like a fish out of water, as he began to speak.

"Good evening. It is indeed an honor to be here this evening for such a worthy cause. On behalf of KCI, my wife Raven and I wish to present two checks. The first in the amount of two hundred and fifty thousand dollars to the foundation, and the second in the amount of twenty five thousand to Little Miss Taylor Anderson for being such a courageous young lady and for giving so much of yourself to help someone else." The room exploded in thunderous applause and I found that fake smile again as I watched as Shayla fuming at Derrick's stunt.

"Checkmate." Angel said as if she agreed with Derrick.

"That's just what she deserves." Angel's voice was quieted by Shayla's voice as she decided to make her move.

"Thank you Derrick. It appears that my ex-husband has gained something in the generosity department while going through his mid-life crisis. You know most men, trade in their cars for a newer model, but not Derrick, he had to go to the extreme and trade in his wife for a newer, flashier one." There was a small amount of laughter.

"But Derrick my darling, you must know that you can dress her up, you can even give her my jewelry but my style and grace is something that can never be replaced." The crowd laughed and applauded Shayla as I pulled slightly on Derrick's hand so we could leave.

85

Chapter Eight: Derrick

Raven pulled her hand away from mine and stormed out of the ballroom. She managed to keep her composure while she was in the spotlight but it was obvious when she did not return to our table that Shayla's comment had gotten to her. I stopped long enough to write a check out to Taylor and then excused myself. By the time I had reached the door, Matthew had pulled off with what I assumed was my very angry wife.

"Can I call you a car sir?" The valet asked.

"No thanks." I replied before turning to go back into the ballroom. Shayla was at the microphone again thanking everyone. She caught sight of me and smiled at her handiwork, I nodded to give her the acknowledgement she was seeking. As expected Shayla surpassed last year's goal and vowed to do it again next year.

"Congratulations. It looks like tonight is your night." I said to my ex-wife when she made a beeline straight for me. She picked up two glasses of champagne from one of the trays on the table and handed one to me.

"A toast?" She said raising her glass.

"What are we toasting?"

"A toast to an overall successful night." She said clanking her flute against mine.

"I guess it goes without saying that you're proud of your behavior tonight."

"What's not to be proud of?"

"When are you going to get over the fact that we were over a long time before Raven came into my life?"

"Derrick let's be honest here. Yes our marriage disintegrated, but in spite of that we remained husband and wife to the benefit of the both of us. You had a wife who was close enough when you needed her and far enough away to stay out of your way. I even allowed you to have your side dishes, just as long as they were aware that they were just side dishes. Did I make some bad financial deals? Yes, but nothing that could have devastated what we've built or us. But you took it too far when you suggested that I was only with you for the money. Darling, if it wasn't for me there would be no money. You seem to forget that it was me who helped you build that empire."

"Shayla, if I recall correctly you were Sheila when I met you, back when you and I barely had two nickels to rub together. I will admit that mistakes were made, but just as soon as life became easier for you, you changed. The difference between you and I is that I know who I am with and without money. If everything I had disappeared tomorrow, I would still be able to live and live happily. Can you say the same?"

"What you fail to realize my darling ex-husband is because of all that I have learned over the years, I will never have to worry about that. Make no mistake about this; as long as you live and have anything, I will have at least twenty-five percent of it. You have already made sure of that." Chanel approached the two of us and placed an arm around her mother's waist.

"You were fabulous tonight. I especially liked the way you handled him and his wife." She looked at me through eyes that looked like she may have been sipping on champagne. I wondered if this was the reason why she was treating me as if I were a stranger instead of her father.

"Chanel, I have put up with more than enough of your blatant disrespect. I will give you this last warning. You will give Raven and I the respect that we both deserve if for nothing more than the fact that we are your elders. I will not tolerate your childish tirades, your smart mouth or your nasty disposition anymore. You will get your act together or..."

"Or what, you can't threaten me like I'm one of your employees. I am not going to give you anything. You made a choice between your family and that woman and you have to live with it, not me. I will never and I repeat never show any type of kindness or respect to that tramp you married. Not now, not ever." I had to restrain myself from grabbing her and to think that Shayla was standing there as if nothing Chanel said out of her mouth was out of line.

"Then my suggestion to you little girl would be to talk to me again after you have grown into that adult you claim to be. You have a lot to learn and to be quite honest, it is apparent you aren't going to learn any of it being with your mother. Have a good evening ladies." I placed the champagne flute on the table and turned to walk away.

"Derrick, we are not finished here…" Shayla's tirade was drowned out when I closed the ballroom door behind me. I got the valet to call a car for me and I instructed the driver to take me to my office.

***

"Sir, should I wait here for you?" The driver asked when the car stopped in front of the building.

"No thank you. I'll call when I'm ready to leave." I said thanking the driver and handing a tip over to him.

"Thank you sir and have a good evening." He opened his door.

"Thank you, I've got it." I opened the door and stepped onto the curb. The security guard looked startled to see anyone especially me at this hour of the night.

"Good evening." I spoke to the security guard as I pressed the button for the elevator; it opened immediately. By the time I reached the executive suite, I was halfway out of the monkey suit. I powered on my computer since I was not ready to go home and face whatever my bride had in store for me.

"Damn." I cursed as another email had come from Regina. I opened it only to find more pleas for a paternity test since the pictures and notes from whoever was trying to blackmail her had started coming to her home.

"Derrick if you really think about this, I am protecting you as well." That last statement closed any opening in my mind that suggested I help her. I deleted the message and began to focus on the next company I was interested in acquiring.

***

"Princess." I whispered knowing that she is a light sleeper and probably heard me when I came in the front door.

"Yes." She sounded calm but I knew it had to be the calm before the storm.

89

"I didn't want to startle you coming in."

"Okay." She turned over away from me as if she was in a deep sleep not recognizing that it was now morning. I undressed and slid into bed beside her and before long drifted off to sleep.

The clock on the nightstand read 11:23. I willed myself out of bed and pulled on my bathrobe. I could hear voices when I approached the second landing and recognized that Raven was on the telephone.

"Sounds good to me. What time should I pick you up?" Raven said as I entered the den and placed a kiss on her cheek.

"Okay, I'll see you in an hour. Bye." Raven ended her call.

"Good morning." I spoke.

"Is it?" She responded icily.

"You're still angry." I said taking a seat opposite her.

"Actually no; I'm not angry."

"What does that mean?"

"What didn't you understand? I said I'm not angry. What more needs to be said?"

"I would have to say nothing. You seem to have made yourself perfectly clear." I said as Raven got up and placed the phone on its cradle and headed towards the front door.

"May I ask where you're going?"

"You may, but I may not answer." She closed the door behind her without a second glance.

Chapter Nine: Wesley

Lily was charming her way into everyone's heart, everyone that is except my wife. Although she wasn't going out of her way to be distant, I could still see that she wasn't comfortable in the presence of my daughter.

"Wesley, she's grown so much since the last time she was down here." Vicky said while playing with Lily.

"I know it's amazing how much she has changed and it's only been a few weeks since the last time I've seen her." I sat down beside Naquia and placed a kiss on her cheek.

"What's up Doc?"

"Nothing." She spoke softly.

"Are you sure?"

"Yes, I guess I'm just tired."

"Vicky, could you keep an eye on Lily for a little while."

"Sure. You two have to go out or something?"

"Or something." I said standing and pulling my wife up to her feet. I knew that Naquia was feeling like she was second and even though I still found that to be silly, I had to meet her where she was. I led my wife upstairs to our bedroom and as soon as she stepped across the threshold, I placed a kiss on her lips. She wanted to speak but I shook my head no. For this moment, I needed her to let me do what I felt she needed. She needed some love and attention and that was what I planned to give her. I pulled the tee shirt she wore over her head and kissed her neck as I unfastened her bra. I kneeled down in front of Naquia and placed kisses on her flat stomach as I unfastened the button fly jeans that hid part of her tattoo. I smiled at the red lace thong that covered the treasure cove my tongue wanted desperately to enter. I pushed the lace to the side and lifted one of her legs to my shoulder. Naquia's hands cupped my head as I began to munch. Her knee buckled once and I was afraid she wouldn't be able to keep her balance. I looked up to find a pleased expression on her face and it took a moment for her to register that I had stopped. I placed her foot back on the floor and rising to my full height, lifted her petite body and placed her on the bed. She lay still as I slid the thong down her hips and took full inventory of the tight toned body my wife worked so hard to keep.

"You're beautiful." Were the only recognizable words spoken for the next hour. I took my time and demonstrated to my wife that she was the most desirable woman in the world. Naquia cooed, sighed, inhaled and exhaled. There was a different sound for each level of ecstasy she reached, peaked and succumbed to. As badly as I wanted to enter her, I denied myself that pleasure so that she would be completely satisfied. It didn't take long before she begged me to give it to her. She turned the tables and began to take control. When we made contact, I felt an immediate urge to release but I remembered that she hadn't covered me with a condom.

"Babe." I whispered.

"Hmm." She responded as she started to cover my lips with hers.

"Hold up a second."

"I can't. I want it, I need it now."

"We need a..." I couldn't finish what I was about to say because she began to gyrate all over my stiffness.

"Go deep." She growled and I obliged. It wasn't long before we were both spent and drenched in sweat, panting to catch our breath.

"I needed that." Naquia smiled as she lay her head down on my chest. There was a few moments of silence and I wondered if Naquia had changed her mind about becoming a mother. I debated internally with whether or not to say anything. I had tried to stop things before they were too far gone, so she can't accuse me of trying to make her do something she didn't want to do. I picked up the cell phone to call downstairs to see if Vicky needed me to come and get Lily. She informed me that they had left to go to Father's over an hour ago.

"I figured you two needed some time to do that "or something" you spoke about."

"Good looking out." I responded.

"I'll keep Lily tonight. You two enjoy yourselves. Be careful or we could end up with another little bundle of joy in the family."

"I'll see you in the morning." I hung up the phone wondering if maybe Vicky and Naquia had talked about my wife having a baby. My thoughts were interrupted when my wife decided she was ready for round two.

***

"Good Morning." I spoke walking into Father's kitchen that was filled with the aroma of Aunt Ruth's cooking. The smell of bread in the oven, bacon, and fried potatoes all had my stomach growling.

"Good morning baby. Gimme some sugar." She held her cheek over for a kiss and I gave her what she wanted and then some when I tickled her side.

"Boy don't you start that." She said between giggles.

"Go wash up and I'll fix you something to eat." She pointed towards the bathroom.

"How do you know I haven't eaten already?"

"I heard your stomach when you walked in here, now stop sassing me and go get washed up."

Father and Mr. Henry were deep in a chess match when I walked past them on my way to the bathroom.

"Happy birthday old man." I patted Father on his shoulder.

"Thank you son." He stood to give me a hug.

"Where's Naquia?"

"She had an early shift; I'm going to pick her up in a few hours."

"Good." He said taking his seat and making a move he must have seen when he was standing.

"Check."

"Check?" Mr. Henry was surprised by his move.

"Where's my lady?" I asked.

"I think she's sleeping. She's grown so much. It's so good to have my little Lillian here."

"I thought she would add something special to your birthday old man."

"Watch it." He laughed. Aunt Ruth yelled out for me to come and eat.

"Coming." I hurried into the bathroom, washed my hands and sat down to eat before she had a chance to call me again.

"Thank you." I said before bowing my head to say my grace.

"You're welcome." She started peeling potatoes.

"So what's been going on with you? I liked it better when you lived in the city. I could count on a visit every once in a while."

"Now that I've hired the contractor to oversee the renovations, I don't have to go there as often as I used to. I basically drive up to see my baby and then I'm back on the road to come home to my other baby."

"So things are better now?" She asked.

"Much better. I had to make some adjustments and so did she. It's not perfect but it's better than it was before."

"Honey it will never be perfect. Everyday will be something. Hell, for as long as I've been with Henry's crazy behind, he never ceases to amaze me."

"How long have you been married?"

"This is our forty-fifth year. I never thought we'd make it past the first year and look at us now."

"You love that man."

"I do, I love him but sometimes he can make me so damned mad. But then out of the blue he says or does something that makes my heart flutter like it did when we were kids. I wouldn't trade him for the world, but I'll never tell him that."

"You just did." Mr. Henry walked up behind her and placed a kiss on her cheek.

"Now fix me something to eat." He said as he walked away.

"You'll starve if you think talking to me like that is gonna get your plate fixed." She said turning the water on over the potatoes she'd finished peeling.

"You see what I have to deal with. She ought to be thanking goodness that I haven't decided to go on out to find me a woman who knows how to treat a man like me." Mr. Henry took the seat beside me at the table.

"Go on out there and find that woman, I bet your behind will be back before the sun goes down. You wanna know why?"

"Why?" I asked instigating their verbal banter further.

"Cause he knows he can't get it nowhere else like he gets it here." She said, placing his plate on the table.

"You've got that right baby." Mr. Henry grabbed his wife's behind, and she swatted at him. I smiled enjoying this exchange between the two of them wondering if one day Naquia and I would enjoy the same.

***

Everyone sang happy birthday, and then sat down to eat the bountiful meal Aunt Ruth had prepared. There was fried and baked chicken, smothered pork chops, potato salad, collard greens, macaroni salad, seafood salad, lima beans, rice, corn pudding, homemade rolls; much more food than we needed for the few people attending the dinner. As the plates went around, I watched as my daughter's eyes followed the movement. It's a shame she just had her baby food instead of tasting the wonderful cooking.

"Aunt Ruth, you have outdone yourself today." Vicky said, passing the potato salad over to Denise.

"Good then I won't have to worry about any leftovers."

"Nope, cause I'm going to pack up whatever is left and take it home with me. Shoot I won't have to cook for at least a week." Denise said and everyone laughed.

"This is good." DJ said and the rest of dinner was pretty silent with the exception of the sounds of forks hitting plates. I watched my wife, who looked very uncomfortable, searching for something to eat.

"Do you want me to go out and get you something else?" I asked.

"No thank you." Naquia responded softly.

"What's the matter?" Aunt Ruth asked.

"Nothing. Everything is good." Naquia said covering.

"It's my fault. I forgot to tell you she's a vegetarian." I said.

"Oh girl, just eat. Nothing here's going to hurt you, might do you some good. You could use a little meat on those bones anyway." Aunt Ruth said before putting some more potato salad on her plate. Naquia smiled but I could tell she didn't appreciate what had been said. She offered to do the dishes and excused herself from the table.

"What?" Aunt Ruth asked as if she didn't know if she'd said something wrong. I excused myself and followed my wife into the kitchen.

"Are you okay? You know Aunt Ruth speaks before she thinks." I said placing a kiss on Naquia's forehead.

"I'm fine, just tired. Would you mind if I took your car and went home?"

"We can all go. Let me get Lily…"

"No, please stay with your family. I'll be fine. Call me later and I'll come and get you."

"That's all right. Go home and get some rest, I'll get Vicky to bring us home." I caressed her face.

"Are you sure you're okay?" I asked.

"Stop worrying, I'm fine." Naquia kissed my lips and then started cleaning the kitchen.

"I got this. You go ahead and go home. Get some sleep cause when I get there it is on tonight." I handed her the keys.

"Okay." Naquia picked up her purse and left. I walked back into the dining room where everyone was watching DJ fill his plate again.

"Boy you are going to bust wide open." Aunt Ruth laughed; she seemed pleased that he was enjoying her cooking so much.

"Hurry up and finish eating boy, so I can put you to work, eating like that you need a job." I said taking my seat again.

"Where's Naquia?" Niecy asked.

"She was tired so I sent her home."

"She's probably hungry." Aunt Ruth said as she started clearing the table. I was about to say something when Lily caught my eye; she had something green on her lip.

"What is this?" I said pulling what was left of a piece of collard green.

"I gave that baby some greens, she needs some real food." Aunt Ruth said from the kitchen.

"Aunt Ruth…"

"Wesley, don't go there." Denise intervened picking Lily up out of her highchair.

"Come here pretty girl, how have you been?" Denise and Lily followed Father and Mr. Henry into the living room where they resumed another game of chess. I took some more of the dishes off the table and walked into the kitchen.

"I'll wash." I offered.

"You sure?" Aunt Ruth was removing some dishes from the cabinet to begin fixing doggie bags for everyone. I reached past her to get the containers from the top shelf.

"Here you go." I said handing the stack of Tupperware to her.

"Thank you. DJ baby, are you finished eating yet?" Aunt Ruth asked.

"Yes." Denise answered for him.

"What is wrong with you people that you don't want these kids to eat?" Aunt Ruth handed DJ the serving spoon and the look on his mother's face told him he was finished.

After the kitchen was cleaned and all of the leftovers evenly disbursed, we all made plans to head home early. Lily and I hitched a ride with Denise to give Vicky the opportunity to leave earlier for her date.

"I thought you said Naquia was going home to get some sleep." Denise said when we pulled into the empty driveway.

"She probably got called in." I said unfastening Lily's car seat.

"When are you taking Lily back?"

"Friday if Naquia can get Saturday off." I said leaning Lily over for a kiss from her Aunt Niecy.

"She's going with you?" Niecy sounded surprised. I gave her a look that told her that I wasn't going there with her tonight.

"Thanks for the ride. Be careful and call when you get home." I gave my sister a kiss and that manly nod to my brother-in-law and nephew. Lily and I went inside, placed the bag of leftovers on the bottom shelf of the refrigerator and then spent some daddy and daughter time on the sofa. When Lily drifted off

97

to sleep on me, I took her upstairs to put her to bed and then decided to page my wife to find out when she would be coming home. Her pager began to beep from its place on top of her nightstand, so I hung up and called the hospital.

"Dr. Charles please, this is her husband."

"I'm sorry sir; Dr. Charles isn't on duty tonight." A nurse whose voice I didn't recognize said.

"Thank you." I said before hanging up the phone. I wondered where my wife could've gone and without her pager. Before I finished dialing her mother's number, the headlights of Naquia's truck pulled into the driveway. I went downstairs to meet her.

"Hey, I thought you were coming home to get some rest." I placed a kiss on her lips.

"I got called into the hospital for a few hours." She responded and walked past me to go upstairs.

***

Lily and I went for a walk through the neighborhood today and I had the chance to introduce her to some people who knew me when I was a baby. Lily smiled and cooed as if she was a campaigning politician. Naturally she was gaining the approval of the masses and was sure to get all of their votes. By the time we reached the driveway, Lily was asleep. A smile crept across my face because I figured; I could now have the chance to put both my babies to bed. I walked into the house and carried Lily up to her room; taking the monitor with me, I took the stairs up to our bedroom.

"You know how I feel…" Naquia stopped talking when she noticed me coming into the room. I placed the monitor on the dresser and then walked over to where she sat on the bed.

"I can't talk now, my husband's here. No. I've got to go." She disconnected the call.

"Who was that?"

"A friend."

"Who?"

98

"Just someone who's mad at me. They seem to think I don't have time for them anymore."

"Jealous huh?" I started to pull up her top.

"I guess. What are you doing?" She smiled and lifted her hands so I could remove the top.

"Taking advantage of a few free moments with my wife. Any objections?"

"Where's the baby?" She asked as I unfastened her bra and set her breasts free.

"Sleeping." I said before taking one of her nipples into my mouth. Our lovemaking had just begun when Naquia's pager went off on the dresser next to the baby monitor.

"Ignore it." I whispered.

"I can't, it's probably the hospital." Naquia removed herself from her seated position on me and whatever chance we had of completing our mission was lost in the cold air. Naquia picked up the phone and dialed. I walked into the bathroom and turned on the shower. When I returned to the bedroom, Naquia was nowhere to be found. I stepped into a pair of sweats and walked down to peek in Lily's room, she was still sleeping. I continued down onto the first floor, still no sign of Naquia and her truck was gone.

Chapter Ten: Raven

"It's good to see you again Raven." Larry said as he walked out to meet me.

"Thank you for meeting me on such short notice. I promise I won't take up too much of your time today."

"Not a problem. Would you like something to drink?" He offered and I shook my head no.

"What can I do for you Raven?"

"I want to draw up an agreement between me and my daughter's father regarding visitation."

Larry looked puzzled; I guess he also assumed that Derrick was Lily's father. I thought Derrick had already shared the truth with his lawyer.

"I'm sorry Larry; I thought you knew that Lily was not Derrick's child."

"No I didn't. At any rate, what are the terms you'd like set in this agreement?" Larry picked up his pen and began taking notes as I talked. Within the hour he had drafted the agreement and said he would messenger it over to me at the office by Wednesday.

"Thanks Larry. I really appreciate you handling this for me on a Sunday afternoon."

"It was my pleasure Raven." Larry and I walked out to our respective cars together. When I saw the new Mercedes he pulled off in, I figured that was why he didn't mind meeting me on a Sunday.

I turned onto the freeway figuring I'd run by to see my family while I was in the city. Mama and Daddy weren't home when I drove by their house, so I headed over to Cee's.

"Hey up in here." I announced my entrance into the house.

"Hi Auntie." Trey came bouncing down the stairs.

"Where's Mommy?" He asked.

"She's not here?" I asked reaching down for my kiss.

"No she said she was meeting you to go shopping." Winston said standing behind me with Tyrese on his hip.

"Oh, I guess she didn't get my message." I said trying to cover for her since I had no clue what was going on. As soon as it was out, the alarm beeped signaling her return.

"Hey. I'm sorry you must have left before you got my message." I said hoping she'd catch on.

"No I got it; I just decided to go anyway."

"And she wonders why I work all the time. Where are the keys? I'll get the bags." Winston handed Tyrese over his wife and Cee gave him her keys.

"Thanks." She said when Winston stepped outside.

"Thanks? Where have you been?" I asked.

"Out." She sat Tyrese down in the walker.

"I think you might want to clue me in the next time you decide to use me as your alibi."

"Trey baby, go help daddy with the bags." She said with a slightly irritated tone in her voice.

"Okay mommy." Trey ran outside.

"Now why would you say something like that in front of the little human tape recorder?" She walked past me and into the kitchen.

"So where have you been?" I asked following her.

"If I don't answer that type of question for my husband what in the world makes you think you would get an answer." She poured something to drink and then offered it to me.

"No thanks. Cee..." The beeping of the alarm at the door interrupted my response. Winston came in carrying bags of groceries and Trey followed with the laundry detergent.

"Are you two going out again?" Winston asked.

"No. Why?" Cee responded before taking another sip of her drink.

"I promised Trey, I'd take him to the park. He seems to miss that now that Raven is so far away."

"I'm sorry Trey; Auntie will make it up to you soon. I promise." I reached down to give my nephew a kiss.

"Ooh Auntie, that tickles." He squirmed to get out of my reach so that he could leave to go to the park.

"Have a good time baby. I'll see you two when you get back." Cee started putting away her groceries. I waited until I was sure that we were alone before I tried to get to the bottom of the mystery of her disappearance.

"I am going to ask you again..."

"Don't. So tell me about the benefit."

"What's to tell?"

"Something happened. You weren't looking too happy in that picture on the front page of the society section."

"What? Where?" I reached over to the paper folded on top of the recycle bin. I opened the paper to find the picture of Derrick, Shayla and I at the podium onstage. I replayed Shayla's comment in my head and got angry all over again.

"So what happened?"

"Nothing worth repeating." I said closing the paper and placing it back in the bin.

"Oh so that's how you want to play this? Because I don't want to tell you where I've been, you don't want to talk about this."

"Turnabout is fair play. I've got to go."

"Have it your way spoiled brat." Cee said as I grabbed my purse and headed out the door. I got in the car and picked up the phone. I didn't know Shayla's number so I called Rick and asked for it.

"Hello?" Shayla answered on the first ring.

"Shayla, it's Raven." I said determined to stay calm and see this through to the end.

"What can I do for you?" Shayla sounded curious.

"I was wondering if I could come by and talk with you and Chanel for a minute."

"Actually we were just about to step out. What is this about Raven?"

"I really don't want to talk about this over the phone. Would it be possible for you to stop by the office sometime tomorrow?" I said stopping at the traffic light.

"We can do that. What time?" She asked and I heard Chanel's voice in the background.

"Any time. I'll make sure I'm available."

"Fine we'll see you then."

"Thank you." I disconnected the call and turned onto the parkway.

***

I decided to go to the office to put the finishing touches on the launch party for Eric. When I returned home it was well after dinnertime and I then realized I hadn't eaten anything since leaving home after breakfast.

"Hi." I said after noticing Derrick working in his office when I started to go upstairs. Within a few moments Derrick stood in the door.

"Are you feeling better now?" He asked.

"I feel fine. How are you feeling?"

"I knew you would be upset, but don't you think you're taking this a little bit too far?"

"Derrick honey, what are you talking about?" I asked before taking a seat at my dressing table.

"I'm talking about last night."

"What about last night?"

"Raven, let's not play games. I know you're upset about the stunt Shayla pulled at the benefit."

"Thanks for reminding me." I reached into my jewelry box to retrieve the necklace that Shayla let the whole world know belonged to her.

"What are you doing?" He asked.

"I am going to return this necklace to its rightful owner."

"You should know me well enough to know that I would never give you something that belonged to my ex-wife." Derrick said extending his hand to me.

104

"Derrick, I can honestly say that right now, I don't know much of anything except, I am so tired of all of this. I thought after we were married, the foolishness would have stopped. It hasn't. I expected you to handle it; you haven't. So I've decided to take matters into my own hands."

"What does that mean?" Derrick asked.

"You'll see."

***

"Raven, Shayla and Chanel are here to see you." Valerie announced over the speaker.

"Send them, no better yet, bring them in please."

"Will do." Valerie said and I took a look in the mirror just to make sure my makeup was flawless. With a light tap, Valerie opened the door and came in with Shayla and Chanel in tow.

"Ladies, thank you for coming." I said walking over to greet them. Valerie stood inside the door not sure if she should leave us alone.

"Where's Derrick?" Shayla asked before taking her seat.

"I don't know I haven't seen him since we arrived this morning. Would you like something to drink?"

"No." Shayla said and Chanel still hadn't spoken a word.

"That will be all Valerie, please hold my calls."

"Will do." She said and walked out closing the door behind her.

"What do you want Robin?" Chanel asked taking a seat on the sofa.

"Chanel, I was hoping that we could come to an understanding. I know that we all love your father very much and I know that the fact that we can't seem to get along is hurting him. So I have come to the conclusion that there is one of two ways to handle this."

"Raven..." Shayla started.

"Shayla please let me finish. Last night, I realized if we allow all of this to continue, we are going to do nothing but hurt Derrick. I acknowledge there is no love lost between us. I don't expect us to end up as friends, but can we find a way to at least be civil to one another, to try and co-exist peacefully. At your benefit, I was ridiculed in front of your friends and Derrick's colleagues. I do not wish to have to go through that again. There are going to be many functions that Derrick is going to ask me to attend as his wife and I don't want a repeat of the other night."

"What is it that you expect of me Raven? You have come in and destroyed my family and you expect me to take that lying down?" Shayla sounded like she was getting agitated.

"No, what I expect is for you to accept that this was not my doing. Derrick and you were over a long time before I entered the picture."

"Is that what he's told you?"

"If that isn't the truth, then why don't you clue me in?"

"Raven, as I have told you on numerous occasions. You were one of the many women I allowed Derrick to have. You were not supposed to be anything permanent, but you did the one thing the rest of them had class enough not to do. You pulled the oldest play in the book; you got pregnant. Derrick should have known better. So please don't fool yourself into believing this man just fell head over heels in love with you at first sight. I've been with him long enough to know he isn't that kind of man."

"Having said all of that let me clear up a few things for you. Derrick hasn't been forced to do or feel anything with me. He has acted on his own accord. Derrick pursued me even with the knowledge that I was very much involved with someone else. When all was said and done, he made a choice, it just wasn't you. I just want to know if we can agree to give each other some respect."

"Respect? Did you respect the fact that my mother and father were still married when you screwed him and got knocked up? You two keep asking for something that you ain't ever gonna get. Mommy let's go."

"Ladies, please wait a moment. Chanel, for the record, I did not disrespect your parent's marriage and I am not going to continue to defend myself for something I did not do."

"Raven, this is really pointless." Shayla joined Chanel at the door.

"One last thing; let me just say that I will not tolerate another embarrassing display like the one you orchestrated this weekend. If you take it there again, be prepared for whatever may result from it."

"Are you threatening me?" All of the class Shayla had purchased over the years was quickly fading away.

"If you choose to take it that way." I said joining them at the door.

"You bitch." Chanel lunged towards me and Shayla grabbed her arm.

"Sweetheart don't; she may have given us just what we need to be rid of her."

"Run to Derrick, maybe then he will illustrate for you again that you weren't his choice. And Chanel, if you ever think about crossing that line little girl, be certain that is what you want to do." I said with a smile as I opened my office door.

"Have a good day ladies." I said watching Valerie rise to her feet. Shayla and Chanel headed off towards the elevator. I was surprised because I figured they would have run straight to Derrick.

"You okay?" Valerie asked following me into my office.

"Yep. I'm fine." I said taking my seat again and opening my email.

"So are you going to tell me or are you going to make me pull it out of you?"

"What?" I acted like I was really engrossed in the email I was reading.

"Don't play with me. What brought the evil step daughter and the evil step daughter's mother here to visit you?"

"I invited them." I said nonchalantly.

"And why would you inflict such pain on yourself?"

"No pain; at least not for me."

"Ray, if you don't turn around and give me your full attention I am going to unplug that damned thing."

"All right, dang girl. This weekend was Shayla's charity benefit."

"Yeah."

Laine Highsmith

"Well let's just say she put on a performance that could have taken the Oscar from any actress up for the award."

"What happened?" Valerie sat back to get comfortable for the drama.

"I'll give you the short version. My husband insisted that I attend this function with him. He even presented me with this beautiful diamond necklace because he said he wanted me to look and feel like the most beautiful woman in the room." I began.

"A night to get all dressed up and a diamond necklace. All of that sounds good to me." Valerie said.

"When we get there, we find out that Shayla has made seating arrangements for Derrick only. Not surprising to me, but my darling husband gets upset and ends up buying a table for the two of us which cost him another fifteen thousand dollars on top of the two hundred and fifty thousand he had already contributed."

"Okay, but you and I both know that's nothing to him."

"Hold on. The festivities begin and I have to sit through all of these people praising Shayla and the wonderful job she's done. People are constantly asking Derrick if he thinks his wife will surpass the amount she raised last year. The time comes for the contributors begin to give their donations. They are going in alphabetical order and my wonderful husband decides that he wants me to make the presentation."

"What?"

"Yeah, so here I am smiling for any of the people that may be watching and pushing the envelope back over to him because there is no way I am going up on that stage. KCI is announced and Derrick stands which brings the spotlight over to shine on our table. He extends his hand to make me go up there with him. To make a long story short, Derrick gave Shayla all the ammunition she needed to go in for the kill. She made a comment along the lines of Derrick being with me because of him going through a midlife crisis and that and I quote, he can dress her up and even give her my jewelry but he can never replace my style and grace." I said in an annoying whiny voice.

"Ouch." Valerie tensed up like she was actually being hit.

108

"Exactly and then to top it all off, he didn't come home that night."

"What? Where did he go?"

"Don't know. Didn't ask."

"He fell asleep and spent the night in his office because he knew his wife was going to be too upset to hear him out." Derrick's voice startled the both of us.

"Hello Valerie, could I please have a moment alone with Raven?" He smiled at Valerie who excused herself and closed my office door behind her when she left.

"What can I do for you Derrick?"

"I came to see if you were free for lunch."

"Actually, I'm not. I have a meeting for the launch party at noon that will probably last for the rest of the afternoon. I'm just going down to the cafeteria to grab a sandwich."

"I see. What about dinner?" He asked as if he was disappointed with my answer.

"Maybe."

"Raven, I have given you enough time and space to deal with your anger. It's been several days now, how much longer do you need?"

"Derrick, I told you, I'm not angry with you. I said what I had to say last night."

"Very well Raven, I'll check with you later regarding dinner." Derrick left my office without looking back. I didn't know what he expected but I knew he was not having his way with this one.

Chapter Eleven: Derrick

Raven hasn't been herself these last few days. I was hoping that Lily being gone for the week was contributing to her foul mood. Wesley had called to say that they would be arriving later in the day; which was good because I could use one of Lily's innocent smiles right about now.

"Would you like some lunch?" Mrs. Hill asked when she stuck her head in the door of my office.

"Yes, that would be great. Have you seen Raven?" I asked noticing that I had been working in the office for at least two hours without realizing the amount of time that had elapsed.

"She left a while ago. She said not to hold lunch for her, she'd eat while she was out."

"Oh, then I guess it's just you and me." I said rising from my chair. I followed Mrs. Hill into the kitchen. She gave me a run down of my choices and I decided on a sandwich and a glass of her infamous iced tea.

"Raven mentioned that Lily would be coming home today. I have to admit; I never noticed how quiet this house without her. I welcome that precious one's gurgles and coos." Mrs. Hill placed the plate in front of me and poured the tea.

"I've missed her too. Just think, in a few months she will be crawling around here; trying to talk, then we'll welcome the peace and quiet." I bowed my head and blessed my food before taking a bite out of my sandwich.

"I remember the days when Rick and Chanel were that age; I didn't have as much contact with them since Mrs. Kincaide insisted that the nanny take care of them. But I feel very connected to Lily, she's a great joy." Just as Mrs. Hill finished speaking, we heard the door open and the click of Raven's heels on the floor.

"Hi." She said entering the kitchen.

"Would you like a sandwich or something?" Mrs. Hill asked.

"No thanks, just some tea please." Raven took a seat on the barstool next to me.

"Are you finished?" I asked figuring that she was still working on the launch party.

"Almost." She said before thanking Mrs. Hill and then taking a sip from her glass.

"Eric needed to do my final fitting and I met with the lighting director to finalize everything. Friday can't get here soon enough."

"Maybe we can take a few days and sneak away afterwards for the weekend."

"That sounds nice. Ooh, what time is it?" Raven jumped up.

"It's almost two. Why?"

"Wesley said they'd be here by now. Has he called?"

"Princess, I'm sure everything is okay, maybe they got caught in traffic or they may have left later than expected."

"I'm going to call him." She had the phone in her hands just as the doorbell rang. Mrs. Hill left to go to the door.

"That's probably them now." I got up and reached for my wife who walked past me and into the foyer. I followed her and watched as a metamorphosis took place when she held Lily in her arms.

"Hi sweetheart. Mommy missed you so much." Raven kissed Lily and hugged her tightly.

"Hello Wesley." I extended my hand to him and offered to take one of the bags.

"Hi. I've got another bag in the car for her, I'll be right back." Wesley turned and walked back out the door. Lily looked around and smiled for all of us as if she too was glad to be back at home.

"How about a kiss for me?" I asked leaning down closer to her cheek. She cooed and melted my heart. Raven walked into the den and took off the pastel colored jacket Lily wore over her jeans and tee shirt. Raven was checking her diaper when Mrs. Hill led Wesley into the den.

"Vicky went shopping for Lily so we needed another bag. She's going to be the best dressed baby in America between the two of you." Wesley smiled as he placed the bag on the floor beside Raven and Lily.

"Would you like something to eat or drink?" Mrs. Hill offered.

"Something to drink would be good. Thanks."

"How was your trip?" I asked offering him a seat.

"Not too bad, we made good time. And before you go there, I wasn't speeding, we left early." Wesley said to Raven who finished changing Lily's diaper instead of responding.

"I wonder who that was meant for." Raven said to Lily and we all laughed. Mrs. Hill returned with a glass of tea for Wesley.

"How was your grandpa's birthday? Were you the star of the party? Did you steal the spotlight?"

"She's got all of us wrapped around her finger." Wesley smiled proudly.

"Wesley, I have something for you." Raven handed Lily over to me and left us alone for a few minutes. She returned and handed Wesley a large manila envelope.

"What's this?" Wesley asked.

"I had our lawyer draw up some preliminary visitation papers. Whatever changes you want to make let me know. I have all of the insurance information in there and like I said whatever you want to change just let me know."

"Thanks." Wesley seemed to be just as stunned as me.

"Go ahead, look at them, and tell me what you think." She reached over to open the envelope for him. Wesley took a few minutes looking at the papers and then said everything looked okay.

"So you can come and get her every other weekend and if we have plans that contradict that, then I am hoping we can work it out."

"No problem." Wesley seemed pleased.

"I'd better get going." He said putting the papers back in the envelope.

"Let your lawyer look over that and make sure there aren't any changes you want to make." I said still surprised by what I had just witnessed.

Raven got up to walk Wesley to the door. Mrs. Hill came over to get her chance with Lily and I returned to the kitchen to finish my sandwich.

***

"She's asleep." Raven came in from the nursery and sat down at her dressing table.

113

"I'm glad she's home; I've missed her so much." I said walking over to her.

"Me too." She picked up the brush from her vanity and I took it from her hand.

"I was pleasantly surprised that you took care of the visitation." I said brushing her hair.

"Why are you surprised?" She asked looking at me through the mirror.

"I don't mean anything by that, I'm just saying that you were so..."

"The key word is were. I can't really fault you for not handling your business with the past and continue not to handle mine. Can I?" Raven reached for the brush and when I handed it to her, she rose to her feet and headed into the bathroom. When Raven didn't return within fifteen minutes, I knocked before joining her in the bathroom.

"Princess, we need to talk."

"What is it Derrick?"

"I know that you have a lot going on right now with the preparations for the launch on Friday."

"Yes."

"I know it's been difficult not having Lily here this past week."

"Yeah and."

"Is that all there is to your foul mood or are you still angry with me?"

"I have already told you that I am not angry with you."

"You are just being short with me for no reason."

"I didn't realize I was being short with you."

"And the smart remarks?"

"When have I not had some sort of smart remark?"

"I don't know if you expect me to believe that but I will. You seem to have found a new method of running now."

"What is that supposed to mean?"

"Nothing. It's obvious you don't feel like discussing the distance growing between us. So I won't press it any further. Good night."

Chapter Twelve: Wesley

"Hey you. This is a surprise." Cee smiled and opened her arms for a hug.

"You always say I don't come and see you when I come to the city, so I decided to prove you wrong." I said closing the door behind me.

"Can you stay for dinner?" Cee asked as I followed her into the kitchen.

"Naw, I got to get back on the road."

"Have you eaten?"

"No, I'll just stop for a burger or something."

"Boy, you know you want a real meal. Go downstairs, get the rest of my family, and let's eat."

"Yes Ma'am." I followed her orders and went down to the basement.

"Westley." Trey noticed me first.

"Hey there." I took the last few steps down and grabbed a hold of Tyrese.

"You get prettier every time I see you little girl." I placed a kiss on her cheek and extended a high five to her father.

"How you doing man? It's been a long time." Winston said.

"I guess I missed you the last couple of times I've been by. What's going on?"

"Everything is everything. What's up with you and Miss Jackson if you're nasty?"

"We're working things out. It's a day-by-day thing."

"I know what you mean."

"I sent you down there to get them not to stay." Cee yelled from the top of the stairs.

***

After dinner, I went back downstairs with Winston to shoot some pool and to catch up. I remembered the last conversation I had with Cee and hoped that things weren't as bad as they seemed.

"Trey is getting taller every time I see him and Tyrese, man she's growing in leaps and bounds." I said after calling my shot.

"I know man; it's hard to believe she's almost a year old. Time is flying. I know you know what I mean. I see Tyrese everyday and I'm amazed, you see Lily every chance you get."

"You're right, I had her all of last week and it seems like she grew in that short period of time. I'm going to try and make sure I see her at least twice a month so I won't miss too much."

"Raven's going for that? You coming here twice a month?"

"Yeah, actually it was her idea."

"What?" I wasn't sure if Winston was responding to what I had said or the fact that I had just sunk the eight ball and took the game.

"She had some papers drawn up with a visitation schedule."

"Damn, that's wild considering how mad she was that night when they came home from the honeymoon." Winston racked up the balls.

"Don't remind me." We both laughed.

"I guess Cee talked some sense into her." I said.

"I doubt that." Winston took the first shot. I waited for him to see if he would finish his thought but he didn't.

"I don't know what happened but I'm glad it did." Winston missed his shot and after another couple of games, I pulled out to hit the road loaded down with a plate of food that Cee had packed for me.

*****

"Wesley, I'm working a double tonight." Naquia woke me up with a kiss.

"Hey, hold up a minute." I reached out for my wife.

"I was hoping we could…"

"No time. I'm running late." She cut me off.

"Go back to sleep and call me later." She left before I could respond. I was too tired to get up since I had only been asleep for about an hour. I figured I'd catch up with her later. I grabbed Naquia's pillow and drowned myself in her scent. Before long, I was in a deep sleep, which was interrupted by the ringing phone. I wasn't sure if it was real or in my dream.

"Wesley?"

"What's up doc?" I answered the phone.

"They just brought Samantha in. It's not good. She may not make it through the night."

"What? Really?"

"Yes, it looks like she's in the final stages, her condition has worsened and all we can do now is keep her comfortable. Have you seen Vicky? She's asking for the both of you."

"No. I was sleeping. Did you try her cell phone?" I asked pulling myself out of the bed.

"I didn't get an answer; it went straight to her voicemail."

"Did you try Father's?"

"Yes, he said he thought she may be at our place."

"Umm. Let me go see if she's here." I took the cordless phone with me and took the stairs down to the second level to see if Vicky was in her bedroom.

"Babe, she's not here. I'll let her know you want to see her when she comes in."

"Okay. Are you coming?"

"I don't think that's gonna happen."

"Come on Wesley. She's asking for you."

"Naquia, Samantha and I don't have anything to say to one another. Besides, if she is as bad off as you say, I don't think I can handle that this soon after Mother."

"I'm sorry, I wasn't thinking about that."

"No problem. How are you doing? You don't sound so good."

"I'm okay, it just hits harder when it is someone you know. I haven't known Samantha very long but we've grown close since I've been treating her."

"Really?"

"Yes. Other than your sister, no one has been here to spend time with her. Her grandmother came once; she's basically been abandoned. She keeps saying how sorry she is for what she has done in the past, especially to you. I thought it would be nice if you would come so she can at least apologize and clear her conscience." I heard an announcement come over the intercom in the background.

"Honey, I've got to go. Will you come by later? Please." Naquia asked.

"I don't know…"

"Please Wesley, it would mean a lot to me. You are asking me to do something that I am not happy with; surely you can do the same." I thought about what she was saying and had to agree.

"Sure thing baby."

"Bye." She hung up and I sat there for a minute with the receiver in my hands.

***

"Hey big brother." Vicky woke me up with a kiss on my forehead.

"What time is it?" I asked sitting up on the couch and patted the space beside me.

"It's five thirty. Your lazy butt has been sleeping all day haven't you?" She asked nudging me.

"Naquia has been trying to reach you; she said she couldn't get through on your phone."

"I forgot to charge it. What's up?"

"Samantha…" Vicky started crying before I could finish.

"You take a few minutes and I'll take you over to the hospital." I hugged her and left her alone for a few minutes. I went upstairs to shower and change; Vicky was on the phone waiting for me in the den.

"Terrence, I'm calling because I wanted to know how you are… Oh you're there." Vicky spent the next few minutes just listening. Before long, she was crying again. I took the phone from her trembling hand and placed the receiver on the cradle.

"Let's get out of here." I extended my hand to her and helped her up to her feet. I wrapped her in my arms and walked out to the garage, sat her in the front seat of the car and strapped her in.

"Thank you. You always take such good care of me."

"Hey, that's my job." I kissed her cheek and closed the door. I started the engine and turned on some jazz. Vicky was silent for most of the ride and when I heard her begin to cry again, I pulled off the road and turned on the emergency lights.

"I know you think I'm crazy." She said between sobs.

"Sometimes you are, sometimes you're not. You want to talk about it."

"Terrence was the first man I ever loved. He hasn't always been the guy he acts like now. I look at what has happened to Samantha over the last few months and I hate the thought of him being sick and alone." Vicky closed her eyes for a moment and I handed her a tissue to dry her eyes.

"I still love him. He has been mean and evil, he's cheated on me, he's hurt me and in spite of it all I still love him."

"If you repeat this, I will kill you. I know what you mean; a part of me still loves Raven." I confessed.

"What's to repeat?" She smiled and that made me feel a little bit better.

"It's hard to just turn off something that felt so right for so long. No one could have ever told me that Raven and I would each be married to someone else and raising our child apart."

"I know you all thought that I was crazy to go back to California after Pookie's funeral. I know it would have been easier to just have a moving company get my stuff, but it was something I had to do. I had to face him and make sure that he was going to be okay."

"You've always had a big heart; no one can hold that against you." I said brushing a piece of tissue off her face.

"Then why can't you understand that I have forgiven Samantha?"

"It's not up to me to understand. You do what you feel."

"Wesley, we can't let her go on carrying this burden of feeling that you haven't forgiven her."

"I have no control over that."

"Yes you do." She said turning to face me again. I started the car and she touched my arm.

"Wesley, don't hold on to that unforgiveness. We have all done some things and needed someone to forgive us. Please forgive her so she can go in peace." I heard the sincerity in Vicky's plea and then Naquia's voice reminding me of what I was asking of her.

"I'll try." I said switching off the emergency lights and turning back onto the highway.

***

I dropped Vicky off at the main entrance and drove around the lot looking for a place to park. I walked into the main doors thinking Vicky would have waited for me; since she hadn't, I walked over to the nurse's station to have Naquia paged.

"Dr. Charles please." I said to the older lady who was probably a volunteer. The phone on the desk rang and after she answered it, she handed the receiver to me.

"Hello."

"Hi. Take the elevator up to the seventh floor." Naquia said and disconnected the call. I thanked the woman at the desk and walked over to the elevator. When the doors opened, I stepped inside and pressed the button for the seventh floor. Before I could get to my floor, the elevator stopped on six and Naquia and another doctor stepped on.

"Wesley?" She seemed surprised to see me.

"Hey Doc." I leaned over to kiss her and she turned her cheek to me.

"You remember Harrison. Harrison this is Wesley." Naquia acted nervously.

"Nice to see you again." Harrison extended his hand to me. The bell rang for the seventh floor and I stepped aside to let Naquia off first.

"Stop by my office when your shift ends, I want to go over that chart with you." Harrison said and Naquia nodded her acknowledgement. The doors to the elevator closed and Naquia led me to Samantha's room.

"Prepare yourself. She's heavily sedated and has a lot of tubing." Naquia squeezed my arm.

"I'm cool." I said hoping she was convinced because I wasn't. Vicky sat next to Samantha who looked like a skeleton with something that was supposed to be skin stretched over her. Samantha turned to face us as we walked in. Naquia walked over to her and ran her hand across her hair.

"Is the Morphine helping?" She asked softly; Samantha nodded.

"Wesley. Come. Don't be afraid." Samantha said hoarsely. Vicky stood and offered me her seat. Samantha extended her bony hand to me and reached for my hand.

"Thank you for coming." She managed to say after a coughing fit.

"You're welcome. You need something to drink." I asked and she nodded. Samantha tried to sit up to take a sip from the cup I held over the railing.

"Thank you." She lay back on the pillows. I tried not to act as if I was uncomfortable but it was hard to see Samantha like this; all I could remember was her stunning beauty and the long shiny black hair that she loved to pull up into a ponytail that actually looked like a pony's tail.

"I know it was hard for you to come here. It really means a lot that you did." She touched my hand and I tried not to pull away.

"You pulled out the big guns on me; between Vicky and Naquia, I was outnumbered." I said with a forced smile that Samantha tried to return but it quickly turned into tears. Naquia excused herself to leave the room when her pager went off.

"I need to tell you something and as much as I want you to forgive me I know that may never happen."

"Samantha what has happened between us, good or bad, it's over. We can't go back and change it so there really is no point in bringing it all back up."

"There you go again trying to do the right thing. You were always doing that for everybody, even me when I was the one person who didn't deserve it. You don't have to say it; I know it's true. You were the one man in my life that ever really loved me and I was too stupid to realize it. You are a good man Wesley, a real gentleman and I was a fool. I am truly sorry for all that I have put you through. I guess a part of me still loved you and was mad because you didn't love me back. I was foolish enough to believe that I could fix things between us when you got out of prison. When you brought that girl Raven home with you, I lashed out and wanted to hurt you because you had hurt me."

"Samantha..."

"Wesley, I have done something this time that I never intended to do and I need to warn you..."

"Samantha, they are going to take you down for some x-rays." Naquia came in followed by a couple of guys with a stretcher.

"I just need a few more minutes alone with Wesley."

"That can wait." Naquia pulled the railing down on the side of her bed and asked me to leave.

"Wesley, I'm sorry." Samantha said as I walked towards the door.

Chapter Thirteen: Raven

"Everything has been sent over to the Excalibur Room. The models are going through their dry run, Eric and his staff will be there by four and you're all set." Valerie checked off the last item on her list and sat down looking totally exhausted.

"Thank you girl, I don't know how I would have gotten through this without you." I sat down beside her and laid my head on her shoulder.

"Me either." She said and we both laughed.

"What did I miss?" Monica stepped into my office. Ever since she and Geoff started dating, we hardly see her anymore.

"Well, well if it isn't my old friend Monica. I never thought that I would see the day when I would get kicked to the curb because she had a man. But miracles never cease." I teased.

"And I never thought I'd see the day when I'd meet a man worth kicking your jealous behind to the curb but I did." She laughed.

"So are things getting serious, you know you are the last one of us to jump the broom." Valerie said.

"If I recall correctly, you two just caught up with me. Been there, done that, and got a tee shirt and divorce to show for it. Don't get me wrong, Geoff is a great guy, but I ain't putting no stock into this. We are basically just kicking it."

"Just hittin' it, you mean." I said and she swatted at me as I walked over to my desk.

"I came here to see if you were straight for tonight. Instead I'm getting abused because Monie's got a man." She sang and we all laughed.

"Yes, Mrs. Alvarez has taken care of everything, I am about to go home to get dressed and then try and enjoy the show."

"Valerie, this would be a good time to ask for a raise." Monica nudged her.

"Get out of my office." I said.

"And if she doesn't want to cooperate, I think I can work something out for you."

"Don't make me call security." I threatened.

"I'll see everybody later tonight. Bye bye." Monica waved and walked past Derrick who was coming into my office.

"Hi Valerie. Are you ready to go home Princess?" Derrick asked.

"Yes. Valerie, are you finished with everything?"

"Yes." She responded.

"Then go home and get changed. I will send a car for you and Ramon around six." I said powering off my computer.

"Okay. We'll see you two later." Valerie exited my office and closed the door.

"I'm ready." I picked up my briefcase and Derrick took it from my hand.

"You're shaking." He said lifting my hand up to his lips.

"I know I've had butterflies in my stomach all day. I know it's just my nerves, but I feel like something is going to go wrong."

"I have every confidence that everything will go as planned and we will have a smash on our hands. You know how you are with your meticulous planning, if you could surprise me with a wedding, this launch party will go off without a hitch." Derrick placed another kiss on my hand and then my lips.

***

"You look awfully handsome." I helped Derrick with his tie.

"Thank you. You're as beautiful as ever. Eric did a good job on this dress." Derrick's hands left his tie and found my waist.

"You know we have a few minutes before the car is scheduled to arrive." He smiled.

"Don't start. I'm nervous enough." I said putting the finishing touches on his tie.

"Take a deep breath." Derrick said looking deeply into my eyes. I did as I was told.

"Now repeat after me. I have nothing to worry about."

"I have nothing to worry about."

124

"I am the most beautiful and desirable woman in the world." He continued.

"Derrick..."

"Repeat it."

"I am the most beautiful..."

"And desirable woman in the world." He repeated himself.

"And desirable woman in the world. And my husband is a prejudiced lunatic." We both laughed.

"I haven't heard that in a while." He said solemnly.

"What?"

"The sound of your laughter. You've been on edge, I'm just glad tonight is here so I can get my wife back." I could tell that he was being cautious with the words he spoke.

"I haven't been that bad."

"I beg to differ."

"You'll be begging for more than that if we don't get out of here. Are you ready?"

"Yes."

Chapter Fourteen: Derrick

Raven did it; she has amazed me once again by pulling together a spectacular event for Eric Jackson Designs. This show looked like it would top any of the launch parties Shayla ever dragged me to. I looked around to see that my wife had every major clothier in the city bidding for the chance to carry her client's line. She had convinced each of them to send at least one buyer because they wanted exclusivity with the retailers. She gave each of the buyers a paddle with a number on it and they would at the end of the show make a bid on the designs they wanted to carry. It looked like my wife was going to make this man a millionaire overnight. The room was beautifully decorated in addition to the phenomenal light show she'd designed with the tech team. The jazz that played in the background added the perfect touch and the champagne and sparkling cider flowed freely through out the room with the help of the wait staff dressed in their black and white with a signature dress shirts designed by Jackson.

"I hope you don't think you're going to get a raise because of all of this." I whispered into Raven's ear before placing a kiss on her cheek.

"Just let me get through this night and then we'll talk about that raise." She placed her ice-cold hands into mine.

"Princess, are you all right? Your hands are freezing." I looked at her dressed in a black gown with a hint of sequins coming through in various places.

"I'm just nervous. Believe me I'm not cold, I'm sweating bullets under this thing."

"Remember your mantra, I am the most beautiful and desirable woman in the world. Like I said, if your gown is any indication of what the rest of the line looks like, you have nothing to worry about."

"That's just it, he refused to share any of the designs with me, so I don't know if I have the right atmosphere going on in here and…"

"And you have done a wonderful job and everything will be fine and I love you and nothing else matters." I kissed her softly and caught the flash of a camera in our faces.

"Do you mind?" Raven asked justifiably irritated by the intrusion. The photographer walked away.

"We're ready to get started Mrs. Kincaide." A young woman dressed in black said to Raven and we took our seats. Raven squeezed my hand as the house lights went down and the stage lights came on. The emcee for the evening gave a brief welcome and then the show began.

"Remember to breathe." I whispered to her. She nodded. The show began with what was called career wear. I watched as the paddles began to rise all across the room. Raven had some of our employees assigned to keep watch of each of the buyers' choices so after the show they could make their respective bids. The emcee announced a ten-minute intermission before the debut of after five. The house lights came up and one of the waiters offered me a glass of champagne; I offered one to my wife.

"No. Thanks." She took her hand away from mine and wiped some perspiration I couldn't see from her forehead.

"It's a success." I said as people began to crowd Raven, many of them buyers trying to get an edge up on the others.

"We will call everyone on Monday to give you the time for the auction. Thank you all for coming." Raven said looking like she finally believed that she had a hit on her hands. I grabbed some hors d'oeuvres and a glass of cider for my wife.

"Take a sip." She looked at me suspiciously.

"It's cider." I said.

"Thank you." She smiled and then gave me a kiss.

"I won't need any champagne tonight." She whispered in my ear.

"Maybe we should get out of here now." I said and she laughed. She looked like she was finally relaxing. The blinking of the lights signaled the end of the intermission. We took our seats again and the show began. The crowd really got excited with the after five collection which was followed by weekend wear. There wasn't as much of a response to that line and I felt Raven tensing up again. Jackson must have saved the best for last, the eveningwear was the last segment of the show and it began with a model wearing the dress he had designed for my wife. A few more gowns came out and then the runway was filled with men dressed in tuxedos all lined up across from each other and the grand finale of the collection made its entrance on Suzanna. She looked absolutely beautiful and she glided down the runway as if this whole show had been built around her. She turned right in front of us and walked back down the runway to meet up with Eric to bring him out. Everyone stood and applauded to show their approval of the line. Eric blew a kiss over to my wife and mouthed a thank you. Suzanna smiled before the two of them exited backstage. The lights came back up and the room was filled with chatter.

"Congratulations Princess." I hugged my wife and kissed her lips.

"Thank you." The brilliance of her smile confirmed her belief in the success of the show. Many well wishes came from passer bys and then Eric came with Suzanna draped on his arm.

"We did it." Raven said.

"You did it; I was blown away when I walked in this place. Thank you." Eric placed a kiss on Raven's cheek and then extended his hand to me.

"Thank you too Derrick."

"You're welcome. Suzanna, it's nice to see you again; please let me introduce you to my wife."

"Regina, it's nice to finally meet you." Suzanna extended her hand to Raven.

"It's Raven." She said shaking Suzanna's hand.

"Derrick, how have you been? How are the children?" Suzanna turned all of her attention to me.

"Everyone is doing well. How have you been?" I asked trying to gauge Raven's demeanor.

"My life is wonderful, you know I was really disappointed when I lost you to Regina but I guess it has all worked out for the best. I have a film career that's taking off and I'm still at the top of my game in this modeling thing. And here you are married again."

"Yes and very happily." I tried to place my arm around my wife's waist but she was whisked away by Valerie and Monica.

129

"That's nice." Suzanna sipped her champagne and Eric excused himself.

"Was all of that necessary?" I asked once we were alone.

"What do you mean Derrick? So I got confused, you have so many women I guess it's just hard to keep up."

"Suzanna you didn't strike me as the jealous type before."

"I never thought of you as the hit and run type either. You led me to believe that we had a future Derrick."

"I never made you any promises; besides you wanted to focus on your career and you needed your space."

"Of course that is the way you would see it. That's the only way you can justify the poor way you handled this."

"What are you talking about?"

"I'm talking about your wife or should I say your ex-wife coming to threaten me."

"What?"

"You expect me to believe that you knew nothing about this."

"When have I ever had a problem telling you or anyone for that matter anything I wanted them to know?"

"That is exactly what was so surprising to me, and then when I came to confront you about it..."

"When was that?"

"I came to see you a week or so after I finished the shoot in England. Barbara said you were out of town with Rick and that she expected you back that evening. She gave me the spare key to your hotel suite and when I arrived, it was already occupied. Your wife didn't tell you? That was when Regina and I met."

"My wife's name is Raven."

"I am sure the woman I met that night was named Regina."

"That may well have been." I sipped my champagne and looked around the room catching the eye of my beautiful wife. I motioned for her to come over to join us. En route to us, Raven got sideswiped by some members of the press.

"Suzanna it was nice seeing you again. You have a good night." I walked away and over to my wife.

"Raven, it must be difficult for you seeing your husband with his supermodel ex-girlfriend here on a night when you are supposed to be the center of attention." A reporter shouted out as I walked up beside her.

"My beautiful wife has nothing to worry about. This is her night. I am her husband and as you so eloquently put it, that was a person who was a part of my past. You should be focusing on what's happening here and now instead of trying to dredge up something from the past." I answered and made it clear that this was the end of the questions for the night.

"Are you rescuing me or yourself this go around?" Raven's remark was dripping with suspicion. Monica asked if she could have Raven for a brief moment.

"I'll meet you in the car." I said before saying goodnight to Monica.

Chapter Fifteen: Raven

"What's up girl?" I asked Monica when we were alone.

"I want that pin striped suit and the camel dress." She said handing a check over to me.

"You know I can't do that. Let me introduce you to Eric and you two work it out."

"Do what you gotta do, I want those two pieces and I don't want to see them on anyone else." She said putting the check back in her purse. We walked backstage where I tried to find Eric to make the introduction.

"Eric. Listen I'm about to call it a night. Congratulations. I will give you a call after we hold the auction with the buyers."

"Sounds good Raven. Again thank you so much for everything."

"You're welcome and to get things started for you; this is my good friend Monica and she has fallen in love with a couple of your pieces and wishes to buy them tonight."

"Nice to meet you Monica." Eric said extending his hand to her.

"I'm going to leave you two to talk business. Monica if you two settle on this, call me so I'll know what to pull out from the buyers."

"Okay girlfriend. Thanks. And congratulations, you pulled it off." I waved goodbye and headed back towards the main door.

"Regina. Regina." Suzanna was trying to get my attention.

"You need to smack her ass if she calls you Regina one more time." Angel chimed in as I stopped and turned to face her.

"Listen, I hope I haven't caused any trouble with you and Derrick. Derrick is a wonderful man and I am happy that he has found happiness even if it's not with me. Regina, you are a lucky woman and I hope you realize that and never take that for granted."

"Why do you insist on calling me Regina, when we've told you that my name is Raven?"

"I'm sorry it's just that when we first met, I could have sworn you told me your name was Regina."

"Tonight is our first meeting."

"Are you sure about that? I thought we met a few months ago in Derrick's hotel suite."

"It's been a long night Suzanna, so if you don't mind..."

"Please tell Derrick that I am sorry if I've upset him and I wish you two the best with your marriage."

"Good night." I said with a wave and I left to join my husband in the car. He stepped out to meet me when I walked through the door. Extending his hand, I stepped inside the car and took my seat.

"Ready to go?" Derrick asked after closing the door. I nodded since speaking was out of the question. Derrick leaned over to kiss me and I turned away.

"What's wrong?" He asked sounding exasperated.

"Umm, let's see. The evening started out nicely, all of the hard work my team and I put in culminated into a successful show for my client. I was nervous in the beginning but as the night progressed I gained my composure. I had a hit on my hands and my handsome husband by my side and then it all came to screeching halt. This talking toothpick shows up on the arm of my client and informs me of her relationship with my husband. One that I am hoping is over and in the past."

"Prin..."

"No, please let me finish; it gets better. You see she then starts off by calling me Regina. Accident? Maybe. Maybe not. You correct her in the beginning. She insists that she's right about my name being Regina. I dismiss it at first until she later explains that she could have sworn that we met a few months ago when she went to see you in your hotel suite."

"Are you done?" He asked.

"Not yet. You see at first I was going to dismiss it all, thinking this is a woman lashing out because she wasn't the chosen one. But this Regina thing has taken me for a loop especially considering that we both know a Regina. One who is known for the infamous use of her body in exchange for whatever she wants. So tell me am I crazy and just imagining things?"

"Yes, you are crazy for allowing Suzanna to get into your head and spoil your evening. Raven, I love you and only you. I am a man who once had a relationship if you'd like to call it that with Suzanna. That relationship is over, completely and you have absolutely nothing to worry about. It would be unrealistic for you to believe that I did not have a life before meeting you. You are an intelligent woman and I know you know better than that."

"Derrick..."

"Raven, I do not wish to spend the rest of this evening talking about this nonsense. You pulled off a spectacular event tonight; you have probably turned that man into a millionaire overnight. I think we should be celebrating instead of having this conversation that's going nowhere." The car slowed to a stop. Derrick opened the door, got out and extended his hand to me.

"Where are we?" As soon as the question was out, I realized we were back at the office.

"What are we doing here? Did you forget something?" I asked as Derrick led me into the building.

"Good evening Mr. and Mrs. Kincaide." The security guard spoke when we walked past him and onto the elevator.

"Are you going to answer me?" I asked still wondering what we were doing back at the office.

"Just give me a moment please." The bell rang and we stepped off into the executive suite. Derrick took me to a stairwell that led to the emergency exit. When he opened the door I thought an alarm would go off but it didn't and we ended up on the roof of the building. When the door closed, I saw a table set for two surrounded by candles, there was a man playing a piano and a line of people waiting to serve us.

"Derrick..." The rest of whatever I wanted to say was swallowed back with the lump of emotion that had filled my throat. Derrick took me to the edge of the roof.

"I want to show you something. Do you realize that what you are doing is placing us on top of the advertising world? Your Jameson campaign, the launch party tonight and whatever else you have in store for us is placing us so high above everyone else, no other company can compete. We have an unprecedented number of companies coming to us asking to be acquired. I don't have to go out and seek anymore; you are bringing them all in to me. The view from up here is phenomenal but with it, there are dangers. Dangers of people trying to undermine and sabotage what we're achieving and their jealousies and insecurities that want to infect what we have. Princess we cannot let that happen. We have to stay focused and united, together as one, as husband and wife and as CEO and Vice President soon to be COO. Do you understand?"

"I do and I appreciate all that you just said. But I don't think I can take another surprise. Surprise that's my necklace you're wearing. Surprise I'm the last woman in your husband's life. Surprise..."

"I love you. I have been open and honest with you. I have tried to protect you and provide for you. I want to spend the rest of my life with you and my kids. You are so precious to me and I am not going to do anything to jeopardize what we have found in one another. We've been through a lot and I don't think there is anything that we can't face now. We've weathered Lily's paternity situation and sharing that with Wesley. We've weathered Shayla and the divorce; and we've become stronger because of it. So please don't let Suzanna or anyone like her into our world who wants nothing more than to do us harm." Derrick removed a stray hair from my face and then kissed my lips.

"Umm... Are you hungry? I got the chef at Julian's to prepare something special for our celebration."

"Don't take this the wrong way but I don't feel like eating right now. I have a lot to digest and process. Derrick, I love you and I appreciate what you've done here tonight for me, but..."

"But what?" He sounded disappointed.

"You keep saying how you appreciate the fact that I see beyond your wealth. But what you fail to realize is that every time something happens, you buy something or do something like this to smooth the waters. Honey, I can't take anymore surprises." I felt tears welling up in my eyes.

"Raven when I planned this evening, it was simply to congratulate you on a job well done and to have a nice romantic moment with my wife. I had no idea that Suzanna would be one of the models in the show; I had no idea she would try to play mind games with you to make you feel insecure. I was not attempting to buy anything." Derrick sounded hurt but I could not let that change the way I was feeling right now. Derrick took me by the hand and walked me over to the table and after we were seated, the food was served. With the piano playing in the background and the warm breeze, on any other night this would have felt like a dream come true, but tonight after the reporters, Suzanna and her insistence on my name being Regina, it felt more like a nightmare. After dinner the staff from Julian's dismantled the table and Derrick instructed them to move the piano in the morning. We walked down the stairs to the executive suite and took the elevator back down to the car. On any other night we would have made love or held onto one another all the way home, but not tonight.

Chapter Sixteen: Wesley

Naquia spent the last couple of nights at the hospital; she said she wanted to be there so Samantha wouldn't feel alone in her last moments. I had to respect her for that but I also told her that she couldn't continue to get so attached to her patients if she was going to continue working at the AIDS hospice. I saw how hard she took both Preston's and Mason's deaths and I could see Samantha's would be just as hard. Since I was on my own, I promised Father I would help him turn my old bedroom into a workshop. Natalie's new assignment was out on the west coast, which meant he was spending a lot of time alone. Vicky decided to stay with him for a while just to keep an eye on him.

"Is there anything you want me to pick up before I come out tomorrow?" I put the last of the tools back in the box after Father measured the doorframe again.

"I still don't think that door is going to fit." Father said going ahead of me towards the kitchen.

"It'll fit." I said.

"Vicky is cooking dinner tonight and bringing home some fella she been seeing. Why don't you and Naquia join us?"

"Don't wanna get food poisoning all alone huh?" I said loud enough for Vicky to hear me.

"I heard that." She said.

"I know." I placed a kiss on her cheek.

"So are you guys coming?" Vicky asked handing me an apple.

"I'll call Naquia and see if she can leave for a few hours."

"Leave? Where is she?"

"She's been staying at the hospice. She said she didn't want Samantha to be alone."

"Samantha's back at the hospice?" Vicky seemed surprised.

"What do you mean back?"

"Samantha went home last week, since her T-Cell count was up, she said she wanted to go home." Vicky placed the prime rib she was preparing for dinner on the counter.

"Let me talk to Naquia and I'll get back to you." I said pulling my keys out of my pocket.

"Dinner is at seven, call if you're going to be late." Vicky said as I walked out of the kitchen and jumped into my car. I headed straight over to the hospital. For weeks now, things have been strange. On more times, than I cared to remember, I had caught Naquia in a lie or what seemed to be a lie. I wanted to call her on it, but I gave her the benefit of the doubt. This time there was no doubt she could benefit from. My cell phone rang just as I pulled into the parking lot of the hospice. I checked the ID before answering.

"Hey Doc."

"I miss you."

"Then come home."

"I can't."

"Why not?"

"Samantha needs me."

"I need you too. What about your patient over here?"

"Wesley, please. Don't you think this is hard on me too?"

"Actually no. I think you find it easy to leave me alone, or else you wouldn't do it so much. Hold on a sec." I put the phone on mute while I turned off the ignition and got out of the car. I looked over into the doctor's lot and noticed Naquia's truck immediately.

"I'm back." I said after walking up to the entrance of the hospice.

"Where are you?" She asked.

"Outside."

"Well honey, I've gotta go."

"Hey Doc, hold up a minute. Vicky wanted to know if we could join her for dinner tonight."

"Dinner? Tonight wouldn't be good."

"You can't get away for an hour or two. It's at seven."

Consequences

"I'll have to see. They're calling me, I've gotta go."

"Doc..."

"I'll call you later." She disconnected the call. I walked into the main lobby and walked up to the information desk.

"Hi, can I have Samantha Nelson's room number please?" I asked the woman behind the desk. She typed something into her computer.

"Did you say Samantha Nelson?"

"Yes."

"I'm sorry sir; we don't have anyone registered under that name."

"Could you check Samantha Charles please?"

"No Samantha Charles either."

"If she had just been discharged, would her information still be in your files?"

"No sir, the computer is updated immediately after a patient is discharged. This is how we know how many beds we have available."

"Thank you." I turned to walk away but then stopped and turned to ask one last question.

"Can you check to see if Dr. Charles is on duty please?"

"Sure." She picked up the phone and dialed a number. After a brief conversation, she returned her attention to me.

"I'm sorry sir, Dr. Charles is on vacation. She's due back next week. Would you like to leave a message for her?"

"No. Thanks." I left the hospice and headed over to the hospital.

***

I stopped off and picked up a cheesecake before heading over to Father's for dinner. Vicky had set the table using Mother's favorite china and table linens. The sight of the table brought back memories of when I would sit and watch her trying to remember which side of the plate the fork should go on.

"I guess you finally learned something. This table looks nice." I said to my sister who was dressed in a beautiful silky dress accented by a colorful scarf tied around her waist. I was just about to compliment her when the doorbell rang.

"You think you can behave yourself long enough to get the door."

"I'll try." I said with a smile before walking over to open the door to this Brooks Brother suit-wearing dude. He was the complete opposite of Terrence and since that was the only guy she'd ever dated, I guess I really couldn't make a comparison.

"Hi I'm Eugene Witherspoon." He extended his free shaking hand; the other had held a bouquet.

"Hi Eugene, I'm Vicky's brother Wesley. Come on in." I shook his hand and opened the door wider.

"Nice to meet you."

"Relax man, you're here now."

"I was hoping..." Whatever Eugene was about to say got cut off by Vicky joining us in the foyer.

"Hi Gene." She walked over and placed a kiss on his cheek and he presented her with the flowers.

"These are for you."

"Thank you; they're beautiful. Are you hungry?"

"Starving." Vicky laced her fingers into Eugene's and led him into the dining room. Vicky served us a delicious dinner and seemed truly pleased that Father and I liked Eugene. He seemed to be a good guy; he told us that he heads up the robotics division of General Motors; he was divorced and has a seven-year-old son who lives with his ex-wife in Seattle. He noticed Vicky at the hospital one day when he was there visiting one of his employees whose wife had just given birth. They told the story while I cleared the dinner dishes.

"Are you ready for dessert?" I asked bringing in the cheesecake.

"I didn't know you brought that. Thanks." Vicky smiled and got up to get the dessert plates out of the china cabinet behind her.

"I figured we'd better have something that wouldn't poison us tonight." I smiled as I cut into the cake.

"Dinner was delicious Vicky and I am going to take your brother into the den to beat him at a game of chess and give you two a few minutes alone. Eugene it was nice to meet you and I am hoping this is the first of many visits."

"Thank you sir. If it is okay with Vicky, then I'd like to come again and get beat at a game of chess too." He stood to shake Father's hand and we took our cheesecake into the den.

***

The doorbell rang and I heard Naquia's voice coming closer to us.

"Hi, I'm sorry I'm so late. When I went outside my truck was gone." She placed a kiss on my cheek and sat down on the sofa beside me.

"Was it stolen?" Vicky asked.

"I don't know, I called the police and they said they'd get back to me. I've been calling you for the last couple of hours. Where's your phone?" She nudged me; I patted my pocket.

"I must have left it in the car." I said acting like I was deeply engrossed in my chess match.

"Are you hungry? I can heat up something for you." Vicky offered before returning to the kitchen.

"No thanks. Are you beating him Mr. Charles?" Naquia ran her hand down my back.

"It's hard to say right now, we're kind of evenly matched."

"Not for long. Check." I announced and got up to stretch.

"Check?"

"Yeah old man. I'll finish you off tomorrow. How'd you get here?" I turned to face my wife

"I caught a ride." She stood up to give me a kiss.

"Yeah with who?" I held her back.

"Harrison dropped me off."

"Oh." I let go of her and walked into the kitchen where Vicky and Eugene were finishing up the dishes.

"You're leaving?" Vicky asked handing Eugene a serving dish.

143

"Yeah. Eugene man, it was nice to meet you. I can see now you are going to be around for a while. She got you doing dishes, she ain't letting go." I laughed and he joined in.

"That's good to hear." Eugene placed the dish on the counter and shook my hand.

"Oh Naquia, excuse my manners. Gene this is Wesley's wife Naquia. Naquia this is my Gene." Vicky smiled as Eugene placed his arm around her waist.

"Nice to meet you." Eugene extended his free hand to Naquia.

"You too. I'm sorry I missed dinner, maybe we can get together and go out one night." Naquia wrapped an arm around my waist and looked up to me.

"That sounds good to me." Eugene said. We said our goodbyes and walked out to the car.

***

Naquia talked most of the way home, talking about Samantha and digging herself deeper in her ditch of lies. When I pulled into our driveway, her conversation stopped mid-sentence.

"What's my truck doing here?" She asked turning to face me; I turned off the ignition.

"I had it towed here earlier today." I said then opened my door and got out.

"Why did you do that?" She said getting out of the car before I had a chance to get over to her to open her door.

"I figured it must have broken down on you since it was parked in the lot and you weren't there."

"When were you at the hospice?"

"The better question is when were you at the hospice?" I said and she walked off without an answer. I followed her inside the house and heard the bedroom door slam and lock. Resigning myself to a night on the couch, I tried to get comfortable until sleep came and took over for a couple of hours. I heard Naquia when she came down the stairs. She probably figured I was still asleep but truth be told I didn't get much sleep at all. I ended up flipping channels and then eventually closed my eyes only to relive all of the times Naquia had misled me over these last few months. I wondered how long it had been going on since she had me believing the only problems we had were all the result of my daughter coming into my life. I listened as she walked past me and headed out to the garage. I wanted to see how long it would take before she came back inside when she saw that the truck was blocked in the garage by my car and that I had changed the codes on my car, the truck locks and the garage door.

"Wesley, I don't have time for this bullshit." She screamed from the garage.

"Wesley? Do you hear me talking to you?" She came back into the house.

"Yeah I hear you."

"I'm going to be late."

"I agree." I said with a smile and I watched her nostrils flare.

"What do you want from me Wesley?"

"Some answers."

"Answers to what. You know where I've been."

"That's not true. You told me you were staying at the hospice with Samantha. Samantha has been at her grandmother's house the whole time you've been away. The hospital and hospice both said you were on vacation. So this is the last time I'm going to ask you. Where have you been?"

"I have told you…"

"You haven't told me the truth. Let me make this clear, I will not share my life, my home or my bed with someone I cannot trust."

"My therapist suggested that I go away for a few days to work some things out."

"Your therapist?"

"Yes. I've been seeing someone twice a month."

"Who?"

"Wesley?"

"Who Naquia? I want to talk to this therapist."

"They won't talk to you. It's privileged."

"They'll talk to me if you're there. Call them and we'll go talk to them today. Right now as a matter of fact."

"I'm not sure..."

"Call them." I handed her the phone. She took the phone from me and dialed a number.

"Hi, it's me. Could you give me a ride to work please? Thanks." Naquia hung up the phone and walked away from me.

***

I ran three miles hoping I could burn off the anger that was welling up inside of me. I didn't realize the time and that I had forgotten about helping Father until I saw his truck pulling into my driveway. I quickened my pace and caught up with him as he was getting out of his truck.

"Sorry about this morning." I said between breaths.

"I figured you needed sometime with Naquia this morning. I could tell things were strained last night. You want to talk about it?" He leaned against the truck. This reminded me of the times we'd spent before the whole prison ordeal when he'd give me some advice about life and how a man is supposed to handle things. After all the things that happened, I never thought we would ever be at this place again. It felt good to know that we were finally past our past.

"Sure. Come on inside." I opened the door and Father looked at the way I parked the car to block the garage.

"I'll explain." I said and he laughed. We walked into the kitchen and each took a seat at the kitchenette.

"So what's going on?" He asked and sat back like he knew he was in for a long story.

"I don't know really. Something just doesn't feel right. I have never been the kind of man that has to know every move my wife makes. She's never had to tell me everything she's doing or every place she's going. But here lately, too many things don't add up."

"Have you asked her about it or are you assuming something is wrong?"

"I tried talking to her today. She said she was seeing somebody, a therapist. I think she's still lying."

"Well if you don't trust her what do you have?"

"Good question."

***

After my talk with Father, I came to the realization that I needed to decide whether I wanted my marriage to Naquia to work or not. I had made the mistake of marrying her on the rebound and I had to recognize that what was going on was a result of that bad decision. I had to find out if we had anything worth salvaging. I ordered Naquia's favorite dinner and picked up a bouquet of flowers for the table. My intentions were not to try and romance her. I didn't want the two of us to end up in bed exhausted and still have whatever it is that has come between us. Tonight we had to make a decision about tomorrow and everyday after that. I paged Naquia and she didn't return the call. I called the hospital and then over to the hospice to find that she had left at five. It was now seven and she was nowhere to be found.

Chapter Seventeen: Derrick

"You have Galbraith at two thirty, and that's it." Barbara closed her calendar.

"Thanks. See if you can get a reservation at Hamiltons. I'd like to surprise my wife with dinner tonight."

"Will do. Any particular time?"

"Six would be good." I powered off the computer and picked up the phone as Barbara exited my office.

"Raven Kincaide." Raven sounded pre-occupied when she answered the phone.

"Princess, how about an early dinner tonight?"

"I don't..."

"I am not taking no for an answer. Barbara is making us a reservation as we speak. I will have a car sent for your Mother and Mrs. Hill can watch Lily until we get home in a couple of hours."

"What time are you talking about?"

"Six, but we are leaving here precisely at five-thirty."

"Well since I am being told that I basically have no other choice, I guess I'll see you at five-thirty."

"Thank you for your cooperation." I said expecting her to come back with something and was surprised when she didn't.

"Okay. Bye." Raven hung up the phone and a sense of uneasiness filled me.

"Excuse me sir, I wanted to bring in those specs on Galbraith before the meeting in case you had any questions." Geoff Grainger came into my office as I was hanging up the phone and handed me the file.

"Thank you. Have a seat." I looked over the information. This looked like it was going to be an easy acquisition especially since Geoff had uncovered some of the company's financial woes that they had reported had been settled and weren't. We were able to then sweeten our offer without tipping our hand to let them know we were aware. They had rejected our first offer because it would have only provided them with a break-even margin. The new offer gave them a slight increase but we are now taking the company in whole without any of their staff. It was Geoff's keen eye that saved us on this one and I wanted to make sure he was adequately compensated for it.

"Everything looks good. You've done a great job on this."

"Thank you sir."

"No thank you. And please stop calling me sir; you're making me feel like an old man. Would you like a drink?" I asked walking over to the wet bar for a soda.

"Yes, thank you." He followed me over to the bar and took a seat.

"We haven't had much time to get acquainted Geoff. I know who you are on paper, but I would like to find out who you are as a man."

"Well I attended..."

"Stop. This isn't an interview. If I am not mistaken, you are dating one of my wife's best friends, not to mention the Vice President of Financial Affairs." I handed him a glass on ice and opened the refrigerator to show his choice of soft drinks. Geoff reached for a bottle of water and seemed to relax.

"Yes. Monica and I have been seeing each other. But we have been very careful to remain professional and to keep our personal relationship outside of the office."

"How do you do it? I haven't been able to and I am the CEO?"

"Well I uh..."

"That was rhetorical. Relax. Why don't you two like to join us for dinner sometime?"

"That would be nice."

"I'll have Barbara set it up on one condition."

"What's that?"

"That Geoff Grainger the man who is dating my wife's best friend shows up and that we are able to have an enjoyable evening with no thoughts of this company. Agreed?"

"Agreed." Barbara buzzed in and announced it was time for the meeting. We finished our drinks and left for the conference room.

***

Lloyd Galbraith and his executive staff were all seated in the conference room when Geoff and I entered.

"Good Afternoon gentlemen." I walked around the table and shook everyone's hand.

"You all know Geoff Grainger." I said taking my seat.

"Yes. Good to see you both again." Lloyd said after taking his seat.

"So let's get down to business." I opened the folder that contained the acquisition papers.

"Derrick before we get started I need to say something." Lloyd looked around the room to his staff.

"Yes Lloyd?"

"We are most appreciative of your recent offer of twenty point five million for Galbraith, but after further consideration, we are going to have to decline."

"Decline?" Geoff spoke first.

"Mr. Galbraith, when we last met; you gave me the figures that you said would be sufficient to conclude this matter."

"That was before I learned of another company's interest."

"Another company?" Geoff asked.

"Yes, we received an offer of thirty-five million yesterday."

"What company?" Geoff asked obviously irritated by this intrusion in his plans.

"I would rather not say."

"Then why should we..." Geoff started but I interrupted.

"Lloyd, then it's obvious that you would rather trade in your honor for a few more dollars. I thought we had an agreement, a gentlemen's agreement if nothing else."

"Derrick as much as I like you and respect you as a businessman; I can not allow that to interfere with the livelihood of my family and the families that have been supported by Galbraith all these years. Really, it's nothing personal, this is just business."

"Very well then; our offer stands until midnight tonight. If you decide to go with the other offer, then I wish you all the best. If there isn't anything else gentlemen..." I stood and Geoff looked concerned.

"Before you take that stance, I should at least let you know that we have just negotiated a deal to sign a multi-million dollar client that could breathe new life into Galbraith. This is the reason why this other company made their offer."

"Like I said, if there isn't anything else, have a good day." I walked over and opened the door. Lloyd and his staff walked through after shaking my hand.

"Sir, I'm sorry. I thought this was a done deal." Geoff spoke once we were alone.

"There's no need for any apology; Lloyd is being influenced. Unfortunately, he doesn't realize that he stands to lose the generous offer we made to him."

"What about the other company?"

"There isn't one."

***

I went back to my office around 4:30 after sharing with Geoff how I knew that Lloyd was being played in a game that he had no knowledge of. Barbara was exiting my office when I stepped off the elevator.

"There are a few contracts that need your signature before they go out. I left them on your desk. Is there anything you need before I leave?" She asked.

"Nothing that can't wait until the morning; remind me to have you schedule an emergency board meeting for early next week."

"I will. Good night."

"Good night." I said and took a seat behind my desk. I opened the acquisition file I had on Galbraith and reviewed all of the scouting reports as well as the finances. There was no mention of any company on the east or west coast that was willing to take on Galbraith with all of their financial woes. While Galbraith had once been a viable competitor in the advertising arena, it struggled with keeping clients that wanted a company like KCI that could give them more exposure. I remembered speaking with Lloyd over a year ago at the CLIO awards ceremony where he'd mentioned that I should just buy him out since we were literally swallowing them whole anyway. I mulled the idea over but when I saw the amount of debt they had at the time, it was not in my best interest to even consider the idea. Three months ago, Lloyd came to me with a reorganization plan and another plea to buy him out. Now he wants to pull a stunt like this. This has Shayla written all over it. Shayla and Millicent Galbraith run in the same circles and I am almost certain that Shayla went to Millicent talking about how she would make sure that they got a good offer from me.

***

"Hello Derrick." Regina's voice cut through the silence in my office.

"Regina. What are you doing here?" I asked without looking up.

"You aren't answering my calls or emails so I figured..."

"We have nothing to talk about." I signed the last contract and closed the folder.

"Derrick, here is the reason why I am here." She said handing me an envelope that looked like the one she had in her office the last time we saw each other.

"What is this?"

"This one was addressed to my husband, I happened to see it before he did. Derrick you may not want your marriage but I want mine. I need that paternity test."

"What do you need?" Raven asked walking towards us.

"The preliminary tests; I had marketing test a new market area for the baskets." I lied.

"Oh. Well it is five-thirty now and I believe I have a dinner date." Raven said coming over to my side of the desk.

"Derrick…" Regina started.

"I'll have that information forwarded to you tomorrow."

"Derrick, I…"

"Regina, my husband and I have a date. You do understand that don't you?" Raven spoke up and I was relieved.

"My wife has spoken." I took my wife's hand and headed towards the door. Regina wasn't pleased with the turn of events but I was just happy to put some distance between the two of them.

***

We were greeted by the maitre'd at the door who escorted us to the private dining room.

"I thought we were just coming in for a quick dinner." Raven said as she was seated.

"This is Barbara's doing. I guess she figured we needed this."

"What have you been telling her?" Raven picked up her menu.

"Nothing; I haven't said a word. Would you like some champagne?"

"Are we celebrating or are you trying to get some?"

"There was a time when I wouldn't have to resort to such methods."

"So you're saying things have changed." She looked at me from the side of the menu.

"Actually, I wanted to celebrate acquiring Galbraith but it appears Shayla has managed to put in her two cents worth."

"I don't understand." Raven closed the menu.

"She has said or done something that has thwarted the deal I made with Galbraith. I can see her handiwork in this but she once again has underestimated me." I opened my menu and began to look over my options.

"How did she know?"

"The board knows about any and all impending acquisitions. I suspect that Gavin and her other allies have aided her in her efforts."

"What are you going to do?"

"Let's just say that I have it all under control. Enough with business; what are you having?"

"I'll have the stuffed flounder with grilled vegetables please." She handed the maitre'd the menu.

"Sir?" He asked.

"I'll have the same and a Brandy please." I handed him my menu and he left us alone.

"So what preliminary tests were you running for Regina?"

"What?"

"The tests that Regina needed, what were they?"

"She wanted..." The ringing of my cell phone cut off my words.

"Excuse me Princess. Derrick Kincaide. No. What's the matter? Yes. Where are you? I'll call my pilot and leave within the hour. What hospital? I'll meet you there. Calm down. Where's Chanel? Very well, I'll call you when I land." I closed the phone.

"Is everything okay?" Raven asked.

"That was Shayla. Rick was in some kind of accident. I couldn't get much out of her so I don't know any specifics. We're going to meet in California. Would you mind if we postponed dinner?"

"Not at all. Call John and I'll get the maitre'd to cancel our order." She rose from the table and I called John asking him to file our flight plan.

"Why don't you go ahead to the airport? I can catch a cab back to the office and call a car for later. I've got some more work to do anyway since we've got a babysitter."

"Princess, I don't know if I should ask you to accompany me..."

"Honey, if you want me to come then I will for you, but if it is going to add stress to an already stressful situation then I think it would be best if I stayed here."

"Thank you. Why don't you drop me off at the airport? Whatever you left undone can wait until the morning." I said taking my wife into my arms.

"Let's just get you out of here." Raven kissed my lips and we walked out to the valet.

***

Raven boarded the jet and sat with me for a few minutes while John continued with his flight preparations.

"I'll call you later to give you an update."

"Give Rick my love and I will send up a prayer for him." She kissed my lips and then got up to leave.

"Princess." I said and she stopped.

"I love you."

"I love you more." She said with a smile and deplaned.

Chapter Eighteen: Raven

"Mama, I'm going back to the office for a couple of hours, if you don't mind I'll come pick up Lily a little later." I said after leaving the airport and instructing the driver to take me back to work.

"I thought you and Derrick were having dinner."

"He had an out of town emergency. Rick was in some kind of accident."

"Oh, I'm sorry to hear that, is he all right?"

"Derrick didn't know; Shayla was too emotional to give him any real details, so I'll wait until he calls when he lands."

"Sweetheart, you could have gone with him, Lily could've stayed right here with us. Is it too late?" Mama said and I heard Lily in the background.

"I didn't think my presence would be a good thing so I declined the offer. Besides I'm too busy right now and he may be gone for a few days. I really didn't want to go; I was just trying to be a good wife."

"Someone here wants to say hi. It's your Mommy, can you say hi to your Mommy?"

"Hi baby girl, Mommy misses you. Are you being a good girl for your grandma? I love you; Mommy will see you in a little while."

"You should see her, she's just grinning." Mama said.

"Okay Mama, I'm just going to finish up a few things and then I'll be right over, probably around eight or eight thirty."

"Whenever baby, she can stay the night and you can pick her up tomorrow or we can get the car to bring us out to you. Why don't you just let her stay? Your father probably wants to hold her all night anyway."

"All right, I'll let you grandparents have your night. Good night. Give my baby a big kiss for me please."

"Surely. Don't you stay out too late."

"I won't. Good night."

"Nite." Mama disconnected the call just as we pulled up in front of the building. The driver opened the door and I headed back upstairs to my office to get some work done.

***

"I thought you were going home." Derrick said before I had the chance to say hello.

"I never said that. How's Rick?"

"He was lucky; he's got some bumps and bruises. His car was totaled when they collided. The passengers in the other boy's car were more seriously injured."

"What happened?"

"The accident is still being investigated, but it appears to be alcohol related."

"I didn't think Rick drank."

"I don't believe he was drinking, it seems they were leaving the same party and the other boy was drinking and did not give anyone his keys to drive for him. I am still wondering why in the world those other boys would get into the car with someone who had been drinking. Thank God Rick and his passengers weren't at full speed when the boy crossed the median. I'm trying to get more details but I can't get a word in edgewise at this point; his mother is screaming that she's suing the other boy's parents. I'm going to have to get her out of here before she gets put out."

"I understand. Tell Rick I send my love and you my darling husband are going to have your hands full. Have you checked in anywhere?"

"Not yet, I came straight here. They are releasing Rick today, so I'll get him settled in and then find a room somewhere. What was so important that it couldn't wait until morning?"

"I have the final reports on Eric's auction and we are reporting to the stores in the morning, the designs they will be carrying. Tomorrow is going to be hectic. I've been fielding calls all week, I'll be glad when it's over really."

158

"That's the price you pay for being so damned good at what you do."
He laughed.

"Well, I have to be good at something; it seems lately I haven't been
good at being a wife."

"I never said that, I just think that you've been very distant. I've tried
talking to you and you say everything is all right, but we haven't been all right in
quite sometime. I'm not talk sexually; I'm speaking of the intimacy we used to
share. I miss that more than anything. You used to just touch me for no reason
and that spoke louder than anything you ever said. I guess I took those light
caresses for granted until I began to miss them."

"Honey, I..."

"Raven, I heard you the night of the launch party. I know that I haven't
handled things the way you think I should have but I've done the best that I can.
That is all that I can do. It hurts me that at a time like this with my son being
injured in an accident that you don't feel comfortable enough to be here to show
your concern first hand instead of sending a message through me. I am not
blaming you; I know Shayla and the games she plays. I am happy that you have
handled yourself with class and grace, because quite honestly, I'm sure any other
woman would have stooped to her level a long time ago. That is just another
reason why I love you so much."

"I appreciate what you are saying but..." I heard Shayla screaming at
someone in the background.

"Princess, hold on a second please." Derrick must have placed his hand
over the receiver.

"Princess, I've got to go, I'll call you once I'm settled."

"Okay. I love you."

"I love you more." Derrick said before disconnecting the call. I finished
the last of the report and decided to check my calendar for the rest of the month. I
figured I could get Wesley to keep Lily for a week and maybe kidnap Derrick and
steal away for a few days. I found a few meetings on my calendar that I could get
Valerie to reschedule and I could probably get Barbara to do the same. I powered
off my computer and called the car to come for me. On my way out, I walked into

Derrick's office to check his calendar. There was an envelope on Derrick's desk addressed to Richie Jameson. I figured Regina must have mistakenly left it when she was here earlier. I put the envelope in my briefcase with Derrick's calendar and made a mental note to have a messenger deliver it in the morning.

***

"Good morning." I peeped Derrick's name on the caller id before I picked up the receiver.

"Good morning. How are you this morning?"

"Good. Why are you up at this hour? It's what about three in the morning."

"I'm still on east coast time. Are you on your way into the office?"

"Shortly, I am going to stop by my folks' place to see Lily this morning."

"What time did you leave the office last night?"

"I didn't stay much longer after we talked, I just figured she'd be asleep and I didn't want to disturb her. Besides I probably would've had a fight on my hands trying to get her away from her grandfather."

"You're probably right."

"So is everything settled? How's Rick?"

"He seemed okay, he's a little embarrassed by the show his mother is putting on. She's insisting that the police arrest the young man driving the car while they complete their investigation. He's already in a lot of trouble and she's not helping matters at all."

"So when will you be back?"

"I'm not sure. I haven't had a chance to talk with Rick. I should have a better idea later today."

"Go back to bed and get some rest, if you need a day or two, go ahead and take them. I'm sure we can keep the company afloat until you return."

"I'm sure you can. Have a good day Princess, and I'll give you a call later."

"Sweet dreams honey." I disconnected the call and finished getting dressed.

***

"Good morning." Barbara spoke as I stepped off the elevator.

"Good morning. Derrick had to go out of town unexpectedly."

"He called me a few minutes ago."

"I told him to get some sleep. Anyway, I'm trying to plan a surprise getaway. Can you check to see if you can reschedule any meetings he has the week of the eighteenth?"

"Let me see." She flipped the pages on her calendar.

"That shouldn't be a problem. Do you need me to make any reservations or do anything?"

"No, I think we'll just go out to the house in Hawaii."

"That sounds nice. Can I ask one favor?"

"Sure, what is it?"

"Turn off the phone this time."

"You know I think I will." The phone on Barbara's desk rang and I left her to take the call.

"Good morning Mrs. Alvarez." I said to Valerie and she stood to follow me into my office.

"Good morning Mrs. Kincaide. How are you this morning?"

"Pretty good and you?" I took the messages she had for me from her hand.

"Good. Let's see. You have a staff meeting with the directors at two; Weaver electronics is coming up for renewal so I've pulled the files. Monica needs to see you sometime today, she said just give her a call or come by."

"Okay. I need you to reschedule anything I have scheduled the week of the 18th."

"The whole week?"

"Yes, I'm going to kidnap my husband for a few days."

"Ooh, that sounds nice. Where are you going?"

161

"I think I'll take him back to Hawaii to finish our honeymoon. I realize now how silly it was for me to spaz out when I heard Wesley had taken Lily to..." The look on Valerie's face reminded me that I had not shared Lily's paternity with her or Monica.

"I guess I forgot to share that bit of news with you huh?"

"Yeah, but I suspected as much and then when you delivered in May, I kinda just put two and two together."

"But you didn't say anything."

"Why would I? That's your little red wagon to be draggin'."

"So tell me what you really think."

"I think you made a mistake. Derrick is a great guy, but you love Wesley."

"Loved. Past tense." The phone rang ending our conversation.

"Raven Kincaide." I answered.

"Are you busy?" Cee sounded like she had been crying.

"No, what's up?"

"I hate to ask this, but could you come over here, I need to talk to someone before I lose my mind."

"Sure.

***

I stopped and picked up some lunch for us, Cee didn't sound good and I wanted to give her my undivided attention.

"Hey, hey up in here." I announced my entrance into an eerily quiet house.

"Cee?" I placed the food on the dining room table and peeped in the kitchen. It was empty. I opened the door to the basement; maybe she was washing and couldn't hear me. The basement was silent as well. A sinking feeling came over me, I was putting the food in the oven when I looked up and saw Cee coming in from outside.

"Hey." She said softly, she looked as if she had been crying.

"Come here." I opened my arms and gave my little sister the hug she looked like she desperately needed.

"Thanks for coming." She sniffled as she placed the phone on its cradle.

"Where's Tyrese?" I asked.

"Daddy came by to pick her up since Lily was over there."

"He must be in grandpa heaven by now." I said and a slight smile came across Cee's face.

"What's that?"

"I brought us some lunch, sit down." I reached into the cabinet and pulled out a couple of plates. Cee poured us some lemonade and I placed the cartons of food on the table. After blessing the food, I waited for Cee to open up and when she didn't I started asking questions.

"So what's up?"

"Are you happy?" Cee asked softly.

"I think so. Why would you ask me something like that?"

"I used to think I had it all together. I met Winston and fell in love, I got married and had two beautiful kids and I thought my life was complete. Now I'm looking back and seeing that I haven't done anything, I haven't been anywhere and I have nothing to show for it."

"You have a happy home, two gorgeous kids and a handsome husband. You have it all."

"You've got it backwards this time. This home is far from happy, and my husband may look handsome on the outside but lately he's been uglier than I've ever seen him."

"Okay so let's stop with the double talk. What's going on?"

"I'm just feeling like all of this has been a waste. Winston no longer has any interest in me. I gave up everything; all of my potential because I thought I was in love and that was all I needed. I'm bored, I have no real friends, and I have no outside interests. Nothing. I mentioned taking on a job and you would have thought I asked him to have his dick cutoff."

"What?" I tried not to laugh.

"Derrick loves the fact that you two share the business, you have more to talk about than bills and what's for dinner. Hell you don't even have to talk about that, you have a housekeeper and accountants to handle that shit. I am the housekeeper and the accountant."

"Okay, so what I am hearing is that you need some time and attention."

"Yes, and guess what? When I told him that, he took that to mean that I wanted him to jump my bones."

"There must be something in the air." I chuckled.

"What?"

"Derrick has been saying the same thing to me lately. He needs some time and attention. The only thing that is different is I think he'd be happy if I just jumped his bones."

"This morning when I tried talking to him, that's what he did and I swear it felt like he was taking it, for the first time in my life with Winston, I hated his touch. I don't think I can do this much longer. I need to figure some things out and lately the only answer I keep coming up with is..." The phone rang interrupting what she was saying.

"Hello." When Cee took the phone into the living room, I started clearing the table. She returned a few minutes later in a better mood than when she left.

"You feel better now?"

"A little." She smiled after hanging up the phone.

"I'm going to surprise Derrick with a short getaway, why don't you do the same thing?"

"Unfortunately, we don't live in the same manner as you two. You can just jump on your airplane and fly off to one of your houses."

"Fortunately, you could do the same; you could use the jet and any one of the houses whenever you want. Derrick has made that clear to you both on many occasions."

"Yeah, but Winston's manly pride wouldn't allow that to happen."

"You let me handle my brother-in-law and you figure out what you want to do and where you want to go. I will take care of everything."

"I'll try."

"Don't try. Do."

"Okay. Well I guess you'd better get back to work. I've got some running around to do."

"I'm serious. We are going away the week of the 18th. Why don't you schedule something around the first of the month?"

"I'll give it some thought. Go to work, I'm feeling guilty."

"I'm outta here. Call me later." I reached over to hug my sister who appeared to be in much better spirits now.

Chapter Nineteen: Wesley

"Hello." I was out of breath because I had quickened my step when I heard the phone ringing in the garage.

"Wesley, are you all right?" Raven asked.

"Hold on a minute." I put the phone down to go and close the door.

"I'm back. Yeah, I'm fine; I was just coming in from a run. What's up?'

"There's a lady here who wants to know if she can come and stay with you for a few days."

"When?"

"I was hoping she could come the week of the eighteenth."

"Yeah sure. I can do that."

"Good. I'll bring her to you on this Wednesday if you don't mind."

"Cool. How long can she stay?"

"If it's not a problem, can she stay until the end of the following week?"

"No problem."

"Are you sure? I mean I realize it is short notice, so if I'm intruding on some plans that you and Naquia have, I can ask Cee to keep her."

"No way. What time Wednesday?"

"I'll call you after John files the flight plans."

"Cool. Give my baby a kiss from her daddy."

"Hold on she wants to say hi to you." Raven's voice disappeared and I heard gurgles on the other end of the phone. After a few seconds, Raven's voice returned.

"Thanks again, I'll call you as soon as the plans are finalized."

"Anytime. I'll talk to you soon. Bye." I hung up the phone and ran to go jump in the shower.

***

After unloading the car and taking all of the things I'd just bought for Lily in its proper place; I threw a frozen pizza in the oven and sat down to watch the game. It surprised me when I heard movement upstairs. Naquia had been by a few times when I wasn't here to pick up her mail and some of her things, but we haven't seen each other since she got caught in her lie. I went upstairs to check things out.

"Hey Doc." I spoke to Naquia who was coming out of the bathroom with her arms full of her toiletries.

"Wesley."

"How are you?"

"Fine."

"I guess this means you aren't here to stay?"

"You don't want me here."

"I never said that."

"You said you would not share your life, home or bed with someone you can't trust."

"Yes, I did say that and I meant what I said.

"Then you have answered your own question because you've made it clear that you don't trust me."

"Naquia, what would you think if I were disappearing and not in the places where I told you I was going to be?"

"What difference does it make now?"

"Help me understand. When I went to the city because my building had a fire and you accused me of running to be with Raven. The difference is I told you where I was going and when you tried to reach me, I was there. Seems to me that this lack of trust thing was on both sides."

"Whatever Wesley; I am tired of arguing with you. It is obvious you want out of this marriage, so make your move."

"Hold up. I never said that. You are the one who has been trying to get out of this marriage since the beginning. I have made my mistakes and I have taken responsibility for the things I've done. I have acknowledged that I handled the whole situation with Lily badly. I have even compromised the time and attention that I owe my daughter to be sensitive to your feelings."

"You are right, I did deceive you. I told you I was going to be at the hospice and I wasn't there. But I also told you that I was advised by my therapist to get away for a few days. But you don't want to believe that."

"Why should I believe it?"

"Because I said it."

"Naquia…"

"No Wesley, I am tired of this. I will come and get the rest of my things this weekend. I'm moving in with my mother and I will make an appointment to see someone about the divorce."

"If that's the way you want it." I said and left her alone in the bedroom.

***

I pulled into the driveway of Samantha's house to take Vicky a package she'd forgotten to take with her.

"Hi Wesley. It's good to see you. Come on in." Mrs. Nelson hugged me before she left to go back to the phone.

"Thank you Mrs. Nelson." I walked in and the memories of the times when Samantha and I were dating resurfaced. I remembered being here having Mrs. Nelson's homemade pound cake, sitting around watching television or just barely escaping getting caught trying to get some on the sly.

"The girls are upstairs. Go on up." Mrs. Nelson said before returning to her phone call. I took the stairs up to Samantha's bedroom. Instead of the posters and newspaper clippings and pictures from her modeling days; all of that has been replaced with monitors and IV poles and other medical paraphernalia.

"Can I come in?" I knocked before walking in since the door was open.

"Hi Wesley." Samantha was sitting up in a wheelchair and Vicky was brushing what was left of her hair. It still hurts to see her like this so I'm trying to hold on to the old images of her from when we were younger.

"How ya doing Samantha? Vicky here's that package you asked for." I handed the bag to her and she smiled.

"Thanks. Let me run this downstairs to Mrs. Nelson." Vicky said leaving Samantha and I alone.

"Have a seat." Samantha said.

"Okay. Can I ask you a question?"

"Sure."

"Do you remember the night I came to see you in the hospital?"

"Yes. I really appreciated your coming; it meant a lot."

"That night you acted like you had something to tell me."

"I needed to warn you."

"Warn me? About what?"

"Your wife. I'm not trying to stir up any trouble or anything but there is something I think you should know. Remember when I told you that I was angry with you when you brought your other girlfriend here after you were released from prison."

"Do you remember that I told you we don't have to go rehash any of that?"

"Yes but you need to know that when I met Naquia, I was still very angry with you. I told her about us, about Corey and about what I did to you."

"That's cool; I told her all about that, it's not a secret."

"When I told her about the money, we made a plan for her to get close to you so that we could take the money. She was supposed to make you fall for her and then start draining you of the money."

"What?"

"I didn't want to leave my grandmother with a mountain of hospital bills after my death. So we made a plan to get you to marry her, get access to your bank account and start to siphon the money. We were supposed to split it in half so I could pay my hospital bills."

"I haven't noticed any money missing."

"She double crossed me. She claims she fell in love with you and that she couldn't do it. But I don't believe her. I have seen her with that white doctor, and I think she's messing with him."

"Every time I want to give you a chance you come up with another reason for me to..." I figured I'd better leave before I said something ugly.

I headed home and went straight to the computer. I replayed the conversation with Samantha in my head and my heart began to get heavy. After thinking about all of the things that occurred between Naquia and I in recent months I wondered if she had changed her mind and had gone along with Samantha's plan without making her aware. I entered the account number and password for the one account Naquia had access to, I scrutinized the check withdrawals and none of them were out of the ordinary. All of them were for known purchases and were recognizable. The cash withdrawals could have been made by either one of us and since none of them were of an exorbitant amount, I just surmised that they were legitimate. But the uneasiness I felt inside did not disappear when I logged out of the account. My mind had me wondering why is it that my judgment is so flawed when it comes to the women I choose.

Chapter Twenty: Derrick

Shayla was insistent upon filing charges against the young man who was driving while intoxicated. The young man was still in serious condition and her only concern was to get to his parents or in their pockets. Rick and I literally had a fight on our hands to get her away from the hospital. Once we were back at Rick's place I called John to have him file the flight plans so I could go home and take care of some business in case Rick needed me to come back.

"Are you sure you don't need me to stay?" I asked Rick who was pouring milk into his bowl of cereal.

"I'll only need you if she is staying." He said.

"Your mother is leaving today; Chanel is not old enough to be in Paris alone. But that doesn't mean she won't turn around and come right back."

"Why did you give her that jet?" He said before stuffing a spoonful of sugar into his mouth.

"You know your mother, did I have much choice?" We both laughed. I placed my hand on his shoulder.

"Call me if you need me to come back." I said after placing a few bills on the table for him.

"Thanks." Rick stood and gave me a hug before walking me out to the car.

***

"We're on our final approach sir." John announced. I closed the laptop and fastened my seatbelt again. In less than ten minutes, I was deplaning and into the limo on my way home to get changed. I dialed Barbara to make her aware of my impending arrival.

"Is Raven? I would like to surprise her."

"Yes, I believe she's in a meeting."

"Do me a favor please? Order a couple dozen roses and put them in my office please."

"Will do; I'll see you in a little bit."

173

"Thanks Barbara." I disconnected the call and dialed the house.

"Kincaide residence." Mrs. Hill answered.

"This is Mr. Kincaide calling, and how are you Mrs. Hill?"

"Good. How's Rick?"

"He's okay. A few bumps and bruises. I believe his real healing process will begin as soon as Shayla's plane takes off."

"I agree. Are you hungry, I can fix you a sandwich or something?" She said after laughing.

"That would be great. How's my little lady?"

"Miss Lily is still over her grandmother's. Raven said she'd bring here home with her after work today." My phone beeped in the middle of her response.

"I've got another call. I'll see you in a few minutes." I disconnected that call and answered the other.

"Hello?"

"Derrick, I can't believe you left without saying what we are going to do about this situation with Rick. You know if you had listened to me and he was enrolled in the School of Business, we would not be having this discussion."

"Shayla, what does his academic curriculum...we are not having this discussion. Goodbye."

***

"Floral delivery for Mrs. Kincaide." I hid my face behind the two dozen roses but I'm sure my height and voice were a dead giveaway.

"For me?" She came over to take one of the vases from me.

"Why didn't you tell me you were coming home today when we spoke?" She asked before placing a kiss on my lips.

"Because I wouldn't have gotten this kind of response if I had." I placed the second vase on her desk and took my wife into my arms. After another long awaited kiss, she hugged me tightly.

"How's Rick?"

"He's probably much better now that his mother is on her way back to Paris."

"No comment." She said and we both laughed.

"So what's going on here?"

"Business as usual."

"You mean to tell me you haven't brought in a multi-million dollar contract in my absence. You're slipping."

"So you keep telling me." She slipped out of my grasp and walked to her side of the desk and proceeded to catch me up on everything that took place in my absence.

"Well done Mrs. Vice-President of Operations. And you thought you couldn't handle it. Other than my signature, I'm obsolete around here."

"No comment."

"No comment huh? What else do you have today?" I asked.

"Dunno, let me check." She opened her calendar.

"Nothing really. Why? What do you have in mind?"

"Some time with my two favorite girls. Let me return a few calls and I'll come and get you in about an hour."

"Sounds good to me." Raven walked me to the door and asked Valerie to call a messenger to deliver a package for her.

Chapter Twenty-One: Raven

"Are you ready to go?" Derrick asked walking into my office.

"Honey, why don't you go ahead? I have a few more things to finish up and then I'll be right behind you." I braced myself for a fight.

"Why don't I stop and get us something for dinner before Mrs. Hill cooks and that way she can have the night off too?" Derrick smiled with whatever other thought that ran through his mind.

"Maybe I should leave Lily with Mama for another night. You look like you have something naughty on your mind."

"I need to see my little girl too."

"You can stop by Mama's; I'm probably gonna be here for at least an hour. I'll call her to see if Lily can stay." I picked up the phone and hit the button programmed for Mama.

"Hello." Daddy answered jubilantly.

"Hey old man, what are you doing home in the middle of the day?" I asked already knowing the answer.

"I have been held captive by these ladies here. It's been a long time since I've had to deal with three women under my roof."

"You loved it then and you are loving it now. Would you mind if one of your ladies spent another night? It sounds like her mother is going to be held captive as well tonight."

"Sure."

"Thanks. And how is the little woman today?"

"Your mother is doing just fine." He said with a laugh.

"Ooh, you know I'm going to tell her what you said."

"Hold on, she's standing right here." Daddy handed Mama the phone.

"Hi."

"Hey. How are you doing with three babies on your hand?"

"Actually, it's been rather quiet. Your father has one on each hip and they love it."

"That's not good. Lily is probably gonna want to be held like that on the regular."

"She'll be fine. She's just grinning and soaking up all the attention. Tyrese keeps looking at her as if she's a doll. I'm just waiting to see when she is going to try and pick her up."

"She tried once and Lily wasn't having it, I think Lily scared her when she started to cry." I said and we both laughed.

"So what time are you coming by tonight?"

"Actually, I was hoping Lily could stay with you another night. Derrick just got in and he wants some time and attention."

"Derrick is going to spend another night away from Lily?"

"No, he will probably stop by there on his way home. I am finishing up some stuff here and then I'm going to meet him at home a little later."

"Enjoy yourself, for as hard as you've been working lately, you deserve it."

"I will. Thanks. Do you need me to bring Lily anything?"

"No, you know she has a whole wardrobe over here."

"I forgot. Okay. Give my baby a kiss for me, shoot, I may even come by on my way home too."

"Okay. Have a good time tonight."

"Will do. Bye."

***

"Raven, Mr. Jameson on line one." Valerie informed me before she transferred the call.

"Thanks Valley." I pressed the button and answered the call.

"Hello."

"Hello Raven."

"Hi, did you get your package?"

"That's why I am calling. What is this?"

"What do you mean?"

"Where did you get this?"

178

"Regina was here the other day and I think she mistakenly left it on Derrick's desk. When I saw it and that it was addressed to you, I just had it sent over."

"Regina left this in Derrick's office?"

"I believe so, that is the only way I can figure out how it was on Derrick's desk. Richie is everything okay?"

"Raven, do you have a few moments? I would like to come over to your office."

"Actually, I was heading out for the day. My husband just..."

"It will only take a few minutes. I'm on my way now."

"Okay..." Before I could finish Richie had hung up the phone. I shut down my computer and went out into the reception area to talk to Valerie. Within a few minutes, the bell on the elevator rang and Richie appeared.

"Hi, that was quick." I said and he just walked into my office without a response.

"Raven I think you may need to sit down."

"Okay." I said and sat down on the sofa and patted the seat beside me. Richie sat down and handed the envelope I sent over to him to me.

"Open it." He said. I opened the envelope to several pictures of Derrick with Regina in compromising positions. I started to cough because my breath got caught in my throat with whatever I was about to say. Richie started patting my back as tears began to fill my eyes.

"I'll get you some water." Richie rose to his feet and walked over to the wet bar.

"Take a sip." He handed me the glass and took the pictures from me. I took a small swallow and opened my mouth to get some air as the tears flowed from my eyes. I wiped my eyes and picked up the pictures again.

"Don't..." Richie took the pictures from me again.

"I..." I started to speak but Richie cut me off.

"I always thought Derrick was a stand-up guy."

"Unfortunately, I can't say the same about your wife. That..."

"Raven, it was the both of them."

"You know what? I need some answers." I got up to go over to my desk and picked up the phone.

"Wait a minute." Richie placed his hand on mine.

"Wait? For what?"

"I want to talk to Regina first."

"You do what you gotta do. I'm going home to handle this right now." I picked up my purse, the pictures with my keys and left Richie there in my office.

Chapter Twenty-Two: Wesley

Sitting here waiting reminded me of when Raven came for Thanksgiving dinner about a year ago. I didn't even know then that she was pregnant and carrying my baby and now this time she's bringing my baby to spend the week with me. I was surprised when she called to say that they were on their way since this was earlier than she had said before. I guess she and Derrick decided to head out earlier on their trip. It didn't matter to me; it just gives me more time with my beautiful one. I peeped the time on the clock and then my watch, Raven said her pilot said they'd be here by nine. It was 8:57 so I got up to walk over to the gate for the private planes. Raven looked like she owned the place when she walked in with Lily in her arms and a guy walking behind her with Lily's bags.

"Hey beautiful." I said.

"Hi handsome." Raven responded with a smile and handed my sleeping angel over to me.

"How was the flight?" I asked while placing a kiss on Lily's cheek.

"Smooth. Where are you parked?"

"Follow me." I turned my attention away from my daughter and led her and the guy with the bags to the car.

"Would you mind if I hung out for a little while with you two?" Raven asked as she got into the front passenger seat.

"No."

"I won't be causing problems for you with the Mrs., will I?"

"Nothing I can't handle."

"Seriously, if it is going to be an issue, I can get a room here at the airport."

"It won't be a problem Raven, but what about your pilot and your jet?"

"I sent them home; I'll catch a flight later." She fastened her seatbelt and I stopped asking questions. There was very little conversation on the way to my house. Lily woke up when I hit the button on the garage door opener. Raven turned around to soothe her until she got acclimated with her new surroundings.

When I turned off the ignition and turned on the interior light, Lily recognized me and gave me her beautiful smile.

"Hey there gorgeous." I said before opening my door and then jumping in the backseat with her. Lily started making some incoherent sounds that sounded like music to me.

"How's daddy's girl? You are just getting more beautiful every time I see you." I placed a kiss on her cheek and unfastened her belt in the car seat. Raven asked me to open the trunk so she could get the bags.

"You take this precious cargo and I'll get that stuff." I handed Lily over to her and then opened the door so they could go inside the house. Raven and Lily stepped just inside of the utility room.

"Come on in." I walked past them and into the kitchen. The light was on in the den so Raven walked over to the sofa.

"Are you hungry little lady?" She asked Lily as she took her coat off.

"What about her mom? Are you hungry little lady?"

"A little." She said with a smile.

"What would you like?"

"Whatever you have is good, I don't want you to go to any trouble." Raven said as she pulled out the jars of food she had for Lily.

"Here let me get that ready for you." I took the jars from her hand and she picked up Lily and followed me into the kitchen. Lily seemed excited about getting into her high chair, she started singing and kicking when she got close enough to reach the colored balls that were attached to the tray in front of her seat.

"Okay baby, Mommy's going to put you in."

"She loves that chair." I said while handing Raven a bowl and the two warmed jars of food for Lily.

"Daddy has been spoiling you down here in South Carolina huh?"

"Absolutely rotten." I said before opening the refrigerator and pulling out the leftover ziti I had cooked earlier.

"Wesley, could you give me a diaper out of her bag please?" Lily had used the peas she was eating to add some color to Raven's blouse.

"Why don't you go change?" I handed her some paper towels.

"I didn't bring anything for me."

"Go upstairs to the loft and look in the chest of drawers behind the door; I have something in there you can put on."

"Are you sure?"

"It's either that or prepare to get rid of your blouse there."

"Okay smarty." Raven handed me the spoon and bowl and walked to the stairs.

"Where's the light switch?" She asked.

"Just take the first step, the lights will come on."

"Fancy. You go boy." She laughed and then kept talking the whole time she was upstairs.

"This is nice. You're talking about me living in a mansion. You got your own mansion right here."

"This house is a mini me compared to yours." I responded and then got a taste of Lily's peas when she reached in her mouth behind the spoon and pulled out what I had just put in.

"I guess that means you've had enough of that yucky stuff huh?" I wiped her face and hands and tried to give her the last few spoonfuls of the vegetable beef dinner she had left in the bowl. She opened her mouth for one last spoon and that was it; when she placed her hand in the bowl, I knew dinner was over.

"Okay, daddy hears you." I placed the bowl on the counter and picked her up to wipe her off. She began to fret and as soon as I put her back in the highchair she started playing with the balls and completely phased me out. Raven's cell phone started to ring and I turned off the water in the sink so she could hear it.

"Raven, that's your phone."

"The voice mail will catch it." She said coming down the stairs. When I looked up to see her dressed in my sweats and a tee shirt, it looked like a remembrance from a past experience.

"What? Did I choose something you didn't want me to put on?"

"No. No you're okay." I turned the water back on and finished washing Lily's bowl.

"I pulled out some ziti I made; you can just put it in the microwave or oven to warm it up."

"You made ziti?"

"Whatcha trying to say?"

"When did you learn to cook?"

"You know Mr. Perelli taught me a few things."

"How come you never cooked for me?"

"I don't think you ever gave me a chance."

"What? What is your daddy trying to say?" She reached for Lily and Lily let her know immediately she was not trying to get out of her chair.

"She's not having it." I said.

"I see. Oh so you want to act all prissy for your daddy. I see the game you're playing. I see it. I see it." Raven tickled Lily who laughed and her eyes lit up with excitement.

"Would you like a salad with that madam?"

"No thanks, the ziti will be fine." She took a seat at the table beside Lily who went back into her world of the colored balls.

"How's the rest of your family?" I asked placing the casserole dish in the oven.

"Everyone's good. And yours?"

"Good."

"Mind if I ask a question?" She asked and I noticed that her tone had changed.

"You just did, so I guess it doesn't matter if I mind."

"Wow, you must have eaten your Wheaties today, you are on a roll."

"What's your question?"

"My being here isn't going to cause any grief is it? I have had a rough day today and to have to go a few rounds with your wife is not exactly what I have in mind for the evening."

"You won't have to go any rounds with Naquia. She won't be coming in tonight."

"Oh. Working late?"

"I don't know."

"Oh." Raven stopped short of what she was about to say next because her phone started to ring again. I noticed she didn't attempt to go and get it.

"May I ask a question?"

"Sure."

"Who or what are you running from this time?"

Chapter Twenty-Three: Derrick

"Good evening Grace. How are you?" I said before kissing the cheek of my mother-in-law after she opened the door.

"Good. How are you? How's Rick, was he hurt badly in the accident?" She asked as she closed the door behind me.

"He just suffered some bumps and bruises; thanks for asking."

"That's good to hear. So what did Raven leave?"

"I'm sorry, I'm not following."

"You must have stopped by to pick up whatever she left when she picked up Lily."

"Raven picked up Lily? When?"

"She left a couple of hours ago. They should be home by now. Can I get you something to eat or drink?"

"No, thank you." I opened my phone and dialed the number to the house. There was no answer. I tried Raven's cell phone and it immediately went to her voice mail.

"Was everything okay with Lily?" I asked after following Grace into the kitchen. She was placing a casserole dish into the oven.

"Yes. When Raven said she was picking up Lily, I just assumed you two changed your minds about Lily staying another night." She placed the potholder on the counter beside me and finished chopping the cucumber.

"You seem surprised." She said offering me a cucumber slice and I shook my head no.

"Raven didn't say anything to you?" She asked before placing the slice into her mouth.

"She probably left a message on my phone while I was shopping. Thanks for everything, and I'll see you tomorrow. Have a good evening, I'll let myself out."

"Good night." Grace said to my back as I walked back into the living room to exit her house.

Raven's car was parked in front of the garage when the driver pulled in front of the house. I tipped him handsomely for all of the stops we'd made since leaving the office more than four hours ago. I opened the door after juggling with the portion of the bags that I could carry and held it open with my foot while the driver followed me in with the rest.

"You can take them into the dining room, to your left." I said while stepping aside so the door could close. After placing one of the bags on the table in the foyer, I punched in the alarm code; which seemed strange since Raven rarely put the alarm on when she came in. The driver came back from the dining room and took some of the bags I was carrying from my hands. I followed him into the dining room and after thanking him; I followed him out to the main door.

"Good night sir." The elderly gentleman said after tipping his hat to me.

"Good night." I closed the door and returned to the dining room. I smiled at the place setting Mrs. Hill had completed for me before retiring for the night. I placed the bouquet of flowers in the vase and lit the candles. The Beef Wellington dinner with all the accompaniments was still warm and I transferred it all into serving dishes. I was surprised that Raven hadn't come downstairs by now after hearing the alarm but figured she might have taken a nap with Lily while waiting for me to come home. After discarding all of the trash and placing the gift-wrapped box from Victoria Secrets in Raven's chair, I ventured upstairs to see my two leading ladies.

I reached Lily's room first and there was no sign of them or any indication that they had even been there. I peeked into our bedroom and found it empty as well. I dialed Raven's cell phone again, still no answer. I tried Selina, Winston said he hadn't seen or heard from Raven and if he did, he'd let her know I was looking for her. I called the office and got the voice mail for both Raven and Valerie. When I walked into our bedroom again, all of the questions I had were answered when I found the photographs of Regina and me and Raven's wedding rings in the center of the bed.

"Dammit." I picked up the photos and put them in the trash where it belonged. After placing Raven's wedding rings went on her dressing table, I retrieved the photos from the wastebasket because I didn't want to embarrass Mrs. Hill when she came to empty it. I needed to find her and talk to her but I knew better than to chase her down while she's mad. She would never hear anything I tried to say to her anyway. Regardless of how mad she may be, she has no right to just disappear; when is she going to learn that she can't run away every time something bothers her? I went downstairs to blow out the candles and put the dinner in the refrigerator. With nothing better left to do, I retired in the den to watch the television. When I woke up and realized it was four in the morning, I picked up the phone to call Raven again.

"Princess, I have been trying to reach you for hours now. I have tried every conceivable place that I can think of. I know you are upset and I won't even attempt to get into that right now. I just need to know that you and Lily are somewhere safe. Could you at least extend me that courtesy to know that you two are okay?"

Chapter Twenty-Four: Raven

I watched Wesley getting Lily ready for bed. This was the first time I had actually seen him in his fatherly role. He was so gentle and careful with her.

"Mommy, come and give our beautiful baby a good night kiss." Wesley said drawing me out of the trance I had been caught up in.

"Good night sweetness." I leaned over the side of the crib to kiss Lily who reached out for my necklace. Wesley dimmed the lights and the ceiling illuminated full of stars. In the corner of the room was a moon that provided enough light to walk around without bumping into anything. Wesley pulled a stool up to the side of the crib and opened a book of bible stories.

"Where did we leave off from your last visit?" He flipped through the pages and Lily's attention turned to him as he started to read. I felt tears welling up in my eyes because this was another one of those times when I felt regretful for the choices and decisions I made. I quietly got up and walked out of the room because I didn't want either of them to see me cry. I went back downstairs and started cleaning the dishes from my dinner. I heard my phone ringing again and immediately the picture of Derrick and Regina came to my remembrance. I thought about the inevitable confrontation with Derrick. I knew that we would have to talk about this but something deep inside of me knew already that I wouldn't believe a word he had to say. I wanted to confront Regina but knowing me and my anger, I'd probably start a fight, which would turn into something worse than those pictures. I finished the dishes and searched in the cabinets for the place where they belonged. I sat down on the sofa and turned off the phone so that I wouldn't have to answer it or anymore of Wesley's questions if it rang again.

"She's asleep already?" I asked when I heard Wesley coming towards me.

"Yeah, I didn't even make it through a couple of pages."

"I guess she's jetlagged." I said looking at my watch.

"Could be; what about you? Are you ready to call it a night?" Wesley sat down beside me and I was surprised when I felt a butterfly in my stomach.

"Actually, I was hoping to beat you at a game of Scrabble, but it's getting late. I'd better call and see if I can get a room at one of the hotels near the airport."

"Hotel? Raven you know you are welcome to stay here in one of the guest rooms."

"I don't want to cause any problems."

"What did I just say?" Wesley got up.

"Where are you going?"

"To get the game since you obviously have missed getting beat." He said with a smile.

"Oh, if I remember correctly, we were evenly matched. If anything, I have won more games than you."

"In your dreams maybe." Wesley placed the game on the coffee table and then the dictionary.

"Yeah? Okay smarty. What are the stakes?"

"Same as usual." Wesley said and then stopped. He looked at me as if he had said something wrong.

"You're on." I opened the box and he walked into the kitchen.

"You want something to drink or something to snack on."

"No thanks." I shook the letters in the bag and pulled out a letter placing it face down on the board. Wesley handed me a pad to keep the score and Wesley pulled out the letter 'a' and had to go first.

"Let's get ready to rumble." He said shaking the letters and drawing out seven letters.

***

"Well if I am reading this correctly Mr. Charles, it appears that you have lost this game by sixty-three points."

"Yeah, yeah. You and your five dollar seven letter word at the end of the game. It was just a lucky break."

"Do you hear that?" I asked.

"Is it Lily?" Wesley got up to check the baby monitor.

"No."

"What do you hear?" He turned to look at me.

"I think it's the sound of a loser." I said and he laughed coming over extending a hand to me.

"Very funny. Okay, so tell me what did I lose?"

"You said the stakes were the same as usual." I said placing my hand in his and standing to my feet.

"So that means you don't remember the stakes." Wesley said with a smile.

"I remember. Are you ready?" I returned his smile and moved over to the stereo.

"What are you doing?" He asked.

"Turning on some music, don't you think you'll need it?"

"For what?"

"My dance. You owe me a dance. Maybe you are the one who doesn't remember the stakes." I pressed the button marked CD and some jazz began to play. Wesley seemed nervous and I was surprised when that one butterfly from earlier seemed to have multiplied. Wesley opened his arms to me and held me as if we were at a dance class just learning how to do the waltz. Neither of us moved with any rhythm.

"You call this a dance?" I asked but it came out in a whisper.

"What's wrong?"

"You are acting like you don't know how to hold me. You never had a problem with it before." I stepped in closer to him and he seemed to loosen up.

"Is this better?" Wesley's voice had been reduced to a whisper also.

"Much."

"You know you can't do this, you're a married woman." Angel decided she needed to step in. The song ended and the disc changer changed CDs. I thought Wesley would have let go but he didn't. Lionel Ritchie started singing and our bodies continued to move.

"I think this is the first time we've ever danced and you didn't sing." Wesley's voice startled me.

"I don't think I would do Lionel any justice."

"That's never stopped you before." He laughed. I tried to break our embrace and Wesley held me tighter.

"Running again?" He stopped dancing to look me in the eye.

"How about another game?" I asked hoping to change the subject.

"You can run but you can't hide you know." Wesley loosened his grip on me and I quickly returned to the sofa. Wesley walked into the kitchen and brought back two sodas.

"What are the stakes this time?" I asked.

"Another dance would be cool with me unless you had something else in mind." He said.

"I'm not the one who will be losing, so it would probably be in your best interest to establish what you are willing to lose." I smiled because I knew that I was about to cross a line that I probably wouldn't be able to turn away from.

"Umm. I could take that to mean that there are no limits to this particular wager. Are you sure you can handle that?"

"Like I said, I won't be losing." I shook the letters in the bag and pulled out a letter.

"Here's an idea. I will write down on a piece of paper what I want my prize to be and you do the same. The winner will choose which slip of paper they want as their prize." Wesley smiled confidently as if he knew with either choice he would win.

"Okay." I said and handed him a slip of paper. Wesley laughed as he wrote his prize. I gave it some thought and then finally settled on another dance.

***

"So what's the score?" Wesley asked knowing full well he had beaten me badly.

"I don't know, I decided to wait until the end to total the scores."

"Let me get you a calculator, I don't want you to make any mistakes." He said as he placed the last of his tiles on the board for another twenty points in addition to the thirteen points I had left on my tray.

"That's not necessary, I have one right here." I said pulling my phone out of my purse. As soon as I turned it on to use the calculator, the message-waiting indicator started to beep.

"Don't." I said to whatever Wesley was about to say or ask. He started picking up the tiles on the board as I totaled his column. Wesley held back his comment and by the time he'd finished, the tabulation was complete and he had beaten me by more than fifty points.

"There must be something wrong with this calculator." I said folding the piece of paper up that contained the final scores.

"Why? By my calculations, I should have won by at least fifty points."

"Your calculations? How could you possibly know that?"

"I just kept track of the points between us." He said putting the top on the box.

"So now you want me to believe in addition to being a cook, you are also a mathematician?"

"You knew I had skills." Wesley sat down beside me and I felt a ton of butterflies take flight in my stomach.

"So you say. Okay, fair is fair. Where's your pick?"

"Right here." Wesley handed me the slip of paper with a smile. That made me even more nervous, if that was possible. With a deep breath, I unfolded the paper and he started to laugh.

"I want whatever you said as my prize." I read his response aloud and he continued to laugh.

"So where's your paper?" He asked between snickers. I handed it to him. Wesley smiled when he opened it and I was glad that I had decided to write down another dance instead of what my body was trying to talk me into. I got up and walked over to the stereo.

"Shall we dance?" I opened my arms and Wesley walked in with a smile.

I closed my eyes trying not to hear the urges that were speaking to me. I could tell that Wesley was fighting demons of his own because I felt an erection that had surfaced between us. The CD changed to Chante' Moore and our first night together came back in a flash.

"You have to sing for me now." Wesley whispered and I felt the first sign of my dampness.

"I don't think that's a good idea."

"If you're scared, say you're scared." Wesley tightened his grip on me probably because he knew I wanted to run.

"And if I call your bluff?" I asked in a voice I didn't even recognize.

"Call it." He stopped dancing and looked directly in my eyes. I closed my eyes to break the trance I was slowly but surely falling under.

"Make love to me." I sang in his ear.

"I don't remember that as one of the lyrics."

"If you're scared, say you're sacred." Before the words were out of my mouth, Wesley's lips covered mine and I felt my strength and the sound of the music fading away. My hands found their way inside his tee shirt and caressed the muscular frame that I had become so familiar with before. I found that spot in the small of his back that held that tiny scar he got when he fell from a tree when he was younger. Wesley's hands cupped my behind and when he lifted me off the floor, I wrapped my legs around his waist and he sat down on the sofa.

"Are you sure about this?" Wesley asked and I knew he was trying to say the right thing but his body and his eyes were telling me that he wanted to do anything but.

"Are you telling me that you want to forfeit your prize?"

"So you do remember?"

"How could I ever forget?" I traced my finger around his lips and he opened his mouth to suck on it. That move alone opened the floodgates as all the memories of the love we made surfaced at once. The look on Wesley's face told me he was reliving something as well. I removed my finger from his mouth and pulled his tee shirt up over his head. My tongue circled one of his nipples and his erection pulsed under me. A gasp escaped his lips and his hands caressed my back until he found my bra and unfastened it. In one quick move my tee shirt was off and the bra lay on the side of the sofa. Wesley smiled before he began to suck on my nipples reminding me of Lily in her early days. He lapped and laved as if he were actually nursing and it sent chills through me. My inner cove was soaked and began to throb in anticipation. I couldn't stand the wait any more and I stood up and pulled Wesley up to his feet. Without a word, his slacks and briefs were at his ankles and I caressed his member that seemed to be throbbing in sync with me.

"Ray..."

"You missed me huh?"

"More than you'll ever know."

"Show me." I said stroking him to make him even harder. Wesley followed his hands as they removed the remainder of my clothing and on his knees; he began to show me exactly how much he missed me. His tongue entering me brought on a sensation that made me feel like I was floating.

"Ooh!!!" I planted the one foot I had on the floor and tried to steady myself on his shoulder. Wesley munched and I relished in the pleasure I was feeling until it stopped abruptly.

"Did you hear that?" He said looking over to the counter.

"What?" I asked placing my foot on the floor as he rose to his feet. I watched his muscular body and tight ass walk over to pick up the monitor.

"She's awake." Wesley stepped into his briefs and slacks before going upstairs. I took a deep breath and thought about what was happening here and decided it was best if I just got dressed.

Chapter Twenty-Five: Wesley

"What are you doing awake?" I asked as Lily looked up at me when I leaned over the edge of her crib.

"Are you wet?" I felt her diaper and answered my own question. After changing her, I picked my daughter up and held her close against my chest. For the first time since she'd been born, I felt like this was the way it was supposed to be. Lily was supposed to be here in her room waking up in the middle of her parents making love. Raven was supposed to be here with me in this house raising our daughter. This evening was supposed to be a regular occurrence when we would have dinner, put our daughter to bed and then spend the rest of the evening dancing in the dark, playing scrabble, watching a movie or just making love. Where did we go wrong?

"You want daddy to finish your story?" I picked up the book and sat down in the recliner. I made it through a couple of pages and she was fast asleep again. I got up and placed her back in the crib and dimmed the light again.

I walked into the guest room next to Lily's and turned on the light. I knew that making love to Raven was not right, she's a married woman and I'm a married man. I changed the linens on the bed and headed down the stairs with my arms full so that I would not be tempted to pick up where I had left off. I was relived when I saw that Raven had gotten dressed and was now asleep on the sofa. I walked past her and placed the linens in the washer in the utility room; after turning off all the lights and checking the alarm and doors, I walked back into the den.

"Raven, come to bed." I whispered because I didn't want to startle her.

"Okay." She responded like she had so many times before when she was sound asleep and not aware of our conversation. I took her by the hand and she woke up when we reached the landing.

"I was hoping you'd wake up before I'd have to carry you up the stairs."

"What are you trying to say?"

"Nothing. You can sleep in the room next to Lily's."

"Okay." She walked into the room and sat on the side of the bed.

"What's the matter?" I asked standing in the doorway.

"I'm sorry." Her voice broke when she spoke.

"There's nothing to apologize for, I am just as guilty as you. I was a willing party too."

"That's not what I mean. Tonight I finally realize what I lost when I messed up with you. I made a stupid mistake, a huge mistake. I should have listened to you; we could have worked through Samantha. I promised your mother that I would take care of you and her family and look at the mess that I have made." Tears fell from her eyes and I walked over to comfort her.

"Listen to me. We both messed up. As much as I would like to, I'd love to erase the past and start again. But we can't. I think we both recognize what we would have and could have had if we had both made better choices and decisions. But tonight, we cannot allow whatever regrets we have to open the door to another bad decision."

"You're right. Please accept my apologies. I had no right to put you in a compromising position like that."

"We're both consenting adults and you didn't do anything to me that I didn't do to you."

"Well that's not totally true." She smiled with a sniffle.

"Don't go there."

"Wesley, I would deny this if you repeated it; but you are the only man who has ever made me feel like...I can't even describe how you make me feel when we make love. You take me higher than I have ever been and I believe that is what making love truly is. It's not just good sex; we are actually making love to one another."

"I feel the same way but..."

"So if this is the last time, we can both feel like this, if this is the last time that we can truly make love, let's not miss this moment."

"Raven..."

"You can't convince me that you don't want this just as badly as I do. My body is aching to feel your touch. I want to feel your lips all over my body, I want to feel you deep inside of me and I want to feel you explode in me. I want to hold you as you tremble afterwards and caress those chill bumps you used to get afterwards." Raven's hand unzipped my slacks. She was right I could not convince her and within minutes we were both naked, kissing and caressing each other. Raven straddled me and started kissing me from my forehead down, stopping at certain places where she knew she would receive a response. Both heads were throbbing and when her lips touched the lower one, I lost contact with the higher one.

Chapter Twenty-Six: Derrick

"Good morning Barbara." I spoke when she entered my office. She had no idea that I was here.

"Good morning. How long have you been here?"

"A few hours." I answered taking some telephone messages and documents she had for me.

"The agenda for the emergency meeting will be ready by noon. Have you decided on lunch yet?" I could hear Barbara speaking but nothing she said registered. I noticed that there were no messages from Raven not that I expected there would be, but I was hoping she would have left one.

"Derrick?"

"I'm sorry Barbara, what did you say?"

"Should I have lunch catered for the emergency meeting?"

"Yes. That will be fine."

"Are you okay?" She asked placing her pen and paper down on my desk.

"Yes. I'm fine. Just a little pre-occupied."

"Your calendar is light today; all you have is the meeting at one. Why don't you go get your wife and sneak out of here for a little while? I'll call you if there is something that needs your immediate attention."

"That's a good idea Barbara, I'll see you later." I picked up my keys and briefcase. Barbara stepped aside so I could leave and within a few minutes I was ringing my sister in law's doorbell.

"Good morning Selina."

"Derrick. How are you? Is everything okay?" She asked opening the door wider so I could enter.

"I was hoping you could help me locate your sister. I feel ashamed to have to resort to sure measures."

"You're not the first one. You two had a fight huh?"

"I guess you could say that."

"Have you had any breakfast?"

"No."

"Then come in the kitchen with me and I'll fix you something to eat and maybe we can put our heads together to figure out where she ran to this time." Selina took me by the hand and led me into the kitchen.

"Do you like western omelettes?" She asked from the refrigerator.

"Sure."

"Wash up in the sink and chop some onions and peppers for me please?" I took off my suit jacket and did as I was told. Selina placed the cutting board and a bowl with the knife on the table. I took the onions and green peppers from her hands and went over to the table to get started.

"So what did you do or didn't do? She was hyped about your trip."

"Trip?"

"Yeah, she said she was going to get Wesley to keep Lily for a few days so she could take you away on a romantic getaway."

"Wesley."

"Did I spoil the surprise?"

"I won't let on. Would you mind if I took a rain check on breakfast?"

"No, not at all."

"Thanks Selina." I grabbed my jacket and headed over to the airport.

***

When we touched down in South Carolina, it was almost ten. The car was waiting on the tarmac. John gave the driver the address and I was on my way to pick up my wife. I noticed Wesley coming out of his garage when the car stopped.

"Good morning Wesley. Are you on your way out?"

"Just going for my morning run."

"Is Raven here?"

"Yeah, she and Lily came last night. I think they are still asleep though. Just go in through the den and up the first set of stairs. Raven is in the room next to Lily's. I'll be back in a few."

"Thanks." I watched Wesley jog off and then I walked into his house. I followed his directions and at the top of the stairs, I found the room with Lily's name above it and saw the closed door beside it. I peeked in Lily's room to see if she was awake. She was sleeping and smiling as if she were playing with the angels. I stepped back into the hallway and knocked lightly on the door of the room where Raven was supposed to be. When she didn't answer, I knocked again and then opened the door slightly.

"Princess." I whispered and she answered me with her half asleep, half awake response.

"Princess." I sat down and touched her softly on her back.

"Derrick?" She said turning to face me.

"Good morning."

"What are you doing here?" She wiped her eyes as if she thought they may have been deceiving her.

"I came to take you home."

"What makes you think I want to go anywhere with you?" She sat up and pulled the covers up to cover her.

"Raven, I realize that you are angry but we need to talk."

"Talk? It's a little late for that isn't it?"

"No it isn't and I don't intend to have this conversation here with you."

"Derrick…"

"Princess please, just get dressed and let's go home." I felt like all of a sudden I was dealing with my daughter instead of my wife.

"Why did you come here Derrick? After what was dropped in my lap yesterday, why would you come here of all places?"

"Because this is where you ran to."

"I wasn't running. I had made arrangements for Wesley to take Lily for a few days so that I could spend some time alone with you. I saw no reason to disappoint him because we aren't going away now."

"And that's the only reason why you ran to Wesley?"

"For the last time, I wasn't running."

"And the purpose of you not answering your phone?"

205

"I had nothing to say to you and nothing that I wanted to hear from you. Why am I even having this idiotic conversation with you?" Raven pulled back the covers to reveal that she was sleeping in a pair of sweatpants.

"Raven..." My words ceased when I heard Lily cry out over the monitor.

"Excuse me." She pushed her way past me and walked out of the room. I followed her into Lily's room.

"Good morning sunshine." Raven's voice was much warmer when she spoke to Lily. Lily looked up and recognized me, I could see that Raven was not pleased when Lily started calling for me.

"Daaadaaa"

"Yes princess." I reached out for her and reluctantly Raven handed her over to me.

"Daddy has missed you." I placed a kiss on her cheek and hugged her. Raven walked out of the room and I took a seat in the recliner beside her crib. After a few moments alone, Raven returned fully dressed in what she wore to the office yesterday; there was a stain on her blouse.

"Are you ready to go home now?" I asked when Raven took Lily from my arms.

"Home?"

"Yes Raven, to our home. I am not in any mood to play games with you. That is not why I came here."

"Oh really? Why exactly did you come here Derrick?" She tried not to sound angry in front of Lily, but it wasn't working.

"To stop you from making a mistake."

"And what might that be?"

"You coming here to try and exact some type of revenge by sleeping with Wesley to get back at me."

"I don't play tit for tat." Raven walked out of the room and I picked up Lily to follow her.

"Raven, we have an emergency board meeting scheduled for one this afternoon."

"We?"

"Yes. We. You are the Vice-President of Operations and your presence is needed as well. As angry as you may be with me, you are still a member of the executive staff and you will have to act in your role in spite of your feelings."

"Fine. Let me tell Wesley we're leaving."

"I don't think he's come back yet?"

"Back? Where did he go?"

"He said he was going for a run."

"Then let me fix my daughter something to eat in the meantime." Raven turned and walked ahead of us into the kitchen. Lily started kicking when we got closer to her high chair.

"She wants to be put in her chair." Raven said before opening the refrigerator door. I turned to sit Lily in the chair and she cooed what must have been a thank you. Within a few moments, we heard a door opening and Wesley emerged.

"Good morning." He spoke to Raven and then turned all of his attention to Lily.

"Good morning Beautiful." Wesley placed a kiss on the top of her head. Lily reached for him.

"Hold on, let daddy get cleaned up." Wesley walked off and Lily's eyes followed him until he left the room. Lily started to cry and Raven tried to soothe her.

"Shh. Daddy is coming right back. He's got you so spoiled." Raven placed a bowl of cereal on the table and a jar of fruit. Lily stopped crying long enough to allow Raven to begin to feed her. I took a seat on one of the bar stools and watched as Raven fed Lily and just as they were finishing Wesley returned. Lily's eyes lit up and she reached out for Wesley.

"Hey there." He spoke to her softly as he picked her up out of the highchair. The two of them sat down on the sofa and Raven walked over to the sink to rinse the dish.

"Wesley, we are going to leave now. Derrick just informed me of a meeting we have later this afternoon."

"No problem, so when will you two be back from your trip?" He asked.

"There is no trip. But I won't let that interfere with your time with your daughter. I'll call you in a few days."

"That's cool. Tell them bye bye." Wesley waved Lily's hand.

"Good bye sweetheart." I leaned down to kiss Lily's cheek.

"Thank you Wesley. Raven, I'll be in the car." I said leaving them alone for a few minutes.

***

"Raven and I are running a little behind schedule, have everyone start with lunch and let them know we're en route." I said to Barbara who called to let me know that the members of the board had started to arrive. I disconnected the call and walked out of my office hoping Raven would be dressed and ready to go.

"Princess, we have to go." I said taking the stairs up to our bedroom.

"I'm ready." She met me at the door.

"You look beautiful. Is that new?" I asked.

"No. Let's go." She walked past me and started down the stairs. I followed Raven out to the car and endured another silent ride. We entered the lobby through the garage entrance and walked right into a waiting elevator. Raven checked her appearance in the mirrored walls and when the bell rang signaling our arrival, I watched a transformation come over my wife.

"Good afternoon everyone." She spoke cordially and walked into the room.

"I'm sorry we're late. Blame it on a fashion emergency." Raven took a seat near the head of the table. I followed her lead and took my seat.

"Thank you all for coming. This meeting has been called for two reasons; the first is to inform you all that we just received word that Jameson has taken the lead in the market share for all regions in the United States. So congratulations, our client is now the number one baby food company in the states." I started the applause and everyone followed.

"Congratulations Princess, all of your hard work has paid off." I leaned over to place a kiss on her cheek not knowing if she was going to allow it. She played along and smiled.

"Thank you, but I can't accept the credit alone. There is a whole creative team and supporting cast that has worked this account day in and day out and I think we should do something special to recognize them."

"That's a great idea. Barbara let's get started working on a celebration." I said and Barbara jotted something down on her pad.

"Now on to the real reason we're here. As you all know, Galbraith was slated to be the next company to come under our umbrella. We were scheduled to finalize the deal a couple of days ago, but Lloyd Galbraith informed us that there is another company that has made a counteroffer. I'm surprised because Lloyd came to me asking that we would acquire his company, so if they were in any condition for sale that conversation would have never taken place."

"What are you trying to say Derrick?" Joyce Mitchell asked.

"I am saying that someone in this room gave Lloyd the impression that he could pull a stunt like this and get away with it. All of my calculations all add up to one individual."

"And who might that be?" Shayla spoke first as if that would somehow take the light of suspicion off her.

"You."

"And why would I do such a thing?" She said with a nervous giggle.

"In all the time I have known you Shayla, I've never been able to figure you out."

"Derrick, this is precisely what we were concerned about in our last meeting. You and your personal distractions." Gavin added.

"Gavin, I know that was a concern for you and you've masked it well considering you are probably working under the promise that you will replace me as the head of my company. Let me assure you, that promise will go unfulfilled. Shayla may have manipulated her way into twenty-five percent of ownership here, but she still comes up short in anything she attempts to do. Word of advice, you can keep her in your bed, but you'd be better off getting her out of your pockets."

"Derrick! I will not sit here and allow you to ridicule me." Shayla squealed.

"Then I would suggest that you leave and anyone who has a problem with that can give their resignations now and follow you." I took the time to look at each person seated at the table making sure they knew I was very serious. Shayla stood to her feet.

"You will regret this. I assure you, it will cost you dearly." She stormed out of the room.

"If there is no other business, this meeting is adjourned." I stood up and walked out of the room and headed straight for my office.

Chapter Twenty-Seven: Raven

"Congratulations." Valerie followed me into my office.

"Thanks but you helped with the original concept, so I guess I should be congratulating you." I sat down behind my desk and went through the stack of phone messages.

"You didn't look too good when you stormed out of here last night. Are you okay?"

"I will be. What's on my calendar for the rest of the day?"

"Nothing that can't be moved." Valerie said.

"Good. Clear me for the rest of the week." I picked up the phone to call Cee.

"Are you leaving early on your romantic getaway?"

"Nope." I said and the phone began to ring.

"Hey sister." I said and Valerie exited my office.

"Hey, I see he found you."

"What are you talking about?"

"I'm talking about your husband standing in my kitchen this morning, chopping onions and peppers, looking for you. Where were you?"

"I took Lily to South Carolina last night."

"You spent the night there?"

"Yes."

"Without informing your husband?"

"Apparently.

"So did you call me for a reason other than to be a smart ass?"

"I needed someone to talk to, but you may not be the right person."

"C'mon over and let me be the judge of that."

"I'm on my way." I called for a car after hanging up with Cee. I walked out into the reception area.

"Valerie, the next couple of days are on me."

"What?"

"Just consider it a part of your bonus for Jameson. Go home and spend some free time with that beautiful baby."

"Thanks Ray. Umm, if you need to talk..." She started.

"I'm fine."

"If you say so. I'll see you..."

"When you see me. I've gotta go and so do you; get out so you aren't drawn into this."

"Okay, you're the boss." The phone on her desk rang and it was the guard telling her that my car had arrived.

"See ya." I said before stepping into the elevator.

***

Walking into the townhouse seemed strange. It had been such a long time since I'd been there. The first thing on my list of things to do was to open a window and let some fresh air in. I took a few moments to look around and immediately all kinds of memories came rushing back to me. When I looked at the sofa, I saw the last time Wesley and I made love in that spot. A smile crept across my face when I realized that was probably when Lily was conceived. I looked at the Scrabble game and all of what happened last night floored me.

After bringing in the last of my things from the car, I sat down and dialed Wesley's number. Butterflies took flight again in my stomach with each ring. I was just about to hang up when he finally answered.

"Hello."

"Hi. Did I catch you at a bad time?"

"Actually, we were just on our way out. What's up?"

"Just missing my baby."

"Yeah? Which one?"

"I only have one. What is she doing?"

"Lily's in her car seat ready to go. Hold on, I'll let her tell you." I could tell that Wesley had placed the phone up to Lily's ear because all I could hear was heavy breathing.

"Hi baby, Mommy misses you. Be good for your daddy. I love you."

"She loves you too." Wesley said.

"What did you say?" I asked.

"What do you think I said?"

"It sounded like we love you too."

"I guess that's wishful thinking on your part huh?"

"Ouch. What did I do to deserve that?"

"You don't know? I guess it was good that I was strong enough to stop anything from happening between us."

"Wesley…"

"Raven, next time you want to do something because you're mad at your husband, please find someone else to play games with. We've got to go now. Bye."

"Bye." Wesley had hung up the phone before I had a chance to say goodbye.

***

I was coming down the stairs after unpacking everything when I heard the doorbell ring. I wondered if Trina had noticed my car and decided to stop by to catch up. I was surprised to open the door to Derrick.

"What are you doing here?" I asked before walking away.

"I came to talk." He said stepping inside.

"Can you make it quick? I have to be somewhere and I am running late." I reached over the back of the sofa for my purse and pulled it up on my shoulder.

"This may take a few minutes so you may want to call whomever to let them know you will be delayed."

"What is it Derrick?" I said in a whiny voice knowing that it would annoy him.

"Princess, please give me a moment." Derrick extended his hand to the sofa, I took a seat on the bar stool beside me instead.

"You've got five minutes, give me your best pitch and then walk." I said and watched as he smiled at the challenge.

"As a human, I am prone to make a mistake. As a man, I have made many mistakes and will venture a guess that there are many more to come. As a husband, I have made many mistakes…"

"Mistake?"

"My five minutes aren't up yet." Derrick said handing me one of the pictures of him and Regina.

"As a husband, I have made many mistakes, but this isn't one of them. Regina was a poor choice that I made long before we even knew each other really. And after it was over, I made a bad decision when I tried to keep this from you. I knew in my heart of hearts that she would probably try to hurt you or to get back at me by disclosing our brief ill-fated liaison. And now because I wasn't completely honest with you, this is the consequence that I must suffer. Princess, I love you. I have not been unfaithful to you and I will do any and everything within my power to save this relationship. You mean the world to me. You are my world right now, you and Lily. It would kill me literally if I lost you." He said and I waited to make sure he was finished before I spoke.

"I guess you expect me to just take what you're saying now as the truth. I am supposed to take you at your word right?"

"I suppose under the circumstances, it is a bit much to ask."

"You're right about that."

"Fair enough. In the meantime, would you please come home?"

"What in the world would lead you to believe…?"

"Princess, we have an appearance to keep up and a company to run together. I know how angry you are, but just like you did not let on in the meeting today, we have to continue in that same fashion. With the stunt that Shayla tried to pull with Galbraith, if this got out we would certainly have a mutiny on our hands with the board. I don't think Regina is worth losing our company."

"I guess you should have thought of that before…"

"Please. We have more than enough rooms in the house that you can move into. I promise. I will not pressure you."

"Derrick…"

"Please give it some thought, and in the meantime..." Derrick handed me my wedding rings.

"Would you please put these back on? I'm hoping no one noticed."

"I'll give that some thought as well." I said taking the rings from his palm and placing them on the counter.

"Now if you don't mind, I've got to go." I stood up and waited for Derrick to walk to the door.

"I love you Princess." He said after opening the door. I punched in the alarm code and walked down the steps. By the time I reached my car, Derrick was in his BMW and driving off.

***

"I thought you changed your mind." Cee said when I walked in the front door. She was braiding Tyrese's hair.

"Hey pretty girl." I walked over and caressed my beautiful niece's cheek and sat down beside her mother.

"Where's Trey?" I asked placing my keys in my purse.

"He and Winston went to pick up a pizza for dinner."

"Pizza? For dinner? What's up with that?" I asked truly shocked that my sister was opting for junk food instead of one of her nutritious balanced meals.

"Yes, Hazel is off today." I detected a little bit of an attitude so I changed the subject.

"What..."

"What's going on with you and the mister?" Cee asked cutting me off.

"A lot."

"Are we going to talk or did you just come over here to play games with me?"

"What's wrong with you?" I asked just as Winston and Trey walked through the door.

"Hi Auntie." Trey made a beeline for me and placed a kiss on my cheek, which was followed by a kiss from my brother-in-law.

215

"Where's Lily?" Winston asked after returning from the kitchen.

"She's with her father."

"Which one?" Tyrese climbed up into his lap since Cee left us to go into the kitchen.

"She only has one. She's with Wesley."

"Excuse me. I guess I'd better quit while I am ahead."

"What do you mean by that?"

"It must be a full moon or something. I just don't know how to communicate with the McNeill girls today."

"I'm sorry; I didn't mean to snap at you; it's not you."

"This pizza is getting cold." Cee yelled from the kitchen. We all got up to go into the kitchen. Cee hadn't done any of the things she normally does to prepare for her family's dinner. Paper plates, plastic cups and napkins sat on top of the pizza box. I thought she may have been in here at least making a salad but I was wrong. After they were seated, Cee reminded Trey to say grace and then we walked out into the living room.

"What is going on?" I asked.

"Nothing. What's up with you and Derrick?"

"He slept with Regina."

"Who?"

"You heard me Regina. The ho I used to work with."

"He's having an affair?"

"I don't know. He claims it was before we got together."

"And you don't believe him."

"I don't know what to believe."

"How'd you find out?"

"Regina's husband brought me some pictures."

"What? She's married?"

"Yeah, remember she married the son of my biggest client. Remember she ended up planning her wedding the same day as Valerie's wedding."

"Not really but go ahead."

As I started talking through the whole thing, it dawned on me that what Derrick said to me earlier must have contained some truth because it was right after Derrick had announced the reorganization when Regina was pissed when she didn't get promoted. Soon after that, she announced her resignation and impending wedding plans. Soon after that, she was...

"Pregnant." I thought and spoke the word at the same time.

"Pregnant? Who? Regina?"

"Yes." I said still halfway in my fog.

***

After talking things through with my wise little sister, she made me feel better and a little bit worse. Feeling beat up nonetheless, I opted for a glass of wine and a bubble bath. I went downstairs to get the bottle of Spumante' that I picked up on my way back to the townhouse and locked up for the night.

I placed a call to Wesley's on my way back upstairs to say goodnight to my daughter but got the answering machine and hung up. I lit the candles around the tub, placed the tray of fruit and the new Essence magazine on the floor and stepped into my warm oasis. This was the first time in a long time when I realized how much my lifestyle had changed since being involved with Derrick. Although I loved my bathtub here at the townhouse, there is a big difference between this tub and the whirlpool tub back at the house.

I took my first sip of Spumante' and opened the magazine. After reading about the lifestyles of several movie stars, I came across an article written from the perspective of the other woman. I had made an immediate assumption that this would be some skank justifying having an affair with a married man because the wife was not doing something she should have been doing at home. I was surprised to find that this article was about a young girl who had been seduced by an older man and got caught up in the whole syndrome of trying to find her father in the men she was having affairs with. I wondered if there was some story like this to explain Regina and her antics.

"No she's just a ho." Angel chimed in and I agreed. I poured myself another glass and finished off the melon balls and strawberries. The CD changed

downstairs and I closed my eyes and sunk deeper into the bubbles. I was startled when the phone rang, because I hadn't realized that I had dozed off.

"Hello."

"I thought I was imagining things when I saw this number on my caller ID." Wesley said.

"No, you're not imagining things. What time is it?"

"A few minutes after eleven."

"Oh. I just wanted to call to say goodnight to Lily and to let you know where to reach me in case you needed me."

"And why are you at the townhouse?"

"I don't want to talk about it."

"So you were running. That's what last night was all about."

"No."

"Yes. Be honest. You came here running from your husband and you ran to the one person that you knew was crazy enough to take you in."

"Wesley it wasn't like that. Yes, I was and still am angry with Derrick. Nothing that was said or done last night had anything to do with Derrick. Last night I was feeling regretful for all that I lost when I lost you. I was mad because instead of going through what I have been going through this last year, I could have been there in that house with you and my daughter or we could have been here in the city together. Last night, I wanted to escape this mess that I've made called my life and I wanted to be with the one man who has made me feel like a woman being loved."

"That all sounds good and I wish I could believe you. After last night, I don't know if I can ever trust myself with being alone with you again. Last night would have been a huge mistake and I promise you that I will never let that happen ever again."

"I'm sorry you feel that way."

"Yeah me too. I was just returning your call, now that I know how to reach you. When do you want me to bring Lily home?"

"Whenever you are ready. She was supposed to stay with you for a week so that doesn't have to change."

"Good. I'll call you when I'm on my way to bring her home so that I will know where to bring her."

"Fair enough."

"Can I just say one thing?" He said.

"Sure."

"It is going to be confusing enough for Lily with us not being together. You have made a commitment to Derrick and he loves my daughter very much. Don't make the same kind of mistake with another man that loves you like the one you made with me. She doesn't deserve that. Good night."

Chapter Twenty-Eight: Wesley

Lily and I spent most of the day with Father. Lily charmed him before her reflection in the glass doors on the entertainment center caught her attention. She laughed at her reflection and then crawled over to her activity blanket, totally oblivious to our presence in the room.

"Chess old man?" I asked pulling the game out.

"Sure." Father got up to get his glasses and stopped by long enough to steal a kiss from his grandbaby. Lily smiled and decided to follow him back to the chess table. She pulled herself up using the table and stood by herself. I watched her to see if she was going to venture and take a step. I have watched her over these last few days and could tell that she was getting up her nerve to try. I fully expected that one-day without any notice; she would just walk over to me as if she's been doing it all along. When she noticed me watching, she grabbed on to her grandpa's leg. It wasn't long before she was up and in his lap and we were struggling with trying to keep the clear and frosted chess pieces on the board.

As Father captured some of my pieces, Lily was content with the ones on the side instead of the board. It only took one stern "No" to get her to realize that these pieces weren't to be put into her mouth. She decided since she couldn't have her way that she wanted to get down and go back to her own toys.

"Hello…" Vicky's voice came in from the kitchen. Lily turned around and crawled over to the end table to pull herself up.

"I think my favorite niece is in here somewhere. I think I see her." Vicky walked into the room. Lily stomped her foot and laughed at Vicky.

"There she is. Hi gorgeous." Lily dropped down to her knees and crawled over to Vicky.

"You didn't tell me she was coming." Vicky said slapping me upside my head.

"She wasn't supposed to come until later." I said as Vicky dropped down to her knees to get Lily.

"How long is she going to be here?"

"Dunno. Raven and Derrick are supposed to be going away, so I guess at least a week. She said she'd call."

"Good. That gives me a little time with my girl." Vicky picked Lily up and started plastering kisses all over her face. That was when I noticed a ring on her finger.

"What's that?" I asked.

"What?" Father asked.

"What is that on Vicky's finger?" I made my move and then got up to get a closer look.

"Eugene asked me to marry him." Vicky said softly.

"Congratulations." I hugged her.

"Thanks."

"So you weren't going to tell me."

"Actually, I was coming over tonight to talk to you. I would like you to be one of the groomsmen."

"Wow. You're planning it already."

"Yes, I think we need a real ceremony and reception since you cheated us out of yours."

"Let's just hope a real ceremony will result in a real marriage for you."

"Here give me my grandbaby and we're going outside to watch the sunset while you two talk." Father took Lily from Vicky's arms and they exited the room.

"How long have you two been seeing each other?" I asked as we both took a seat on the sofa.

"I know it's only been a few months but this just feels so right. Wesley, I have never been with a man that makes me feel like this. I thought that I was in love with Terrence, now I know that I was wrong. That was nothing compared to this. For once I have a man that treats me so good, it's like he believes if I am not taken care of; he has not done his job. He makes me feel like I am his number one priority, like nothing else matters until I am satisfied. And what is really so special is the fact that we have both decided to wait until our wedding night before we are intimate. I remembered what you said to me about being a priceless, precious jewel that's meant to be treasured. That's how Eugene makes me feel and you are right, this is what I deserve."

"I'm glad you realize that." I said pulling her close to me and giving her a kiss on her cheek.

"Thank you for rescuing me once again. You are my knight in shining armor."

"That's what I'm here for."

"Would it bother you if I asked Naquia to be in the wedding?"

"No, this is your day."

"I was asking because from the sounds of it, you two aren't doing too good."

"Hey, you know Naquia, I could go home tonight and she'll be there acting like we're cool again."

"Wesley, do you love her?"

"I love her, I just don't like who she's become here lately."

"Then tell her that. I think she loves you, she just doesn't know how to love you the way you need to be loved."

"Are those your words or hers?" I asked.

***

Lily and I had finished her dinner and bath, I let her play for a few minutes while I cleaned the kitchen. I locked up, set the alarm and picked up my powder fresh smelling daughter and headed upstairs. These last two weeks have been fun, everyday Lily shows me something new she can do or has discovered. I sat Lily down in her crib and reached over to get the book of Bible stories.

"Maaaa." Lily looked at me with her bright eyes.

"You miss her? You want to call mommy?" I reached over and picked her up and we went upstairs to my bedroom. I hit the programmed number for Raven's house.

"Kincaide residence."

"Hi Mrs. Hill, it's Wesley. Is Raven available?"

"Hi Wesley. Hold on a minute please." Mrs. Hill asked before clicking over to the music. It was less than a second before Raven's voice came on the line.

"Hi Wesley. Is everything all right?" Raven asked. I placed the phone to Lily's ear and she began to speak in her language. I heard Raven responding and watched the excitement in Lily's face. When Lily began her attempt at saying goodbye, I put the phone to my ear.

"Did that answer your question?"

"That answered my question and made my day. Thanks."

"I thought I'd better call since she called your name."

"I miss my baby, are you ready to let her go yet?"

"Nope, not yet."

"When will you be ready?"

"Never." I laughed and she joined me.

"I'm finishing up the project I was working on, so if it's okay with you, I can come and get her on Sunday."

"I'll check with her and let you know."

"I know my baby misses me that's why she made you call me tonight."

"Okay, you ain't got to rub it in. We'll see you Sunday."

"Okay, thanks again for calling me. Good night."

"Good night."

***

After reading a few pages to Lily she fell asleep with a smile on her face that showed all of the traits she received from her mother. I dimmed the light and turned on her monitor before exiting her room. It was still early for me, so I went downstairs to see what I could catch on the tube. It didn't take long before I was waking up to an infomercial that came on some two hours after I sat down in the recliner. I turned off the television and stopped momentarily by Lily's room only to replace the covers she'd kicked off in her sleep. I debated on whether or not taking a shower right now would wake me instead of aiding in my attempt to fall back into my slumber. The thought of the warm bed won out over the shower and I undressed and was immediately reminded again of the emptiness of this king-sized bed without my wife. Trying to escape those thoughts, I punched the pillow and curled up for the night.

***

I thought I was dreaming when I heard the doorbell, when it was followed by a knock I knew it was real. I checked the clock on Naquia's nightstand, which read 3:27. I quickly jumped up and went downstairs to the door.

"Wesley man, I'm sorry to wake you up but I need to see Vicky." Terrence stood in front of me drenched in sweat, which seemed strange considering it was probably around 50 degrees with a breeze that had a chill to it.

"Terrence, you all right man? What are you doing here?"

"I need to see your sister man, it's important. Please, I don't want to cause any trouble. Is she here?" His breathing was labored like he had been running.

"Come in." I opened the door wider and when he took a step over the threshold, his knee buckled so I reached out to grab him. I walked him over to the sofa and helped him sit down. I picked up the phone and paged Naquia, luckily she called right back.

"Hey Doc, I need you to come over here right now it's an emergency."

"What's wrong? Is there something wrong with Lily?"

"No, it's not Lily. I'll explain when you get here."

"I'm on my way." She disconnected the call.

"My wife's a doctor, she's on her way. You need anything, some water or something." I said to Terrence who had started shivering as if he was cold. I walked over to the hall closet and pulled out a blanket.

"Lay down, she should be here in a minute." I placed the blanket over him and then picked up the phone to call Vicky. Not wanting to alarm everyone in the house, I tried her cell phone first. Her voicemail came on so I assumed she'd turned it off for the night. When I pressed the button to call Father's number, I saw Naquia's headlights turning into the driveway. I saw her running over to the front door and went to meet her.

"What's the matter?" She asked looking me up and down.

"It's Terrence. He's in the living room and he don't look too good to me." I said stepping aside so she could go in. Naquia kneeled down beside Terrence and began asking him some questions. His words were few and after a while, he started to just respond with nods or by shaking his head.

"Wesley, dial 911 we need an ambulance."

***

Natalie made me leave Lily with her when I went to pick up Vicky. I expected her to be emotional which was why I thought it best to just go by Father's house to pick her up instead of telling her about Terrence over the phone.

"I didn't think to bring her anything; I'll take Vicky over to the hospital and go back home for her bag." I said when Natalie came back from laying Lily down.

"Don't worry about that, I'll take care of her. Just call and let us know what's going on."

"We will." Vicky was dressed and pulling me out of the door.

"What happened? What is he doing here? Tell me everything."

"I really don't have anything to tell. He showed up out of nowhere, he didn't look good, so I called Naquia, she came over and then we called the ambulance." I said before closing her door. I thought I would be met with more questions but she was quiet the whole ride over to the hospital. When we walked into the emergency room entrance it seemed unusually quiet. I walked over to the nurse's station and asked for Naquia. The nurse sent out a page and Naquia came out from one of the rooms.

"He's been admitted, we couldn't get much information from him because he was slipping in and out of consciousness. Do you know any family members we should call?" Naquia said to Vicky in a soft calm voice.

"No, when we were together, Terrence didn't keep in contact with his family. He kept saying they were all after his money. I can try to find a number for his mother. What's wrong with him Naquia?"

"We're running tests, but it looks like he may have developed pneumonia."

"What does that mean?"

"It means that I don't want to speculate. Let's get the test results and then I'll let you know more when I know more. Don't worry; I will do everything within my power to take care of him."

"Thanks." Vicky reached over to hug Naquia.

"No problem. You might as well go back home and let me call you later in the morning."

"No, I can't leave him. I want to stay here. Can I see him?"

"Not right now, he's in isolation. Let me get the results back and then I'll see what I can do. I've got to get back now, Wesley take her home where she'll be more comfortable."

"I said I want to stay." Vicky's tone of voice told me that this was not up for discussion.

***

"Wesley." Naquia nudged me as she called my name.

"Huh." I looked around trying to get acclimated to my surroundings.

"Where's Vicky?" She asked just as I noticed that Vicky wasn't at my side.

"Dunno." I stood up to stretch and Vicky came around the corner.

"What happened?" She hurried over to where we stood.

"Terrence has stabilized, you can see him now." Naquia extended her hand to Vicky and I took the cup of coffee she held. I watched the two of them disappear down the corridor. I looked at my watch, it was after eleven and it then dawned on me that I hadn't called Natalie.

"Hello." Natalie answered with a chuckle in her voice.

"Good morning. How's everything going over there?"

"We're fine. Lily is here charming your father out of his fruit."

"That's my girl."

"So what's happening over there?"

"Naquia said Terrence has stabilized but he has pneumonia."

"How's your sister holding up?"

"She just went in to see him."

"I thought something like this would happen. He refused the nurse I referred to him."

"I don't know what's going on but I just hope Vicky doesn't get caught up in his mess again."

"I agree. When you speak with her, tell her that Eugene has been trying to reach her. He's called her cell phone and then he called here, I think he was worried when they told him she didn't come into work today."

"I will. Give my baby a kiss for me and I'll try to get there as soon as I can."

"Take whatever time you need. If you need to go home and catch a nap, do that, she's fine."

"Thanks Natalie, I really appreciate it." I disconnected the call and waited for Vicky and Naquia to return.

***

I caught a glimpse of Naquia on my way back from the cafeteria; I needed some coffee so I could stay awake. I walked over to where she stood talking to another doctor and waited.

"You look tired Doc." I said offering my cup of coffee.

"I am, this is my twentieth hour and I'm due back on duty at five."

"I'm sorry, I didn't know. Why don't you go home for a couple of hours?"

"I would, but my truck is at your house."

"I'll take you home. Are you ready?"

"In a minute, I just told Vicky that we need to run some more tests, so I gave her a few minutes alone with him. As soon as she comes out, we can go."

"So what's the deal?"

"I can't say it's kind of a moment by moment thing. Our biggest challenge right now is to get the fluid out of his lungs so the medication can get in and do its job." Naquia yawned and I noticed Vicky coming towards us.

"You okay?" I asked placing an arm around Vicky's waist. She just nodded as if words were too difficult at this moment.

"He's getting the best possible care." Naquia offered and Vicky nodded again. We left the emergency room and all got into my car. It didn't take long before the ride on the highway lulled them both to sleep. I decided to just go to my house; they could both get some sleep there before going back.

"Ladies, come in and get some sleep." I said after turning off the ignition. Naquia looked into her purse.

"Don't even think about it. Get in there and get in the bed." I said sternly and she smiled. Vicky walked straight to the room that used to be hers. I watched Naquia who looked like she didn't know where to go.

"Has it been that long?" I asked taking her by the hand and leading her up to our loft. Naquia walked over to her side of the bed and laid down on top of the covers with her back to me. I picked up my pillow and went down into one of the guest rooms.

***

'Thanks for picking me up." Naquia said when she got in the car.

"No problem, I promised you breakfast, I wanted to make sure you didn't blow me off."

"Blow you off? When have I ever blown you off?" She said and then we both smiled when we thought about what had been said. I put the car in gear and we headed off to the waffle house. Our breakfast was nice, we talked about current affairs, asked about each other's family and then when all the safe talk was over, we ventured into talking about us.

"When are we going to talk about..." We both started to say.

"You first." I said to Naquia.

"I have been thinking a lot lately about us. Probably because of Vicky and the wedding. I recognized that I haven't given our marriage a fair chance. I

229

think I knew that you still had feelings for Raven, but I thought I could make you forget her. When Lily was born and you told me that you were her father, I felt very threatened by that and I did the wrong thing by taking it out on her."

"Doc…"

"Please, I've been kind of rehearsing this all night."

"Go ahead."

"I want to come home. I know we have something special, I know I haven't been the best person that I could be. I want another chance to show you that I love you and I want to be your wife. Do you think we can give this another try?"

"We have a lot to work out, but I'm willing to try if you are." I reached over for her hand.

"I am. I love you Wesley. I know I've messed up, but I want this, I want you."

"I love you too." I reached over to kiss her lips and was met with the taste of maple syrup.

"I hope you won't take this the wrong way." Naquia said when our lips parted company.

"What is it?"

"I don't know if I should…"

"What is it?"

"We always seem to fall back into bed together without ever really resolving anything. I don't want to fall into that trap. I really think we should get some help."

"Counseling?"

"Yes. I think it would help. Will you just think about it?"

"Yeah, I can do that."

***

Vicky had decided to stay with me so that she could be closer to the hospital if Terrence needed her. She was doing just what I hoped she wouldn't and that was falling back into his mess. Vicky has spent every available hour at that hospital, she's taken a leave of absence from her job and I haven't seen Eugene in days.

"What are you doing pretty lady?" I asked Lily while I got down on the floor where she sat playing with her toys. Vicky had dressed her and combed her hair in anticipation of Raven's arrival. Lily pulled herself up and held onto me like she was going to take a step.

"Where do you think you're going?" I asked her as she grabbed my hand and I helped her get over to my face where she graced me with a wet sloppy kiss and then giggled.

"Thank you." I grabbed her and squeezed her in a big bear hug. Vicky came in from the kitchen with a cup for Lily and I lost my baby to the juice.

"What time is Raven coming?" She asked.

"She said around three, what time is it?"

"Ten after two. I'm going to run over to the hospital and check on Terrence."

"Have you seen Eugene?"

"We've talked."

"That wasn't my question."

"Wesley, let's not go there."

"Too late. What are you doing?"

"What am I doing? What great advice do you have to share big brother?"

"I'm prepared for this fight. I know all about your loyalty and how you probably still care about Terrence. All I'm saying is don't forget about that brother who has shown you nothing but love and respect since you met him. Don't let Terrence take that away from you."

"Terrence isn't taking anything from me, how can you even say that under the circumstances?"

"Vicky..."

"No Wesley, you listen to me. We are all adults now and you should have grown out of that jealousy you have of Terrence. He is not well, he has come here to make amends with me and he said since he's going to die, I am the one person on this earth that he wants to be by his side. In spite of what you all think, that man loves me and if you and Eugene can't understand what I have to do here; then I feel sorry for you. I've got to go." She jumped up from the sofa and stormed out of the den.

"You think she's mad with your daddy?" I asked Lily who seemed unfazed until we heard the doorbell.

"Let's go see who's at the door." I stood Lily up to her feet and helped her walk to the front door. I slowly opened the door to Raven and Lily started to jump.

"Hi baby." Raven dropped down to her knees to greet Lily. She grabbed her and held her close while planting kisses all over. I left the two of them alone and within a few minutes they joined me in the den.

"Hello Mr. Charles."

"Mrs. Kincaide, how are you?"

"I'm great now. Wow, she's grown so much in two weeks."

"It's that good old country food, water and air."

"You're probably right. So how have you been?"

"We're good. I think our daughter is going to venture and take a few steps on her own pretty soon."

"I'm having a hard enough time trying to keep up with her in the walker."

"You'd better get your running shoes, cause she's ready." I said and the conversation seemed to stop.

"Let me get her stuff." I started to get up but Raven stopped me.

"Wesley, before you do that. I owe you an apology. The last time I was here I behaved horribly and I put you in a compromising position and that was very wrong of me. I am ashamed of my behavior and it was not fair of me to toy with your emotions because of something going on in my life. I am very sorry for taking advantage of you in that way." She spoke but she couldn't look at me.

"I accept your apology. One thing I have learned about you Raven is that you tend to act before you think. I am just as guilty as you when it comes to behaving badly. I should have never allowed things to get out of hand like it did. If anything, we should both know by now that we can never go there again. Despite the fact that we are both married, there is still a forbidden temptation there and we are not strong enough to handle it. I'm just glad we didn't do it after all." When I looked up, Naquia was standing in the kitchen. I didn't know how long she'd been standing there but the look on her face showed that she had heard more than either of us wished she had.

"Excuse me." Naquia walked past us with her suitcase and went upstairs.

"I think we'd better go." Raven said.

"I'll get Lily's things." I left and went up to the nursery. After taking the bags to the car and kissing Lily goodbye, I went back inside and straight up to the loft.

"Do you want to talk about it?" I asked.

"Not right now." Naquia responded from the closet.

***

I waited a few hours to give her a chance to finish what she was doing. I wanted to talk about this because if we were going to do this, we were going to do it right. This was not a time to sweep anything under the rug. I went upstairs and knocked on the doorjamb before going in.

"Is this a better time?" I asked.

"For what?" Naquia sat on the bed looking through one of her medical books.

"Let's not do this. We have to talk about what you heard."

"I didn't hear anything that I didn't already know. You still have feelings for Raven; she used them against you and almost got you to break our vows. You are the only one in denial about her. What is it that we need to talk about?"

"I owe you an apology."

"Actually you don't. We were separated, right? Isn't that the only reason why you could even justify sleeping with another woman other than me?"

"No. I can't justify it, it would've been wrong if it had happened. But it didn't."

"You know every time I think we have a chance to work on this marriage, that woman comes in between us. If you are serious about reconciling, you are going to have to do something about her. I can work through my feelings about Lily, but I cannot work through Raven. I made an appointment with Dr. Winters for tomorrow at three. I hope you can make it."

"I'll be there."

"Good. Is there anything else we need to discuss?"

"I guess not." I picked up the rest of my stuff and moved it into my new bedroom.

***

"How about some lunch?" I asked as Naquia and I were leaving the marriage counselor's office.

"No time. I promised Tara that I'd come in early to cover for her. She has some relatives..."

"Okay Doc. I was just asking." I interrupted her before she went into one of her lengthy explanations. Ever since Dr. Winters told Naquia that her disappearing acts were not conducive to a healthy relationship, she has been detailing her comings and goings as an attempt to rebuild the trust in our relationship.

I fought this counseling thing in the beginning but after hearing everyone's opinion on what I should do under the circumstances, I gave in to the pressure. When we first started, I thought that it would end up being a lot of talk about how we should not have gotten married in the first place. I was surprised when the counselor started by asking about our family life and our relationships with our family members. It seemed odd but as we began to talk, he showed us how the things we saw growing up formed who we became as adults trying to relate to one another as man and wife.

Marjorie had explained to me all the changes Naquia had gone through when her father left them. When Naquia finally opened up about it in one of our sessions, I could see how she was feeling about the things that were going on early in our marriage. The counselor got her to admit how she was angry with

234

her father and taking it out on the men in her life, including me. Samantha had warned me to be careful of Naquia; she wanted me to be aware because she didn't think that Naquia was all that she was claiming to be. I took what Samantha said to me with a grain of salt. Now with the things that are being revealed in the sessions, I have to wonder. Naquia pulled up to the emergency entrance of the hospital and put the car in park.

"I don't know yet what time I'm getting off, so I'll call you." Naquia said before leaning over for a kiss.

"Okay. Do you want me to go and get you some lunch?"

"No, I can just get something in the cafeteria." She placed a quick kiss on my lips and opened her door. I got out and met her on the parking lot.

"Are you okay?"

"I'm fine. I'll see you later."

"I know our session today was kind of rough..."

"Wesley, I'm fine. See you later." She kissed me again and then walked off.

Chapter Twenty-Nine: Derrick

"This looks great." I said to Barbara who had done a wonderful job in pulling this celebration together on such short notice. I placed a kiss on her cheek and whispered in her ear.

"I owe you one."

"Try two." She said with a smile. I walked around to the bar and picked up a glass of champagne. Raven hadn't arrived yet, she said she wanted to stop by and pick up Selina on her way in. The guests had started arriving and I began greeting many of the employees as they filed in. The Jamesons arrived and I walked over to greet them.

"Good evening." I spoke and extended my hand to Richard.

"Hello Derrick." He spoke.

"Mrs. Jameson, you are looking quite lovely." I leaned over to kiss her cheek.

"Thank you. Where's that beautiful wife of yours?" She asked.

"I'm expecting her any minute now. She took the car to pick up her sister." I responded.

"Good."

"Follow one of these young ladies, they will escort you to your table and I will see you in a few minutes." The Jamesons left me and Lloyd and Millicent Galbraith approached me.

"Good evening, I'm glad you two could join us." I said shaking Lloyd's hand and kissing his wife's cheek.

"I'm glad you invited us. I figured now that the acquisition has been completed that our business relationship was over."

"I bought your company Lloyd, that's it, nothing else has changed."

"Has Shayla arrived?" Millicent asked.

"I haven't seen her, but I am sure she will be here. Follow one of these ladies and they will show you to your table." I looked around the room as it was beginning to fill and my eyes met with Regina and her husband as they walked in. My attention was then directed to Shayla and Gavin when they walked in together looking like the couple I had suspected they'd become. We hadn't seen or spoken to one another since the board meeting four weeks ago.

"Derrick." Shayla made a beeline for me.

"Shayla, you are looking lovely this evening."

"Thank you for noticing. Your...Raven has done a phenomenal job in here."

"Actually this is Barbara's doing, she has spearheaded this whole affair."

"I must commend her on a fabulous job."

"I'm sure she would appreciate that." Gavin joined us handing Shayla a flute of champagne.

"Derrick. Good to see you."

"Likewise Gavin. If you two would excuse me." I said noticing Raven and Selina coming in. I walked over to meet them.

"You two are the most beautiful women I've seen all night." I said placing a kiss on Selina's cheek.

"Thanks, you don't look too shabby yourself brother-in-law."

"Looks like a nice turn-out." Raven said eyeing the room.

"I asked Barbara to make sure there was some cider for you. She said to tell you that it's in the rounded flutes."

"Thanks." She said and smiled. Things haven't completely gotten back to normal between us, but I'm grateful that we're bridging the gap.

"Let's get seated so they can begin." I said extending my hand towards the table reserved for us.

"I'll be right there; I'm going to the ladies room." Selina said before walking away.

"Good evening everyone. Thank you for coming; I am Victor Truell, President of Accounts. Tonight is a night of celebration. Tonight KCI wishes to recognize a major milestone, our client Jameson Foods has taken over the number one position in the market share arena for baby foods international." Victor stopped for applause. "Tonight we want to show our appreciation to all of you who are responsible for this monumental achievement. After much consideration, on behalf of Derrick Kincaide our CEO, we would like to present these awards to the following people." Victor went through all of the names of everyone in each department and gave them an engraved plaque with their names and the date they made our client number one. Attached to each plaque was a check for $1000. Raven had convinced me that in the scheme of things, this was a grand but ultimately inexpensive way of showing immediate appreciation and gratitude. It would definitely improve employee morale and give the incentive for other employees to reach beyond the minimum.

"Have you seen Cee?" Raven leaned over and whispered.

"No."

"Where could she be? I'd better go and make sure she's okay."

"Princess wait. Let me send one of the ushers."

"And last but certainly not least. Raven Kincaide would you please come forward." Victor said and the spotlight turned to our table. Raven smiled graciously but pinched me when she walked by. On her way up to the podium, as expected she stopped by the table beside us and took Valerie with her.

"Raven Kincaide and Valerie Alverez, on behalf of Derrick Kincaide and the KCI Board of Directors, we would like to thank you for all of the time and effort you two have put into this project from its inception. We are presenting you two with a one week all expense paid trip to Martinique and a check for $2500 dollars." Victor handed each of them, their award and placed a kiss on their cheeks.

"Thank you." Valerie said and moved away from the microphone. Raven took her cue and decided to share a few words.

"You never really know when you start a project how far it is going to go or even if it will make it off the development floor. From the beginning with this project, I think everyone that heard it felt connected to it and it was solely because we were working with an outstanding product. With gratitude I accept this generous award but I cannot let this moment go without saying thank you to everyone from the security guards who kept us safe when we worked late at night to all the vice-presidents that found the financial backing to get this project out to the public. But mostly, I would like to thank the Jamesons for putting their trust in the team and me. Everyone please give the Jamesons and their delicious baby food, which by the way my daughter simply adores a round of applause." Raven started the applause and then everyone in the room gave them a standing ovation. I turned to the usher who whispered that Selina was not in the ladies room.

"Thank you." I responded and turned my attention to the podium where Richard and his son stood beside Raven.

"Raven, I just want to thank you personally for challenging me to take the steps necessary to get to where we are. Son, do you have anything you want to add?"

"Yes. I too want to thank you Raven for all of the hard work you have put in for our company. A business relationship is much like a marriage. It must be built on a foundation of trust and respect. I am sure when you got married a few months ago, not only did you marry Derrick because you loved him but also because you trusted and respected him. I know when I made the decision to marry Regina; those were definitely two components of my decision. So like a marriage, our company put our faith in KCI if for no other reason then the fact that we trusted the people that we were working with and that we had great respect for them. Unfortunately, all of that has changed and now our relationship, much like my marriage is headed for a divorce."

"Richie…" Raven's words were drowned out when she covered the microphone. Richard removed her hand to continue.

"I recently discovered that the woman I married, the mother of the young man that she claims is my son has been involved with the CEO of the company that handles my company's account. Listen to the conversation that took place in the office of my so-called wife a few months ago." Richard pressed a button on a hand held recorder and my voice became amplified when he held the recorder up to the microphone.

"Regina, I just want to deal with this situation for the last time and cut off any further communication or interaction between us. So if you want to offer me anything, offer me the assurance that this is the end of this nonsense."

"Derrick, if this wasn't important, I wouldn't be bothering you. You do recognize that I did not create this situation alone. It takes two to tango and the two of us tangoed quite a bit. Now that you have become involved with Raven..."

"This has nothing to do with my wife. Is this another one of your competitive jealousies? I can assure you, you won't win."

"Jealousy? Please there is nothing Raven has that I would ever be jealous of."

"And the point of all of this is what exactly? Regina you are a married woman and you knew I had no real interest in you. Whatever it was that we had was purely of a physical, sexual nature. At your prompting, if I recall correctly, you wanted to show me how a man like me should be treated. I did not deceive you; I did not mislead you. You were involved in a relationship and so was I."

"And if I recall correctly, you never once tried to stop it. There is no need to continue to rehash all of this; we see things very differently. You should know that someone else knows about us."

"There is no us and whatever anyone thinks they know is strictly speculation."

"Actually its not, they saw us together."

"What is this?"

"This arrived while you were on your honeymoon." Richard clicked off the recorder.

"Effective immediately, Jameson Foods is severing all ties with KCI, our account will now be handled by AD-Vantage Advertising which has just recently come under the helm of Lloyd Galbraith. I am advising you Derrick Kincaide to turn over anything that AD-Vantage will need so that my company feels little to no impact of this transition. Anything less than your full cooperation will result in further embarrassment and loss of clientele." Richard walked away from the podium and I tried to establish eye contact with my wife; I wanted to make sure this didn't hurt her. I didn't care that Richard had lashed out at me; I expected somehow this ugliness would all surface. I just never expected it would happen here. There was a loud hush of voices all around the room, each person whispering whatever their thoughts were.

"Excuse me. May I have your attention please?" Raven spoke into the microphone. The room immediately quieted.

"Who knew we would receive good food, drink, cash and awards for some and now a drama filled soap opera like show all on a Monday night? If I were you, I'd give them all a round of applause." Raven stopped and clapped her hands but everyone else sat in awe wondering what she was going to say next.

"I asked Mr. Jameson not to do this in public in this forum. But I guess emotion got the best of him, and I understand that because when we stumbled across the pictures that were further evidence of this…I don't even know what to call it. Anyway, we were both disgusted by what we saw. And since we are uncovering things, exposing people and airing dirty laundry, let's take it a step further." I could see the anger rising up in my wife and as much as I wanted to stop her, I knew better.

"Respect and trust; those are the words that Richie chose to use in describing the components of his marriage and this business relationship. Well for those of us who know Regina Daniels-Jameson and has worked with her for a number of years, we would have to wonder how in the world you could have used that as the criteria in choosing Regina to be your wife. Didn't you know who you were getting involved with? Everybody knew that Regina was infamous for using that old adage, you've gotta use what you got to get what you want. What she's got has been used so much; I don't know why this surprises you. My husband and I talked about this situation a few weeks ago and he said something to me that I didn't want to hear but after some time had passed and I processed what he said, it all became crystal clear. What he said to me in a nutshell is that as a man he is prone to make mistakes, but as a husband this was not one of them. At first the anger in me wouldn't allow me to hear what he was saying, but later it was reason that forced me to listen. And after putting my shock and anger aside, I was able to clearly see that whatever happened between the two of them, happened before Derrick and I became a couple, before we were together. But for you Richie, it meant that while you and Regina were together, she did this nasty deed with no regard for you or your relationship. Your wife has closed many of her deals either on her knees or on her back. I would even venture a guess to say that she may have used that very tactic with you. So why you would be surprised to hear that she has done something she's been doing all along perplexes me. It's like your wife just said, it takes two to tango." Raven turned to Richard's father.

"Mr. Jameson Senior, you know how hard we have worked to put your company in the place that we were supposed to be celebrating tonight. You cannot possibly think that taking your account from KCI because of this fiasco created by your daughter-in-law is going to guarantee that you will remain in the number one spot. I understand your son's anger; I understand the hurt he feels. I have felt the same and I have said and done some things that weren't very well thought out. Please do not make the mistake of taking this account away because your son is making a decision out of anger and emotion. Don't get me wrong, I am in no way excusing Derrick's behavior and I definitely am not condoning what has been done. I am sure there are some people in attendance here tonight that had a hand in trying to discredit my husband and make him look bad. But I must ask that you consider what my husband said to me; as a man he is prone to make mistakes, but as the CEO working for KCI, this was not one of them." Raven looked at me and then walked away from the podium. I got up to go to her but got stopped by Shayla and Gavin.

"Another one of your personal distractions?" Shayla asked with a gigantic smile on her face.

Chapter Thirty: Raven

A night that was supposed to be a celebration has turned into a nightmare. I can't believe Richie did this in front of everyone, in front of all these employees, the board and the press. There is something else going on here, I don't know what it is but there is something else. I walked out of the ballroom looking for Cee, she wasn't in the lobby, and she wasn't in the bathroom. People started leaving and as the crowd thinned, I still couldn't find her.

"You didn't have to do that?" I heard Regina's voice coming from behind me; I took a deep breath before turning to face her.

"Regina, I don't have anything to say to you."

"You seemed to have a lot to say to defame me up there."

"Defame you? That's funny. If you think you have a case then take me to court. Judge Judy, Judge Mathis, The People's Court; choose one, sue me."

"Listen you..." Regina reached out and grabbed my arm just as I was about to walk away.

"You want to add an ass kicking to everything else that's gone on here tonight?" I looked at her and felt years of anger and rage rising up. Mr. and Mrs. Jameson must have overheard the two of us.

"Ladies..." Mr. Jameson removed Regina's hand from my wrist and walked her away from me.

"Raven, I am ashamed of all of this but I was simply trying to open my son's eyes."

"You orchestrated this?"

"I wanted him to see her for the slut she really is."

"Mrs. Jameson..."

"I know honey; I will take care of this."

"I think you've done enough." I walked off from her and walked back into the ballroom. I looked around and did not see Derrick or Cee, so I walked outside and asked the valet to call my car. I was surprised to see that Derrick wasn't home when I got there. I went into my dressing room to change thinking he'd be home shortly; I was surprised when he hadn't arrived by midnight.

***

"Morning." Valerie spoke as I exited the elevator.

"Good morning. What's happening in Peyton Place?" I asked walking past her and into my office.

"It's been quiet believe it or not." She said handing the mail and messages to me.

"Have you seen Derrick?"

"Not yet. You didn't see him?"

"No he left before I got up this morning. I thought maybe he had an early meeting that he didn't mention."

"I don't know. You want me to check with Barbara."

"No that's all right; I'll try to catch up to him later. Any news on Jameson?"

"Nothing."

"Well let's hope that no news is good news." I said picking up the phone, I had a message from Cee and wanted to return her call. I dialed the number and Valerie left me alone for the call.

"Hello." She answered on the first ring.

"Morning. Are you on the other line?"

"Yes, I am. Can I call you back?"

"Yep. See ya." I disconnected the call and waved to Valerie to have her come in again.

"Whatcha need?" She asked.

"What's on my calendar today?"

"You have the staff meeting at one and there is a conference call with Weaver Electronics at three; other than that you are pretty much open."

"I know this is going to sound crazy but indulge me."

"I'm used to you sounding crazy." She said with a smile as she took a seat opposite me. We spent the morning pulling together a list of all of our

246

clients, and new prospects. Valerie created a phone list for each account manager to make personal phone calls to find out where we stood after the nightmare celebration. My list contained all of the high profile clients that would really impact us if we lost them. I went downstairs to grab a salad for lunch before meeting with all of the account managers and explaining their assignment. It was surprising to see that there were more people who supported Derrick in all of this than I would have thought. After the staff meeting, I went back to my office where I noticed for the first time that Cee hadn't returned my call. First she disappears and now she's not returning my calls; I picked up the phone to call her but Valerie came in to remind me of the Weaver call.

"Conference on line three." Valerie said holding up three fingers.

"Thanks." I pressed the button for line three and waited until the introductions were done before announcing my arrival.

"Raven Kincaide, KCI. Good afternoon everyone."

"Good afternoon." Everyone on the call chorused in. I listened as Leroy Hanks went through the client's state of affairs and asked if there were any questions. When Leroy finished his part, I took my cue to find out Mr. Weaver's position after last night.

"Mr. Weaver, I am sure that you've heard about the festivities."

"Yes, I did but before you go any further Raven let me just say; as long as my ads are in the paper on time with no errors, as long as my commercials are getting regular rotation and my sales stay above sixty percent over last year. I could care less who Derrick Kincaide is sleeping with."

"Thank you Mr. Weaver. I think." I said and got a laugh out of everyone on the call.

"You're welcome sweetheart. You and KCI have done a remarkable job for my company and I would be crazy to walk away. So you can lay that worry aside."

"Thanks again. If there isn't anything else, everyone have a good day and Mr. Weaver we will talk again soon. Goodbye." I disconnected the call and then made all of my calls and surprisingly got pretty much the same response as the one that I received from Mr. Weaver. I asked Valerie to call around and get a two-page spread in all of Thursday's morning papers. I called all the account managers and asked them to get usable quotes from the clients that we could use to describe their feelings about KCI or their reason for staying. I gave them a deadline of 10am and put the copy department on alert. This felt good, even though Derrick and I had been at odds these last few weeks; I still knew that I loved him. It hurt seeing him in this funk; he was back to the quiet man suffering silently that I saw when Shayla was putting him through changes with the divorce settlement. It appears she was behind this source of pain as well. After answering the last of my emails, I decided to call it a day and stop by my sister's house on my way home.

***

I heard the bells on my baby's shoes coming towards me when she heard the alarm beep. I am still amazed that she's actually whizzing around in her cousin's walker.

"Hi sweet face." I dropped my briefcase and purse and grabbed my bundle of joy.

"Maaamamama" She said and laughed as I smothered her with kisses.

"Where are Grandma and Mrs. Hill?" I asked placing Lily back in her walker. Lily took off towards the kitchen and I followed.

"Good evening, it smells good in here." I spoke taking a seat at the breakfast bar.

"Your mother's car just left and dinner will be ready in about ten minutes. Is Mr. Kincaide back yet?"

"Back?"

"Yes, he said he had to fly to California this morning?"

"I didn't know."

"Oh. I'm sorry. I thought he spoke to you about his trip."

"That's okay. Is everything all right with Rick?"

"I don't know, he just mention going, he didn't say anything further."

"Okay. Let me go get washed up and then you and this little one get ready to join me for dinner please. I'll be right back." I went upstairs to change clothes and then came down to enjoy a quiet evening of good food and conversation with the ladies of the house. I practically had to fight Mrs. Hill to get her to let me clean up the dinner dishes. After that battle, Mrs. Hill took Lily upstairs for her bath and got her ready for bed while I went into the den to go through the mail. I picked up the phone and tried to reach my sister again.

"Hello." Cee answered.

"Did you forget your Geritol or something?"

"What?"

"I thought you were going to call me back today."

"Oh yeah."

"Where have you been?"

"What?"

"I stopped by on my way home; no one was there."

"Where could I have been? You know my life; if I go anywhere it's within a five mile radius of this house."

"That's not true. You disappeared on me at the KCI celebration last night."

"I got bored and went home."

"Bored? How could you have been bored with all the drama?"

"You call that drama? I guess you've been living the glamorous life for too long big sister. Anyway, I got bored and caught a cab home. Listen I have some stuff to do, I'll talk to you later."

"Are you okay?"

"I will be. Bye." Cee disconnected the call. Realizing that I wasn't getting any answers from her, I gave up on that until I could get to her face to face. After opening all the mail, I moved on to the catalogs. Christmas was just six weeks away and I hadn't started any of my shopping. By this time last year Derrick and I had practically bought enough to replenish the dying economy. This year we hadn't even talked about spending a dime. After the whole disaster with the Galbraith acquisition, I wasn't sure how much of a loss we had taken. Derrick found out last Saturday that Lloyd Galbraith had defaulted on several loans that he had said were paid off before the papers were signed. Mr. Galbraith had also written checks on the Galbraith account for monies that weren't there. Larry is supposed to be working on taking legal action against him. I went through all of the catalogs and started folding over the corners of the pages that I wanted to revisit.

"Good night." Mrs. Hill said from the doorway.

"Sweet dreams." I said and looked at my watch, it was almost ten and I was concerned that Derrick hadn't called. I picked up the phone and dialed his cell. No answer. I called the office. No answer. I called the plane. No answer.

***

I decided to get off on Derrick's side of the floor this morning. I was hoping he was there or to at least talk to Barbara to find out where he was. I figured last night that he must have been giving me a taste of my own medicine after I pulled that disappearing act with Lily a few weeks ago.

"Good morning Barbara." Barbara raised a finger to me in response since I hadn't noticed that she was on the telephone. I mouthed an apology to her.

"Morning." She spoke as she hung up the phone.

"Boss around?" I asked.

"Raven I know that you two have been on the outs…"

"I just want to know that he's okay. I haven't seen or heard from him in a couple of days."

"He's fine. He went to California for the hearing."

"Hearing?"

"Yes for the driver in Rick's accident. He wanted to make sure Shayla didn't cause any real harm. He's coming back tonight."

"Thanks."

"Raven, can I say just one thing?"

"Go ahead."

"I've worked for Derrick for almost twenty years now and he has always put his family ahead of his work. When he and Shayla became estranged, it became his kids and then his work. As the kids became older, it became all work.

250

He stopped living until he found you. I can't remember seeing Derrick happier than he has been since the two of you met. Lately, I've seen him reverting back to that man with no life in him. Please..."

"Barbara, you don't have to say another word." I reached over and hugged her.

"Thank you." I whispered and fought back some tears that surprised me.

"I hope I haven't spoken out of turn."

"You and Mrs. Hill are probably the only other women that love him just as much as if not more than me. You can speak any time you think something needs to be said. Thanks for giving me the kick in the butt that I needed."

"You're welcome." She said with a smile.

"Since your boss is away, why don't you go play? Valerie can handle your phones."

"Are you sure?"

"Yep. Enjoy your day."

"Thanks." Barbara started preparing to leave and I walked around the corner to my office.

"Good morning Valley."

"Morning." She said and followed me into my office.

"Can you cover Barbara's phones for me please? Derrick's out of the office so the calls should be light."

"No problem. All of the account managers have responded to your email and the copy department is on standby. I've printed all of quotes and..."

"Whoa, who are you and what have you done with my assistant?"

"Stop playing. This is important; this is about more than just Derrick and Regina. This is our job, our bread and butter; we can't let this go without a fight."

"You know what; I was so busy being worried about people thinking I was a fool and about how Regina got the best of me again. I never thought about what you just said."

"That's because you're selfish and always thinking about yourself." She teased.

"There's my assistant, the one I know and love."

"You can't fool me. I know that's why you spent over three hundred thousand dollars to take out a two page spread in every newspaper in the tri-state area."

"It cost that much?" I was surprised by the figure.

"Yep and worth every penny. Sign this check requisition while I'm thinking about it." She handed the manila folder over to me and I signed everything in it.

"You think you know me. You don't know me. Give me the quotes so I can go through them and make sure we are getting our money's worth." Valerie handed me the file and I went downstairs to the copy department. I ordered lunch in and we completed the spread in time to get it out to all of the papers before their deadlines. After all was said and done, I felt like I had really accomplished something. Valerie had several phone messages for me when I returned to my office. I looked through them and decided they could all wait until morning. I needed to get over to Cee's and find out what was happening with her.

***

"Hey up in here." I spoke coming into the front door. I didn't get a response to my greeting so I walked through the kitchen to see if Cee was out back. No sign of her there, I tried downstairs hoping that the washer or dryer silenced my call. I went back into the kitchen hoping to find a note that she may have left for Winston. Nothing. It dawned on me afterwards that the alarm wasn't on, that was strange because she never leaves home without setting the alarm.

"Cee." I called out again before completing the flight upstairs to the bedrooms. There was still no sign of her. I went back downstairs, out the door and drove home.

***

Mama and the girls were seated on the floor in the den watching Sesame Street. Mama was making sounds with Lily while Tyrese was saying the words or at least her version of them.

"Hi." I said before joining them.

"This is a surprise." Mama said as Lily crawled over to me.

"I see you've got your hands full. Where's Cee?"

"She said she had some business to take care of, she dropped Tyrese off this morning before the car came for me."

"Did she say what time she'd be back?"

"No, I just told her I'd call her when I get home."

"Ask her to give me a call when you talk to her please."

"Sure baby. Tyrese, give your Auntie and Lily a kiss." Mama said standing to her feet. I gave my niece a hug and a kiss and Lily tried to do the same. Lily and I walked them to the car and then went back inside to spend some time together. The phone rang while we were in the middle of playing patty cakes; Mrs. Hill brought the phone to me.

"Hello."

"Hey. Where's Mama?"

"She went home about an hour ago. Where are you?"

"Running errands. I'll call her at home."

"Hold up. What's going on with you? Lately..."

"I've gotta go, I'll call you later." Cee cut me off and disconnected the call. I picked up Lily and we went in to see what Mrs. Hill had in the works for dinner.

"Whatcha cooking good looking?" I asked walking past her to place the phone on the cradle.

"Beef Stroganoff."

"Wow. What's the occasion?"

"Mr. Kincaide is coming home tonight and I thought he would appreciate a real meal."

"You ladies take such good care of that man. If I were the jealous type I'd have a fight on my hands trying to get rid of you and Barbara."

"It wouldn't be much of a fight believe me." Mrs. Hill laughed and we heard the alarm beep. Lily started kicking because she wanted to get down. As soon as her hands and knees hit the floor, she took off for the foyer and I followed.

"Hi Princess." Derrick dropped his briefcase and suitcase and picked up his treasure.

"Daaaadaaaa" Lily said and the smile on Derrick's face was evidence that he had just received all that he could possibly need.

"Welcome back. How's Rick?"

"Thank you. He's good. The young man pled no contest and we asked that he get a community service sentence and pay restitution for all the damages."

"That's good. Are you hungry?"

"Yes." He said before taking a bite out of Lily's cheek. She blushed and giggled. Like mother like daughter.

"Let me take her off your hands so you can get cleaned up for dinner." I said reaching for Lily who was not at all pleased with my intrusion on her time with Derrick. When she started to cry, he gave in and took her upstairs with him. I retreated to the kitchen and helped Mrs. Hill by setting the dinner table and carrying in the serving dishes.

***

After helping Mrs. Hill with the dishes, I left Derrick and Lily alone to spend some quality time together. I went for a walk and when I got back I walked into the den to find the giant sleeping with the little one on his chest.

"Why don't you go to bed, I'm sure it's been a long day." I asked taking Lily from his grasp and waiting for Derrick to follow.

"I'll be right there." Derrick said wiping sleep from his eyes.

"Okay." I took Lily up and got her settled for the night. Afterwards, I walked into the guestroom that had been my bedroom for the last month. I took a shower and was about to call it a night when I realized that Derrick had not come upstairs to go to bed. I wrapped my robe around me and stuck my feet into some slippers before going down to get him to come to bed.

"Derrick?" I spoke softly into the darkness.

"Yes."

"Why are you sitting in the dark?" I asked walking over to the wall, reaching for the dimmer switch.

"Please don't." He said when he saw the first glimmer of light. I respected his wishes and walked over to the sofa taking a seat beside him.

"Do you want to talk about it?" I asked.

"Where would I begin?"

"At the beginning." I said scooting over closer to him.

"I would be the first to admit that I have made my share of mistakes, but it seems that here lately that is all I seem to be making."

"You're not still talking about that whole Regina thing are you?"

"No. It's more than just her. I must be losing my focus. I didn't go the extra mile with this Galbraith thing and it is going to cost us. Between the twenty million I gave him and the additional millions in debt that he covered up, we could take a significant hit after losing Jameson."

"Derrick…"

"I have a son who wants absolutely nothing to do with the legacy I have created for him and his sisters. I honestly wished that he would want to run the company when I decided to retire. My oldest daughter hates me because I no longer love her mother. The mother of my children hates me enough to risk her livelihood just for the satisfaction of ruining my reputation and me primarily because I fell in love with someone else. The woman I love and adore can't stand to sleep in the same room with me because of something foolish that I did months before I knew her." I heard his voice crack and knew immediately that emotion had gotten the best of him because my tears fell with his. We sat there together in the darkness because I knew it would hurt him for me to actually see his tears. I gave him the moments he needed to get it all out of his system. I could tell that he had been holding all of this inside of him for quite sometime and that he must have reached his enough is enough point.

"Honey, let's go upstairs." I felt around in the darkness to grab his hand.

"I think I'll just sleep down here tonight."

"No you will not, tonight you will sleep in our bed." I stood up and he followed me. When we reached the illumination of the night-lights in the foyer, I stopped and turned to look at him. I saw the weight of all that he had been carrying all over his face and in the slight evidence of the tears that remained in his eyelashes. We walked upstairs together and into our bedroom. I pulled back the covers while he walked into the bathroom to change his clothes. When Derrick came out of his closet, he stopped and looked at me.

"Come here baby." I said opening the covers. Derrick got in the bed and like a little boy placed his head on my breast and grabbed a hold of me. In a matter of minutes our breathing had become synchronized and he was asleep.

***

I woke up around five and looked over to Derrick who looked like he was getting the rest that he had been neglecting his body. I quietly rolled out of bed and into the shower. Within an hour, I was on the freeway headed for the office. I stopped and picked up all of the papers so that I could see the ads before mentioning them to Derrick. They looked better than expected and finally I could breathe a sigh of relief. When I walked into the lobby I was surprised to see that Valerie had come in early as well.

"Good Morning." I spoke and she held the elevator for me.

"Morning. Have you seen it yet?" She asked when I joined her.

"Yes, it looks great. I know, I could barely sleep, when I heard the paperboy this morning, I jumped up." The bell rang and we departed the elevator on our floor. I left a message for Barbara asking her to call me when she got in. Valerie went to leave messages in all of the departments asking them to meet in the cafeteria at ten. I called the cafeteria's manager asking her to setup a continental breakfast and then called Mrs. Hill asking her to prevent Derrick from leaving before nine. The copy department blew up a copy of the ad from the paper to display on the wall in the cafeteria. At precisely 9:45 I placed a call to Derrick's cellular.

"Derrick Kincaide."

"Good morning. How'd you sleep?"

"Better than I have in weeks. Thanks Princess."

"You're welcome. So are you going to stick around the house today and get some rest?"

"No actually, I'm on my way into the office. We are just exiting the freeway now."

"Oh. I thought you might want to take the day off and catch up on your rest and daddy time."

"That sounds good, but I'm sure my absence is raising some questions at the office."

"You know I can handle all of that." I said.

"Yes I am sure that you can but it's not fair for you to have to weather this storm alone. I want to call a department head meeting for this afternoon so we can get our thoughts together collectively."

"That sounds good. Listen, I'll meet you in the lobby and maybe we can meet in the cafeteria for a quick bite to eat."

"I'm sorry, but Mrs. Hill made waffles this morning so I'm not hungry."

"Then you can keep me company while I grab a Danish."

"I'll see you in a few minutes." Derrick disconnected the call and I made a mad dash to go on all the floors to make sure that everyone was already in the cafeteria by the time he got there. Valerie had a few stragglers set aside so that nothing would look out of the ordinary. I took the elevator down to the lobby checking my appearance in the mirror. Other than my hair being a mess, I looked presentable. George smiled when I came out of the elevator and walked down to the main doors. Derrick was coming up the steps. He smiled when he saw me.

"Good morning again." I said placing a soft kiss on his lips.

"Good morning." Derrick switched the briefcase over to his other hand and placed his arm around my waist.

"Have you had a chance to see this morning's paper?" I asked hoping the surprise hadn't been spoiled.

"No, I was on a call with Larry prior to your call."

"Anything new?" I asked.

"Nothing really. It looks like we are going to have to bite the bullet and pay for everything." He said just as his cell phone began to ring.

"Can it wait?" I asked as he looked at the display to see who was calling.

"It's Bob." He said as he opened the phone.

"Let me say hi." I grabbed the phone hoping to prevent Bob from spoiling the surprise.

"Good morning Bob. Can Derrick give you a call back in a few minutes we're kind of in the middle of something?"

"Sure Raven."

"Thanks." I closed the cover on the phone and started walking towards the cafeteria entrance where we were met with a thunderous greeting.

"Good morning Mr. Kincaide." Almost all of the two hundred and seventy three employees were standing and applauding. I watched Derrick's eyes as they surveyed the room and then stopped on the ad on the wall. I walked up to the podium and asked everyone to be seated.

"Thank you everyone. Derrick, on behalf of the employees and clients of KCI, we just want you to know that we are here with you, we support you and we are not going to allow anyone to take us down. In other words..."

"We got your back!!!" Everyone said and then there was loud cheering and applause.

"Speech. Speech." Someone chanted and Derrick moved over to the microphone. I started to walk away and he grabbed my hand to stop me.

"You're asking for a speech and you have rendered me speechless. First let me say thank you. I thank each and every one of you for this wonderful outpouring of support. I cannot even begin to find the words to articulate what

I am feeling at this moment. Gratitude and appreciation aren't strong enough to convey the feeling. I just want you all to know that in spite of what has transpired in these last few days, I am still committed to making this company the number one advertising agency in the world. I am still committed to running a profitable business that will benefit each and everyone one employed here financially. I am still committed to you and your success as well as mine. We are more than just a team, we are a family here, and I am humbled by the love that you have shown me here. Thank you." Derrick turned and placed a kiss on my cheek.

"Everyone please enjoy some breakfast on us and have a great day." I said and people all started coming towards Derrick to share a few private words.

"You never cease to amaze me girlfriend." Monica gave me a hug.

"I couldn't have done it without my partner in crime here." I said placing a kiss on Valerie's cheek.

"So now you know the truth." Valerie said to Monica after wrapping her arm around my waist.

"Yeah, that you are the real brains behind this operation." They both laughed.

"Don't believe the hype." I said excusing myself to go and join my husband who was receiving words of encouragement from several employees as they picked up their breakfast and ventured back to their respective desks and offices.

"Thank you." Derrick was saying to the last person who waited to speak to him individually. The young lady smiled and she and her friends all walked off together.

"I can't believe you did this." Derrick said pulling me into his arms not even considering that we weren't alone.

"Why? You don't think there are others that love and respect you besides me."

"Thank you so much for this. I know none of this has been easy for you."

259

"I guess this is one of those things that would fall under for better or for worse huh?" I said with a smile. Derrick placed a kiss on my lips that ignited a fire in me that hadn't been lit in a very long time. Monica and Geoff clearing their throats and extending an invitation to lunch interrupted our kiss.

***

Derrick and Lily were spread out on her activity blanket in the den when I came in from the office. Derrick went to meet with his legal staff after our lunch with Monica and Geoff. Lily turned to smile at me when she heard my heels clicking on the floor just outside of the den. The ad in the paper had sparked some interest within the business community and it turned into eleven new prospective clients that had entertained the prospect of signing with AD-Vantage. I was excited about sharing that news with Derrick.

"Guess what?" I said stepping out of my shoes and taking a seat on the blanket.

"What?" Derrick asked turning his attention to me.

"It seems that this attempt to hurt you has turned out to be a more profitable venture in the long run. We have meetings with eleven new prospects scheduled for next week." I waited to see what Derrick's reaction would be and when it was delayed I didn't know how to take it.

"What's wrong?"

"You have no idea how wonderful you are?"

"Oh, I have some idea." I said with a smile. Derrick smiled but he was overcome with emotion again and I saw tears welling up in his eyes.

"Daddy's turning into a crybaby Lily." I said reaching over to caress his face. He kissed my hand and then turned away.

"Have you eaten?" Mrs. Hill's voice broke the silence in the room.

"No." I responded and picked Lily up for a hug.

"I'll warm your dinner." She said leaving us alone again.

"Let's give daddy a moment. You wanna come eat with mommy?" I took Lily with me into the kitchen. I heard the alarm beep while we were in the kitchen and figured that Derrick just needed some time to get his head together.

After dinner, Lily and I took a walk around the grounds and the cool night air sent us back inside a lot sooner than expected. I gave Lily her bath, read a bedtime story to her and then decided it was time for me to get ready for bed. I walked into our bedroom through the adjoining door between our room and Lily's and heard the water running and music playing. I walked in to get a closer view and was stopped in my tracks by the room which was totally illuminated with candles, roses were everywhere including in the bubble bath and my handsome husband was dressed in a silk robe seated beside the tub.

"What's this?"

"Come in, this is my way of thanking you for being the most incredible woman I have ever met. You have shown me what real love is supposed to be about. If my only experience with love had been with Shayla, I would have never known what real love is supposed to be. Thank you for loving me faults and all. I don't think I have given you not even half of what you have given me, but as of this moment, all of that is going to change." Derrick walked up to me and began to remove my clothing. Then he led me to the tub where he bathed me and washed my hair.

***

"Good morning." Derrick woke me with a kiss on my forehead.

"Where are you going?"

"I have a breakfast meeting with Larry. Why don't you take the morning off?"

"No can do." I said opening my eyes.

"You just went to sleep." He sat down beside me with a smile and an obvious recollection of the love we made last night.

"Wonder why?" I ran my hand down his thigh.

"I don't know why but we can try and figure that out tonight."

"It's a date."

"Go back to sleep, meet me around one for some lunch." Derrick said standing to his feet again.

"Okay." I turned over and listened as Derrick left the room.

***

When I woke up it was almost eleven so I got up, showered and dressed and then went downstairs to see my beautiful daughter.

"Good morning." I spoke walking into the den. Mama was crocheting and Lily and Tyrese were playing with a cartoon singing the numbers in the background. I stepped out of my shoes and got down on the blanket with the little ones. After a barrage of kisses and a round of tickling my two favorite girls, I crawled over to where Mama sat.

"You're gonna wrinkle that pretty suit. " Mama said without taking her eyes off her hands.

"It will be okay. How are you this morning?"

"Good. And you?"

"Great." I said with a smile as one of those recollections that Derrick must have had earlier crept into my mind.

"So where's Cee today?" I asked as Mrs. Hill came in bearing treats for the girls.

"Oh, I didn't know you were still here. Would you like some breakfast?" Mrs. Hill asked while handing the girls their cups.

"No thanks. I meeting Derrick for lunch."

"Mrs. McNeill can I get you anything?"

"No, I'm fine; thank you." Mama said still focused on her project.

"Mama, you didn't say. Where's Cee?"

"I guess she's home, she called this morning and said Tyrese wanted to come with me to play with Lily."

"That's good. Well let me get out of here, I have a lunch date."

"Have a good day baby."

"Thanks." I reached up and gave her a kiss and then kissed my ladies again before picking up my shoes and heading out the door. Since I hadn't called a car, I decided to drive in this morning. I went into the garage, looked on the wall for my keys and then walked over to my car. It has been several months since I last drove this car, every time I get in this car it reminds me that my 500SL is being driven by someone else now. I pressed the button to open the door to the bay for my car and within a few minutes I was on the freeway. I decided to stop by Cee's on my way so I called Derrick and asked him if we could push our lunch back.

"Sure Princess, is everything okay?"

"I just need to make a stop, I shouldn't be longer than a half hour."

"Take your time. I'll have Barbara order from Julian's unless you'd rather go out."

"No ordering in is fine."

"Good, we have some decisions to make and I was hoping we could handle that over lunch."

"Yes, we can do that. I'll see you around one thirty."

"See you then. I love you."

"You too. Bye." I disconnected the call just as I got to Cee's exit. I turned on her street and was stopped by a trash collector's truck. By the time they waved me past them, I noticed a black Lincoln Town Car in her driveway and Cee walking out of the house dressed to the nines. The back door on the passenger side of the car opened and Cee got in the car and then the car drove off.

"What is she doing?" I said aloud as if someone was going to answer me.

***

Valerie wasn't at her desk when I stepped off the elevator. I walked into my office and found the mail and several phone messages. I powered on my computer and checked my email messages. Since nothing needed immediate attention, I left a note on Valerie's desk to let her know I was in Derrick's office and then left to go meet with him. Barbara was finishing a call when I rounded the corner.

"Hello pretty lady." I spoke to her and then walked over to give her a hug.

"Thank you." I whispered in her ear.

"You're welcome but may I ask for what?" She whispered back.

"Let's just say for putting me in check." I said in my normal voice.

"No problem. I have to keep you two in line that's in the fine print of my contract. Lunch will be here in about fifteen minutes."

"Thanks again." I opened the door to Derrick's office and walked in.

"You're early." He walked over to take me in his arms for a kiss.

"I figured we could get a head start on those decisions you said we need to make." I wiped lipstick off his lips and Derrick led me over to the conference table. There was every imaginable Christmas catalog on the table.

"Is this what you were talking about?" I asked.

"This is Lily's first Christmas, it has to be special. Here look at this." Derrick opened the FAO Schwartz catalog and handed it to me. We spent the next few hours shopping for everyone through the catalogs and online. Derrick spent an enormous amount of money, every time I started to say something; he gave me a look that told me not to say it.

"All right Santa, we've taken care of everyone on our list with the exception of you. What does Derrick want for Christmas?"

"A peaceful, joyous holiday with my family."

"That's a given, isn't there something that your wife can give you to open under the tree."

"There is one thing but it's not something material that can be wrapped."

"Then what is it?"

"I want a second chance."

"What do you mean?"

"We've been through something unfortunate that has shaken the foundation of our trust. It bothers me that as soon as something went wrong, you ran to Wesley. Your actions told me that he still has your heart."

"Wesley is very dear to me, he probably always will be, mainly because of Lily, but I love you."

"I believe that. You do love me but you still love him. I know that and I thought I had made peace with that."

264

"Derrick, I'm going to be honest with you. I was very angry with you when I took Lily to South Carolina. Angry enough that if the opportunity had presented itself, I would have crossed the line with Wesley. Thankfully, Wesley cares enough about me that he recognized that something was wrong and he did not allow anything to happen. Just another reason why I treasure our friendship, he knows me even the parts of me that I refuse to recognize sometimes. You don't have to feel threatened by our friendship. After what we just went through, I think our relationship has proven to the both of us that we love one another in spite of ourselves; faults and all."

"I guess you've got a valid argument."

"Besides do you think I would allow just anybody to do the things that you did to me last night."

"Another great point." Derrick sealed this with a kiss.

"So are we having the open house this year?" I asked.

"You're the lady of the house."

"No, Mrs. Hill is the lady of that house. I'm just the wife."

"If you say so. Why don't we have your family over for Thanksgiving and put up the tree?"

"That sounds good. I'll run it by Mama tonight."

"What do you want Santa to bring you this year?" Derrick asked opening another catalog.

"I'm not sure I've been good enough to get anything this year."

"You have been naughty and nice and I am sure Santa can overlook a couple of things."

"Then Santa will just have to surprise me."

"Santa likes that answer." Derrick smiled. The phone on his desk ringing interrupted our chat and I excused myself to let him take his call.

***

"That was quite an experience." Derrick said after closing the door of the car.

"It is humbling." I said.

"I have always given monetarily to the homeless and other causes but that's not enough. I want to do more. I want this to be something we do every Thanksgiving. Thank you." Derrick leaned over for a kiss.

"You're welcome. Now let's get home, we have some more hungry folks that will be coming to dinner in a few hours." I said wiping my lipstick from his lips. Derrick started the car and I dialed Mama's number on my cell phone.

"Smells good." I said when she answered the phone.

"How are you baby?" Mama asked.

"Good. I'm just calling to see if you need anything. Derrick and I are leaving the city now if you want, we can stop by and pick up whatever you have that is ready."

"That's okay we can handle it."

"Do you want me to send a car for you and daddy?"

"You know your father, he will want to drive himself."

"All right. We're asking everyone to come early so we can spend some time decorating the tree before we sit down to dinner."

"We'll be there by four."

"Have you talked to Cee?"

"Not today, I figured she was busy cooking." Mama said before asking me to hold.

"I'm back. We will see you at four sweetheart."

"Okay Mama. Bye." I disconnected the call and dialed Cee.

"Hello." Winston answered.

"Hey. Something smells good." I said.

"I don't know what you're smelling, nothing is cooking here."

"What?"

"Your sister decided she wasn't cooking dinner since she was sure we'd have plenty of leftovers from your house."

"That's probably true but you and I both know that she has always cooked something for your house, regardless of where we were having dinner before."

"That was the old Cee, this new one doesn't cook anymore."

266

"Can I speak to whichever Cee is there?"

"She just left to go to the store. I'll tell her you called."

"Oh okay. I just wanted to remind you guys to get to my house by four so we can decorate the tree before dinner."

"I'll pass on the message."

"See ya later then. Bye." I disconnected the call and my mind went immediately to the remembrance of seeing Cee a few weeks ago getting into that car.

***

The doorbell was ringing precisely at four and I was surprised that both my parents and Cee and her family were together on the other side of the door.

"Happy Thanksgiving." I said opening the door. Everyone came inside each placing a kiss on my cheek as they stepped over the threshold. Mrs. Hill came out to help with the dishes and daddy followed her into the kitchen with the boxful of goodies that Mama had prepared.

"Derrick and Lily are in the den, I think he has one of the football games on." I said taking Winston's coat. Cee opened her coat to a beautiful sweater dress that looked like cashmere.

"Go ahead sexy Ida." I whispered in her ear when I took her coat.

"You like?"

"Very much."

"I'm glad my dress caught somebody's attention." She said louder; it was obvious she wanted Winston to hear her.

"Tell me what's been up with you lately. You're never home anymore and I used to receive regular phone calls. It seems like ages since we've talked."

"I've been busy trying to find things to occupy my mind. I decided to get myself together so I can get enrolled in some classes."

"Yeah? When did this come about?"

"A few weeks ago." Cee responded and when she unwittingly pulled her hair behind one of her ears, I noticed a beautiful pear shaped diamond earring.

"Wow." I said moving in closer to get a better view.

267

"What?"

"Nice earring. Did I miss a special occasion or something?"

"Girl, this is something I picked up on one of the shopping channels."

"Cee, I know the difference between glass and ice. That's ice baby."

"Believe what you want." She pulled the hair back over her ear and changed the subject when Mama and Mrs. Hill joined us.

"When are we going to start on the tree?" Cee asked.

"They are watching the game, we can't just go in there and..."

"Why not?" Cee headed off towards the den.

"It's time to trim the tree." She announced just as Mama and I reached the den.

"Mommy, it's the fourth quarter." Trey articulated just what the rest of the men were thinking.

"We didn't come here to watch football, we are supposed to trim the tree and eat dinner."

"Selina, what's the big rush? We're here with all of the family, we don't have anything else to do or anyplace else to go." Winston spoke as if he was irritated by Cee's impatience. She rolled her eyes and walked out of the room.

"Come with me." I followed her and took her by the hand so she wouldn't have a chance to tell me no. I pulled Cee into Derrick's office and once we were behind the closed door, I locked it.

"Have a seat." I said and sat down beside her on the sofa. Cee looked irritated but she obliged my request.

"Talk to me Cee."

"What do you want to talk about?"

"What's going on with you?"

"Didn't we already have that conversation?"

"Okay, let me come from another angle. What are you doing?"

"What are you talking about Raven?"

"A couple of months ago, you were upset about your life, you said you were bored, you wanted a job and Winston wasn't hearing you when you tried to talk to him."

"Yeah and?"

"Has that all been resolved?"

"As far as I'm concerned."

"What does that mean?"

"It means that it is about time I started putting myself ahead in some things in my life. I mean my children are my world and they will always come first but everything and everyone else is going to have to take a step back."

"Including your husband?"

"Yep. I've tried everything I can think of to get through to him. It's not that he doesn't hear me; he doesn't want to hear me. So I'm tired of talking, I'm doing what I gotta do to make me happy."

"What is it that you're doing that's making you happy?"

"Taking care of my business."

"Are you sure you know what you're doing?"

"Positive."

"I don't think so. I saw you the other day."

"You saw me? Where? What are you talking about?"

"I came over to your house the other day, I watched you getting into a strange car."

"So what's the problem?"

"Who was it?"

"A friend."

"You looked like you were dressed for a special occasion or a date."

"Raven, you are probably blowing whatever you think you saw out of proportion as usual."

"All I'm saying is if you are doing something or about to do something that you have no business doing, you ain't being very smart with it. You can talk all the double talk you want to but I know that those are real diamonds in your ear, diamonds that your husband probably couldn't afford to give to you on the spur of the moment. That dress looks like Prada and I have a hard time buying clothes like that with the money that Derrick has so I know Winston didn't swing that one either."

"Anything else Sherlock Holmes?" Cee stood up to walk out of the office.

"Be careful." I said but her walking out and closing the door cut off my words.

***

Mrs. Hill sat the turkey down in front of Derrick and he rose to seat her. Derrick walked back to his seat and then asked us all to grab hands.

"Lord, we thank you for this day. We thank you for the gathering of our family for this occasion. We thank you for our many wonderful blessings, even the ones we sometimes overlook or take for granted. We pray for special blessings for the less fortunate, and for the families that cannot or will not come together today to show their gratitude for one another. We thank you and pray for your continued and constant covering over our lives and families. We thank you for showing us forgiveness so that we know how important it is to forgive and to be forgiven when we do things that fall short or disappoint the ones we love. We thank you for the tender mercies that you bless us with everyday because you love us enough not to give us everything that we deserve. Lord, we praise you and glorify your holy name and lastly Lord, we thank you for this bountiful feast that has been lovingly prepared for the nourishment of our bodies and ask that you bless the hands that prepared it. In Jesus' name we pray. Amen."

"Amen." Everyone chorused in and Derrick stood to carve the turkey as the other dishes began to get passed all around the table. We heard the alarm beep when the front door opened. Derrick looked surprised but I smiled when I realized that my invitation had been accepted. Despite my better judgment, I felt it was only fair to invite Derrick's kids to join us. The look on Derrick's face showed me that I'd done the right thing when Rick and Chanel walked into the dining room.

"Good evening everyone." Rick spoke and walked over to greet his father.

"Good to see you son." Derrick hugged Rick and then opened his arms to Chanel.

"Chanel?" Rick said and she began to move towards Derrick.

"Have you eaten?" Mrs. Hill was already on her feet before she asked the question.

"No, we are having dinner at the new house. Since Raven called, I wanted to come by to at least wish everyone a Happy Thanksgiving." Rick came over to give me a hug. Chanel was unusually quiet which was strange. I figured this would've been one of those occasions where she would have tried to embarrass me in front of my family. Instead she hugged Derrick and then moved back to the place she held at the door.

"Where is this new house?" Derrick asked after taking his seat again.

"In the Hamptons."

"Your mother bought a house in the Hamptons?" Derrick seemed surprised.

"Yes. She didn't tell you?" Rick asked before he stuffed a slice of turkey that Mrs. Hill handed to him in his mouth.

"Sit down and have something to eat. Just enough to hold you over for the drive." Derrick walked over to Chanel.

"No, I'd rather not. Rick I'll be in the car." Chanel turned to leave and Derrick grabbed her.

"Please Chanel don't do this. Stay inside with us; stay long enough so you can help trim the tree. You know that is our Thanksgiving tradition."

"It was our tradition. You gave that away when you dumped us. Remember?"

"Chanel..."

"Save it. Your family is here; share it with them. I only came here because of Rick, now I see that was a mistake. He has defected too." Chanel stormed off and within a few seconds we heard the opening and closing of the front door. Derrick was crushed and it seemed that my intention to do good was not a good idea after all.

"I'd better go." Rick walked over to give Lily a kiss, said goodbye to everyone and then he and Derrick walked out into the foyer.

***

Moving from the dining room table to the den proved to be quite challenging for most of us. It seemed that we all enjoyed a good number of helpings of almost every dish on the table. No one had room for dessert, we decided to wait until the tree was done to see if we could even fit the thought of something else to eat into our stomachs. Lily enjoyed seeing all the lights and different colored ornaments that we placed on the tree. Trey enjoyed being hoisted up to place the star on the top and we let Tyrese press the button to turn on all the lights. After a few minutes of marveling at the sight, Trey announced he was ready for his dessert.

"Coming right up." Mrs. Hill headed off towards the kitchen with a small crowd who followed. I grabbed the hand of my handsome husband.

"Are you okay? You've been a little quiet." I asked.

"I'm fine. This has been an enjoyable evening."

"I thought I was doing a good thing when I invited Shayla and the kids."

"I know and I appreciate it but I guess they just aren't ready."

"I'm sorry if what I intended for good hurt you."

"There's nothing to apologize for. Come let's get some of your mother's sweet potato pie." Derrick kissed my hand and we joined the rest of the family in the kitchen.

"When and where are we getting together to exchange gifts?" I asked after taking a bite from my most favorite dessert in the world.

"You can all come home on Christmas night for dinner. That will give the kids a chance to open their gifts from Santa and have a chance to play." Mama said handing Derrick a large slice of pie. He grinned like a little child and then placed a kiss on her cheek while purposely avoiding eye contact with me.

"Sounds good to me." I said patting the space on the window seat beside me. Derrick sat down and put another forkful of pie in his mouth. I looked to see who was going to respond from the Moore family.

"Cee?" I said before another bite.

272

"What? Mama said dinner at her house."

"Yeah but normally you'd have something to add."

"Things change."

"Ain't that the truth." Winston added.

"What is that supposed to mean?" She icily responded.

"It means that it's hard trying to keep up and trying to figure out who you are these days."

"Trey, why don't you take the girls upstairs to play some video games?" I asked.

"Okay Auntie." Trey stood up and took his sister by the hand. I picked up Lily to follow but Mrs. Hill said she'd take her.

"You two sound like you need your Christmas present now." I said looking at Derrick, hoping he'd just follow along.

"What are you talking about now?" Cee was obviously aggravated.

"Derrick and I have decided to give you two a romantic getaway on us." I grabbed Derrick's hand to confirm his support.

"Anywhere you want to go." Derrick added.

"Sounds great but it will never happen." Cee said walking past Winston to place her dessert plate in the sink.

"Why?" I asked.

"Because Winston thinks if he doesn't work everyday, all day long that we will end up homeless or something."

"What's wrong with a man providing a roof over his family's head?" He asked her as if no one else was in the room.

"Nothing is wrong with it. You just keep on doing what you're doing."

"Selina. What has gotten into you?" Mama could not hold her silence anymore.

"I'm sick and tired of being everything for everybody. When can I get what I want for a change?"

"What you want? Don't I give you any and everything you ask for? Look at you, this dress, those earrings. You go shopping all the time and I work to make that happen."

"You are missing it. And no matter how much I try to talk to you, you just don't get it. Sis thanks for the offer but a romantic getaway is the last thing we need." Cee walked out of the room and Mama followed. Daddy hunched his shoulders and gave Winston a knowing glance. The two of them left Derrick and me alone in the kitchen.

"Thanks." I said before getting up.

"Not a problem." He followed me to the sink.

"I saw that pie, notice I said pie and not slice of pie you had for dessert."

"Your mother was just being generous."

"There's something to be said about that charm you have. You have a way of getting anything you want out of us."

"It's a gift." He said with a smile and I leaned over to give him a kiss that was interrupted by the phone.

"Hello." I answered when Derrick held the phone to my ear.

"Hi Raven, it's Wesley."

"Happy Thanksgiving. How are you?"

"Good. Listen I'm calling to ask a favor."

"Sure, what do you need?"

"Denise and I are planning an engagement party for Vicky and we are trying to do this while her fiancé's son is here for the holidays. So I was hoping that Lily could come for the party and she can have her Christmas while she's here a little bit early."

"When is the party?"

"Saturday, December 20th."

"I don't see a problem with that. Are you coming for her or do you want me to drop her off?"

"If you and Derrick don't have plans, you two are welcomed to come with her. We are just doing a family dinner and then exchanging gifts with Lily."

"Hold on a sec." I placed my hand over the receiver.

"Honey, Wesley has invited us to an engagement party he's giving for his sister. He wants to give Lily her Christmas at the same time; it's on the twentieth. Do you want to go?"

"We don't have any plans, so if you want to go, it's fine with me." He responded.

"Wesley, we'll see you on the twentieth. What time?" I said.

"Dinner's planned for six."

"Okay, we'll be there by six. Thanks for the invitation."

Chapter Thirty-One: Wesley

I finished hanging all of the Christmas lights outside and put all of the bows on the windows. Vicky and Eugene's engagement party is in a few hours and we are all excited. Denise and I have put our all into this party for the two of them and for the first time in a very long time, we have our Vicky, our baby sister back. She looks so happy and beautiful, she is actually glowing. Denise has been teasing her that she's anxious to get married because she wants to jump Eugene's bones. She has yet to deny it.

"Okay DJ, hit the switch." I yelled to my nephew and then he ran around to see the fruits of our labor.

"That's looks good." DJ said pleased with his work.

"Good job." I gave him a high five. We picked up the ladder and all the boxes that the lights came out of.

I can't wait until Lily comes to see all of this. The tree has been up for weeks and the floor has been flooded with Christmas presents so I didn't have any room to put out all of her unwrapped toys. My family thinks I have gone overboard but nothing is too much for my baby. I invited Derrick and Raven to the engagement party since Vicky wants Lily to be the honorary flower girl for the wedding. She should be walking by the time of the ceremony. Aunt Ruth is still fussing because we decided to have the party catered, but there is no stopping her, she had already made some food anyway. This will be the first official meeting of our family and Eugene's family. We planned the engagement party three days before Christmas because Eugene's son is here for the holiday and we wanted him to met his future family.

"DJ, go and get in the shower." Denise was dressed for the evening and covered in an apron since she was setting up the table for the food.

"Okay. Where's my stuff?" He asked.

"Your father is on his way, he'll be here by the time you get out of the shower." She said.

"I told you we could have hired some people to serve." I said grabbing a celery stick off one of the trays.

"For what?" Denise asked.

"Never mind. I have been beat up enough for hiring a caterer; I ain't starting that up again."

"Good then you get in there and get dressed too. What time is Raven coming?"

"She said they should be here by six." I said before swiping another celery stick.

"Get out of here." She grabbed the tray and moved it into the dining room. I put the Christmas CDs in the changer and went upstairs to get dressed.

***

"There's a limousine coming in the driveway." DJ shouted from the window.

"That's Lily. Stop yelling." Denise said walking over to join him at the window. I watched as the driver got out to open the door. Derrick got out and Raven handed Lily to him and then Raven joined them. Derrick handed Lily over to Raven and the three of them walked towards the front door.

"Happy holidays." Denise said as she opened the door.

"Hi. It's good to see you." Raven said handing Lily over to Denise.

"Derrick, this is Wesley's sister Denise and her son DJ."

"Nice to meet you both." Derrick said as I joined them in the foyer.

"Wow. How tall are you? Do you play basketball?" DJ asked.

"I'm 6'8 and I used to play basketball when I was younger." Derrick answered with a smile.

"He's probably still got some game DJ." I said extending my hand to Derrick.

"No, these knees are too old, my game is golf now."

"Hey beautiful." I said and was surprised when Raven did not respond. Denise handed my daughter over to me and we walked into the den to join the rest of the family. Raven made introductions and then gave Father a hug.

"It's so good to see you. How are you?"

"I'm doing good. And you? You are as beautiful as ever."

278

"Thank you. Hi Natalie. How have you been?" She reached over and hugged Natalie next.

"I'm fine and look at this little lady. She's grown so much since the last time I saw her." Natalie came over to where I stood with Lily.

"Aunt Ruth, I'm loving that dress." Raven said.

"If I could fit into that one you have on we could trade." Aunt Ruth opened her arms for a hug.

"How you been baby?" Aunt Ruth asked.

"Good. And you? How are you?" Raven stood back to look at Aunt Ruth taking her by the hand.

"I guess I'm doing all right, I'm still here. Thank you Lord."

"Yes, thank you Lord." Raven said and walked Aunt Ruth over to meet Derrick. Just as they were getting acquainted Vicky, Eugene and his family arrived; I handed Lily over to Natalie so that Denise and I could greet our guests.

***

I noticed Naquia coming in as we were all preparing to exit the dining room. She was taking off her coat when I got to her.

"Hey Doc." I kissed her and helped her with her coat.

"Sorry I'm late, we had an accident come in right as I was about to leave.

"No problem. Your plate is in the refrigerator. Are you ready to eat right now?"

"No I can wait."

"Let me hang this up for you; come I'll introduce you to everyone." I hung her coat in the closet down in the utility room and then taking her by the hand we walked together into the den.

"Hi." Naquia spoke as we entered.

"Sorry I'm late. I got held up at the hospital."

"No problem." Vicky came to meet her and then took her around the room to make the introductions. I watched Naquia to see how she would react to Raven and Lily being here. Ever since she's been back we've talked about what needed to happen to make this relationship work. Time out for the childish games, the secrets and lies and disappearing acts.

"Can we help Lily open her gifts now Uncle Wesley?" DJ and Eugene's son had me surrounded.

"Yeah, but give me a minute." I said running my hand across DJ's head. Vicky and Naquia were talking to Derrick and Raven when I walked over.

"So I'm hoping Lily will be my flower girl since she should be walking in June." Vicky said when I joined them.

"We'll have to ask her, I can tell you now that my daughter has a mind of her own; she may want to be a bridesmaid instead." I said and got a laugh out of everyone.

"Stop talking about my baby." Raven said after punching me in the arm.

"Ouch. She can't help it; she got it honestly. Listen, the boys want to help Lily open her gifts. Do you mind?"

"No, she's too young to notice the difference. Let's see what Santa bought." Raven said taking Lily from Derrick's arms and together they sat down next to the tree. The boys followed their lead and began distributing the presents. It didn't take long for the adults to get caught up in the gifts while Lily played with one computer game that lit up and made noise when she touched it. It didn't really dawn on me how much money I'd spent on things she probably wouldn't play with more than once or twice.

"I guess we both got caught up in the Christmas spirit." Derrick said.

"You too? I didn't realize until now, how caught up." We both laughed.

"You know the two of you are going to have to seek some help." Raven came over to where Derrick and I stood.

"That little girl has the two of you so wrapped up. What's going to happen when she's talking and can actually ask for what she wants?" She wrapped her arms around our waists.

"We'll probably need a bigger house." Derrick responded. I noticed Naquia watching the exchange between the three of us and I walked out of Raven's grasp to ease her obvious pain.

"I'll just send her stuff to you in the bigger house." I laughed and then excused myself.

"Doc, are you okay?" I whispered in her ear.

"Fine. You and Denise really did a good job with the party."

"It was Neicy; I just did as I was told." I kissed her cheek.

"Lily seems excited with all her toys."

"It's her first Christmas; I wanted to make sure it was special."

"Uh huh." She said and then yawned.

"Why don't you go upstairs? You've been up since five and I know you're beat. Vicky will understand." I said to my wife who looked dead on her feet.

"Understand what?" Vicky said obviously overhearing our conversation.

"My wife is tired and I'm ordering her to bed." I said wrapping an arm around Naquia's waist.

"Ordering? Is this what I have to look forward to?" Vicky asked and looked up to Eugene standing by her side.

"I'm not walking into that one." Eugene said.

"Smart man." I extended a hand to him.

"I'm just coming over to thank you again, we want to get all of Eugene's family settled for the night. We're going to have brunch at Eugene's house around eleven, can you guys make it?"

"What's your schedule doc?" I asked.

"I'm not on duty until seven, so we'll be there." Naquia said before yawning again.

"I'm sorry. I think I'll follow my husband's orders and call it a night." Naquia gave Vicky and Eugene each a hug and then started saying goodnight to everyone as she made her way to the stairs. Within a few minutes, everyone was saying they had to go. I checked my watch and noticed that it was after ten. Aunt

Ruth had packed goodie bags of food for everyone and she and Mr. Henry went home with Father and Natalie. Raven started picking up the wrapping paper and Derrick was on the phone when I came in from walking everyone out to their car.

"The car has been delayed; it should be here in about forty-five minutes." Derrick said after closing his phone and placing it in his pocket. Lily was fretting and Raven handed her over to him.

"I think she's sleepy daddy, do you mind?"

"Not at all." Derrick kissed Raven's lips and then sat in the recliner and placed Lily on his chest. Raven went back to her pile of paper and I went into the kitchen to grab a trash bag.

"Need some help?" I offered opening the bag.

"Thanks."

"No, thank you. You're doing a great job cleaning up."

"Consider it your Christmas gift." She laughed.

"You ain't getting off that easy." I reached under the tree and pulled out a present for her.

"What's that?"

"A present for you and one day for our daughter."

"Wesley..."

"Raven..." I sat the gift-wrapped box down on the floor beside her.

"I can't accept that."

"You can and you will. Open it."

"No."

"What is your problem?"

"The last gift you gave me made me cry. Remember?"

"I have no control over that. Are you going to open it or what?"

"Let's finish cleaning up and then I'll open it." She said placing an arm full of paper into bag. We separated the toys and gifts and put them into piles of what was going home with them and what was staying here. After taking all of the trash out to the garage, I returned to the den where Raven was watching Derrick who had fallen asleep with Lily.

"That's it for the trash. Do you want to take the other things out to the garage?"

"Sure." She whispered. We started carting everything down to the garage and on the last trip; I picked up Raven's gift and placed it in my pocket.

"That's the last of it." I said leaning against the truck.

"It's a beautiful night out here." Raven had walked outside to the star filled night.

"That may be, but it's cold out there. Come inside." I walked out and grabbed her by the hand.

"In a minute, look." Raven pointed up to the stars and it was like a premonition of something I would be experiencing with Lily one day.

"It's beautiful and it's cold. Come on Miss Lily." I pulled Raven by the hand thinking this is exactly how it would end one day with our daughter. Once inside the garage, I pulled the box out of my pocket and handed it to her.

"This better not make me cry." She said and leaned against the deep freezer. She ripped open the paper to the velvet jewelry box and stopped to sigh.

"I'm serious." She opened the top of the box to find a pair of emerald and diamond earrings. She took another deep sigh and then I saw her eyes tear up.

"Already told you I have no control over that."

"They're beautiful. I can't accept these."

"I knew you would say that so..." I cleared my throat before continuing.

"These earrings are a gift for you and for Lily. I wanted to get something to say thank you for blessing me with our beautiful daughter so I decided to get you her birthstone. I had them add the diamonds because maybe on her wedding day or some special occasion like that, you will give these to her from the both of us. It's supposed to be like a heirloom that maybe she will pass on to her daughter and so on."

"You make me sick." She said as the tears began to fall.

"Aw. But you love me." I joked and she nodded her head in agreement. Raven stopped what she was just about to say, when I noticed that she was looking past me.

"Wesley, the hospital just called; I think you should give your sister a call."

"Sure thing." I walked over to the phone on the wall and dialed Vicky's cell then turned to see if there was going to be any drama with Naquia and Raven.

"Raven, I believe your car has arrived." Naquia said pointing to the lights behind Raven.

"Thanks. Let me go and get my family." Raven said walking past Naquia and back into the house.

"Vicky and Eugene are going to meet us at the hospital." I said hanging up the phone.

"What was all of that?" Naquia asked.

"It was nothing. Come on let's go." I took Naquia by the hand.

***

"I'll park the car and meet you in the lobby." I said to my wife who was still very angry with me.

"Fine." She got out and slammed the door. I drove around to the visitor's lot and found a space next to Eugene's car. I jogged across the lot and met up with my family in the waiting room, since my wife evidently had no intention of waiting for me in the lobby.

"Hey." I spoke before sitting down next to Vicky.

"I wonder what's wrong. This could be it; I know he signed the papers so they would not resuscitate him." Vicky's face was soaked with tears and so was Eugene's shirt.

"I don't want to make a mistake and say the wrong thing, so don't take my silence the wrong way."

"Vicky, Terrence is asking for you." Naquia came in followed by a nurse.

"Okay. Eugene will you come with me?" She turned to face him.

"Are you sure sweetheart?"

"Yes, I'm sure. I want him to see that I am happy and that I have someone who will love me and take care of me. He's been worried about that."

"I understand."

"Wesley?"

"What?"

"You too. You need to bury the hatchet between the two of you. Come on." She stood in front of me extending her free hand.

"I don't think…"

"Do it for me."

"Vic…"

"Please." I took my sister by the hand and followed everyone to the room. Terrence was hooked up to several monitors and propped up. He looked to be in better health today then he did on the night he appeared on my doorstep.

"Terrence, I brought someone I want you to meet. This is my fiancé Eugene. Eugene this is my friend Terrence." Eugene extended his hand reluctantly and Terrence looked like he tried to reach out but his arm wouldn't cooperate.

"So you're the new guy. Nice to meet you man. You got a real special lady there and I wanted to meet you so I make sure you measure up." Terrence attempted to laugh but it turned into a cough instead.

"Wesley, I bet she had to damn near break your leg to get you to come in here."

"Nothing that drastic."

"I know we ain't never been friends, you and I always had that healthy competition thing going on. Looks like this time you are finally gonna beat me at something." He coughed again.

"If that's how you remember it, I'll let you have your moment. But I remember many a game when I beat you even if your team won the game."

"True that. You always had game, I have to give you that." He reached over to the bedside table and Vicky picked up the file he was trying to get.

"Vicky, this is for you."

"What is it?" She took a seat on the bed beside him and Eugene looked like that made him uncomfortable.

"I did those things you asked me to, go ahead and open it up." He coughed again and this time one of his monitors started to beep.

"Do you need your oxygen?" Naquia asked. He shook his head and Naquia leaned over to listen to his chest through her stethoscope.

"No, I'm good."

"Terrence, this is not what we discussed. I told you I don't want any of your money."

"I heard you, but in all the years we've known each other when have I ever done exactly what you said. If you don't want it, then you give it to whoever you want to. All I want you to do is take me back to my house and throw me off the balcony into the water." Terrence's monitor started beeping again and this time Naquia gave him his oxygen without asking. Eugene looked like I felt, very uncomfortable so I decided to try and get out hoping to save him in the process. I tried to think of what to say under the circumstances. I couldn't say something as casual as see you later, or take care and this made me feel worse.

"I've got to go. Bye." I walked towards the door without looking back hoping no one was going to try and stop me. I walked out to the waiting room to see if Naquia was coming out, she didn't. I left a message for her at the nurse's station and went home.

***

"Hey Wesley, how ya doin'?" Eugene walked up to where I was shooting hoops.

"What's up? Did Vicky leave yet?" I rebounded the ball and bounced it over to him.

"Yes, her flight took off about an hour ago." He aimed and took his shot.

"How is she?"

"I don't know. She's trying to be strong and act like she can handle all of this on her own. I just wanted to be there for her, she fought me tooth and nail. She didn't want me on this trip. It's making me feel like I'm invading on his territory."

"You don't have anything to worry about. My sister loves you, and this is probably what they call closure for her. Terrence was her first love, at least that's what she thought."

Chapter Thirty-Two: Derrick

Being out of the office for two weeks was something I'd never done before. Christmas and the week after were like pure bliss with Lily and Raven. Mrs. Hill went to visit some friends and family so we had the house all to ourselves. Lily is more of a wonder everyday, and it made me a little bit regretful that I had not spent the same time watching Rick and Chanel grow up like this.

"You want to join us for lunch?" Raven asked walking into my office with Lily.

"Give me a few minutes and I'll be right there."

"Okay." Raven said and Lily tried to repeat. The phone rang just as they exited my office.

"Hello." I answered powering off the computer.

"Derrick, it's Reginald. Happy holidays."

"Happy holidays to you too. How are you Reginald?"

"Great. I heard you were on vacation so I apologize for infringing on your family time."

"No problem Reginald. What's up?"

"Can I speak frankly?"

"Of course. What is it?"

"I've been your accountant for years, and you know I am not one to tell you how to spend your money, but don't you think you two went a little overboard this Christmas?"

"No more than usual."

"Two million dollars is not usual Derrick."

"That can't be correct?"

"I can forward you an electronic copy of the file."

"Please do that. So I'm guess you want permission to accelerate the next advance to the liquid account."

"Yes, I'll include the release form with the file."

"Good. Thanks Reginald, I need to go have a talk with my wife to see how generous we were this Christmas."

"Very well. Have a good day."

"You too." I hung up the phone and powered on the computer again to wait for the file.

***

"Can I help you sir?" The heavily accented greeting came from a petite Hispanic girl who couldn't have been more than twenty.

"I'm Derrick Kincaide, I'm here to see Shayla."

"Senora Kincaide. Yes, please come in."

"Thank you." The girl closed the door behind me and disappeared down the hall.

"Derrick? What is he doing here?" Shayla's voice grew louder as she walked over to me dressed ever so stylishly.

"Nice house." I said watching as her anger continued to rise.

"What are you doing here?"

"I'm answering your call."

"What call? What is this all about?"

"Surely, you knew I would eventually find out."

"Find out what Derrick?"

"Hand them over Shayla." She actually looked at my extended hand like she had no idea what I was talking about.

"The credit cards." I said.

"Why do you want my credit cards?"

"I've seen you do better, the innocent act needs a little work."

"Answer me. Why do you want my credit cards?"

"Because I signed papers that said I'm no longer financially responsible for you or your shopping sprees."

"You my darling will always bear some responsibility for me for the rest of our lives; we have children remember?"

"I don't have time for this mental chess match. I just got the bills for your latest shopping spree and I'm here to tell you that it all stops right here, right now."

"I don't have any idea what you are talking about."

"I'm talking about that hundred thousand dollar car you bought for Rick, the two chinchilla coats and the thousands you just spent in furniture for what appears to be another home you won't spend any real time in."

"Once again, you have the wrong perspective darling. You just purchased a replacement vehicle for your son and furnished the home your daughter needed for the times when she comes to the states."

"Oh, I see. Thank you for making things clearer. I'm sorry to have bothered you."

"It was no bother." She opened the door and I opened my cell phone.

"Larry, this is Derrick. Shayla is up to her old tricks, and it looks like she has had some advice with this one. Seems that our children were in need of some things that were purchased without my prior knowledge using my funds. To remedy this, call Reginald and get the total spent and have her portion of those costs deducted from any future alimony payments she's scheduled to receive starting immediately. Please call me if you have any questions." I closed the phone and drove out of her main gate.

***

"Are you okay?" Raven asked as soon as I walked into the foyer.

"Yes, I'm fine."

"Where did you disappear to? We thought you were joining us for lunch." She placed her hand in mine.

"I had something to take care of, I'm sorry I should have said something before leaving."

"It's okay, I was just a little concerned. Did you eat?"

"No. Will you keep my company?"

"Sure." We walked together to the kitchen.

"Where's Lily?"

"She's asleep in the den. She had a little crying spell when Cee and Winston came to pick up the kids."

"So how did the honeymooners seem?" I turned on the water in the sink to wash my hands.

"Good. I think this trip may have given them the chance to get some things in order." Raven handed me a paper towel and then opened the refrigerator.

"What do you want for lunch?"

"Anything, a sandwich is fine." I took a seat on the barstool at the breakfast bar and Raven brought all of the fixings for the sandwich over. I let her know what I wanted and she prepared my sandwich.

"Thank you." I blessed my food and took a bite of my sandwich while Raven poured me a glass of tea.

"I'm going to go into the office tomorrow, I've got to prepare for my strategic planning meeting." Raven said as she sat down beside me.

"No you're not. We are not due back until the fifth."

"Derrick, you are going to have to remember that I am my own woman and you trying to tell me what I will and will not do is not going to fly."

"What happened to love, honor and obey?" I laughed.

"You never heard me say anything about obeying." She nudged me.

"Yes, you did."

"Did not, I was very careful about that one."

"Get the video, I'll meet you in the den." I picked up my plate to place it into the dishwasher while Raven went ahead of me into the den. My phone rang just as I left the kitchen.

"Hello."

"Derrick, it's Larry; I just got your message." He laughed.

"She never ceases to amaze me." I said.

"You know she is not going to sit still for this one."

"What can she do? She made purchases without my consent on my accounts."

"You haven't cancelled those cards?"

"It keeps slipping my mind, but I don't think we'll have anymore problems after this. Do you?"

"Probably not. I'll make sure her check doesn't go out and I'll wait to hear the fallout. Tell Raven I said hello and I'll see you Saturday at the club."

"Thanks Larry." I closed the phone and sat down next to my wife who pressed the play button on the remote.

"You looked so handsome." She inched in closer to me.

"Looked. Past tense?" I turned to look her in the eye.

"You know what I mean." She kissed my lips. We watched the video and I couldn't help smiling as the memories of all that I felt that day resurfaced. Raven looked so beautiful and I could see the love she feels for me in her eyes. Raven's family and friends all looked happy and pleased, but whenever the camera caught sight of Shayla, Chanel and Vonda there was another story.

"No, I can't believe it." Raven said when she heard herself saying her vows.

"Believe it. Now as I was saying." I pulled her in closer to me and placed a kiss on her lips that was interrupted by the alarm signaling the opening of the front door.

"Hey you guys." My son said as he joined us in the den.

"Hi Rick." Raven said before leaning over to check on Lily in her playpen.

"Mom said you came by the house today."

"I did."

"I figured you came by to see me before I left to go back to school."

"That wasn't my sole motivation. As a matter of fact, I wasn't aware of you leaving this soon." I said trying to gauge Raven's reaction to this.

"I wasn't but when you guys got me the car, I figured I'd leave a few days earlier so I could drive." Rick smiled and I assumed it came from the thought of his upcoming travels.

"You just be careful, you know that is a powerful automobile you have there."

"I know; I can't wait to show all my boys. We just saw this car in that James Bond movie. I can't believe you guys bought it for me. It was the best surprise."

"A surprise to us all." I said and caught Raven's eye. Lily started stirring and all conversation with Rick stopped when he turned all of his attention to his little sister.

"Rick, you want something to eat or drink?" Raven asked.

"Sure. Whatcha got?"

"A little bit of everything. Help yourself while I get her changed." Rick handed Lily over to Raven before leaving us to raid the kitchen.

"You want to talk about that?" Raven laid Lily on the sofa beside me and walked over to pick up a diaper.

"Maybe later." I placed a kiss on Lily's forehead and she giggled.

***

Barbara and I were in the middle of dictating some letters when Shayla blew into my office like a hurricane force wind.

"You are not going to get away with this."

"Good afternoon Shayla." I said and Barbara excused herself.

"Derrick surely you don't believe I am going to sit idly by and allow you to do this; where is my check?"

"You spent it." I laughed.

"This is not funny and I am not amused." She fumed.

"Get on that phone and call Reginald and tell him to cut my check immediately or I'm going to the judge."

"I doubt that. You don't want to involve the authorities with this because you after all are the one that committed a crime."

"I did no such thing."

"Call the judge, explain why I have withheld your check and see what he calls it."

"You bastard. I never thought I'd see the day when I would truly hate you and what you've become."

"I have only become what you've made me."

"Be careful Derrick. Be very careful, one day all of this is going to catch up with you."

"Not if I'm careful as you say." I got up and walked over to open my door.

Chapter Thirty-Three: Wesley

"Wesley, we're leaving." Naquia shouted from Lily's room.

"Hold up a minute Doc." I went down the stairs from the loft and met them in the hall.

"Come on, we're late. We were supposed to be at the church ten minutes ago. I still have to get dressed."

"I just want a picture of my two beauties." I snapped a photo of Naquia and Lily.

"Say bye to daddy." Naquia said to Lily.

"Bye daddy." Lily said and waved her hand.

"I'll see you in a few." I went back upstairs to get into my tuxedo.

***

DJ and Eugene's son JR were busy ushering all of the guests to their seats. Denise was trying to keep Lily occupied because she was anxious to make her debut as the flower girl. I watched as the wedding coordinator walked around getting everyone lined up so the ceremony could begin. It had been a long time since I'd seen Samantha looking this beautiful in her gown. It was good to see that young girl whose face used to grace all the magazines blossom into a woman in spite of her being ill and in a wheelchair. Since JR was standing at the best man post with his dad, DJ was responsible for wheeling Samantha down the aisle. When they left, Naquia and I took our places and I winked at my radiant wife when she placed her hand in mine. We walked down the aisle and parted ways at the arch. When I turned, my heart was stolen when my daughter came half running down the aisle dropping white rose petals along the way. She walked right over to Naquia like we had practiced last night and it made me feel good to see the two of them together. The music changed and all eyes turned to see my gorgeous baby sister and Father about to make their grand entrance. I turned to see Eugene's expression and was surprised when I saw tears falling. Father had tears in his eyes as well when he reached the altar and answered that he gives his daughter to be wed. All through the ceremony, I found myself watching Naquia and wondering if she felt cheated not having a ceremony like this. Since we've been through therapy these last eight months, I've felt closer to her now than I've ever felt before. We have even discussed working on our family now that her schedule has slowed down at the hospital. After Terrence's death, she had given up working double shifts and we've spent most of her off time together alone, basically falling in love again. Lily's visits have been well received and the hostility she feels for Raven has either lessened or she's gotten better at hiding it.

***

"Vicky looked beautiful, didn't she?" Naquia walked over to me to help unzip her gown.

"Stunning but my eyes were glued to someone else."

"Yes, your daughter was gorgeous too."

"She looked all right, I was speaking of you."

"Why thank you Mr. Charles."

"You're welcome. Do you regret not having a real wedding?"

"I wouldn't say regret."

"Do you want to have one?"

"Are you serious?"

"Very. Your schedule has calmed down, you have more time on your hand to plan it and I'm sure Vicky and Denise will be more than happy to help you. You women seem to like that stuff."

"I'll think about it."

"We could have a real honeymoon this time. You said you wanted to go to Maui."

"I said I'll think about it."

"I'm serious."

"I said…"

"I heard you. Hungry?"

"Starving."

"I'll be right back." I checked on Lily on my way down to the kitchen. My angel was out for the night; it had been a long and eventful day for her. I kissed her cheek and pulled the rail up on the side of her bed. I went downstairs and raided the refrigerator to get something light for our late night snack. After setting the alarm, with an armful of fruits and vegetables I went to join my wife in what had been renamed our den of passion. Seeing her on the telephone when I reached the top landing told me that my intentions had been thwarted.

"When did you get back? I can't wait to see you; I want to hear all about the country and your research..." Naquia noticed me and toned down the excitement in her voice.

"I'm scheduled off tomorrow but I'm coming by, maybe we can have lunch. Okay. I'm so glad you're home. See you tomorrow. Good night." She disconnected the call and I sat the tray down in the middle of the bed.

"That was Harrison, he's back from Africa."

"Oh."

"He's been over there doing the work that I want to do. He's actually making a difference in the fight against AIDS. Did you know he wants to start a research hospital so that he can continue in treating the patients with the new medical discoveries that we are finding everyday?" Naquia continued talking about all the work this guy was doing and I could hear in her voice how passionate she was about her work and her patients. We finished the tray of goodies and then she turned off the light because she wanted to get an early start in the morning.

Chapter Thirty-Four: Raven

John asked us to prepare for landing, as we were about to start our final descent into Charleston International. Derrick closed his laptop and left the conference table to join me for the landing. We had been in Seattle checking out a new company Derrick was interested in. It still amazes me to see the transformation from gentle husband to astute businessman as soon as we walk into the meeting room. Before we left, Derrick had this owner practically begging KCI to take over his company and bring him aboard our staff. While I had seen my husband on many occasions take pleasure in the conquering aspect of other mergers and acquisitions, he was strangely quiet with this one. The last time I'd asked him what was going on he answered me with something else Shayla was putting him through and asked me to allow him to handle it on his own. I noticed a few weeks ago that things between the two of them had gotten progressively worse, to the point where Shayla was actually issuing threats.

"Derrick. What is going on in here?" I walked in to find my husband breathing heavily with veins filled with anger pulsating at his temples.

"Raven, I need a minute."

"No, what you need to do is calm down."

"No, what I need is for you to give me a few minutes alone with my ex-wife." I remembered that Derrick's tone of voice left no room for misinterpretation so I exited quietly from his office. I looked over to my husband who looked like his mind was miles away.

"Ready to see your little girl?" I asked taking his hand in mine.

"Can't wait. She's probably just what I need right now."

"I don't know if I like the sound of that." I said with a chuckle.

"You know what I mean. There are certain pains that she can soothe and then there are the others." Derrick raised my hand to his lips.

"I think I'll let you slide with that one." With a feather light touch we were down and John joined us in the cabin to open the doors.

"Are you okay John, you look tired?"

"I think I may be coming down with something Ma'am." John answered softly. I placed my hand on his forehead to check for fever.

"John, why don't you get some rest in your quarters, I'll place a call to get us another pilot." Derrick said.

"Sir, that's not necessary."

"Like I said, get some rest and I'll get a pilot."

"Yes sir." John resigned knowing full well that this was not an argument he would win. We deplaned and stepped right into the car waiting on the tarmac. I called Wesley once we were in route to his place and told him we'd be there in about fifteen minutes.

"We're out back so just come around." Wesley said.

"Okay. See you in a little bit." I said before disconnecting the call. Derrick was reading the paper and still seemed very distant and quiet. Not wishing to start anything, I turned my focus to the sights passing by and quietly remembered the places I remembered Wesley showing me when we came here. His mother quickly came to my remembrance and I remembered her letter again. We turned into the driveway to Wesley's house and the driver got out and opened the door.

"Thank you." I stepped out and straightened my skirt. Derrick stepped out behind me and took my extended hand. We walked to the back yard where Wesley was having a cookout. Derrick noticed the men playing basketball and we parted company when he walked towards the court and I walked over to the picnic table.

"Hello everyone." I spoke reaching the table.

"Hi." Denise spoke while tending to the grill as Natalie walked over carrying a tray of meats.

"Need some help?" I offered.

"You are not dressed to help." Denise said

"Girl please, you know how I like to shop. A stain will just give me a reason." I said taking the tray from Natalie.

"Your little lady is still sleeping, she had a late night trying to stay up with DJ and JR last night." Denise said taking a slab of ribs off the tray.

"What were they doing?"

"They were playing one of those video games, they gave her an unplugged controller and she was pressing buttons like she was playing. She had a ball; and I had to fight her to get her in the bathtub which was strange because she loves the bubbles but last night she was more interested in getting a touchdown." Denise pointed to the bowl of barbeque sauce and I handed it to her.

"I'm hoping that was a one time occurrence." She said.

"Ditto." We laughed and then our attention turned to Naquia and Vicky walking towards us.

"It's blue." Vicky was overflowing with whatever had given her this great joy.

"Congratulations mommy." Denise hugged her sister.

"Ssh, I don't want to jinx it. Let's wait until I see a doctor. I'm sorry, hi Raven." Vicky turned to me.

"Hi and congratulations on your wedding."

"Thank you. Excuse me ladies, I need to see my husband." She whispered before skipping off.

"Hi Naquia, how are you?" I decided to speak since she didn't act like she was going to.

"Hello Raven. Are you here alone?"

"No, Derrick's with me. He's over there with the men."

"Good." She said before walking away. I wondered if this was another one of her insecurity episodes. We hadn't seen or talked to one another since the night of Vicky's engagement party and I still wasn't sure if she was angry at what she thinks she walked in on. I couldn't tell by Denise's demeanor if she was in the know of all that had happened or if she was oblivious to it all. My eyes followed Naquia as she walked over to where Derrick stood and then the two of them took off walking together. Vicky and the guy I assumed was her husband came out of the house, my eyes went straight to my bundle of joy in Vicky's arms.

"Mommeee." Lily's outstretched arms and greeting was the sweetest thing I'd seen or heard in days.

"Hi baby." I grabbed her and kissed her all over her face.

"Hey Eugene, you mind going over there to get the rest of the crew? It's time to eat." Denise asked.

"Be right back." Vicky's husband walked away and I watched Vicky as she eyed the man she loved. I wondered if I still did that when Derrick walked away from me. I wondered if I did that today would it be because of my being in love or because I wasn't sure if Naquia was trying to upset the harmony that I currently share with my husband. The two of them joined the rest of us at the picnic table and Wesley's father blessed the food. Derrick took Lily from my arms and I noticed that he was in a much better mood now; was it because of Lily or his disappearance with Wesley's wife.

***

It was a two-hour wait before we could get a replacement pilot. John didn't look any better when we landed at home and Derrick requested a car so John could be driven home.

"Thank you Mr. Kincaide. I really appreciate this."

"No problem John, you just get to the doctor first thing in the morning; please have your wife call me if you need anything."

"I will sir. Thanks again. Good night."

"Good night." We both said before walking over to get into our car. Derrick held Lily until I got in and then handed the sleeping cargo over to me. I placed a kiss on her forehead and tried to lull her back into her sleep. The last thing I needed tonight was for her to wake up and be fully rejuvenated because I was beat. I tried to kick my shoes off and Derrick reached down to help me out.

"It's been a long day." He said massaging my foot.

"It's been a long week and it's not over yet."

"Why don't you take tomorrow off? Or work from home?"

"I don't know, we've got renewals…"

"And if we'd stayed over in Seattle for another day, those renewals would've waited until you returned."

"You've made a very good point. Why don't you stay home with me so we can spend some catch up time with the little one?"

"I wish I could, I made an appointment for tomorrow afternoon that can't be missed."

"What happened to that logic you just threw on me?"

"That only works for you." He smiled.

***

"What's all the buzz?" I asked when I got to Valerie's desk.

"What are you doing here? Derrick said you were tired and taking the day off."

"Wasn't as tired as he thought. So what's all the commotion?"

"Someone said they spotted Janet Jackson coming into our building."

"What?"

"I think it's one of those stories you know that change between the first person and the last. When the truth comes out, they probably said they saw Freddie Jackson going past the building." She handed me a stack of messages.

"Where are we with the renewals?"

"They're all here, I just need to get you and Derrick's signatures, then we can setup the meetings." She pointed to a file.

"Give it to me, I'll get them signed and back to you. Have you seen my husband lately?"

"Not since he came to tell me you weren't coming in."

"I'm going to his office, I'll get these signed. Call me in there if you need me."

"Will do." Valerie handed me the file and I walked around the corner to Derrick's corridor. Barbara wasn't at her desk so I tapped on his door and then walked in.

"Derrick…" I wondered if they were as surprised as I was to see Naquia of all people in Derrick's office.

"Princess, I thought you were taking the day off."

"I told you I had a lot of work to do. Naquia this is a surprise."

"Hello Raven. Harrison this is Derrick's wife Raven. Raven this is one of my colleagues Harrison."

305

"Nice to meet you Mrs. Kincaide." He stood and extended his hand to me.

"Thank you; nice to meet you too Harrison." I said looking to Derrick for some type of explanation.

"Naquia, I am impressed by the information you and Harrison have presented. Give me a little time and let me make a few phone calls and I'll see if I can get some more dollars for your research." Derrick walked over from behind his desk and over to where I stood.

"Thank you Derrick, you don't know how much this means to me. We'd better get going so you can get back to work and so your jet and pilot can get back to you at a decent hour." Naquia opened her arms to embrace Derrick and looked directly at me. Harrison extended his hand to shake Derrick's.

"Take your time. I'll give you a call in a few days." Derrick walked them to the door. I took a seat in one of the chairs opposite his desk because I had to know what this was all about. Derrick's phone rang just as he was about to take his seat again.

"Derrick Kincaide." He answered and I noticed what must have been Naquia's purse on the corner of his desk. I picked it up and motioned that I was going to take it downstairs. I stopped at Barbara's desk and called security so they could stop her from leaving the building.

"Tell her to wait right there, I'm on my way down now." I said just as the bell for the elevator rang. Naquia was standing at the desk when the elevator doors opened and people were standing to the side whispering. Maybe they actually thought she looked like Janet Jackson and I just didn't see it.

"Thanks Raven."

"You're welcome."

"I bet you've been asking yourself, what am I doing here with your husband." She said with a smirk.

"Now you know how I feel." She laughed and walked off to meet Harrison at the revolving door.

"*Bitch*." Angel said what I thought. I turned to walk over to the elevator and waited with a few people.

"I can't believe it. Janet Jackson right here, I wonder if we are going to do a campaign for her or something." The girl speaking realized I was standing next to them and turned looking to me for an answer.

"Sorry but that wasn't Janet Jackson."

"So is she one of those look-a-likes that we can use in a commercial."

"You really think she looks like Janet Jackson?" I asked but the bell rang signaling the elevator before she could answer. We walked on and the girl responded to my question.

"We don't have any campaigns involving Janet Jackson or any look-a-like. Sorry to disappoint you." The bell rang for her floor and she thanked me before exiting with her friends. My floor was the next stop and I headed straight to Derrick's office.

"I thought you were taking the day off." Derrick was coming back from his wet bar when I walked into his office.

"I see." I sat down in the chair after picking up the file of renewals.

"So what was so important you had to come in?"

"I told you I'm in the middle of renewals. Why all the questions? Was there a reason you wanted me to be out of the office today? Are you anticipating the arrival of any other unexpected guests?" I handed the file over to him.

"These need your signature." I said and Derrick took the file with a smile.

"What's so funny?" I asked.

"You're upset."

"There's nothing for me to be upset about." I said trying to sound convincing.

"Then why are you?" Derrick started signing each document.

"I'm not."

"It's almost three in the afternoon; you aren't going to get any of these renewals delivered today; so what was so important you couldn't stay home?"

"I had no reason until I got here. Tell me, what were Naquia and her colleague doing here?"

"She's looking for funding for some research."

"How do you fit in?"

"She remembered my offer to help her when she finished medical school. Why is there a problem?

"It's your money." I said collecting the signed documents and placing them back in the folder. Derrick laughed at some thought he must have had.

"How much longer will you be here in the office?" Derrick asked.

"What's the deal? I don't know Derrick. Are you hiding something else?" I stood up to begin my exit; Derrick met me at the door.

"I wanted to take you to dinner. Listen, I am not hiding anything. Naquia asked me not to mention this because she feared you'd talk me out of helping her because you dislike her."

"When have I ever swayed your decision because I disliked someone? I dislike your ex-wife and I can't seem to sway your decision when it comes to you continuing to deal with her." I opened the door and continued my exit.

Chapter Thirty-Five: Wesley

"Hello."

"May I speak with Mr. Charles please?" A lady's voice asked.

"Speaking."

"Hi, this is Amanda from Klein's Jewelers. I'm calling to let you know that your ring is ready."

"Thanks, I'll be in a little later today to pick it up."

"Great. Just ask for me."

"I will. Thanks." I disconnected the call and went back to finish packing for my trip. Raven mentioned that she had to go out of town on business and asked if Lily could stay with me for the entire week. There was no way I was going to miss this opportunity so I conferred with my wife and asked what her schedule would be like for the next few days. Since she said she'd be on duty for at least the next five days, she suggested that I go to the city and stay there with Lily.

"Are you trying to get rid of me?" I asked teasingly.

"I can't keep an eye on you if I'm not here." I remembered Naquia saying with a smile. I looked around the room to make sure I wasn't forgetting anything and then walked down the stairs to the garage.

***

The nurse at the desk recognized me when I entered through the emergency room door.

"She just went on break, try the cafeteria." The nurse said with a smile.

"Thanks." I returned her smile and pressed the button for the elevator. The doors opened and I noticed that all of the ladies in the elevator smiled to see me with my arms full of flowers and a stuffed bear. When the doors opened again on the lower level, I got a lot of attention walking into the cafeteria. I noticed Naquia sitting at a table with a couple of nurses I had seen before but didn't remember their names.

"Hey Doc." I said walking to meet her.

"What's all of this?" She beamed.

"I have a question to ask you?"

"What?" She took the flowers from my hands and sat them with the bear on the table. I dropped down on one knee and pulled the ring box out of my pocket.

"Will you marry me again?" I looked at her and watched as a blush came across her face. There was a collective sigh from the audience we'd gained. Naquia could not speak as tears rolled down her cheeks and she just nodded her head.

"Is that a yes?" I asking rising to my full height and pulling the other wedding set off her finger to replace it with the new ring.

"Yes." She whispered and placed her arms around my neck before kissing me.

"I get off at eight." Naquia whispered when our lips parted.

"I'm on my way to the city, remember?" I watched as her elation turned into another emotion.

"Oh yeah." She whispered.

"I'll go pick up Lily and come back tonight."

"You don't have to do that."

"I know I don't have to, but I want to."

"I've got to get back to work. Call me later." She pulled away from my grasp.

"I love you Doc."

"Uh huh." She said as she scooped up the flowers and bear from the table. The ladies that sat with her walked over to see her ring and I watched as they walked past me. Naquia smiled but I could tell it was not real. I walked over to the elevator and pressed the button to go up.

***

"I don't know what time we'll be back. If you have to go home, call me and we'll stop in South Carolina and pick her up." Raven said placing our sleeping beauty on the sofa.

"I'll call you to let you where we are." I said closing the door behind the driver who brought in Lily's bags.

"Okay. I've gotta go. See ya." Raven said before leaning over to kiss Lily. She caressed her face and then waved goodbye to me before opening the door. I walked into the bedroom to pick up a blanket to place over Lily and then sat down beside her and started flipping channels. The look on Naquia's face when I reminded her I was on my way here kept resurfacing. I replayed the conversation we had about her being on duty all weekend and wondered if she was going to make the effort to try and get someone to cover for her. I picked up the phone and paged Naquia.

"Hi Daddy." Lily's sweet voice woke me out of my nap and it was then that I realized Naquia never called back.

"Hey beautiful. How you doing?" I scooped her up and placed a kiss on her cheek.

"I'm fine."

"Yes, you are but have you been good?"

"Yes."

"Are you sure about that?" I reached over to tickle her.

"Yes." She giggled.

"Are you hungry?"

"Yes." I picked her up and we walked towards the bathroom so we could get cleaned up. After a tickle battle in the mirror we made our way into the kitchen for some dinner. Lily wanted cereal but I convinced her to get her shoes so we could go out for some Chinese food.

"Okay daddy." Lily ran over to the sofa and took a seat. I dialed Cee's number and put Lily's feet into her sneakers and laced them up for her.

"Hello." Cee answered after a few rings.

"Hey there. Are you busy?"

"Wesley? Where are you?"

"In the city. What are you and the kids doing?"

"Nothing, why?"

"Lily and I are going out to get some Chinese food, want to come along?"

"Sure."

"We'll be there in about ten minutes." I said after grabbing my keys and cell phone.

"We'll be ready." Cee disconnected the call after telling Trey and Tyrese that we were going out.

"You want a juice box beautiful?" I asked taking the phone back to the kitchen.

"Yes please." She answered with a smile. I grabbed a box for the both of us and we headed out to the car. Lily sang along with the radio and I was surprised at how many songs she knew the melody to. She may not have known all the words but she had the harmony. We reached Cee's place within a few minutes and Lily raced me to the door, she was reaching up on her toes trying to ring the bell.

"Need some help?" I reached down to give her boost up and she rang the bell.

"Thank you daddy." Trey answered the door just as Lily spoke the words.

"Hey little man." I said as Lily rushed past Trey to get to Tyrese. I closed the door behind me and saw Cee waving from the dining room; she was on the phone.

"What's up? How's school." I asked as I sat on the sofa

"Good. I just my report card; I got four A's and two B pluses." He said handing me the report card.

"Good job. We are going to have to do something to celebrate that."

"Can we go shoot some hoops at Chuck E. Cheese instead of eating Chinese food?"

"No, but I'll ask your mom if we can go afterwards."

"Let's ask if we can go Sunday instead, cause tonight she'll say no cause I have school tomorrow."

"Okay." I said and Trey smiled. Lily and Tyrese were in the corner in their own little world. Cee ended her call and came in the room with us.

"Ready?" She asked.

"Yep."

"Good. Come on children let's go eat." The girls joined us and within a few minutes we were all seated and strapped in.

***

After dinner, no one had any room for dessert, so we drove back to Cee's.

"Winston working late?" I asked after noticing that his truck wasn't in the driveway when we got out to go inside.

"As usual." Cee said before asking Trey to take his father's food into the kitchen.

"Okay mommy."

"Did you finish all of your math homework?" She asked as he walked away.

"Yeah, you checked it already?"

"Okay, then you can get your bath and watch television for one hour before you go to bed."

"By the way, Trey showed me his report card. I want to take him out to celebrate his grades. Can we get together on Sunday after church?"

"Sure. I know he wants to go to that Chuck E. Cheese doesn't he?"

"We're gonna shoot some hoops."

"What are you going to do with the girls?"

"They'll probably be in the room full of balls. I'll take care of everything."

"Why don't you leave the girls with me? Trey probably wants you all to himself."

"Cool." I said noticing that Trey had returned and was listening to the end of our conversation.

"Sunday after church little man." I said and he balled his fists up with an exclamation of "yeah" for approval.

"Now take the girls upstairs with you so I can talk to Wesley for a few minutes." Cee said pointing towards the stairs.

"Daddy can I spend the night with Reesey?"

"You gonna leave me..." I saw the answer in her eyes before I finished my question.

"That's okay, you can leave me. Ask your Auntie Cee."

"Can I stay?" Lily asked.

"Of course baby. Go upstairs and find something to sleep in."

"Thank you. Good night daddy." Lily walked over to give me a hug and a kiss.

"Good night beautiful, I'll pick you up first thing tomorrow morning."

"Okay." She smiled and waved before following her cousins upstairs.

"So mister man what are you going to do now that you're all alone."

"Dunno, probably flip channels until I fall asleep. So what's going on with you? What's new?"

"Ain't nothing changed but the date. Same old stuff."

"The last time we talked you was talking crazy about leaving your husband. What's up? Talk to me."

"I don't know what you're talking about."

"If you say so."

"What about you? How are things with the Mrs.?"

"Cool. We are actually planning to get remarried. I just asked her today and gave her a new ring."

"Yeah? That's great. Congratulations."

"Thanks."

"So I guess this is a reality. You ain't gonna be my brother-in-law after all."

"C'mon Cee. Your sister is happily married to Derrick and I am about to be happily remarried to Naquia. Everything is the way it was intended to be."

"Funny how you said intended to be instead of meant to be." Cee smiled before she got up and asked if I wanted anything to drink.

***

I got home around two and clicked on the television before going to bed. I had already resigned myself to sleeping on the couch since Lily was going to be here, so I decided to sleep out here anyway.

"Welcome back to the KCI celebrity golf benefit. Up next we have the Derrick Kincaide the CEO of KCI who is three stokes behind our celebrity leader Gary Payton." Hearing Derrick's name brought my attention to the television screen where I was surprised to come face to face with a picture of my wife standing in the crowd watching the golf tournament.

Chapter Thirty-Six: Derrick

I stood on the balcony of our suite and watched the sunrise over the golf course. It was a beautiful site to see and I was pleased with my wife who had done an excellent job in pulling this whole event together. Today is the last day of the tournament and we have far exceeded the goal we had projected. Naquia was pleased when I told her we had surpassed the three million dollar mark. The celebrities had been more than generous with their financial contributions in addition to their time here this weekend. Several of them had approached Raven about taking a job as their personal assistant. I had to flex my muscles on several occasions to show them that I was not interested in my wife leaving KCI or me. The surrounding towns and cities were all booked solid because of all the publicity that Raven had generated to promote the event and it caused a stir within the fan base of the celebrities. Last night both the mayor and governor approached me to ask if we would consider making this an annual event.

"I would have to defer to my wife on this one." I placed a kiss on Raven's cheek and she smiled.

"Let me get through this year and I'll let you know." She answered gracefully before we departed the ballroom. Raven looked exhausted and I knew that I would have to do something extra special for her after all of this was said and done. The bellman opened the penthouse elevator door and inserted his key to begin our ascent.

"How does a hot bubble bath sound?" I whispered in her ear.

"Heavenly."

"Then my angel, let me draw you a bath and wash you from head to toe."

"That sounds good."

"It will be." The door opened to our suite and the bellman said goodnight before departing. Raven walked over to the phone to check for messages and I went in to start her bath.

"Raven your bath is getting cold." I said hoping this would encourage her to end the call.

"Coming." She replied and I lit the candles and dimmed the lights before submerging my body into the warm bubbles. Raven smiled when she saw me in the tub.

"I thought this was supposed to be for me."

"It is; I promised to bathe you from head to toe remember?"

"Yes, I remember." She said as she extended her hand to me to help her step inside. I spent the next few minutes rubbing the loofah across her back and trying to control my animalistic urges as she moaned.

"This feels so good." She cooed.

"I'm glad you're enjoying it."

"I'm not the only one." She laughed as she backed in closer to me. We shared a laugh and then a few quiet moments before she filled me in on her conversation with Wesley.

"I couldn't talk to Lily, she was asleep; Wesley said they have been spending a lot of time with Cee and the kids."

"I didn't think they would have stayed in the city, but then again I should've guessed that they would considering that Naquia was here for the benefit."

"I'm not sure that had anything to do with it, because Wesley asked me why I didn't tell him about the tournament. He acted like he didn't know anything about it."

"That's strange. Why wouldn't Naquia tell Wesley about the benefit?"

"Dunno."

"Well that's something the two of them will have to work out. I have something I want to talk about with you."

"What's that?" Raven said turning to face me.

"What would you say if I told you I wanted another baby?"

"I'd say you're crazy."

"Why?"

"Are you serious? There are many reasons."

"Give me one."

"We have a baby."

"Yes and she needs a sister or brother to grow up with."

"What?"

"Raven, this may sound selfish but I want the two of us to create a child together out of our lovemaking."

"What's really going on here?"

"There's nothing going on. Why are you against this?"

"It's not so much that I'm against it. This just isn't a good time."

"Why not?"

"Let's see. We are very busy at work right now. Lily is still a baby. Mrs. Hill can't handle two little ones at the same time, not to mention my mother."

"Work will slow down, Lily is almost two and we can hire some help for Mrs. Hill and for your mother."

"Derrick, why is this so important to you right now? Is there something you're not telling me?"

"Why would you ask me that?"

"Because I don't recognize the voice of the man I speaking with. Who have you been talking to?"

"No one."

"Then where is all of this coming from?"

"What's wrong with a husband wanting to share a child with his wife?"

"We share a child."

"No, we share Wesley's child."

"Whoa. Where did that come from?"

"Never mind. I'm sorry I brought it up." I knew I couldn't hide the disappointment I was feeling.

"Derrick, I'm not trying to be difficult but I really am at a loss. This is a surprise. How long have you been feeling like this?"

"Raven just forget it."

"No. You obviously have given this some serious thought or else you wouldn't have brought it up. I just want to know where it came from and how long have you felt this way."

"It's nothing."

"It's something or else we wouldn't be talking about it. How long have you felt like you were sharing Wesley's child instead of raising your other daughter?"

"You're taking that out of context. You took it the wrong way."

"I took it the way you said it. I just hope Lily doesn't feel it." Raven excused herself and stepped out of the tub. Recognizing that she needed some time alone, I toweled myself off, extinguished all of the candles and turned off the music. Raven was in the bed when I entered the room so I quietly walked into the living area of the suite and switched on the television. I replayed the conversation I'd had earlier today with Naquia and wondered if I had been influenced by her to make this request of my wife.

"The latest tabulation has us over the three million dollar mark for the weekend. When Raven gets the final total from the silent auction, KCI will make up whatever the difference is to bring the total to an even amount." I said as Naquia gave the waitress her order and handed over the menu.

"Wow. I guess for you this is like talking about three dollars instead of three million dollars. Talking about that kind of money gives me chills, you are just as cool as a cucumber." She said as the server placed our drinks on the table.

"I used to feel that way too in the beginning, now it's just business talk."

"How do you deal with it?" Naquia asked before sipping her iced tea.

"You get used to it with time."

"That's not what I meant; how do you deal with Wesley and Raven?"

"Where did that come from?"

"Maybe if I could learn to deal with things like you, it wouldn't bother me so much."

"There's nothing to deal with really. Wesley is a great father to Lily and other then the two of them spending time together, we really don't have much contact with Wesley."

"That's funny because it seems to me that every time I turn around, Raven is either on my phone or in my house."

"It probably seems that way because of the time you spend at the hospital."

"That has nothing to do with it. Raven is always in contact with Wesley. I believe she's using that child as an excuse. I'm only saying this because I want my husband and I want my marriage and if there was someway we could disconnect that one and only tie they still have; I believe we both would be happier spouses."

"Naquia..."

"I don't know about you but I am going to talk to Wesley about having a child of our own. If we had our own baby, maybe he wouldn't feel the need to be so connected to Lily and continue to make those ridiculous trips every other week to get her or to be there with her. Honestly, I believe he's doing it more so to be close to your wife." She said before the waitress came to the table to bring our lunch.

***

I thought I felt when Raven got out of bed, but when I opened my eyes I was surprised to find her still sleeping. I looked over to the alarm clock that read 7:30 and realized we'd both overslept.

"Princess." I whispered not wanting to startle her.

"Yes."

"We're late. It's after seven and tee time is eight this morning."

"No, we're okay. One of the camera crews had a discrepancy so we pushed back the tee time for the live feed at eleven."

"Oh I must have missed that. I'm sorry go back to sleep."

"No, there's still a lot to do. I might as well get up."

"Wait."

"What's wrong?"

"Nothing's wrong. I just want to apologize for upsetting you last night. You know I love Lily to death."

321

"I know you love Lily but what does that have to do with you wanting another baby?"

"Maybe I'm just feeling my age."

"And you wouldn't feel it chasing another rug rat around?"

"I guess you've got a point there." I laughed hoping it would lighten the mood.

"Derrick, it's not that I'm against the idea of us having a baby. I would love to have your child but it's just not a good time right now. Let's talk about this later when Lily is a little bit older and can do more for herself."

"I can live with that." I reached over and kissed Raven's cheek then spent a few moments sharing my love for my wife. We got showered and dressed and then went down to grab some breakfast so that we could be prepared for the eleven o'clock taping.

***

"Derrick, again thank you so much. You don't know what this means to me." Naquia placed a kiss on my cheek.

"You're welcome but you really should be thanking Raven, she pulled all of this together and this is all the result of her hard work."

"You're right but she wouldn't accept it coming from me. You know she doesn't like me."

"Try. I did what you asked me to do, can you return the favor?" I asked just as Raven approached the place where we were standing.

"Honey are you ready?" Raven asked without even acknowledging Naquia's presence.

"Yes." I said taking my wife's hand and looking at Naquia.

"Uh Raven, I um just want to thank you. This whole weekend, the tournament and everything was great. The money we've raised will help a lot." Naquia said politely.

"You're welcome." Raven smiled and then pulled on my hand. Once we were out of earshot I had to ask.

"What was that?"

"What?" She turned to me as we continued to walk towards the hotel.

"Why the lukewarm response to Naquia's gesture?"

"That's all she deserved for a lukewarm gesture."

"You really don't like her."

"Don't like her and I don't trust her. And if all of my hours of watching crime dramas has taught me anything, then I would say that it was Naquia that convinced you that you wanted another child."

"What would lead you to believe that? What evidence do you have?"

"That comment you made about sharing Wesley's child; that screams Naquia."

"I keep telling you, you are too damned smart." I said stepping into the elevator to go up to the penthouse.

Chapter Thirty-Seven: Raven

"Good morning." I was so excited about seeing Lily, just as soon as I woke up I drove right over to Wesley's to get my baby.

"Good morning. What time is it? I thought I said I'd bring Lily to you." Wesley said wiping sleep from his eyes.

"You did. I couldn't wait; I've been missing my baby and just couldn't wait to see her. I'm sorry."

"No problem. She hasn't come in here asking for her cereal so I think she's still asleep."

"Do you mind?" I pointed in the direction of his bedroom.

"Could I stop you if I did?" He smiled.

"Nope. Go back to sleep." I left him in the living room, kicked off my shoes and curled up on his bed beside Lily.

***

"Good morning mommy." Lily's voice woke me up from the nap I had no intention of taking.

"Good morning baby. Mommy has missed you so much." I grabbed my daughter and began plastering her face with kisses that were met with her laughter.

"I missed you too mommy." She said between chuckles.

"Ready to go home?"

"Yes."

"Then let's go." I sat up, stepped in my shoes and then wrapped Lily up in an afghan that Wesley had draped across a chair in the room.

"What about my stuff?" Lily asked.

"We'll pick it up later." I said picking Lily up in my arms and whisking her off into the living room.

"Hi daddy, bye daddy." Lily said when I stopped to pick up my purse and keys.

"Hold up. Let me get the door." He said laughing at my bout of craziness and me.

"Thanks. We'll pick up her stuff later." I said pressing the button for the elevator.

"I'll drop it off on my way home." He said lifting the gate to the elevator and getting on with us.

"Are you sure?"

"Yeah, it's no problem. I'll probably be over there around noon."

"Okay. Thanks for everything. Tell your daddy thank you."

"Thank you daddy. I love you." Lily said just as he lifted the gate again when we got downstairs. Lily waved to Wesley as I put my giggling daughter in the car and fastened her in her car seat snuggly. We hit the freeway within minutes and were welcomed by the smell of bacon when we opened the front door.

"Miss Lily is that you?" Mrs. Hill called out as she approached us.

"Yes. Hi Mrs. Hill."

"I've missed you so much. Have you been a good girl?" She reached down to hug Lily.

"Yes." Lily responded after kissing her cheek.

"Are you hungry? I made your favorites for breakfast."

"Yes."

"Good then let's go get washed up and get your daddy out of bed." I said and Lily took off running. I followed her upstairs and put my finger up to my lips so we could be quiet and surprise Derrick.

***

Derrick and Lily were out back since Lily wanted to know how to play golf. I watched them for a few minutes until I heard the doorbell and remembered that Wesley was going to drop off Lily's things.

"Hey you." I greeted his smiling face.

"Hi." Wesley walked in and placed the bags beside the door.

"Do you have to leave right now?"

"No. I can stay for a few minutes. What's up?"

"Nothing, I just wanted to thank you again for keeping Lily for us and ask how everything went."

"Everything was cool. Like I told you the other night we spent a lot of time with Cee and the kids. Other than that, nothing out of the ordinary."

"Oh. Can I ask you a question?"

"Yeah."

"Naquia didn't tell you about the tournament this weekend?" I asked because curiosity was getting the better of me.

"No. I guess it slipped her mind."

"That's funny because we've been working on this since June. She approached Derrick about funding for the AIDS hospital that her friend Dr. Baines is starting."

"Maybe she did mention it and it just slipped my mind."

"How did you find out?"

"I was flipping channels and they were showing it on television. Why? What's with all of the questions?"

"Nothing.· Just curious." I said to him but my detective's intuition was thinking something else.

"Come on out back so you can see your baby trying to golf." I said taking Wesley by the hand and leading the way. We walked through the kitchen and out to where Lily and Derrick were. Lily looked so cute holding onto the bottom of the club while Derrick was trying to help her hit the ball.

"We did it daddy. It went in the hole." She squealed and when she turned she noticed us coming towards them.

"Did you see me daddy I did a one in hole?" She ran into Wesley's arms.

"It's a hole in one sweetheart." Derrick said when he reached us.

"A hole in one." Lily repeated.

"I saw you baby, you did good." Wesley hugged and kissed her.

"Good to see you Wesley." Derrick extended his hand.

"You too. I saw you had a good game at your tournament." Wesley said shaking Derrick's hand.

"I didn't know you followed golf. You should have come to see it first hand. Do you play?"

"Putt Putt. That's about it." Wesley laughed.

"We'll have to get Lily to teach you since she seems to have mastered the game. What do you think Princess, can you teach your daddy how to play?"

"Yes." She giggled when Derrick poked a finger into her midsection.

"Sounds good to me. Listen baby, I've got to get on the road." Wesley placed a kiss on Lily's lips.

"Okay daddy." She said before he put her down.

"Be careful." I said.

"I will. Be good baby and I'll see you in two weeks." Wesley started to walk away and we followed.

***

The three of us spent the rest of the day together and Mrs. Hill was obviously happy to have her family back because she cooked a meal that was just short of a feast. Derrick and Lily ate themselves silly and I wondered how long it would be before I'd be hearing the moans of my stomach hurts. I was betting myself that Derrick would moan first.

"Where are you going?" Derrick asked when I excused myself from the table.

"I can't possibly expect Mrs. Hill to clean the kitchen after all of this." I said and watched as she began to rise from her seat.

"Don't even think about it; I have the kitchen, you can take the bath duty." I said watching the smiles that both she and Lily displayed.

"I think I can handle that." Mrs. Hill smiled and she sat back down. Derrick started collecting the dishes and I started removing the serving dishes to take back into the kitchen. Mrs. Hill let Lily convince her to go into the den and watch a new video that Wesley had bought for her.

"Did you get much work done last night?" I asked Derrick when he came in with the last of the dishes.

"Not really. I didn't realize how tired I was." Derrick said tying up the garbage bag.

"I know; it feels good to be home and sleeping in my own bed." I said placing the dishwashing powder in the compartment and replacing the cap.

"I was surprised to wake up to an empty bed." He said leaning against the counter.

"Why were you surprised you must have known I was gone to get Lily?" I said after returning the powder to its place under the sink. I turned on the dishwasher and then the water in the sink to wash down the counters.

"When we spoke to Wesley last night, he said he'd bring her home in the morning."

"You know I couldn't wait that long." I said moving over to where he stood.

"You couldn't wait that long to see Lily or Wesley?" Derrick's words stopped me in my tracks.

"What?"

"Who was it that you couldn't wait to see?"

"You've got to be kidding me."

"That's not an answer."

"That's the only answer you're gonna get. You can let Naquia manipulate you and send you through these changes but you will go through them alone." I placed the dishcloth in the sink and walked out of the kitchen. Mrs. Hill and Lily were still in the den so I picked up my keys and walked out the door destination unknown but ended up at Cee's house.

"Hey family." I announced my arrival coming in the front door.

"We're in the kitchen." Winston responded. I closed the door and made my way into the kitchen.

"Hi Auntie." Trey and Tyrese chorused.

"Hi everybody. Ooh that looks good." I commented on the Cee's infamous Strawberry shortcake that was being consumed by my family.

329

"Grab a saucer and join us." Cee said sounding like my sister again.

"Where are Derrick and Lily?" Winston asked.

"At home." I said before taking a seat and handing my saucer to Cee.

"When did you get back?" She asked handing me the cake.

"We got in late last night. So what's been happening with the Moores; I understand Lily spent a lot of time with you guys this weekend." I said before placing a bite of the cake into my mouth. As expected it was delicious; and probably something I shouldn't be eating.

"Yeah, it was good to see them and to spend some time with Wesley." Cee said and Winston nodded.

"We took Trey to Chuck E. Cheese to celebrate his report card and had a boys night out." Winston said before leaving the table.

"Which was good because me and the ladies had a night of beauty with bubble baths and the works." Cee added and Tyrese nodded in agreement.

"We had a good time. Look mommy did my fingernails." Tyrese extended her hand to show me that Cee had given her a fake manicure with clear polish.

"That looks good. Trey what did you get on your report card?" I asked.

"I got four As and two B pluses."

"Wow. That is great. Boy you are going to break me. How much do I owe you now?"

"Twenty dollars." He said grinning.

"Let me see what I've got on me." I got up to get my purse off the counter. I checked in my wallet and remembered that I had used the last of my cash in Georgia.

"I'm sorry baby, I don't have any cash. Can I write you a check?" I asked.

"Okay." He said but I could tell his heart wasn't in it.

"Are you sure?"

"Yes." He replied but I wasn't convinced.

"You know what, I need to go to the ATM anyway so when I finish my dessert, I go around the corner and get your cash." I said.

"You don't have to do that, he can take the check and we'll go to the bank and cash it after school tomorrow." Cee said.

"That's okay, I don't mind." I placed the last bite in my mouth.

"Then you men can clean up the kitchen and I'll ride with Raven to the bank." Cee said and asked Tyrese if she wanted to go with us.

"No but can I watch cartoons?" Tyrese asked.

"Just for a little while. Are you ready?" She got up and placed her saucer in the sink and motioned for Winston to pass her the rest of the cake.

"Yeah." I placed my saucer in the sink and placed my purse under my arm.

"See ya in a little bit." Cee said before exiting the kitchen. I followed Tyrese into the living room and watched as she punched in numbers on the remote control until she found the channel she wanted. Cee came down the stairs with her purse and opened the door. I followed her to my car and within minutes we were on our way.

"Can we drop by the grocery store for a minute, I need to pick up something from the deli for lunch?" Cee asked.

"Sure. It's good to have you back?" I said hoping she wasn't going to blow up on me.

"Don't start." She said shaking her finger at me.

"What?"

"Let's talk about why you're here instead of being home with your family."

"Derrick said something that set me off, so instead of going off I decided to put some distance between us."

"No you did what you always do, you ran."

"I didn't..."

"Yes, you did Chicken Little; when are you gonna grow up?"

"Shut up. So are things better between you and Winston?"

"They are getting there. I have to admit; your Christmas gift helped a lot. I didn't think it would but it did."

"I'm glad."

"Yeah me too. I can honestly say that I learned something in this."

"What?"

"I learned that I could either continue to be miserable in a bad situation or I could do something about it."

"And what did you do?"

"I changed my perspective. I was talking with Wesley the other night and he was telling me all about the things he's been going through and trying deal within his marriage. For the most part, we are all going through the same thing. We give all that we have to give and sometimes it just isn't enough, so you get to the point where you have to make a decision. He decided to meet his wife half way and now they are going to get married again to start anew. I decided to redirect my energies and change my focus. I decided to stop looking at what I don't have and focus on what I do have and how to make it better."

"That's good. I'm happy for you."

"Thanks. What about you? What did Derrick do this time?"

"He's letting someone get in his ear and now he wants to act like an insecure teenage boy. We both know he's too damned old for that."

"Who's getting in his ear?"

"Believe it or not, Naquia."

"Whaaat?"

"It's hard enough dealing with her and her insecurities, now she is trying to convert Derrick."

"How's she doing that?"

"I don't know if I told you but she talked Derrick into this charity fundraiser thing. He didn't tell me about it before he committed to doing it because she told him I would've talked him out of it. That was probably the only thing she's ever been right about. Anyway to save face, I took the lead on it and actually it turned out pretty nice and raised over three million dollars."

"That's good."

"Yeah it was until I found out this trick told my husband he needs to convince me to have another baby so he won't have to share Wesley's child." I parked the car so we could go into the grocery store.

"Share Wesley's child? What the hell did she mean by that?"

"I don't know what she is trying to do but I ain't having it."

"So what are you going to do?" Cee asked as if she was hanging on to a cliffhanger.

"I have already dealt with Derrick since he actually fell for it and decided to come to me with it. What makes me so mad is that he is a smart man, he is the head of a multi-million dollar business and he has no common sense. Naquia can say a few words and now he suddenly believes that I am still involved with Wesley."

"What do you mean suddenly? You have fueled that fire many times on your own." Cee said and stopped to see my reaction.

"What are you talking about?"

"Wasn't it you who cut your honeymoon short and had a fit in my living room when you found out Wesley took Lily to South Carolina? Wasn't it you who ran to Wesley when you thought Derrick was having an affair? Can't you see that would make even the strongest man feel insecure?" Cee picked up a hand basket and we walked towards the deli.

"I love my husband. Yes I have made some mistakes, I have made some poor decisions but I have never given Derrick a reason to think I would leave him for Wesley."

"Are you sure about that?"

***

It was quiet when I walked into the house; I punched in the code and went upstairs. My first stop was the nursery to see my gorgeous daughter who was sleeping soundly with one foot sticking out from under the covers, just like her mother. After pulling the covers over her again, I walked into our bedroom through the adjoining doors. Derrick was asleep on top of the duvet fully dressed. I sat down beside him and rubbed his back as I spoke.

"Honey." I whispered.

"Yes." He responded softly.

"Get up and get undressed so you can get in the bed."

"I'm good." He said turning to face me.

"Good because I want to talk." I said and he slid up to lean against the headboard.

"Okay."

"I don't like the way things went down this afternoon. I probably could have; no, I should have handled things differently. I was wrong to do the one thing that seems to be what I do best." I paused waiting for him to say something but he didn't.

"I don't know what it is that makes me run whenever I have to face a difficult situation I don't do it when it comes to business, but it seems like I just do it when it comes to my heart."

"Have you given any thought to why that is?"

"No, I can't say that I have. Let me ask you a question; have I given you any reason to believe that there is something going on between me and Wesley?"

"No."

"Then where is all of this coming from?"

"I don't know. Maybe you were right when you said I let Naquia manipulate me and take advantage of my vulnerabilities."

"Why? I thought things were good between us. We worked through that whole Regina thing and…"

"You're right Princess. I apologize but this morning when you disappeared without a word, I heard Naquia's voice telling me about all of the phone calls and visits over the last few months."

"What phone calls and visits? I have not been to South Carolina without you since the night of the Regina thing. Any phone calls have been for Wesley's visitation, coordinating times. Other than this morning, when have we been apart long enough for me to even go to see Wesley?"

"I know; you're right and I'm sorry."

"I don't want you to be sorry. We have to get past all of this. It is hard enough dealing with Naquia and her stupidity. I can't handle two of you. I can't undo the fact that Wesley and I are Lily's parents. I can't help that he wants to take an active role in our daughter's life. I am happily married to a man that I love and adore. I can't fix her insecurities about her relationship with her husband; that's not my job. But I can do something about her interfering in my relationship, and I'm starting with you."

Chapter Thirty-Eight: Wesley

The church was decorated with all kinds of flowers and I'm glad that this time it was for an occasion other than a funeral. I can't believe how nervous I am, I am actually shaking standing here at the altar in front of all of our family and friends. I felt sweat roll down the back of my neck and I looked over at my father who stood by my side as my best man. The organist began to play and the soloist began to sing and then Vicky and two of Naquia's friends began to walk down the aisle towards us. I smiled when DJ and JR rolled the runner down and then felt my heart swell with pride when my daughter who had now become a pro at being a flower girl walked down the aisle dropping rose petals along the way. I looked over to see Derrick and Raven smiling proudly and knew that they too were feeling what I was feeling.

"That's Grandpa's girl; look at her, she's beautiful." Father whispered in my ear.

"She is." I felt tears coming to my eyes and smiled at my big girl. The doors at the head of the church closed just as the wedding march began. Everyone in the church stood and then the doors opened to Naquia who stood there alone waiting until the coordinator told her to come forward. The male soloist began to sing his version of A Ribbon in the Sky by Stevie Wonder. I felt my trembling again as Naquia got closer to me but everything settled when she placed her hand into mine.

"Dearly Beloved…" Those were the only words I could hear until it came to the place where I had to repeat what the pastor was saying. After placing the ring on Naquia's finger and the kiss, this grand affair that took months to plan and thousands of dollars was over and we were being announced as Mr. And Mrs. Wesley Charles Jr. again. We walked down the aisle as the coordinator had instructed us last night and exited into the pastor's study to wait until we were allowed to go back into the church for the pictures.

"I love you." Naquia said before placing another kiss on my lips which was much more passionate than the one we had just shared.

"I love you too, Mrs. Charles." I said caressing her cheek.

"You looked so handsome standing there."

"You took my breath away when the doors of the church opened again."

"If you think that took your breath away, wait until you see what I have on under this gown." She chuckled.

"Let me see." I reached for the side zipper on her gown.

"Down boy." She said just as the coordinator came in to take us back into the church.

***

After all of the pictures taken, we were escorted into the limo and driven over to the reception. We stopped as instructed so everyone could be announced and then made our grand entrance and were seated at the head table. After the food was blessed, the caterer had his staff on point to begin serving. I looked around the room to see that everyone was being served plates of food that still had steam coming from it. I smiled at the remembrance of me being pressed to contribute something to the wedding plans.

"I am contributing something, I'm paying remember." I said to Vicky who punched me because she didn't think my comment was funny.

"C'mon boy. You haven't told us one thing that you want." She said pushing a brochure showing plates of food over to me.

"All I want is some hot food. I am tired of going to these things and after waiting forever to eat; you get a plate of food that is ice cold. My contribution to the wedding plans is I want some steam coming from my food when it's served." I smiled again at the remembrance.

"What?" Naquia leaned over to whisper.

"It's nothing. I'm just happy." I kissed her lips lightly.

"Eat; we have a long night ahead of us." She smiled and placed a fork full of steamed vegetables into her mouth. We ate our dinner while stopping every once in a while to have our picture taken. Lily got up and walked over to the table where Raven and Derrick sat and I wondered if something was wrong. I slid my chair back to go check things out.

"Where are you going?" Naquia asked placing her hand on mine.

"I'm going to check on Lily."

"She's fine."

"I just want to make sure. I'll be right back."

"Wesley she's fine. You insisted that her mother be here on my day; let her take care of her daughter." Naquia's tone changed.

"I didn't insist on anything, I simply invited them to our wedding since they were bringing Lily. What's the problem now?" I sat down hoping we hadn't drawn any attention to ourselves.

"This is my day, my wedding day and I'll be damned if I'm going to share it with her. You told me that things were going to be different now; I'm going to hold you to that." She said before adding a smile to it as if that would make a difference. Having lost my appetite, I placed the fork on the plate and a server came over to pick it up. The wedding coordinator came over and asked if we were ready to cut the cake.

"Yes. C'mon honey." Naquia said putting on a show for everyone. My focus remained on Lily who sat with her head in Raven's lap. Naquia nudged me to follow her to the cake table. We went through the motions and had already talked about not smashing the cake in one another's faces. We posed and cut the cake and then fed each other. Naquia kissed me after licking some of the icing off my lips and the crowd cheered her on. Father gave his best man speech and then the music for our first dance began to play. Father came to cut in on the dance and I walked over to check on Lily.

"Is everything okay?" I asked kneeling down to whisper in her ear.

"My stomach hurts." She said softly.

"She doesn't want to leave because she wants to see the fireworks." Raven said.

"Baby, we can go see some fireworks anytime. I don't want you to stay if you don't feel good."

"Daddy can I stay please I want to see the sparkles." Lily was on the verge of tears.

"Okay baby. Don't cry." I stood up to my full height again and searched the room for my wife. Derrick walked over followed by a guy that looked familiar to me.

"Princess, you remember Dr. Baines don't you?" He asked and then I realized who this was.

"Yes. Nice to see you again." Raven extended her hand and he kneeled down to where Lily was.

"I understand you're not feeling well, can you tell me what's the matter?" He asked Lily.

"My tummy hurts."

"Can you show me where?"

Lily sat up and ran her hands all around the front of her dress. He nodded his head and then asked if he could touch it. She nodded.

"Right here?" He asked.

"Yes."

"How about here?"

"Yes."

"Umm, I see. I think I know what you need to fix this problem."
"What?"

"It's a medicine called Castor Oil. Have you ever taken it before?" He asked with a smile and Lily looked up to Raven.

"What's that?" Lily asked.

"You take it like a cough syrup."

"And it will make my stomach stop hurting."

"Yes just as soon as you go to the bathroom." He said with a smile.

"Daddy, can you go get the medicine so I can go to the bathroom and stay for the sparkles?" She looked at me but Derrick responded.

"Just tell me how to get to a pharmacy." Derrick said to me.

"You don't have to do that, I think we have some at my house. I'll be right back."

"You'll be right back from where?" Naquia asked walking up on us.

"I've got to make a run back to the house for a minute."

"Wesley you can't leave. We are in the middle of our wedding reception or haven't you noticed."

"Wesley, really the driver and I can go. We'll call Onstar." Derrick interjected.

"Thank you Derrick." Naquia said with her eyes planted on me. She placed her hand in mine and led me away from them.

"We have to get ready to toss the garter and bouquet." Naquia walked to the front of the room where a decorated chair had been placed. She took a seat and the wedding coordinator made an announcement to get everyone's attention. The band started playing softly as I was instructed to go up under Naquia's gown to get the garter.

"Let's hurry up and get this over with." I didn't care how it sounded because I have had my fill of Naquia and her attitude.

"I know you can't wait to get me out of here." She said loud enough to be overheard. I didn't reply, I just turned to the coordinator to let her know I was ready. She called all of the single men to come forward and then asked me to turn around to throw the garter. I did as I was asked and was surprised to see that Dr. Baines had caught it.

"Come on ladies, that's a doctor who caught the garter, so the lucky lady that catches the bouquet may catch him too." Naquia laughed. My eyes and attention went over to Raven's table. Lily had returned her head to Raven's lap and I wondered how much longer it would be before this charade was over. Naquia played around for a few minutes teasing the ladies before she actually threw the bouquet. One of the nurses from the hospital caught the bouquet and after the pictures were taken, the coordinator asked everyone to dance.

"I can't believe you were going to leave me here on tonight of all nights." Naquia said as we danced.

"Lily isn't feeling well, I was going to run home and get the stuff for her to take."

"Lily's parents are here; don't you think they could have handled their daughter and her ills?"

"That's just what I was trying to do."

Laine Highsmith

"Honestly Wesley, you are going to have to recognize that Derrick is Lily's father for more than ninety percent of the time. He is with her day in and day out. You and your part time visits are just breaks in her normal routine."

"What did you say?" I stopped dancing.

"I think you heard me. You are going to have to..."

"You are going to have to get your head together because I will not go through this bullshit again." I released her from my grasp and she turned to walk away. Following her lead, I took at seat at the table with Raven and Lily.

"Baby, it's almost time for the fireworks." I said to Lily who I had just realized was sleeping.

"Funny, I thought they had started already." Raven said under her breath.

"Was it that obvious?"

"To anyone watching."

"Damn."

"I don't think many people noticed, I was watching because of the exchange that took place over here earlier." She said rubbing Lily's back.

"I'm sorry you had to witness any of that."

"You don't have to apologize; I know what you're dealing with." Raven said with a smile.

"I think we'd better change the subject." I said not knowing where the conversation would end.

"Okay. Well it was a beautiful wedding. You looked really handsome."

"Thanks, but I think our daughter was the showstopper."

"I agree. She looked just like me." Raven said and we both laughed.

"I think her beauty is a combination of the both of our genes."

"You're right, you're right." She agreed just as Derrick returned.

"Did you find one open?" I asked before I noticed the bag in his hand.

"Yes, but it looks like I'm too late. Should we wake her?" He reached down to caress Lily's face after handing the bag over to Raven.

"You want to be the one to explain to her how we let her miss the fireworks." Raven said and I noticed Vicky trying to get my attention.

"Excuse me." I left them and walked over to where Vicky, Naquia and Eugene stood.

"What's up?" I asked.

"You know you are making all of this harder than it has to be." Vicky said. I looked at Naquia wondering what she might have said to her. I was glad that Vicky spoke again before I could respond.

"Since you won't tell us where you're going for the honeymoon, how are we supposed to know if we've packed the right stuff? She said wrapping her arm around me.

"We're not leaving until morning. I will either pack a bag for my wife or tell her what to pack tomorrow."

"Why are you being so secretive?" Vicky whined.

"Why are you being so nosey?" I said before kissing her cheek.

"You know I'm glad you didn't tell me, she's been badgering me all week trying to get me to tell her something I don't even know." Eugene said.

"Badgering? I didn't badger you." She said walking over to kiss her husband.

"Are you ready to go?" I asked Naquia who was looking off to the other side of the room.

"In a minute. Excuse me." Naquia walked away in the direction of her doctor friend. At that moment, Samantha's warning came back to me but my focus was redirected when I watched Derrick lifting Lily up from Raven's lap.

"Excuse me, I want to say good night to Lily." I left before Vicky and Eugene could say anything. I caught up with Derrick and Raven just as they entered the foyer of the hall.

"Don't go; we're about to leave. The fireworks should be in just a few minutes." I said and watched as Lily's eyes lit up.

"Can we stay?" She asked.

"Yes, we'll wait in the car and I will open the roof so we can see everything." Derrick said and Lily seemed satisfied with that.

"Good night baby. I love you." I kissed her cheek.

"Good night, I love you too." She yawned.

"Good night and congratulations." Derrick said before they turned to leave.

"Thank you." I responded.

"Good night." Raven said but she looked as if there was something else she wanted to say.

"Good night, I'm glad you and Derrick came." I said just as Naquia walked up on us.

"I thought you were so ready to go." Naquia remarked.

"I am, I was waiting for you."

"Naquia, can I have a moment please?" The doctor said before extending his hand to her.

"Sure. I'll be right back." Naquia placed a kiss on my cheek that I am sure was for Raven's benefit.

"I ain't trying to get in your business or anything but you need to keep an eye on that." Raven said watching the two of them walking away from us.

"What?"

"Just be careful. I don't trust your wife and I don't think she's all she pretends to be. I would hate to see you get hurt."

"You can't say something like that without an explanation."

"Remember when we did the charity golf benefit? Remember when you asked me why I didn't tell you about it?"

"Yeah."

"Remember when I asked you if Naquia said anything to you about the tournament?"

"Yeah, I told you I couldn't remember if she did or didn't."

"Did you two ever talk about it?"

"No. Why?"

"Did you know that the doctor was at the tournament?"

"The tournament was for him right? Why wouldn't he be there?"

"But did she tell you that they were going to be there together?"

"Raven what are you trying to say?"

"All I'm saying is be careful." She stopped speaking when Naquia joined us again.

"Be careful of what?" Naquia asked.

"Are you ready? Let's go." I said.

"Not before I get an answer to my question. What should my husband be careful of Raven?"

"You."

"What is that supposed to mean?" Naquia said speaking louder than she had before.

"I'd better go before this gets out of hand. Good night." Raven said.

"When are you going to stop trying to get in between me and my husband?"

"That's funny you would ask that considering it's you that keeps trying to put me in between you and your husband. Isn't that what you tried to convince my husband of when we were in Georgia?"

"Ladies..." I tried to calm things a small crowd started to gather.

"I didn't try to convince your husband of anything, I simply made him aware of you and what you're doing."

"Then I guess you can say I'm returning the favor. Tell you what, you stay the hell out of my relationship and I'll do the same."

"You're not capable of that; you should just give up. This is my husband, he has made that clear not once but twice." Naquia said showing her ring off to Raven, which I'm sure was for the benefit of the audience.

"And it's a shame that you don't feel anymore secure the second time around than you did on the first."

"I'm not scared of you."

"Oh but you should be. You see all I have to do is change my mind and say the word and all of this will be over. Believe that." Raven turned and walked out of the door.

About the author

Laine Highsmith is a romantic at heart who frequently finds her escape through the lives of the characters she creates. Employed in the health insurance industry for almost twenty years she greatly anticipates the day when the boss she has to report to is her computer at home and the only dress code she has to adhere to is which pair of jeans and tee shirt she will wear today. Surrounded by the love and support of her family and friends, Laine is currently pursuing her dream and working on the completion of her fourth novel with these same characters tentatively entitled Repercussions.

Please feel free to contact Laine at www.lainespromise.com or lainespromise@hotmail.com. Your insight and feedback is always welcomed.

Printed in the United States
82064LV00003B/124